FOR TIME AND
ALL ETERNITIES

FOR TIME
AND ALL
ETERNITIES

Mette Ivie Harrison

Published by Soho Press, Inc.
853 Broadway
New York, NY 10003

Library of Congress Cataloging-in-Publication Data

Harrison, Mette Ivie
For time and all eternities / Mette Ivie Harrison.

ISBN 978-1-61695-866-4
eISBN 978-1-61695-667-7

1. Women private investigators—Fiction. 2. Murder—Investigation—
Fiction. 3. Women detectives—Fiction.
4. Mormons—Fiction. 5. Domestic fiction. I. Title
PS3608.A783578 F67 2017 813'.6—dc23 2016041363

Interior design by Janine Agro, Soho Press, Inc.

Printed in the United States of America

10 9 8 7 6 5 4 3 2 1

For my sister Mama Dragons

"Families are forever" isn't a promise.

It's a threat.

A gag order.

A lock on a door with one key.

Families will be together because we belong to one
    another.

I believe in a God of big tents and open doors,

A God present at the first and last gasps of life.

Family is who we choose and whom we mourn.

God does not hold families hostage.

If there is a sealing power on earth, it is love–

The messy, patient, inconvenient kind of love

The dirt under fingernails, spitup in hair, cool hands on
    fevered brow kind of love

The boisterous exuberant dandelion-flowers-
    rammed-into-a-vase kind of love,

The love that witnesses

The love that waits

The love that doesn't ask questions

The love that asks the right questions

The love that shows up tired, but shows up–relentless love

God is a God of that kind of love.

Families are forever because we carve them together,

Build a home inside ourselves for them of clay and sticks,

Feather them with kind words and apologies.

They are as strong and as fragile as life itself.

Family keeps out the cold.

Family isn't binary,

In or out of the circle.

Family is the circle.

Kristen Shill

CHAPTER 1

My fourth son, Kenneth, pulled into the driveway as I was cleaning up the breakfast dishes. I had a sense of foreboding at the troubled look on his face and guessed that he'd waited until my husband, Kurt, was gone to work and I was alone. Kenneth had been distancing himself from the Mormon church lately, which had put a serious strain on his relationship with his father, the bishop of our ward.

"Mom? You home?" he called out, not bothering to knock on the door.

"In the kitchen!" I answered. I wiped my hands off and wished that I looked better, but he was my son. He'd seen me in my pajamas before, and without my hair done.

He came over and gave me a big hug. "I love you, Mom," he said. He smelled like he'd been sweating on the drive over. "You know that, don't you?"

This only made me feel more nervous about whatever Kenneth had come over to tell me. Of my five sons, he was the one I worried most about—well, after Samuel, my youngest, who had come out as gay last year and was currently far away in Boston on a Mormon mission.

"What's up?" I asked cautiously.

"I'm getting married," he said simply.

"What? How? To whom?" Was he so estranged from the family that he had gone as far as to get engaged without even introducing us to the woman?

"Her name is Naomi Carter," Kenneth said.

"That's a lovely name," I said, trying to act normal about this. If he loved her, I was sure the whole family would love her, even if I had to make them do it.

"She's great, Mom. I'm a lucky guy."

I wished that I knew anything about her. I wished I could see them together, make sure they seemed happy together, right for each other. But I trusted Kenneth, and in the end, I hugged him fiercely. "Oh, sweetheart, I'm so happy for you." He wasn't hugging back, though. Something was wrong. "So?" I said, when I released him.

"So what?" said Kenneth.

"Well, what aren't you telling me? Why did you make sure I was alone to spring it on me? Does she have two heads or something? Is she a felon?" I was trying to joke, but I could tell it wasn't going over well.

He sighed. "Naomi's part of—well, her family is only kind of Mormon."

"Kind of Mormon? What does that mean?" With Kenneth's doubts about the church, I really hadn't expected him to marry a devout churchgoer. But that was obviously why he was nervous about telling Kurt. He must want me to act as an intermediary, to get Kurt used to the idea that they weren't going to get married in the temple—sealed as Mormon couples are in an eternal family in this life and the celestial kingdom, not just married till death, as in other religious traditions.

Kenneth sighed again, and rubbed at his head in a way that

reminded me of Kurt, if Kurt had had more hair. "I guess there's no easy way to say it, Mom. Her family is polygamous."

I was so shocked I had to gather my thoughts. Of all my sons, Kenneth was the last one I would have expected to be interested in a polygamous branch of Mormonism. I was really not sure how I was going to handle it if Kenneth were about to tell me he'd be having multiple wives, if that was what he planned for the future with this Naomi Carter. I'd never really accepted the polygamous past of the Mormon church and had always assumed I'd never have to. I thought I'd raised Kenneth to think the same way.

"Are they FLDS?" I asked slowly. The Fundamentalist Church of Latter-Day Saints was the most infamous polygamist branch of Mormonism, led by the now-jailed "prophet" Warren Jeffs, who had been indicted for statutory rape after he married dozens of barely teenage girls, some of whom were also his close blood relatives. Just the idea of Kenneth sitting down for Sunday dinner with men who did that made me sick. I suddenly wished that Kurt were here, after all.

"Not the FLDS, Mom," Kenneth said. "Her family is independent. And very modern. Her dad is an OB/GYN at Salt Lake Regional. One of the wives is an investment broker and another is an artist. Naomi is in med school, too. She wants to be an OB/GYN like her father." He held my gaze as if he were begging me not to judge him just yet.

I struggled not to make a remark about it being a lot cheaper to have a lot of babies if you were a baby doctor yourself.

"Okay," I said, hoping I knew my son as well as I thought I did. "Are you two planning to be polygamous?"

He snorted. "Of course not. Mom, I'm just trying to make sure you understand her history. And when you meet her parents— her father and her mothers—you aren't caught by surprise."

I felt an enormous wave of relief. Mormons hadn't been polygamous since the late 1800s, when the prophet and president Wilford Woodruff had ended the practice. Sometimes I heard older Mormons say that God was polygamous or that polygamy was still going to be required in heaven, but it wasn't a topic I'd heard mentioned in General Conference and I figured that was clear evidence that it wasn't part of the modern church anymore.

"How did you meet her?" I asked, glad to get back to being a nosy mother.

There was a long pause and I realized we weren't done with the difficult part of the conversation. "We met at a former Mormons group. We call it Mormons Anonymous."

Mormons Anonymous—like Alcoholics Anonymous or Gamblers Anonymous? As if my religion were some kind of addictive behavior that you had to recover from?

"I knew you were having trouble with the church," I said carefully, waiting for him to explain.

"Mom, the final straw was the exclusion policy."

I felt a gut punch at this and found myself holding onto the kitchen counter to keep from sinking to the floor. The exclusion policy had been leaked to the press in November of 2015, and it directed that all same-sex married members must be excommunicated and their children disallowed saving ordinances like baptism, as well as participation in other church activities. I had always loved my church, but this was the one thing about it that I simply could not defend. Samuel had struggled with the policy right after he turned in his mission papers, but he had decided to go anyway. Kurt and I had argued viciously about the policy, especially its consequences for Samuel.

I had never even considered that the new policy might have

affected Kenneth, as well. I must have been too wrapped up in my own anger and pain.

"You weren't one of the people who went to that mass resignation event, were you?" I asked Kenneth. It had been all over the news. Ten days after the leak, thousands of people had lined up in City Creek Park in Salt Lake City to have their names struck from the Mormon church's register in protest.

I hadn't thought seriously about resigning, but I hadn't known how to go to church the next week, or the week after that. My marriage had been on edge ever since because Kurt, who was the kind of man called to be bishop, would never admit that he thought the policy might be a mistake, that it could be anything less than a revelation from God. Kurt hoped that Samuel could find a nice woman to marry who could accept him as he was—that Samuel would reject his sexuality and live a heterosexual life. This had infuriated me on my own account as well as Samuel's—Kurt knew that I'd been married to a gay man—my first marriage, to Ben Tookey—and he knew how awful that experience had been for me. How could he want that for his own son, or for the poor woman?

I'd also argued with my best friend, Anna Torstensen, who had defended Kurt. We hadn't spoken since. I couldn't get her words out of my head—she'd told me I should be open-minded about the idea of Samuel's marrying a woman, that I had hit the jackpot with Kurt as a husband and didn't understand that other women accepted much less in marriage in order to find someone to be sealed to for time and all eternities. But how could I hope anything less for my sons than a loving marriage to a partner they were actually sexually attracted to?

So over the last few months, as I struggled to accept what was happening in my church, I couldn't share my pain with my husband or with my best friend. The only thing that had saved me had been joining a closed Facebook group called "Mama Dragons," a group of Mormon women who were fierce in defending their LGBTQ kids. I could say anything I wanted to them and no one else (including Kurt) would see it. Some of them had left the church, but others were trying to stay, like I was, and change it from the inside.

"We didn't go to the mass resignation," Kenneth said. "Actually, Naomi and I hadn't met yet in November. And I didn't want to do anything rashly that would affect the rest of my life and my relationship with all of you. But ultimately, I felt sick about having my name connected to the church in any way. So I looked for a support group and started going to the Mormons Anonymous meetings. Naomi was there, too."

"But you've officially had your name removed since?" I had to ask. It would hurt Kurt deeply, and even though I understood Kenneth's choice, it hurt me, too. It meant our eternal family now had a Kenneth-sized hole in it, since he would not allowed to be part of our family in the celestial kingdom of heaven. The covenant that sealed us forever to our children even before they were born had been broken by the resignation.

"I knew you were busy getting Samuel on his mission, Mom, and I didn't really want to open it up for family discussion. But yeah, I went to see a lawyer who said he'd file the letter officially, so I didn't have to go through the harassment and the waiting period the church wanted to set. It was official in March." His words were clipped and sounded almost rehearsed.

"Oh," I said softly.

Then Kenneth started apologizing. "Mom, I know I should have told you about all this before now. I kept telling myself I should bring it up at every family dinner, let it all hang out. But

I guess I was a bit of a coward. I knew how disappointed you and Dad would be."

"I love you, Kenneth. I will always love you." That was the most I could manage.

Kenneth sat on one of the stools and after a little silence said, "I've never told you this before, but one of my companions during my mission, Elder Ellison, was gay. He told me in confidence, but I was scared of him. I'd been told so many times that gay people were pedophiles and perverts that I believed it. I called the mission president and outed Ellison to him." Kenneth shivered at this.

"What happened?" I asked, feeling a well of sympathy for the poor gay elder who must have felt so alone in the world.

"The mission president immediately came to interview him and Ellison was transferred to the mission office, assigned directly to the Prez instead of another missionary companion." He took a shuddering breath, and couldn't seem to look at me. He was ashamed of himself. "And then, two months later, I heard Ellison was sent home because of 'emotional problems.'" There were air quotes around those two words. "He committed suicide the day before I was released from my mission. He was only twenty-one." He looked at me, and then looked away.

I'd never known any of this back when Kenneth had returned from his mission, and I could see now why he hadn't told me. I thought of Samuel, who could be hurt by a companion who treated him like this. At least Samuel wasn't in the closet, but there had to be hundreds of other missionaries who were. I was glad Kenneth was ashamed of himself. I felt a bit of shame, as well, that I had raised a son who could do this.

But sadly, it made sense of so many things. No wonder Kenneth had refused to go back to church for weeks after coming home from his mission. No wonder he hadn't done the typical post-mission talk in church, telling everyone about his converts and funny stories about his companions. No wonder he'd become inactive since then, and had struggled with the new policy.

Kenneth rubbed at his face, and his hand lingered there, half-obscuring his eyes. "Mom, I've been sorry about this every day of my life since then. I've tried to think of some way I could make it up to Ellison, but I never will. The only thing I can do is to figure out how to prove to myself that I'm not the person I was then, that I'm never going to be like that again. I'm not going to be part of making more gay Mormons commit suicide. I'm doing everything I can to make sure they know I'm not like that, that I understand them."

I reached for Kenneth's arm, but he pulled away, as if he didn't believe he deserved my sympathy.

"The truth is that Ellison was the best companion I ever had," Kenneth added, talking more to himself than to me, I think. "He was a really good person. He wanted to help others. And he believed in God. Really believed that every prayer he said was being heard and answered in some way. And still, I was afraid of—I don't even know what." He clenched a fist and then looked back at me, his eyes bleeding emotion.

"Whenever I think about Samuel on a mission," he said, his voice almost testimonial, "I can't help but think of Ellison, and how things turned out. I really hope Samuel never has a companion like me. But the way the Mormon church talks about gay people, I don't know if the average church member is any more enlightened now than they were when I was a missionary. Or maybe they're worse, if they think that their prejudices have been justified by this ridiculous policy."

I felt horribly guilty about this. What kind of person was I,

that I hadn't talked to my sons about loving the whole rainbow
spectrum before now? I hadn't even told them about my marriage to Ben until last year, as if I was ashamed of it—and him.

"I had planned to tell you after I resigned, but it was harder
than I thought it would be. I mean, I probably hadn't gone to a
church meeting in my own ward for a year. But that Sunday, I felt
horribly guilty. I couldn't sleep for fear that God would punish
me somehow." He rubbed at his eyes.

"Punish you? You mean about Ellison?"

"I don't know if it was about anything specific. But maybe.
You grow up believing that God protects the people who are
righteous and obey Him, and that everyone else has to deal with
hurricanes and droughts and stuff. And yeah, even if you're trying to give it up, it can be hard to stop thinking about God that
way, as someone who punishes."

I wanted to ask him if he'd given up belief in God entirely or
if he was thinking of joining another church, but it seemed too
invasive of his privacy somehow, even if I was his mother.

"I was so jittery I started buying some pretty hard liquor to
try to combat it. And maybe to flip off the church's rules. But I
didn't actually want to get drunk to numb myself out. I needed
to figure out how to deal with the change. So I called up Naomi,
who I'd met in Mormons Anonymous, and talked to her about
everything, and well, we got closer and closer after that."

"I'm so sorry you went through all that alone, Kenneth." I wish
he'd told me. But it was so tricky now, with Kurt as bishop. Even
with my own son, maybe I couldn't be completely honest about
my feelings for the church anymore.

Kenneth shook his head, "No, Mom. Samuel was the one who
needed your attention the most. But I just needed to explain to
you what was going on at the time so you'd understand how

much Naomi means to me. And why we're not getting married in the temple. Or in the church."

I let out a long breath. "If Naomi was from a polygamous family, did she even have to have her name removed from the records like you did?"

"It's complicated," Kenneth sighed. "Her parents were married in the Salt Lake Temple and they weren't polygamous until way after she was born. So, yes, her name is on the records of the mainstream church."

"And did she leave for the same reason that you did?" I asked. "The new policy?"

Kenneth's mouth twisted. "Partly that, and partly other things," he said.

"Such as?" I prompted

"Well, to be honest, she couldn't stand the way the mainstream church covers up so much about polygamy in church history. Joseph Smith and Brigham Young are treated like these heroes who never did anything wrong."

"But the new essays on Joseph Smith and polygamy admit he married a fourteen-year-old girl," I pointed out. There was a new series of "Gospel Topics" essays on the church website, even if they weren't that easy to find if you didn't know about them. Kurt still had people in church complaining about teachers teaching them because they didn't believe they were official.

"They admit it but don't condemn it. Naomi thinks that's even worse. It's okay to take a fourteen-year-old bride if you're the prophet?"

That was definitely a problem in my book, as well. But how could the church condemn Joseph Smith's polygamy without simultaneously disavowing the other things he had done, like translating The Book of Mormon, and restoring the sacred temple rites and proper priesthood power? Without Joseph Smith's contributions, we'd just be the same as most other Christian churches, not the "one true Church."

"I'm confused," I said. "If her family is polygamist, wouldn't they all have been excommunicated?"

Kenneth seemed almost amused. I guess now that he was out of the church, this wasn't his problem anymore. "The bishop of the Carter family ward excommunicated her father but thinks the wives and children aren't culpable. Naomi thinks it's all hypocritical. A wink and a nod kind of thing."

I mulled this over, hoping that I would like Naomi as much as I agreed with her views of polygamy. "So if Naomi resigned from the church because of polygamy, does she still have any contact with her family?" Kenneth had sounded as if he expected me to meet them in the near future.

Kenneth drummed his fingers on the countertop. "Some contact. She's trying to figure out how to negotiate things."

I heard uncertainty in my son's voice. He didn't know how he was going to negotiate things with his family, either. This was all such a mess.

"Will they be attending the wedding?" I asked, because it was easier to focus on the particulars than on the emotions behind them.

"She wants to talk to you about all that herself. I'm hoping that you and Dad will come to dinner with us next week. We can meet in Salt Lake whenever is convenient for you two."

"You want me to smooth things over with your father by then?" I asked.

"Could you? If you need more time than that, I can postpone it for a few more weeks, but we're hoping to get married this summer," Kenneth said.

Kenneth so rarely asked for anything, how could I say no? I thought about how careful I'd have to be and how strained my relationship with Kurt was at this point. I could have tried to explain to Kenneth, but he didn't need to have more on his plate than he already did.

"I'll do my best," I said.

CHAPTER 2

That night I made a special dinner, Kurt's favorite pot roast and mashed potatoes with peas. Homemade rolls were just coming out of the oven when I heard the garage door open. I tensed, worried that the conversation I would have to initiate about Kenneth would lead to another big argument between us. Kenneth had left this for me because he thought I could deliver the message to Kurt better than he could, but I wasn't sure it was true.

Kurt stepped into the kitchen through the garage door but stopped on the threshold. "Are we having guests tonight?" he asked.

"No, just us," I said.

He loosened his tie. "Did I forget something?" he asked. I could see he was going through the list of occasions in his head. It wasn't our anniversary. It wasn't my birthday or his.

"Kenneth came over this morning and told me some things we should talk over," I said.

Kurt nodded. "Let me get changed, all right?"

"Do you have any church appointments I'm not thinking of?" I asked, because I wanted to make sure we had plenty of time to talk this through. It wasn't something he could start and then leave off while he went to do interviews at the church.

"No, nothing tonight," he said. Right then, his phone chirped at him.

"Go ahead, check for messages," I said. If there was a ward emergency, I'd eat this lovely meal all by myself. Or maybe I could pack it up and send it to another ward family who would enjoy it.

Kurt looked at his phone. "It's fine," he said. "Nothing important."

"Do you want to go answer it and then come back?" I asked, trying to be understanding.

He hesitated a moment, then nodded. "I promise I'll be back in just one second," he said, and headed into his office.

It was actually about five minutes until he came back, but luckily, by then, the rolls had cooled just enough for me to put them on a plate and set the table with the nice china (I never used it for family occasions because we only had four settings). I'd put down the lace tablecloth Marie had given us for Christmas last year.

"This looks delicious," said Kurt stiffly. "Thank you."

I passed him the roast and then the potatoes. I'd already eaten one of the rolls fresh out of the oven, so I wasn't as hungry as I might normally have been. I watched Kurt. He was clearly nervous, and he kept glancing up at me as if he were afraid of me.

"I need to talk to you about Kenneth," I said.

"Right," he said. "Kenneth." He swallowed hard and then put his fork down, waiting.

"I don't know how to put this," I said, hesitating.

"Just get it out, Linda. I'm a grown man. I know bad things sometimes happen."

But it wasn't as if Kenneth had a terminal cancer diagnosis. Except that to Kurt, this might be even worse. Dead, Kenneth would still be part of our eternal family. We would know he would be in the celestial kingdom, the highest part of heaven, if he was a baptized and temple-endowed Mormon and died without sin. But resigning from the church would mean no matter how good he was, he could never be with us in heaven. He had rejected the truth and denied his temple covenants. That was worse, much worse, than never being a Mormon in the first place.

"Kenneth resigned his membership in March," I said. After I got it out, I expected to feel relief, but it didn't come. I waited for Kurt to respond. It wasn't as if I thought he'd throw things, but I also knew he wasn't going to just accept this.

"He resigned without even talking to me?" said Kurt in a pained near-whisper.

"It was because of the policy change," I said. Maybe it was selfish of me to say that, because I was using Kenneth to prove my own point, that the policy change was a big deal, that it wasn't just an extension of everything the church already taught, as Kurt had argued with me before.

"I see," said Kurt.

There was a long silence. I had more to say, but I wanted Kurt to react to this first. When several minutes had passed and he still hadn't spoken, I finally blurted out, "Don't you have anything to say?"

"I don't see that what I have to say matters, does it? Kenneth has already done this. He clearly didn't want my opinion."

That was true. He hadn't asked either of us. A part of me wanted to defend Kenneth and mention his mission companion, Elder Ellison. But I couldn't bear to hear Kurt's dismissal of a young gay man's suicide as his own problem and not the church's, so I left it unsaid.

"I think we need to make sure Kenneth sees that we'll treat

him exactly the same as before and show him our love for him will never change, no matter what."

Kurt shook his head. "Linda, I will love Kenneth with every part of my being for all of eternity, but that doesn't mean I will treat him the same. I can't just pretend he hasn't done this."

It was about what I should have expected from Kurt. I started to tear apart one of the rolls I'd buttered, which was entirely unfair to the long strands of beautiful gluten I'd worked so hard to create with my kneading. "He's just as much our son as he ever was. He's a good person."

"Yes, he is," said Kurt mildly. "But God is a god of order. There are rules in heaven, as there are in any place of order."

Again, I didn't want to argue this point with him. So instead, I said, "Kenneth also came to tell me that he's engaged."

Kurt's eyes widened. "To get married?"

I smiled for the first time in this conversation. "Yes, to get married. Her name is Naomi Carter. She's also resigned from the church."

"Ah," said Kurt.

Was he going to ask anything about her? I could only tell him what Kenneth had told me. I hadn't even seen a photograph of her.

"She's in med school," I said. "She wants to be an OB/GYN." I was deliberately avoiding her family's polygamy for the moment. It wasn't like me to do that, especially to Kurt, but everything had changed between us in the last few months. None of our old marriage habits worked anymore. We weren't strangers, but there was now an unspoken contract for how we interacted and avoided conflict. We both followed the rules because we still loved each other and wanted to keep from inflicting pain. So all the pain got held inside.

"Well, that sounds good for both of them. She'll have a steady career if they stay in Utah. Are they planning to stay in Utah, do you know?"

This was like the kind of stilted, polite conversation I had with my parents on the occasions when I called them on the phone dutifully to make sure they were still healthy and alive. The night before Mother's Day, the night before Father's Day, and Christmas Eve, so that the actual days were unspoiled by the bad taste in my mouth my extended family left me with. We were all politeness now, no recriminations about the past and how they had treated me after my divorce, more than thirty years in the past.

"I don't know," I said. "I didn't ask him that." Kenneth hadn't said anything about leaving Utah, but there were a lot of ex-Mormons who were happy to get away from a state where Mormonism was so much a part of the culture and politics.

"Well, I hope they are very happy," said Kurt. There was clearly part of that wish left unsaid.

"But . . . ?"

He shook his head. "But nothing. I hope they are happy."

"You hope they're happy, but you think it's unlikely if they both have left the church."

Kurt looked down at his plate, took a long drink of water, and then set down his glass deliberately.

I said nothing.

Finally, he offered, "I just meant that I don't know how a marriage will work if the two people in it can't depend on each other absolutely for commitment."

It was hard for me not to feel that this was an indictment of me for being disloyal to the church, as well. But I took a breath, and focused on our son and his marriage again. "What do you mean by commitment?" I asked. Was Kurt going to say that he thought only Mormons could have good marriages? Because that was demonstrably false. Our divorce statistics were not that different from the rest of America.

"Well, when someone has been baptized and has made certain promises to a church, and then they turn their back on those promises . . ." He didn't finish. He didn't have to.

"Kenneth was eight when he was baptized. Do you really think that's old enough to make a promise for the rest of his life?" I asked.

"He said he was ready. He was very certain about it," Kurt said.

I wanted to roll my eyes at him. At eight, most children just wanted to please their parents. It was one of the reasons I didn't like it when children bore their testimonies in Sacrament Meeting. They were just too young to do any more than repeat what they'd been told. They hadn't had spiritual experiences of their own. But in Mormonism, eight was supposed to be the "age of accountability."

"And he wasn't eight when he went through the temple. He was nineteen," Kurt added.

Yes, but nineteen is still a teenager, and that was a kid in many ways. "People can change their minds, you know," I said. It didn't make them incapable of committing themselves to other things.

"Yes, they can. But it doesn't bode well for marriage."

Did Kurt see me as a covenant-breaker, too, because I'd been divorced before? "There are covenants on both sides," I said. "When one side breaks them, the other side is free, don't you think?" I felt strongly that a covenant had been broken between the church and members, including LGBTQ Mormons—for example, the covenant to treat people with Christian kindness.

"Yes, but God will bless us if we keep our covenants, even when we're the injured party," Kurt said.

Did he have any idea of the implication of what he was saying? How could he not be thinking about me and Ben Tookey?

"Maybe that's true, but God blesses us all the time, no matter what we do. He loves us, and He wants us to be happy."

"Happiness is not the same as doing whatever we want," said Kurt.

It was so hurtful, I felt a pain in my chest and couldn't speak for a long moment. "She's from a polygamous family," I blurted out.

Kurt paled visibly. "She's what?"

"Not the FLDS," I explained. "I guess they're an independent group. Kenneth said that her father was excommunicated, but it sounds like the children and the wives are still active members of the Mormon church." Sort of.

Kurt muttered something to himself that I decided I didn't want to ask him to repeat.

"He wants us to go meet her for dinner in Salt Lake City, if we can find an evening that works."

Kurt looked away. "Fine. I can do that."

Was that all he had to say?

He stood up. "Thanks for the lovely dinner. It was delicious."

He'd barely touched it, but he was scraping the plate and putting it in the dishwasher before I said anything else.

"I'm going to spend some time reading scriptures and praying in my office," he added as he walked out of the kitchen.

I suspected he'd be praying for Kenneth and Naomi. And me, too.

Fine, let him. God wasn't going to change who I was. That was a fundamental principle of Mormonism that I loved. We all had free agency. It was the reason that Christ had made the Atonement, so we could all choose and learn from our mistakes. I didn't know if Kenneth was making a mistake or not, but I was going to honor his choices and not try to pray them away.

I cleaned up the kitchen, packaging the leftovers into containers for Kurt to take to work with him the rest of the week. He often forgot to eat if I didn't pack him a lunch. Despite all our problems since November, I'd packed him a lunch every day. It was easier to do things like that, and not just because it was a habit. It was a concrete expression of love that didn't imply I agreed with him in any way. If only Kurt could figure out something equivalent to do for Kenneth.

An hour later I passed by his office on the way to putting away my coat and stopped by the door. The sound of weeping was clear, even through the door.

My heart clenched and I thought about going inside to comfort him. I could hold him, at the very least, and tell him that I loved him. If I were a better, more Christ-like person, I would have done it. I wouldn't have thought about my own pride or giving him the false impression I was admitting I was wrong. I would have cared only about showing my husband that I loved him.

I went to bed alone instead, and thought about how long an eternal marriage could really be. Forever. Eternity. That's how long Kurt and I were supposed to be bound together. And I had always, through every disagreement we'd had before, felt comforted by this idea, buoyed by the thought that we would work everything out eventually. But things had changed.

We should have been celebrating our son's decision to marry, but at the moment I wondered if our own marriage would survive. And if I wanted it to. Forever was a long time to be sealed to someone you thought was profoundly, deeply wrong about the nature of God, and about marriage itself.

CHAPTER 3

Kurt and I didn't talk about Kenneth and Naomi again except to confirm the details of our dinner two Thursdays later. Kurt came home from work early to pick me up and drive his truck north to Salt Lake City. I was dressed in a nice maroon suit I'd last worn to Adam's wedding five years ago. Kurt was wearing one of his two black suits and a pink tie I suspect he did not know might look like subtle support of the LGBTQ community.

"We need to be nice," I said after we were on the freeway. I wished conversation were easier.

"I know that," Kurt said. "I love Kenneth, you know. Even if I don't approve of his choice to resign his church membership."

"Can you let that go for the moment?" I asked testily.

Kurt let out a breath, as if he was trying. "Do you think he's marrying a girl from a polygamous family just to tweak us?"

That's what Kurt thought of Kenneth? "Of course he's not," I said immediately. Then after some thought, I added, "Besides, we're all basically from polygamous families, if you go back far enough in church history."

"That's not true," Kurt retorted. "Only twenty percent of Mormons lived a polygamous life even back in the late 1800s."

What apologetic Mormon had he heard that from? Clearly, he'd been poking around on the Internet, since I was pretty sure he hadn't had that statistic in his head before Kenneth announced he was engaged to a woman from a polygamous family.

"Well, if that's true, then those twenty percent are related to the other eighty percent one way or another. Everyone's inter-married in Mormonism by now. At least all of us in Utah," I said.

Kurt wisely didn't argue with me on this point. "Every time I hear about people who practice polygamy now, it's always a testimony to me that once God has withdrawn His support of any way of life, there is nothing holy left in it."

Well, that was convenient, I thought. Just like the Manifesto of 1890 that had banned polygamy in the Mormon church. The manifesto had been conveniently received from God after Wil-ford Woodruff had been threatened by the US government with seizure of all church assets—not to mention imprisonment of every church official practicing polygamy.

The truth was, polygamy had always been one of the most unsavory elements of our Mormon past. Joseph Smith received the revelation to practice polygamy in 1839 and he'd practiced it in secret, even from his first wife, Emma, and some of the husbands or fathers of the women he married. Joseph spent years hiding the truth from Emma, and then wrote a scripture about how if the first wife didn't accept polygamy, the husband had no more obligation to ask her permission.

The first rumors about polygamy started spreading in Nauvoo, Illinois, when the First Counselor in the Presidency of the Church, William Law, who had committed adultery and been denied a temple sealing, got angry that his wife asked Joseph Smith to seal her to the prophet instead. He bought a printing press with the express purpose of exposing the secrets of Mormonism, including polygamy, to the public. The *Nauvoo Expositor* printed but one issue before Joseph Smith demanded the destruction of this private property by church members. This was the reason Smith was thrown in prison, where he was martyred in Carthage, Illinois.

The true historical facts are available on the Internet, but in Sunday School lessons, the story tends to be that Joseph Smith was murdered by those who hated the popularity of the Mormon church and were jealous of the wealth of Nauvoo.

But now was not the time for Kurt and me to come to an agreement on the place of polygamy within the church. All I wanted from my husband tonight was for him to treat Naomi Carter politely. If he could add a little warmth in, that would be a bonus. Her goodwill as a daughter-in-law could mean the difference between our remaining part of our son's life and being relegated to the outside, looking in.

Soon we were pulling to a stop in front of The Melting Pot downtown, where there was fortunately a parking spot. Kurt paid the meter and I went inside to give our name to the hostess. Then we were being led toward a table in the back of the restaurant.

The woman sitting next to Kenneth had long blonde hair, large hazel eyes, a strong Roman nose, and a Julia-Roberts-esque mouth that was emphasized with dark red lipstick. She was leaning into Kenneth's arms and looked up when he pointed at us. I saw wariness cross her features before she could stifle it. I felt an instant of nervousness, as well.

"Mom, Dad, this is Naomi," Kenneth said. "Naomi, my mom and dad, Kurt and Linda Wallheim."

Kurt held out his hand and shook Naomi's. She and I did a "Mormon hug" between women, where you touch across the chest, get a brief whiff of the other woman's perfume, and glance sideways at her ear and cheek in simulation of a kiss. I was left with the faint impression of roses.

"Mrs. Wallheim, it's so good to finally meet you," Naomi said formally. "Mr. Wallheim, Kenneth talks about you all the time."

"Mr." and "Mrs." were almost never used in the Mormon church. "Brother" and "Sister" were far friendlier, but we weren't in a church situation now.

"Call me Linda," I said. Marie and Willow called me "Mom," but Naomi and I weren't there just yet.

Kurt didn't offer his first name, however. I wished he could just speed up whatever mental processes he was going through, but for now I waited for the awkward silence to pass.

"This restaurant is very nice," he said at last, without bothering to even look around to make the statement believable.

We sat down, Kurt and I on one side of the booth and Kenneth and Naomi on the other. Kenneth was dressed in a white shirt, thin red tie, and the dark suit he probably hadn't worn since his mission. It had grown too small for him in the shoulders, an apt metaphor for his church life, I suppose.

Naomi was dressed modestly in a plain white blouse and houndstooth patterned A-line skirt. There was nothing remotely old-fashioned about her that would make me think of polygamists or the FLDS church.

"It's lovely weather tonight, isn't it?" Naomi said.

"Yes, lovely," Kurt said.

"I've never been to The Melting Pot before, but I've always wanted to. What a good idea to meet here," I said.

"Kenneth picked it," said Naomi, looking at him briefly with that intimacy that comes with long months spent together. "He thought it would be good to have, well, neutral ground, I guess."

I stole a glance at Kenneth. On neutral ground? I wasn't that scary of a mother-in-law, was I?

"Any night I don't have to cook is a good night for me," I said.

"You love cooking, Mom, and you know it," said Kenneth.

"Well, for family, that's true," I admitted.

There was another awkward pause. Kurt still didn't seem to have anything to say.

"So, I understand you and Kenneth have been dating for about six months?" I said.

"More or less." Naomi turned to Kenneth and put her hand over his. That was when I saw the ring, which was rather untraditional. Instead of a diamond solitaire it was a band of twisted gold with a leaf pattern.

I didn't have a diamond solitaire either. I thought fondly back to that time, nearly thirty years ago, when Kurt had given me the simple gold band I still wore. He kept insisting he would buy me a more expensive ring after we were married and settled, but it had never happened. I was pregnant with Adam within months of the wedding, and all our money went toward saving for his birth.

Later, when Kurt could have afforded another ring, I didn't want one. I was used to the ring I had. To me, it signified all the years we had suffered in poverty together and still been madly in love and committed to raising our kids. I looked at it now and reminded myself that whatever hard times we were going through, we'd had wonderful times before and might well have wonderful times again. I let out a long breath and felt the first sense of oneness with Kurt since November.

"Kenneth tells us you're in medical school," Kurt said to Naomi.

Well, this seemed to be moving in the right direction now. I kept quiet and let Kurt do his thing. After more than a year of bishoping, he was good at introductions and small talk.

"Just finished my first year. The easy year," she added with a smile.

"There aren't any easy years, and you know it," Kenneth said. He lifted her hand and kissed it across the knuckles, then remembered we were watching and blushed slightly.

"So, tell us more about yourself, Naomi," Kurt said.

"Well, uh—I think Kenneth has told you about my unconventional upbringing?"

I supposed that was one way to put it. "But we'd like to hear your own version," I said.

She looked at Kenneth, then took a deep breath. "My mother was the first wife of my father, Stephen Carter. I'm the oldest of all his children. But neither of my parents was raised polygamous. They were both born mainstream LDS. When they married, my mother never thought she would be anything other than my father's only wife."

"What happened, then?" Kurt asked.

"Well, it was about ten years later that my father felt . . . called by God to become polygamous." She hesitated over the word "called." "He told my mother about it and she was the one who ultimately chose the second wife for him. He's never married another wife without her consent." She sounded like she didn't understand it, and I didn't either.

Kurt's lips twisted, but he didn't comment, no matter how tempted he might have been.

"Our family was already living on the big tract of property on the hills that his parents had left him when they died. It was easy for him to build another house there. And then another after that, as he added wives."

"There are five wives in all, right, Naomi?" Kenneth prompted.

Naomi nodded. "And twenty-one children as of now. Carolyn is expecting in a few months, so that will be twenty-two."

That seemed far too many children for any one man, but many

of our polygamous ancestors had managed larger families than that.

"And I understand that you were never excommunicated?" said Kurt. "Despite the polygamy in your home."

"Well, our ward bishops so far have kind of looked the other way when it came to the wives and children," Naomi said.

"But you left the church anyway?"

She shook her head sadly. "There are so many things I love about the Mormon church. Or there were, I should say. I loved The Book of Mormon and the hymns. I loved the Young Womanhood Recognition program, with all the values. And I loved the sense of shared community."

I couldn't help but feel a twinge of regret at Naomi's mention of the Young Womanhood Recognition Program, the equivalent of the Eagle Scout program for boys. Until Georgia's death, I'd always imagined I'd have a daughter who'd complete the program.

"But all that wasn't enough, for some reason?" said Kurt. This was turning into precisely the kind of grilling session that I had been trying to warn Kurt against. Did he want Naomi to ever talk to us again?

"It's not that," Naomi replied levelly. "I started to have doubts about the church itself when I started asking questions about polygamy. I knew what my father taught us, but it was so different from what Mormons in our ward believed. No one could give me straight answers about polygamy's place in the church. Some people said it was wrong and had nothing to do with being Mormon. Other people said it was the law of the celestial kingdom—I mean some people who aren't even polygamists believe that." She shrugged. "So I started reading to see if I could answer my own questions. The more I dug into the history of the church, the more problems I saw in it. There were so many situations besides polygamy where the church refused to apologize for mistakes in the past, or even to admit them at all. The Mountain Meadows Massacre. The Martin and Willie Handcart Company. The Adam-God Doctrine. Blood Atonement. On and on."

Well, she had certainly done her research. I couldn't disagree with her on any of those examples. They were all unjustifiably wrong and tended to be buried rather than talked about.

"The church belongs to Christ," Kurt said. "Even if the apostles or prophets make mistakes, apologizing sounds like apologizing for Christ Himself. But even so, the church has admitted to mistakes. Not allowing blacks to hold the priesthood, for instance."

"And how long did that take?" Kenneth interjected. "More than a hundred and fifty years after the Civil War."

This was surely not the place for this fight between Kurt and Kenneth about the pros and cons of the church. It was too public and Naomi shouldn't have to deal with that.

"Let's get practical about the wedding day itself," I said, as cheerily as I could manage. "How many people should we plan on your side bringing to the wedding? What kind of venue have you and Kenneth thought about? Do you have plans for a photographer, a florist, or a caterer? Do you want live music or a DJ?"

Kurt leaned back against the bench and looked at the menu as if it were hieroglyphics.

Kenneth cleared his throat. "It's up to Naomi, really. She's the bride."

I wished he wouldn't say that. I was trying to help and I didn't know the bride at all.

"We're working on pinning down a date and a venue. I don't have anything else decided on," said Naomi, more graciously. "Though I'm open to suggestions."

"I'll ask around. It's been a few years for us, and of course it's not the same when you're planning a non-church wedding," I said.

"Are you really all right with marrying without any religious covenant?" Kurt asked Kenneth. "It seems so cold, so contractual. Not to mention the fact that there's no guarantee you'll be together after this life."

I wished Kurt could be more politic about this, but I could see how deeply he had been hurt.

"We don't feel like we need a divine blessing on our marriage. It's all about us living up to our promises," said Kenneth. "And besides, a lifetime of love is plenty for us."

"And a lifetime is longer than most people manage," I said as smoothly as I could. "So if you do, it will be something to be proud of." Please let this be the end of this topic, I thought, but apparently, Kurt was not reading my mind.

"But your children won't be sealed to you," Kurt went on. "Have you thought about that at all, Kenneth?"

Naomi was sitting up very straight and I wondered if that was what she did when her own father stuck his foot in something.

"Dad, I don't believe in an afterlife. I'm not so sure about God, either," said Kenneth.

There was my answer to the question about Kenneth's belief system. It seemed very lonely to me, as someone who had once been an atheist and had come back to faith. But I shouldn't close any doors on Kenneth's behalf.

"Well, maybe you shouldn't be getting married while you're unsure about something so important," said Kurt.

And maybe Kurt should shut up when it came to other adult's decisions—even his son's. I could see from the set of Kenneth's jaw that he was finished letting his father poke and prod inappropriately. Good, I thought.

He said, "Naomi is the one surest thing in my life, Dad, and if you don't want to be part of our wedding, that's fine. We can move on without you." There it was, the gauntlet thrown. Kurt could keep his mouth closed about the eternities or he could get himself disinvited from his third son's wedding.

Kurt was, after all, a grown-up, and kept his mouth closed.

After that, Kenneth leaned back in his chair just like father, leaving me and Naomi to keep up the conversation. In any other situation, I might have thought it rude, as if he was saying that weddings were women's work, but right then, I was just relieved.

"We should plan on you coming to the family dinner this month, Naomi," I said. "Then you can meet Kenneth's brothers. Except for Samuel, of course. He's on a mission in Boston."

"Yes, I've heard a lot about Samuel," Naomi said. "Kenneth is very proud of his brother."

I glanced at Kenneth and was surprised to find myself getting a little teary-eyed. "We all are," I said.

The waitress came and took our orders after that. They soon brought pots of oil for cooking. While we waited for them to warm, Naomi looked directly at me and took a breath. "Linda, I asked Kenneth to set up this dinner for more than one reason. I know we aren't ready to discuss wedding details, but I have a favor to ask." She seemed very young in that moment. "This isn't related to the wedding. It's personal."

I felt flattered at this. "Of course, just name it. Whatever I can do to help you." Within reason, of course.

"I'm asking because—" She stopped, steeling herself. She pulled her hand away from Kenneth's, as if to prove she could do this on her own. "Kenneth told me about the woman in your ward who went missing. And how you helped find her when the police couldn't."

Now I was confused. What did that case have to do with Naomi? "I'm sure I just did what anyone else would have done," I said. It hadn't been anything to be proud of, really. Kurt had been embarrassed by my nosiness and the way I'd put myself into dangerous situations, and I could see his eyes narrowing.

"Kenneth also told me about the man who was murdered in your church building and how you made sure that the police investigated the right person," Naomi continued.

I wouldn't have put it quite that way. "I'm afraid he may have exaggerated my real involvement," I said, shifting in my seat uncomfortably.

Naomi hesitated again. "I need help with a family problem," she said at last. "And from what Kenneth has told me about you, I think you might be able to help me." Her hands twisting in her lap. "I'm worried about my younger sister Talitha. Something is wrong, and I was hoping you could try to find out what. I think she's being abused. Maybe by my father, or possibly by someone else."

This had not been what I was expecting. I thought she'd ask me to manage some fight between the various wives about who was going to stand in the line as her mother.

"How can I help?" I asked slowly.

"I thought maybe you could talk to her," Naomi said. "See if she'll open up to you."

I felt terrible for Naomi, and for her little sister. I assumed a polygamous childhood was difficult even if there was no abuse. But I wasn't the person to help. "You should have a professional talk to her, Naomi. Someone who has studied how to communicate with troubled children. I don't have that kind of experience. I could do more harm than good."

She shook her head. "I don't want to go to a professional until

I'm really certain there's a problem. If I talk to the police or DCFS, they might take all the children away from my mother and the other wives, just because they're polygamists."

Possible. A case worker negatively disposed to polygamy might argue that the Carters' living situation was damaging to the children. But the problem was, I wasn't sure I disagreed. "I'm not sure what you're asking me to do," I said.

"I—it's complicated," Naomi said. "I don't agree with the way my father lives, or how he runs his family. But that doesn't mean I think he's necessarily worse than any other Mormon man who thinks he has the right to tell his wife what to do because he has the priesthood."

Kurt twitched at this. I wished I could tell Naomi that the kind of male privilege and superiority she was talking about wasn't part of the church, but I had seen enough to be embarrassed by how often it was.

"Or any man," I said. "It's not as if Mormons invented the patriarchy."

Naomi nodded to acknowledge this. "But my father was never abusive when I was a kid. I don't want to get him in trouble for nothing. But I know something is really wrong with Talitha, and I need to figure out what it is and how I can help her before Kenneth and I start our new life together. I can't just leave her behind in distress."

"Surely you'd be in a better position to get her to open about it than I would." I said.

Naomi looked up and shook her head again. "She's spent her whole life being told not to talk about things at home, even with me. I'm afraid I'm missing something basic because I'm too used to the patterns of their daily life. I can't bear the thought of not doing something to help her." She put a hand to her heart. "So when Kenneth told me about everything you've done to help people, it just seemed like—well, to be honest, it seemed like the hand of God in my life." She took a shuddering breath and I could see tears shining in her eyes. She looked at me with a direct and vulnerable expression.

My heart pinched and I couldn't help but feel an urgent desire to help. She was a young woman asking for my help on behalf of her vulnerable younger sister. How could I say no? I hadn't been able to save my stillborn daughter, Georgia, over twenty years ago, and whenever I heard about a vulnerable young girl, I couldn't help but want to help her in Georgia's place.

Naomi went on, "And I have to tell you that I had almost come to stop believing in God at all. But if I fell in love with Kenneth in part because God wanted you in my life, then I'm going to use you. I need to know if Talitha is okay. It's the only way I can marry Kenneth and pursue my career without constantly looking back and worrying about her. And about everyone else."

Kurt made a "hmmm" noise, but otherwise did not make a comment about the wisdom of my getting involved in Naomi's family drama.

The waitress brought our meats on heaped platters that looked far too big for us to actually consume everything in one meal. We all gamely started skewering meat and cooking it anyway. When I'd taken my first too-hot bite and then gulped water to cool down my mouth, I put down my skewer to let it cool.

"I still don't understand what you think I can do," I said to Naomi.

She hadn't eaten anything on her skewer yet; she was too busy fiddling with it. "Well, I was thinking that maybe if you went to visit them, you'd see things with a more objective eye than I can. And maybe you can get people to talk to you when they won't talk to me. I don't know."

It seemed equally likely that I would see nothing more than Naomi could. But she sounded desperate and I wanted to help her. I liked her already, and I sympathized enormously with her desire to help her younger sister. What did I have to lose?

"Visit them?" Kurt asked, around a bite of his own meat. "Just show up on the doorstep and announce herself?"

Naomi made a negative gesture with her hand. "My father has already said he wants to invite you two up to the house to meet the families. He'll expect Kenneth and me to be there, too. But if I delay for a bit and tell him I have to do some studying, that might give you enough time to see things without my interpretation coloring it all." She looked directly at me at this.

"We'd be up there by ourselves?" said Kurt dubiously.

Did he think that polygamous cooties were going to get on him?

Naomi turned to him, flushed. "My father will probably make you listen to a lecture on the history of polygamy and why it's God's holiest path."

"You mean, he's going to try to convert us," said Kurt darkly.

"Not convert, exactly," Kenneth explained. "Believe me, I've already heard the spiel. It's annoying to listen through the whole thing, but he can take no for an answer. You just let him talk about it and then tell him you feel differently and that will be that."

Clearly Kenneth had lived through it. I was sure Kurt and I could do the same. After all, he and I both knew about how sacred polygamy had been in the early days of the church. We also knew it had been rejected by every prophet since Wilford Woodruff, so it wasn't as if we were going to change our minds about its current practice.

"I'll see what I can see," I said.

"Thank you so much," said Naomi, letting out a long breath.

"How old is Talitha?" I asked, starting to gather information.

"Ten," Naomi said. "And she's my aunt's daughter, not my mother's."

"What?" I said, confused.

Naomi sighed. "My father is married to my mother, Rebecca, and to my mother's younger sister, Sarah. So technically, Talitha is only my half-sister and my cousin, but we grew up in the same house and I've always thought of her as my baby sister."

I cringed at the thought of two sisters being married to the same man. It wasn't incest exactly, but it seemed too close to it for my tastes. Still, I knew that it had happened fairly often in the history of the church. If a man made one sister happy, people seemed to think he could make another sister happy. And the two sisters would already know how to live with each other, right?

"I see. Well, as long as you're not expecting a trained investigator or anything," I said.

"I understand and I want you to know how much I appreciate your willingness to help," Naomi said, smiling tremulously. "Talitha is so bright, so gentle and innocent. Sometimes I think she's who I would have been if I hadn't had all that pressure on me as the oldest. I want the best things in the world for her."

"You sound like a wonderful older sister," I said.

"You haven't met Talitha yet," said Naomi, her smile widening. "She's the wonderful one."

After that, we focused on eating, and even ordered a chocolate dessert course. I have to admit, it was the most fun I've had in a long time, reaching over people, nearly burning myself, and trying all the different combinations of meat. Even Kurt seemed to loosen up, at least for a few minutes. And yes, we did eat all of it.

Afterwards, Kurt and Kenneth argued over the bill, each trying to pay. We women didn't bother with more small talk. Naomi said she'd call her father and tell him we were waiting for an official invitation.

Kurt and I drove home in silence, except for one remark from Kurt: "I just wish you weren't getting encouragement to meddle in other people's business, again."

"They're practically family, now that Kenneth is marrying Naomi." And wasn't that my job, to take care of family, as a woman and a mother? "Besides, I feel that God is calling me to do this," I added. It was the one thing Kurt wouldn't contradict me on, if I said that I felt inspired to do something by God. And I did feel a warmth in my chest at the thought of this little girl, which I was sure was the Spirit telling me to look after her.

"All right, but please be careful," he said. And then after a moment, "You know I love you eternally, Linda."

I sighed. "I love you, too." It had been too long since we'd both said that.

CHAPTER 4

I wrote a letter to Samuel the next day, opening as usual with some inspirational copied-and-pasted pieces from the "Mormons Building Bridges" Facebook group, which was a safe place for LGBTQ Mormons and their allies to talk online. I also found a new essay up on the Huffington Post by Mitch Mayne, who was a personal hero of Samuel's. Mitch was an openly gay man who had served in his ward's bishopric in California. I'd never met him, but all his writings I'd read seemed not just progressive, but spiritually inspired.

After that, I gave a quick report about baby Carla and Joseph and Willow, about Adam and Marie, and about Zachary. I was pretty sure my other sons wrote to Samuel, but not as regularly as I did, so it was my job to fill in the gaps and make sure that Samuel's relationship with his brothers didn't fall apart while he was on his mission.

I took a break to shower and get dressed for the day, then came back to attempt a fair and honest account of our dinner with Naomi and Kenneth, omitting the part about her worrying that her sister was being abused. I also refrained from talking about how strained things still were between his parents because of the new policy. When he was at home, Samuel had been intuitive enough to sense things like that anyway, but I didn't want him to feel like I was asking him to take on responsibility for any of this.

I always sent real paper letters to our missionary sons, though many parents, including Kurt, used email. Samuel wrote back to both of us on "P-day," his preparation day, which was every Tuesday. He went to the public library in Boston and used the computer there, since he wasn't allowed to have access to one in his own apartment, according to his mission president's rules. Some missions had more computer access than Samuel's, but for him it was P-days only. Missionaries were also restricted from calling home except on Christmas and Mother's Day, or if there was a death in the family and they got special permission.

Samuel had spent Christmas and New Year's last year at the Missionary Training Center in Provo. He had been open about his sexuality with the mission president when he'd introduced himself on arrival in Boston, and with his trainer and his companion when they met and started serving together. So far, he claimed there hadn't been any problems, but I wasn't sure if I was hearing the whole story. Missionaries were instructed to write positive letters home, so if he was being harassed, I might never know of it. I couldn't help but think of Kenneth's companion Elder Ellison as I wrote, and prayed silently that if Samuel began to feel depressed, he'd get help.

I'd sent four of my five sons on missions now (my second oldest, Joseph, hadn't gone), and as a mother I always worried about my sons dying in a car crash or bike accident, getting held up at a grocery store or kidnapped (though that happens less in the United States), or having a sudden allergic reaction to something they'd never tasted before. You felt so disconnected, far worse than when you were just sending them off to college, where you got to talk to them or even visit whenever you wanted.

The church quoted statistics that proved that missionaries were safer than any other population of young men and women the same age, but somehow that didn't help me. The newspapers in Utah were always reporting on missionaries who died serving the Lord. It wasn't something that a mother's fervent prayer could stop.

Writing helped me feel just a little more connected, but I wanted to do more. I imagined that if I could just bake something delicious for Samuel, it would help him somehow—all my prayers for his safety packaged up in flour and sugar form. I wasn't sure how well my baked goods would travel to Boston, but we would find out. I put on my apron and got to work.

I didn't bake lemon Danishes often because they took a lot of time. But the work made me feel better—or maybe it was just a distraction from the pain of an empty house and a suddenly difficult marriage.

I kneaded until I felt the rich, sweet dough start to form a soft ball in my hands, then let it be. For Danishes, you don't want to work the dough to death. Next, I grated lemons for zest, then squeezed them. Juicing the lemons, I discovered the hard way that I had a tiny cut on my left hand that I hadn't noticed before. I rinsed my hands and patted them with a towel. The cut wasn't even big enough to bother putting a Band-Aid on, so I left it and moved on to boiling water for the lemon sauce. When the lemon sauce was finished, I put plastic wrap over the top to prevent a skin from forming, then let it sit in the refrigerator to cool.

The dough wasn't quite ready yet, so I put in a load of laundry and did some light cleaning in the upstairs bathroom. After that, I came back down and got started on rolling the Danishes out.

After I put the trays in the oven, I went downstairs to our storage room and found a box that would survive the US Postal Service. I brought it back up, along with some pieces of foam for padding.

When the timer beeped and the Danishes came out of the oven, they were perfect, just the tips golden brown. I stood over them, breathing in the scent of butter and lemon. I couldn't resist plucking a couple from the batch and eating them right then, when they were still hot and gooey. They fell apart in my fingers before I even got them to my mouth. I groaned with pleasure as the deliciousness burned my tongue.

I resisted eating a third until they had cooled down a little more, and this time I poured myself a glass of milk. This wasn't what I'd planned for lunch today, but it had fruit, grains, and milk—three food groups, right? All I needed was some spinach on the side and it would be a well-balanced meal.

When they had cooled completely, I packed them in Tupperware, then in paper towels. Finally, I headed to the post office with my care package, the letter inside. I knew it cost me more to send my Danishes than it would have for Samuel to buy some from a bakery in Boston. But these were from home and filled with more than calories. They were made with a mother's love, and as much as possible, I hoped that was a bulwark against life's storms.

CHAPTER 5

Naomi came to the family dinner the end of June and was received well by everyone. Willow and Marie joked with her and told her a few ribald family stories that I studiously ignored. I found out Naomi hated chicken breast and always asked for the drumstick on Thanksgiving, which would be useful for me to know in the future, since I usually just put those in soup. Adam found a connection with a friend of a friend who had gone to college with Naomi at the U. And Naomi was very good with baby Carla, who spit up on her. Only Kurt seemed less than ebullient, but he was at least kind and welcoming.

The second week in July, on Sunday night, Kurt fielded the actual phone call from Stephen Carter, Naomi's father, who invited us over to his family compound. After he'd hung up, I asked him what the man was like, but Kurt said, "I only talked to him on the phone. How would I know?"

"You can tell things from a person's voice," I insisted.

"Well, all I could tell was that he was well educated," said Kurt. But we already knew that.

I texted Kenneth, who said that he and Naomi wouldn't be coming for dinner, but they'd drive up and join us the next morning. "Did you understand that Stephen expects us to stay overnight?" I asked Kurt with raised eyebrows.

"We'll see," said Kurt, who was usually unfailingly polite in social situations, but clearly felt pushed to the limit here.

If we didn't stay overnight, I wondered if there would be any chance to find out what I needed about Talitha.

I packed bags for both of us Sunday night, while Kurt was still busy at the church. Since it was summer, it was convenient for Kurt to take some time off from his accounting business (Mormon bishop is a lay position, and doesn't pay the bills.) On Monday morning we headed out.

There was no Googling the address—the Carters lived off the map. At least the frustration Kurt felt at taking wrong turns made the drive less quiet than most of the time we'd been spending together lately. He didn't curse, but he came close a couple of times, eventually pulling over and asking for the instructions he'd scrawled down during his phone call with Stephen Carter. I handed them over because I couldn't read his handwriting. After heading north again on I-215, we finally took the correct exit, then a series of turns in the foothills behind the commercial section of town. The roads were narrow and potholed, and Kurt checked the directions twice more before stopping the truck in front of a gated complex.

"Is this it?" I said.

Kurt grunted in response.

There was no name emblazoned on the gate and no mailbox to be seen.

With all the pine trees that hadn't been cleared here, I could only make out one building on the property, though I assumed there were five houses somewhere in there, one for each wife. The large house looked some thirty years old. I didn't know when the fence had been erected. The iron gate looked ancient and a little rusty, and there was a padlock on it rather than an electronic keypad.

Kurt got out of the car and yanked on the gate, but it didn't budge. But while he was getting back in the truck, a boy who looked about eight years old, very blond and dressed in jeans and a long-sleeved blue-and-white checked shirt, appeared at the gate. He used a key on the padlock, opened the gate for us, waited solemnly and silently for us to drive through, then locked it again, and ran down a hill and out of sight.

Looking back at the gate and the thick metal fencing around it, I noticed how difficult it would be to get out if we didn't have permission, and I wondered how many people had keys. Was this one of the ways Stephen Carter made sure his wives and children remained under his control? I shivered at the thought and wondered why we were here, after all.

Naomi, I reminded myself. And little Talitha, who might be in danger.

The sound of gravel from the unpaved road hitting the underside of Kurt's truck reminded me of visiting my uncle's old farm in Idaho with my parents and brothers back when I was a little girl. Though I could see the Salt Lake Temple from here, this place was more wilderness than city, with native scrub oak and pine huddling together near a small stream that ran down the mountainside and leading eventually to either the Jordan River or the Great Salt Lake.

The big boulders that were usually removed from cultivated lawns had been left intact here, and I imagined that these ten or twelve acres looked very much like they had when the pioneers had first come into the valley in the 1840s and '50s. There were no sprinklers on the lawn, no flower gardens or

ornamental bushes, though I thought I could see a large vegetable garden as we wound around the gravel road toward the
big house.

It was three stories with white pillars in front, and it looked
like it could use a new coat of paint. The western wing had been
built more recently and seemed tacked on. On the rest of the
property, I made out only two buildings to the north and what
looked like a shed a little to the south of the main house, but the
terrain hadn't been leveled, so other buildings might have been
discreetly concealed by nature. The fence around the gate had
seemed to cover any access points, and I assumed it ran around
the property lines, even if I couldn't track it fully.

We rang the doorbell at the main white house, and a woman
in a close-fitting sheath, floral on black, answered the door. I was
surprised at how young she looked, though she clearly had the
same facial shape and nearly the same hair as Naomi. Surely this
couldn't be her mother, and Naomi was the oldest of the children,
which left . . . who?

"Good morning," she said.

"Kurt Wallheim," Kurt said, from behind me. "And this is my
wife, Linda."

There was a lot of noise behind her, children's voices.

"Come inside and I'll go get Rebecca," said the woman, waving
us in without either smile or warmth.

Ah, I thought, relieved to recognize a familiar name. Naomi
had told me that her mother's name was Rebecca.

Kurt and I stepped into a small foyer with wood flooring.

"I'm her aunt Sarah," explained the woman.

So she was Talitha's mother, I thought. "You and Rebecca
share this house?" I asked aloud.

"Yes, because we're sisters, but the other wives all have their own homes close by." There was that wide smile again, and it almost seemed to have something wolfish underneath it now.

"That makes sense," I said, though my head felt like a butter churn, trying to imagine what it would be like to live like this, behind a padlocked gate in a location that even Google didn't seem to know about. I was trying not to leap to conclusions, but Sarah did not strike me as a happy person, despite her nice clothing and her handsome features.

Sarah showed us into the front room, which was filled with musical instruments, including a baby grand piano in a strange shade of pink. There were also several recliners and a white-and-green plaid couch. The wallpaper was busy and floral, peeling at the edges.

"What a lovely room," I said politely. I felt acutely uncomfortable and wished at the moment that Kenneth and Naomi had been here with us to ease the way, but Naomi had wanted me to have this unfiltered view of her father's world.

"Our sitting room, but it doubles as our music room," Sarah said. "Carolyn comes to give lessons here when she isn't pregnant." She gestured to the couch, and Kurt and I sank into it. "Rebecca will be here shortly," she said. "She's been waiting for your arrival all day."

There was a long moment of silence until I said, "This seems a lovely, private piece of property."

"Oh, it is private, all right," said Sarah.

That didn't sound very positive. I glanced at Kurt, who was studiously not looking at Sarah. He did that sometimes when he found a woman attractive. So that left polite conversation to me. I wanted to ask a thousand questions, from how long Sarah had been married to why she'd decided to join her sister in polygamy and how they dealt with things like food preparation and, well, jealousy.

Instead, I tried something innocuous. "How many children do you have?" I asked.

"Five," she said. "Two boys and three girls."

I nodded. "I have five children, too." We had something in common now, which should open things up. "How old are they?"

She shrugged. "Far too young," she said.

I was left trying to figure out if she meant they required a lot of care or something else. "My sons are mostly grown," I said, guessing at the former. "I have one granddaughter now, but I remember the days when they were all at home. It was very noisy, very chaotic. Sometimes I would wish for just one moment to myself."

Sarah stared at me. "And would that help?" she asked. "One moment to yourself, I mean. Were you able to pretend for a little while that they didn't exist, that you were the woman you had once been?"

I didn't know how to answer that. My suspicion about her being unhappy seemed confirmed now.

Kurt put a hand on my shoulder. "I think Linda has always been the same person," he said gently.

Sarah looked sour at this, though I thought it was a nice compliment—and a surprising one considering our relationship right now. "Really? No changes? Then what did you do before you had children?" Sarah asked.

"Do?" I echoed, trying to refocus.

She waved a hand. "As work. Or were you one of those women who never thought she would do anything but be a mother, like my sister Rebecca?" There was clearly a nasty judgment in that phrase. All was not "well in Zion" here.

"I studied psychology, but I never went to work in it." Unless you counted my trying to help troubled families behind the scenes as a bishop's wife, I suppose. It certainly wasn't paid.

"Then you never had grand ambitions that you gave up?" Sarah said.

"What? I guess not." I'd heard younger women talk about regrets about being stay-at-home mothers, but that had rarely fazed me. I was happy with my choices in the past and my prospects for a future.

"Ah." Sarah turned to Kurt, as if her interest in me was over. "And you? Were you always the bread and butter type?"

He didn't wince at this blunt assessment, though I found myself wanting to defend him. Kurt was an accountant, but that didn't mean that he was boring. He helped people, which he did by using numbers. He wasn't a cog in a wheel. He was an individual and she didn't know anything about him just by looking at him for two minutes.

"I always believed that earning a living honestly was nothing to be ashamed of," Kurt said.

"Honestly? That means you think other people make a living dishonestly? People who don't follow the rules like you do?" Sarah said, one eyebrow raised.

For a first meeting, she seemed to be making a lot of judgments about us. Maybe we were, too, but I felt like we weren't blurting them out. I wondered if Sarah met people so rarely she didn't have a good sense of what was socially acceptable or if it was just a mean nature that made her like this.

"And what's your profession, if I may ask?" Kurt said, somehow managing not to sound accusing in return.

"My purpose in life is my painting," Sarah said.

I'd never met a painter before and wondered if this made sense of her dislike of company. Maybe we were interrupting her painting time. But then again, if we were, having so many children couldn't be good for her art, either.

"That sounds fascinating," Kurt said genuinely. "I've always loved the great painters."

She sniffed at him. "Oh, really? Who is your favorite?"

I was sure she was waiting to hear that Kurt admired da Vinci or perhaps Rembrandt. Instead, Kurt said, "Kandinsky."

It stopped her for a moment, and she blinked at Kurt. Recovering, she said, "Ah, Kandinsky. You've seen reproductions, I suppose."

"I traveled to Europe in college and saw as many of his originals as I could find when I was in Berlin," Kurt responded. I'm sure he was enjoying her surprise at this new facet to his character.

"Excuse me. I think I hear one of the children calling for help," Sarah said abruptly, and went out the back door.

I could see nearly a dozen children playing in the backyard, but Sarah didn't go to any of them. She headed past them, disappearing into the shed. Was she going to get some outdoor toy or gardening implement? I didn't see her come out and after a minute, I gave up waiting for it. She wasn't the one I'd come for, anyway, and even if she was a painter, I didn't particularly want to spend more time with her.

I watched the children outside. Which one was Talitha? They all looked alike to me, though the girls were dressed in denim or khaki skirts rather than shorts or pants as the boys were, and their long hair was braided. I was impatient to talk to the little girl I'd come to help, but I reminded myself I could do that later, once we'd met Stephen Carter. I was already steeling myself for his defense of polygamy.

"Do you ever wonder what would happen if the Supreme

Court ruled that polygamy was legal?" I whispered to Kurt. It seemed a real possibility, now that same-sex marriage had been ruled legal throughout the country.

He shook his head. "I really think it's unlikely we'd suddenly hear about a revelation to return to polygamy. The church doesn't want to be associated with Warren Jeffs or anyone like him."

"*Sister Wives* doesn't look that bad on television," I said, trying to joke around.

Kurt wasn't amused. "It doesn't look normal, and the church needs to look normal for the missionary work to go forward," he said practically.

"Hmm," I said. I suddenly wished I had done more research on fringe Mormon polygamy. I'd assumed I knew enough about it, but now that I was here, I felt like a kid caught unprepared for a test.

CHAPTER 6

There were footsteps down the stairs and the woman who appeared looked like a much older version of Sarah. Her belly sagged in the loose cotton gown she wore, and her wrinkled face was marked with age spots.

Kurt and I both stood to greet her.

"Oh, you're here already. I was just doing some laundry. I thought . . ." Her gaze drifted to the backyard and I figured she knew where her sister had gone. "Well, anyway, I'm Rebecca Carter." She offered a tired smile that seemed very familiar to me. "I'm so glad to meet you. My husband, Stephen, will be here in just a few minutes. He had some business to attend to." She shook our hands formally, her two hands over each one of ours in turn. "Brother and Sister Wallheim, it's so good to meet you now that our children are planning to bind our families together."

"Please call me Linda," I said.

"Call me Kurt," Kurt said after a long moment.

I'd never thought of his name as a description of him before. Maybe it hadn't been before now. My curt Kurt. I'd always liked his honesty, but not everyone did.

"Sit, sit." Rebecca moved to sit on one of the recliners and motioned us back to the couch. Behind her was the pink piano.

There was also a cello in a stand-up case, a bass, and several violins and violas, as well as some wind instruments.

"Did anyone get you refreshments yet?" she asked. "I'm sure it was hot outside and you've come quite a ways. I have some lemonade freshly made."

"No, thank you. We're fine," said Kurt, though I would have liked to have tasted her lemonade, just to see how it compared to mine. Did she put lemon zest in it like I did?

"Something to eat?"

"We've eaten," Kurt answered for both of us again.

"All right, then. We can focus on getting to know each other," said Rebecca. She folded her hands in her lap. "I understand you're an accountant, Kurt. Is that as fascinating as I've always imagined it to be?" There was just a faint flicker of a smile in contrast to her sister's wolfish and cold smile.

Rebecca might have more children than I did, and her life circumstances were certainly very different, but her manner made it easy to feel at home with her. I felt an instant connection to this woman. I'd heard some Mormons say that when that happened, it was a sign that you had been friends in the premortal life, as spirits, and destined to find each other again.

Kurt laughed gently, as easy with her as I was, it seemed. "It pays well and I'm good at it. It's been a blessing to our family."

"Except perhaps around April fifteenth?" Rebecca said.

"Well, it feels like less of a blessing then, certainly," Kurt said. "But not all blessings feel like blessings when we're getting through them."

"That's certainly true." Rebecca's face tightened and I wondered what "blessings" she was thinking about right then.

"Being the wife of a physician must be difficult, as well," Kurt said.

Rebecca's mouth twitched. "Relatively speaking, that is not the most difficult part of my life."

We were all dancing around the elephant in the room at this point. Where was Stephen? Where were the other three wives? Why hadn't he made sure they were all here in a row to greet us? I answered the question myself—because he wanted us to see how normal they were. Rebecca was normal. This one main house was normal. All of this was supposed to feel normal to us.

Except that it wasn't.

"And you have five boys, I understand," Rebecca said, turning to me. "Kenneth is, what, the third?"

"He's the fourth," I said, and then listed them off in order. "Adam, Joseph, Zachary, Kenneth, and Samuel. In fact, Samuel, the youngest, just left on a mission to Boston, so we're empty nesters now." There was pride in that, and just a tinge of sadness for me.

"I hope to meet the others some time. They must be good men, if Kenneth is a measure of them. I'm sure you're very proud of the kind young man he is. He's certainly won Naomi's heart, which is no easy thing, let me tell you," Rebecca said warmly. "When she left the house for college and I asked her how she would manage telling men she dated about her family, she said that she didn't plan to date. I think her exact words were, 'No man is worth that kind of trouble.' And for more than four years, she continued to believe that. Until Kenneth."

I felt oddly touched by this tribute to Kenneth, and I could see that Kurt was struck speechless.

"Thank you," I said. "You must know, as a mother of grown children, that it's always nice to hear good things about them when they're out on their own."

It occurred to me belatedly that I ought to say something nice about Naomi, but Kurt got there before me.

"Naomi seems very intelligent and ambitious. But to be honest, I was most impressed with how attached she is to her younger brothers and sisters. She must have a big heart," he said.

I tensed, worried Kurt was going to say too much about Talitha and why we were really here, but he narrowly avoided it.

"Well," Rebecca said, "Naomi has always taken good care of her younger siblings. She started babysitting when she was very young and I worried she would become resentful about it. When she was a teenager that was certainly a problem between us. She hated it when I asked her to watch the other children instead of doing her schoolwork. Then she would be up till all hours of the night finishing while everyone else was asleep. I thought going to college away from the family might make her selfish, but she still comes home and brings treats for the younger ones every time."

Other teenagers argued with their mothers about spending too much time with friends; Naomi had apparently resented not having time to do schoolwork. That told me something about Naomi, and about how strict the rules of the family here were.

"I suppose you have another older daughter who has taken her place now as the main babysitter at home," I said. I was thinking about Talitha, and how maybe it was possible that it wasn't an adult who was abusing her at all, but one of the other trapped, older children.

"After Naomi, the next two oldest are Aaron and Joseph," Rebecca said. "But they are both at the U of U and don't live here, either. After that comes Ruth, who spends weekends at home, but goes up to USU during the week for school."

So she had four children who were out of the house, similar to my five. But she had a younger family, as well. What would my life have been like if I'd had five more children after Samuel?

What if I'd had to deal with other wives and children, and a gated compound that was difficult to leave? I could hardly imagine.

"Were they all homeschooled?" Kurt asked.

"The younger children are, yes. But Naomi, Aaron, and Joseph had already started high school by the time our family situation had changed such that it became expedient to keep more to ourselves," Rebecca said.

She must have practiced many times talking about polygamy without talking about it, I thought.

"The older three petitioned to finish public school as they had begun, and Stephen negotiated with them to make sure that they didn't neglect their other duties for schoolwork. Ruth moved to a hybrid model of homeschooling and public schooling."

I'd heard Mormons talk about children needing to continue to do chores around the house when they were in high school, or contribute financially to the family, but Stephen Carter's "negotiations" sounded like overkill.

"A hybrid model?" Kurt repeated. "What do you mean?"

"Stephen has the same rules for all of the children about how many hours a week they must spend helping at home," Rebecca explained. "It increases with each year of age, to compensate for their food, clothing, and other expenses. For Ruth, it's been easier if she comes home on weekends to manage those hours."

I cringed. Counting hours of housework against family expenses? College girls who had to come home and do chores around the house? I wanted my children to have their own lives, not keep paying me back for raising them. Perhaps independence was not as valued for young women in a polygamous family, however.

"What about the boys?" Kurt asked. "Do they also come home to help around the house?"

"Not with housework. They have other ways of repaying Stephen. Helping tutor the younger children via Skype, for instance," Rebecca said, smiling as if it all made perfect sense.

I wasn't sure if I was angrier about the whole idea of how children owed their parents or the way that the boys seemed to get off easy. I changed the subject. "Are your older sons planning to live—like you do?" I asked, not sure if Naomi was an anomaly. This compound was big enough for one polygamous group, but it could easily get very crowded in another generation. And I hated to think about how much control over his children's lives Stephen would exert if they all married and raised children right here, under his thumb.

But Rebecca shook her head emphatically. "No. Stephen is very insistent that living the Principle has to be an individual call from God. He doesn't know why God called him, but he couldn't turn away from it. He knows how hard the life is, though, and wouldn't force it on any of his children."

I felt relieved, but confused. Obviously, Stephen thought his lifestyle was more godly than monogamy. Why wouldn't he want the highest law for his children?

Rebecca must have guessed that Kurt and I were trying hard to suppress our curiosity, because she added, "Stephen said that I was to answer any questions that you had about living the Principle while we're waiting for him to return."

I admit, I was there to help Talitha, but I was dying to ask questions.

"Go on, ask whatever you like," Rebecca said, smiling faintly.

I wanted to ask about hand-me-downs and chore charts and how much it cost a day to feed this many people. I wanted to ask if anyone ever forgot how many children they had, or which ones were theirs or whose house Stephen went to each night for dinner. I wanted to ask if the wives fought over Stephen and what their sex lives were like. But Kurt got there first.

"Naomi said that Stephen didn't talk about polygamy with you until some years after you were married," Kurt said. "How did that happen?"

Rebecca leaned back on the couch, smoothing out her dress with overly intense concentration. "We'd been married ten years, actually." She paused to take a deep breath. "Stephen had always studied church history very carefully. Then one day he took me to the Salt Lake Temple. He made sure we had time to stay in the celestial room afterward. He told me everything, holding my hand on the white couch, whispering directly into my ear. How he'd been called to the Principle—how we'd both been called. He begged me to accept it." She sounded choked up about a precious memory.

I could see Kurt was rigid in shock at this. I felt much the same. Stephen had used the temple for this conversation? And the holiest of holy places, the celestial room? The celestial room was the place you were only allowed to enter after you had been through the sacred endowment ceremony, a place of pure peace and utter silence, so clean you would never see a piece of lint on the floor, and everything in it was perfectly white. And Stephen Carter had used that sacred space to tell his wife he wanted to marry other women?

"I see," I murmured, trying to disguise my disgust.

"We've never been back to the temple since that day. Stephen was excommunicated not many months later," said Rebecca, her tone mournful. "And though our bishop hasn't excommunicated me, I haven't been back. I think the bishop sees us as victims of a wayward man and keeps trying to help us in various ways." She gave a brief, watery smile.

Kurt's expression was pinched, but he managed to keep quiet. I suspected he, too, felt pity for the wives and children involved in this.

"Ten years after you were married," I said aloud, thinking about what I had been like ten years after Kurt and I had married. All those young children in so few years—my body had been exhausted and flabby and I might not have always been pleasant to be around. "Did Stephen marry someone younger?" I hoped I wasn't prying, but she had said to ask anything.

"Jennifer was a little younger, but age had nothing to do with it," Rebecca said. "She was the person we were both led to by the Spirit to invite to join us in living the Principle for the first time."

Kurt and I shared a look again, a real moment of communion. Led by the Spirit my ass, I thought.

"People from the outside always think it's about the sex. That's the last thing it has anything to do with it," Rebecca went on, utterly sincere and straight-faced. "It's a spiritual marriage first and foremost. Everything else is just figuring out what works best for whom."

"What about your sister?" I asked. "When did she join the—uh—group?"

Rebecca looked down. "Sarah was the fourth wife, the third spiritual wife. She's fifteen years younger than I am. She was just a child when I married Stephen."

I couldn't read Rebecca's emotion here. Was she jealous of her sister, or sad for her? I didn't have any sisters so I tried to imagine sharing a house with one of my brothers. No. We'd never survive.

"Have you ever considered joining one of the other polyga-mous groups?" I asked. I'd heard of various groups, like the

Kingston clan and the Apostolic United Brethren in Utah County, and I thought there were some in Arizona, as well.

"No, no. Stephen thinks they're all completely crazy. Or evil," said Rebecca with a sad expression.

Kurt put a hand to his mouth at this, stifling a laugh, I think. I covered the gaffe by saying, "Why is that?"

"The way they treat their wives and children is scandalous. No education. Nearly enslaving them. No freedom to choose their own lives. It's one of the reasons Joanna is here."

"Joanna?" asked Kurt.

"She's the youngest and newest of the wives, and she's from the FLDS. She ran away when she was only sixteen years old and her daughter Grace was a baby. She had to seek legal emancipation from her parents before she could be assured she wouldn't be sent back. Poor child."

Which one, mother or daughter? Both, probably.

I didn't disagree with Stephen's assessment of the FLDS. Young girls in that community were often denied an education past the sixth grade, forced to provide childcare, cooking, cleaning, and other unpaid labor, and then married off by age thirteen or fourteen to begin a life of bearing a dozen or more children for an older, authoritarian man who had ten other wives and a hundred children. Many of the women never escaped because they were too caught up in mothering children they could not leave or care for financially without the help of the FLDS community. But this one girl had gotten free—only to join another polygamous life. Why? Was it just too hard for her to stop thinking of the world—or herself—in that way?

"A marriage with one other partner seems hard enough," said Kurt. "With so many, it must magnify the problems exponentially." The mathematical metaphor was very Kurt, and I tried not to wince at the implication that he thought marriage to me was difficult.

"It can go bad, I know that," Rebecca said. "We all went in with our eyes open, though. I've seen the problems some people have with the Principle. But they are all human mistakes. Jealousy, gossip, greed, anger. What God grants is the capacity to overcome these. That is why the Principle is the way we must live. It's the only way to really become godlike and reject all of our mortal flaws."

The way she spoke about it seemed so devout. Of course, she was converted to it, but it wasn't that she thought she was better than anyone else, just that this was one way she'd found to live the gospel's command to be less selfish. Who couldn't use more help in that quest? I certainly could, even if I couldn't believe God expected me to do what Rebecca had done.

"Jealousy and gossip are certainly problems for everyone," said Kurt, who was clearly less moved by Rebecca's speech than I was.

"If I hadn't come to my own conclusion that God had called me to practice polygamy, I would never have agreed to it. And Stephen was serious when he told me that I had to agree or he wouldn't do it," she said earnestly.

"What are your thoughts about Emma Smith?" I said, going back to the history of Mormon polygamy, where my opinions were more solid. "She didn't agree and Joseph married other women anyway." Emma Smith had hated polygamy so much that when she learned Brigham Young planned to continue the practice even after Joseph Smith's death, she refused to follow him and the Saints west to Utah—instead, she left and created the first off-shoot of the Mormon church, now called the Community of Christ. Rebecca had done what Emma Smith had not—condoned her husband's desire to marry other women. But Stephen Carter had done what Joseph Smith had not—waited until his first wife agreed.

"Joseph Smith was a prophet of God who was asked to do a nearly impossible thing," Kurt had said almost automatically. He always tensed when people mentioned Joseph Smith in a way that was less than reverential.

"Well, at least we can agree on that," said Rebecca, and at that, the back door opened and Stephen Carter himself was home.

CHAPTER 7

Standing up to shake his hand, I was immediately impressed by the energy of Stephen Carter's presence even though he was probably only five foot nine or ten, average height. He was a handsome man, with dark hair containing only a hint of gray, a strong chin, a Roman nose just like Naomi's, and bright, penetrating blue eyes. I could understand why some women might find him very attractive.

"But what about Kenneth and Naomi?" Stephen asked, looking around the room after we had made the necessary introductions. "I thought they were going to be here, as well."

I looked at Kurt, hoping no one would blame us for this change in plans.

"Naomi texted and said that she had a test she had to study for," Rebecca said calmly. "She and Kenneth will be here as soon as they can make it."

"All right, then. I suppose we don't need them to explain our way of life to you," said Stephen. "Has Rebecca already talked about our conversion to the Principle?"

He turned to face Kurt and the question seemed addressed to him alone, almost as if Rebecca and I were not in the room. It wasn't the first time I'd been ignored by another Mormon man talking to my husband, and it probably wouldn't be the last, but it was still annoying. I glanced at Rebecca and she met my eyes with apology.

"Yes, she did," said Kurt diffidently. His chin was lifted, making the difference in their heights clearer. He was several inches taller than Stephen.

"Sit, sit," Stephen said, waving his hands to include me this time.

After a moment, we complied. I regretted accepting his invitation to sit almost immediately because Stephen stepped forward and loomed over us, as if speaking on a pulpit. "Do you know what Brigham Young said when he first heard about the Principle?"

I watched as Kurt twitched. He was used to being in control of the pulpit every Sunday. But he remained seated by me and shook his head. "I don't," he said.

That seemed to give Stephen full license to expand, and expand he did. "He said that he saw a hearse passing and wished most fervently to trade places with the man in the coffin. That was how much he hated the idea of plural marriage. But he was converted to it because God spoke to him. It was a restoration of an ancient and holy practice." A grand gesture with outstretched arms. "Abraham and Jacob had multiple wives, and if the true church was to be restored, it had to include all of the tenets from the past."

"I know why Joseph Smith restored polygamy," Kurt said tartly.

But Stephen continued the lecture anyway, going all the way back to the 1830s, adding in details I'd never heard of before, including a promise to Joseph in the First Vision that he would become like Abraham, that Joseph's seed would also "number as the sands of the sea" through his progeny, and the claim that all of the prophets of the Book of Mormon had practiced polygamy, from Lehi and Nephi to Alma and Samuel the Lamanite, who had prophesied the birth of Christ.

"Have you never wondered why so few women are named in The Book of Mormon?" Stephen asked, turning to me.

"Well, uh—" was all I got out. I don't think he really wanted me to say more. This was his chance to shine, his own sermon he was expecting us to listen to with rapt attention. I felt that discomfort I sometimes feel when I attend other Christian worship services, where there are so many notes that are exactly what I think, mixed in with things I don't like at all or even find rather offensive, like the curse of Eve or celibacy for priests.

"Women were scrubbed out of the Book of Mormon," Stephen continued, "ever since Heber J. Grant worked to spread the missionary work worldwide. He felt that all references to polygamy in our own past and in our doctrine had to be wiped away and he did his best to convince converts and lifelong Mormons that the LDS church is simply another Christianity, rather than a radical return to the old practices of Judaism."

I couldn't help but glance at Rebecca, who was staring at her husband with awe, like the man she knew as a mortal had become rather more than that in an inspired speech. I'd had a couple of moments like that with Kurt, I admit, although maybe not as many as he would have liked since he became bishop.

Stephen continued, "When an angel came with a sword of destruction and threatened Joseph's life if he did not begin to practice polygamy in 1839, it had to come three times over a period of months before he listened. He waited as long as he possibly could before he spoke to Emma about what God had revealed to him.

"And then when Emma would not listen, Joseph had no choice but to begin to seek out those women whom God had reserved for him to be sealed to. Emma's reluctance meant that he no longer had to ask for her permission, but it also taught him that he had to keep this most sacred of all parts of Mormonism secret because the agents of Satan would try to destroy him even as he showed those who were willing to hear from him how to become gods."

Becoming gods in the celestial kingdom wasn't something Mormons talked about much anymore, though it had certainly been part of polygamy and there were remnants of this belief in the temple ceremony. You had to promise some pretty hefty rewards, in my opinion, to get people to do something so inherently difficult.

"One of the women Joseph married was Eliza R. Snow, the great poetess and future president of the Relief Society. But it was only recently revealed by the historian Andrea Radke-Moss that Eliza had been gang-raped by enemies of the church, and injured in a way that meant she would never be able to have children. Marrying her and other stalwart women like her was a way for Joseph to show them that God still loved them and that they would not be left out of the promises of the temple sealing in the eternities. She might never have her own increase, but she could share with her sister wives in theirs. And when Joseph died, Brigham Young stood in and took his place, giving Eliza his name and his honor and protection for the rest of her days. How could anyone argue that such a use of polygamy was wrong or in any way sexually motivated?"

Though I didn't trust everything Stephen said, I felt something within me stir at this explanation of Eliza Snow, who had been a great Mormon poet and leader of women. Her beautiful song

"O My Father" was one of my favorites and I had always wondered why, when she disagreed with him so often, she had married Brigham Young. For a moment, I found myself nodding with Stephen Carter, agreeing with him that at least for Eliza, polygamy might have made sense.

Then I shook myself. I'd better be more careful listening to Stephen Carter's incantatory storytelling or I was going to end up thinking Kurt and I should start looking around for another wife. Stephen Carter was so charismatic that I could see how I could be taken in, despite disagreeing so strongly with him.

"In 1841, after Emma had refused to embrace the doctrine of celestial marriage, Joseph led another woman to the temple and was sealed to her first. Can you imagine how that made him feel? The woman he had fallen in love with as a young man, the woman he had gone through so much sorrow with, had shared his children's births and deaths with, was not with him on that most important day of his life?" asked Stephen.

I had always imagined it from Emma's perspective. Had Joseph told her coldly what he was planning to do that day? Had she argued with him? Threatened to leave him? Had he done it secretly, furtively? Had she found out the truth from the other woman, now sealed to Joseph for time and all eternities while Emma was his in this life only?

I looked at Rebecca, who was waving at one of the children in the backyard, trying to mouth some encouragement. It was exactly what I thought a good mother would do, but Stephen's body language showed irritation at the distraction for a moment before he decided to ignore her and focus on me and Kurt again.

"Joseph Smith said, 'a religion that does not require the sacrifice of all things never has the power sufficient to produce the faith necessary unto life and salvation.' And Brigham Young took up that challenge. After the Saints were chased from their homes in Nauvoo in 1844 and so many died that terrible winter waiting by the Mississippi River for spring, Brigham Young was inspired by God to lead his people to a place where they could practice the Principle in peace. And under his leadership, they made the desert blossom as a rose in the great new state of Deseret."

Brigham Young had been a great secular leader. The American Moses, some called him. His spiritual ideas had been downplayed by church leaders since then, from the Adam-God doctrine—the belief that Adam was himself God, an idea the LDS church has rejected—to his insistence that black skin was a sign of a curse from God and that no white person could ever marry someone of any other race without losing their temple blessings.

"Brigham Young thought he had left the government that had rejected his people and his religion, but the United States could never stop pressing its borders. And so the only hope for statehood and real political power for the Saints was to give into the demands of an ungodly government. That was why John Taylor, the third president of the church, gave the priesthood keys to the Council of Seven Friends, who continued to practice the law of the celestial kingdom secretly."

What? I'd never heard about any Council of Friends, but I figured this was something else that Stephen had invented and pressed into the history of the church to support his own choices.

"Wait. What about Wilford Woodruff?" Kurt asked. "He was the next president and had all the keys of the church."

"No," explained Stephen patiently. "After John Taylor gave the keys of the priesthood to the council, Woodruff only had the keys of the presidency of the church, which is why he had no power to alter the true and everlasting Covenant when he gave the unholy Manifesto of 1890, which banned polygamy."

This was complicated and unconvincing and I looked around the room. Rebecca looked distant, and I suspected she was impatient and wished that she could be doing something useful, like laundry or dishes or food prep, instead of listening to this long conversation for what must be the upteenth time for her.

"The Manifesto of 1890 was a revelation from God," Kurt argued, "recorded by His only true prophet on the earth at that time. It was the will of God for us to practice polygamy until 1890, and then it wasn't His will anymore and anyone who continued practicing it was going against not only the precepts of the church, but against God Himself."

"You say that when the very apostles of the church were continuing to practice polygamy themselves?" Stephen asked. "And when they continued to perform temple marriages for other polygamists for at least another decade?"

"That's a convenient story promulgated by polygamists and enemies of the church," Kurt said.

Was it? I'd heard that Mitt Romney had ancestors in Mexico practicing polygamy after 1890. Maybe there were others, too.

"Have you never heard of the Second Manifesto given in 1904 by Joseph F. Smith? Why did there have to be a Second Manifesto if the apostles were obeying the first one? John W. Taylor, the son of John Taylor himself, was excommunicated along with Matthias Cowley, both in the Quorum of the Twelve Apostles, because they believed that the 1890 Manifesto was a political document only, meant to deceive the United States government until the Saints could continue to live the Principle openly." Stephen's tone was smug.

"Even apostles can be deceived at times," said Kurt stiffly.

I thought of the recent policy that so harmed LGBTQ members. If Kurt could admit the apostles could be wrong about polygamy, why couldn't he admit they could also be wrong about that?

"Deceived? But the many polygamous marriages in Mexico and Canada after 1890 were done officially by men authorized by the presidents of the church, from Wilford Woodruff to Lorenzo Snow and Joseph F. Smith. George Q. Cannon, who performed these marriages, was a counselor in the First Presidency, and Brigham Young Jr. was also officially asked to do marriages in Mexico and Canada for those Mormons who still wanted to live the Principle after Utah was made a state," said Stephen.

He was throwing names at me too quickly for me to process. I felt overwhelmed by his information; I had no idea if he was making it all up or not.

But Kurt said, "It was unclear for a time if the Manifesto of 1890 was only meant to rescind polygamy where it was illegal. It was not illegal in Mexico or Canada."

That sounded like a weak excuse to me, but Stephen was ready with a reply.

"Then what about the fact that there were still apostles of the church living polygamously in the United States in the 1940s?" he said.

What? I was so shocked at this I could hardly breathe. It felt like my head was floating above my neck by several inches. That wasn't true, surely. I made a squawking sound, but I couldn't get out any words.

"That isn't possible," Kurt said.

"Look it up. You'll see it's true. In 1943, apostle Richard Lyman was excommunicated for living in a polygamous marriage. Rebecca, can you get that essay by Michael Quinn?" He nodded toward the bookcase and Rebecca moved to obey him.

But when he offered the ancient and well-read copy of the magazine *Dialogue* to Kurt, Kurt simply put it down, unopened. I didn't blame him. Rebecca handed it to me and I glanced at it briefly, but not closely. Maybe I didn't want to know the truth. I wanted to remain a Mormon. I was clinging desperately to my faith, even now.

"Whatever you say about the past, polygamy is no longer a part of our doctrine" Kurt said.

"What about Doctrine and Covenants Section 132?" asked Stephen. He began to quote: "*For behold, I reveal unto you a new and an everlasting covenant; and if ye abide not that covenant, then are ye damned; for no one can reject this covenant and be permitted to enter into my glory.*"

"That's referring to marriage in the temple forever," said Kurt. "It has nothing to do with polygamy."

I certainly wanted what Kurt said to be true, but I had read that section of the Doctrine and Covenants, the scriptures that Joseph Smith had written during the early days of the church in the 1830s and 1840s, and I wasn't sure you could get around reading it as about polygamy.

Stephen continued, still quoting, "*Abraham received concubines, and they bore him children; and it was accounted unto him for righteousness, because they were given unto him, and he abode in my law;*

"*And again, as pertaining to the law of the priesthood—if any man espouse a virgin, and desire to espouse another, and the first give her consent, and if he espouse the second, and they are virgins, and have vowed to no other man, then is he justified;*

"*Then shall they be gods, because they have no end; therefore shall they be from everlasting to everlasting, because they continue; then shall they be above all, because all things are subject*

unto them. Then shall they be gods, because they have all power,
and the angels are subject unto them."

I got so tired sometimes of all the old scriptures about men becoming gods. Women were supposed to become goddesses, too, according to the temple, but we also promised to obey our husbands, so what did godhood mean to us?

"Polygamy continues to be the law of the holy priesthood," Stephen said. "God Himself is bound by laws and that is one. He cannot offer the blessings of the holy priesthood to those who do not abide by the laws He has instituted."

I shook my head adamantly. "No," I said, but Stephen was waiting for Kurt's response.

"It sounds like you're commanding God, when God works within the laws of the countries the gospel has to be spread within," Kurt said, his fists clenched. "He has done that many times. Many of the policies of the church are changed to deal with different cultures. Polygamy was a law God used for a time, but it isn't a requirement. It's not part of the church anymore."

I wasn't so sure about that. My friend Anna had been angry that her husband hadn't been sealed to her after his first wife died, when he could have been. Men were routinely allowed to be sealed to more than one spouse, while women could only be sealed to one in this life. Even if they had children with both, it was routinely said that the children would be sealed to the first husband alone because there was no polyandry in heaven, only polygyny.

Stephen went on, triumphant now that he could see he had gotten to both me and Kurt on an emotional level. "And I suppose you also did not hear that a resurrected Joseph Smith appeared to John Taylor in 1886, four years before the first Manifesto? He warned John Taylor that the church would be led astray and that he had to give the priesthood keys in secret to those who would wait and continue to practice God's law until Joseph himself and Christ appeared to take the keys back. The true law of the church has been polygamy all this time."

"A resurrected Joseph Smith? But his bones rest in his grave, with his wife, Emma," said Kurt. "I've been to that grave in Nauvoo. Hyrum's bones are there, as well."

We'd taken all our children there, in fact, years ago.

But Stephen waved this idea away. "I don't know who told you that those were Joseph's bones. Perhaps they are Hyrum's, but Joseph was resurrected only a few years after his death. Of course, he would be. Why would God not make use of one of his most valiant servants, a man powerful in the priesthood?"

I was annoyed by this argument. I didn't really care whether the bones in the grave we had visited were real. But I seriously doubted that a resurrected Joseph had told John Taylor to send the priesthood keys not to the next church president but to some random group of men. Why would God work in such a backhanded way?

"So now you have those priesthood keys?" Kurt asked, red-faced and genuinely angry now. "And the church itself doesn't? You're saying all the men in the church who think that they have the power to call God's blessings down on their children are wrong? You're saying that the very temples that seal couples and families together throughout the world don't have the keys to do so?"

Rebecca had tensed and was looking back and forth between her husband and Kurt.

Stephen leaned in to Kurt, making me acutely uncomfortable since he was now crowding my space, as well. "I'm making you feel attacked, Kurt, and I don't intend to do that. Of course, the mainstream LDS church has continued to do the work of God since the Manifestos, as far as is possible under the legal restrictions that it follows. Milk must be drunk before meat for most of the world, and that is what your church is. The church of milk, which is nothing to be ashamed of."

Kurt was boiling mad by now. I thought about Kenneth going through all of this rigmarole. It would have bothered him a lot less because he no longer believed in Mormonism and had had his name removed from the records of the church. But wouldn't Kenneth have seen how much these accusations would bother Kurt? Or had Stephen deliberately hit harder at Kurt than he had at Kenneth?

"The Lord will never allow the prophet to lead us astray," Kurt said. "We've been promised that. God would take the prophet's life before that happened, and raise another in his place."

Considering the policy and all the other times the prophets had said things that turned out to be wrong, like about blacks and the priesthood, I wasn't sure I could agree with Kurt on this anymore. Though that didn't mean I agreed with Stephen, either.

"Ah, well. If you cannot believe that Wilford Woodruff or any other prophet has been wrong, I must talk to you about this in a different way." Stephen had pulled back at last, allowing me to take a breath. He templed his hands and closed his eyes for a moment. Then he said abruptly, "Did you know that I lost my parents when I was only eighteen years old?"

I stared at him, surprised at the sudden vulnerability in his moist eyes. Then I looked at Rebecca, who had tensed at this reference. Why? Was this too personal for her?

"My younger brother, Edward, died in the same tragedy, a house fire on this very property." He gestured to the window that looked out on the compound. "It was a horrific life event, and I was never the same afterward. I suffered from depression for many years, something I didn't share with anyone." His brow creased with sorrow.

I hated that he was making me feel sympathy for him. I only wanted to feel sympathy for his wives and children. After all, a tragic past didn't mean he wasn't an abuser, I reminded myself.

Stephen continued, "But that sorrow is part of the reason I clung to my religion so desperately. I had to believe that I would one day be reunited with my parents and brother. And the first time I went through the temple, I saw a glimpse of my father, a flash of the coat he used to wear as I was going through the veil into the celestial room." Reliving the moment itself, he lifted his right hand as if he was raising the cloth curtain to move through to the other side. "I heard my mother's voice the next time I went. After that, I went to the temple as often as I could, because it was as close to heaven as I could get in this life. I wouldn't give up my access to the temple lightly, you must understand."

Kurt had his arms folded across his chest. In contrast, Stephen had his arms spread wide open, as if he were inviting everyone into his heart.

"But as I read and studied more about the gospel in an attempt to make sure that I was living every law in accordance with God's will, I became convinced that polygamy was right." He pointed to his substantial bookcase full of church books, including *History of the Church* and *Journal of Discourses*, books I kept meaning to get around to reading, except that they were so many volumes long. And also, I preferred fiction, which seemed in severely short supply on the shelves here. Did Rebecca ever have a chance to read a juicy murder mystery? Probably not.

"The first time I mentioned living the Principle to Rebecca, I was terrified." Stephen's voice had gone very soft, and I could see a tremor on the left side of his face.

Something about his dramatic whisper made me wonder if he had practiced this speech down to the tiniest detail, like an actor playing a part.

"I couldn't imagine loving anyone the way that I loved Rebecca," he continued with a hand to his heart.

She was looking down, whatever spell he had temporarily cast over her now apparently gone.

"But you eventually found someone?" asked Kurt with a touch of sarcasm.

"What happened was that Rebecca and I knew Jennifer already through her work for us as an investment broker, but it was Rebecca who first thought of her in the role of one of my wives. It took some months before I felt the Holy Spirit whispering its confirmation to me." He was speaking as earnestly as if in prayer. Oh, yes, he was the devout and righteous man in all of this. He could never do anything manipulative or self-serving. It was all about God's will.

I couldn't help but wonder what Jennifer was like, and how this conversation had gone with the three of them. Had Stephen had Rebecca start the ball rolling, so to speak? How do you say to someone in an inoffensive way, I think you'd make a good second wife for my husband?

"I prayed night and day for several months before I found the courage to speak to Jennifer about the possibility of a second marriage. But then she agreed to study the scriptures herself, and found her own testimony, both of Mormonism and the Principle, which was proof that I had been right all along," said Stephen.

So Jennifer hadn't originally been Mormon. Interesting. That seemed to put Stephen in a position of ecclesiastical power over her. Did she defer to him on all gospel points? Was that Stephen's attraction to her, that she was a child in the gospel if not in reality?

Kurt asked, "Just out of curiosity, if you weren't married in the temple or a church building, who married you? It couldn't have been a civil ceremony, either, I assume." Since then Stephen could have been arrested for bigamy, was the unspoken end of Kurt's sentence.

"Rebecca did it," Stephen said with head held high. "I thought it was appropriate, even necessary. She has performed all of the spiritual weddings to make it clear she approved of them all."

"But she doesn't have the priesthood!" Kurt objected.

He was hung up on the fact that a woman was performing ordinances? It was kind of amusing, considering the fact that Kurt wouldn't have thought anyone, male or female, had the power to perform an eternally binding polygamous wedding ceremony.

"All women hold the priesthood," Stephen said, to my surprise. "It is part of the temple rites. They are ordained as priestesses and queens and they do the washings and annointings in the temple, as you must know. The priesthood is simply the power of God, and it flows through women as much as men."

I had not expected Stephen Carter, of all men, to start talking like a Mormon feminist. Maybe that was one of the ways he convinced women polygamy was going to be good for them.

I knew Kurt, who believed devoutly that only men could be endowed with the Mormon priesthood, was angry about this, even if it was a marriage ceremony he considered a sham anyway. "You know, you can't just change the doctrine of the church because you think you're right. You're not a prophet. You haven't been called to that authority."

Of course, the only authority in Kurt's mind were the fifteen men, apostles and prophets, who had all agreed with President Nelson's revelation on the new policy.

"But I don't think that the church's doctrine has changed," Stephen said patiently. "It is the same as it always was. If a man wants to be in the highest order of heaven and become a god, he must follow the higher law. If a man expects to rule worlds, he must have wives to serve as Heavenly Mothers for each of them, as God Himself does now."

Kurt's fists clenched and unclenched.

Finally, Rebecca spoke up, trying to lessen the tension. "Well, I guess we'll have to agree to disagree on this for now."

"It's interesting seeing how the same history has led us to different points in the present," I added, to go along with her.

At that moment, Sarah came in from the backyard then, a bit of red paint on her nose. "All finished with the indoctrination?" she asked with that same false smile.

"Sarah, please," said Rebecca, clearly embarrassed.

"What? I should have waited longer? I can go back out and do more painting. You know I'd rather be there than here. But I thought Stephen wanted an official appearance from all of us. All the adoring wives, right in a row." Her tone was acid and I would have sympathized with her more if she hadn't seemed so determined to antagonize everyone.

"Sarah, you can go to your room and stay there," Stephen said, his stern tone like a father to a small child, not like a husband to his wife.

Rebecca looked back and forth between them but did not intervene.

"I can? Well, I'm not going to. You can't frighten me into obedience anymore. There's nothing left I care about that you can take from me." Sarah seemed to be trying to goad Stephen. Why?

"These are our guests. I think they deserve better behavior from you than that," Stephen said with the same stern tone.

"Maybe they do. But they're not going to get it. You've told me too many times that I'm not capable of being an adult, so why should I bother to try anymore? I think I'm going to go for a walk. Don't expect me back anytime soon." Sarah went out the front door this time, slamming it behind her.

It was quite the display in front of guests. A part of me had to admire her courage, however uncomfortable it made us all socially.

"I'm sorry," Rebecca said softly to Stephen.

I thought I could see a tiny twitch underneath one eye, but that was all the emotion he showed in reaction to Sarah's temper. "We'll continue as if that hadn't happened. Sarah isn't always in the best of moods. She has her cycles. You know what I mean, don't you, Kurt?" he said, the humorous tone falling flat in this company.

And this from the man who had acted like he was a feminist, telling us that women were priestesses and goddesses. I didn't know what was going on with Sarah, why she had married Stephen and remained all these years, but there had to be a bigger story here. Maybe it connected to Talitha's situation and maybe it didn't, but I had to find out. Call it my nosiness. Call it a sisterly feeling. I needed to know why Sarah was so angry when her sister was so devoted to Stephen.

CHAPTER 8

"Excuse me," I said, needing a break from the tension of the theological argument and the strange scene with Sarah. "Do you mind if I go get a drink from the kitchen?"

"Oh, I can do that for you," said Rebecca, standing up.

I waved her back down. "I can manage on my own. I'd hate to put you to any trouble," I said, and stood up before she could protest.

Kurt followed me to the door. "Are you okay?" he asked.

I wasn't even sure what I was most upset about. The revelation about polygamy going on in the official history of the church for so much longer than I thought? The way Stephen and Sarah interacted? Or just my general suspicions about there being something deeply wrong here under the surface?

"Not really," I said, finding it impossible to try to explain to Kurt.

He held the door for me politely, then stepped into the kitchen after me.

"What a piece of work he is," said Kurt.

He meant Stephen Carter, but the egomaniac wasn't my only problem here. I wished I could honestly talk to my husband about all the church issues, but he'd just dismiss me and I'd get angrier. In any case, this wasn't the time or place for us to have it all out. "It's all so exhausting," I said, which was true. I rubbed my temples, but it didn't help me relax at all.

"We could just leave," Kurt suggested. "I don't think Naomi or Kenneth would really blame us, considering."

Maybe Kenneth wouldn't, but Naomi would. "I have to see what's going on with Talitha. I promised Naomi, and we haven't even met her yet," I pointed out.

He sighed and shook his head. "You can't let that go?"

"No, I can't," I said, annoyed.

Kurt tensed, but didn't argue. "All right," he said, and left me to go back to the other room.

I drank a tall glass of cold water, enjoying the moment of delicious quiet and privacy, since none of the Carters' children came in and interrupted me, as I half-feared. I considered praying for calm and discernment here as I tried to find out about Talitha, but the words wouldn't come. I found I was angry at God as much as Stephen Carter at the moment. How could everyone claim God was on their side, no matter what evil they were doing? It seemed like some good old-fashioned Old Testament smiting with lightning might be in order, but the sky outside the kitchen window didn't have a cloud in it.

So instead I did some quick meditation and focused on breathing in and out. I hadn't done that since my atheist days. I hadn't needed to.

When I went back to the living room, Stephen called the children in from outside for an official introduction.

Finally, a chance to see Talitha and put away my other concerns! But I had to pay careful attention. Even from up close, the children all looked remarkably alike, Stephen's strong features stamped on every face.

Stephen Carter put his hands on the shoulders of each of his young sons as he introduced them. The older two, Joseph and Aaron, whom Rebecca had mentioned, weren't there, since they were at the U. The ones still at home were Nephi, Lehi, Brigham, and Ezra. All good Mormon names from The Book of Mormon or after modern prophets. Nephi was a little older, but the other three looked all around the same age of eight, and very much alike. I recognized Brigham as the young boy we'd met at the gate, who had opened it with the key for us and then disappeared.

The girls were Esther, Leah, Rachel, Talitha, Madeleine, and Hannah—biblical names, since so few women were actually named in The Book of Mormon. Ruth, whom Rebecca had mentioned before, wasn't here. The others ranged in age from toddler (Hannah) to what looked like nearly fully adult (Esther and Leah). But they must still be in their teens, or they'd have gone off to college, wouldn't they? Were some allowed to go and others not?

But I set aside my other questions to focus on Talitha. She was blonde, but not as fair as the others, and her smaller cheekbones and darker eyes set her apart. I noticed she seemed to pay very careful attention to her father, but I could see no visible bruises or signs of injury. She clung to a mangy striped cat, which was missing patches of fur and looked like it had seen much better days.

"What's his name?" Kurt asked Talitha, bending down to offer the cat a hand to be sniffed. He was hissed at instead, and he put his hands up in a gesture of surrender I doubted the cat understood.

"It's a vicious thing," said Stephen.

"It's not an it. She's a cat and her name is Lucy," Talitha said pertly.

If I hadn't had Naomi's prompting, I couldn't help but think I would have gravitated to Talitha of all the children in any case. She was bright-eyed and I loved that she spoke back to her father. But it also might be a reason she among the children drew his particular wrath—if she did.

"Well, Lucy seems to like you a great deal," Kurt said to Talitha. "And that's a hard thing to manage with a cat. They're usually pretty standoffish." I appreciated that Kurt was paying attention to the girl.

"Not Lucy. She loves me," Talitha said. "We're family."

"An animal can't be family," Stephen said shortly, interrupting the exchange. "If you don't mind coming to see the other wives," he said, beckoning for me and Kurt to follow, "they'd all like to meet you."

I gave Talitha a smile as her father led me and Kurt away—we had many people still to meet, but I would seek her out again as soon as I could. She returned my smile shyly, hugging Lucy to her chest.

From one high point on the property, Stephen pointed out all four of his houses rather grandly: the main one on the gravel road; the flat rambler on a green hillock where I learned Carolyn, the musician, lived; the small blue house, almost entirely obscured by a thick curtain of trees, which was Jennifer's home; and the unfinished house in the gully, where the newest wife, Joanna, lived with her children.

It was a relief to be out of doors in the beautiful summer sunshine, especially this close to the mountains where there was a breeze, but I felt a little guilty leaving Talitha behind. I told myself that I needed to see the whole picture here, not just one household. But the truth was, I was also hoping to regain some sense of balance before I could focus on the task Naomi had set me.

We went to meet Carolyn next. I estimated her to be some-where in her thirties. She had lank, strawberry-blonde hair that fell into her face and she made no attempt to hold it back. Her skin was tinged with gray pallor, and she held her hands over her bulging pregnant belly.

"This is Linda and Kurt Wallheim. They're to be Naomi's mother- and father-in-law," Stephen said.

"Nice to meet you, Carolyn," I said, and offered my hand.

Carolyn moved closer to Stephen, as if for protection. Her handshake to me, when prompted by Stephen, was limp. She wouldn't touch Kurt at all, however, and I couldn't help but won-der what the story was behind that.

"Carolyn is our musician," Stephen said. "She brings the song of the angels to our whole family. Though she was never formally trained, I think it's amazing how much she has learned through her sheer commitment."

"We'd love to hear you play sometime," I said, trying to sound kind and encouraging.

Carolyn shook her head and made a dismissive sound.

"She becomes a little emotional when she's expecting," Ste-phen said. "It's hard for her to play and not to hear all the tiny mistakes she makes. But in a few months, all will be well, won't it, my love?" He patted her shoulder and left his hand resting there.

He hadn't called either Rebecca or Sarah "my love." What did it mean that he'd used it with Carolyn?

"Tell them about our children together," Stephen prompted.

Carolyn spoke in a quiet monotone, as if reciting. "Elizabeth is thirteen. She plays piano, like I do. Jonathan is eleven and I think he's going to end up on a French horn, but right now he's learning trumpet."

"He needs to practice more before we invest in another instrument," Stephen said.

Carolyn tensed at this. "I know that. We already have so many instruments and of course, you can't afford another one for no reason."

This made me consider Stephen's financial situation. Even a well-paid OB/GYN would struggle to pay for four homes and twenty-one children, wouldn't he?

"It's not about the cost," Stephen said. "It's about teaching Jonathan that hard work means reward. I wouldn't want him to have an instrument he hadn't earned through practicing."

"And of course, you're the musical expert," said Carolyn, her voice trembling a little now. She looked away from Stephen.

Something about her nervousness made me think that a physician would know how to hurt people without leaving visible signs. It was a cold thought, but I wondered more and more about whether Stephen Carter used violence to control his wives.

"And what about the other children?" Stephen encouraged.

"Noah is nine and he plays the oboe. Judith is seven and she plays the violin." Carolyn seemed to struggle for a moment.

Stephen squeezed her shoulder. "Go on," he said.

Eventually, she did, but her tone was more subdued. "Little Martha is three and she doesn't play anything yet, but I think I'm going to try her on a flute when she's ready. She seems like a flute player, I think."

"A flute is a good instrument for a young girl," Stephen replied, nodding in approval.

"Instruments aren't for boys or girls," said Carolyn, the first open disagreement I'd seen her show Stephen. "Music is for everyone. Isn't that what the scriptures say? Make a joyful noise."

Stephen's eyes flickered, but he patted Carolyn's hand and

said, "The stress of your pregnancy is making you fractious today, I'm afraid. You must remember how much you are loved and cared for. Anything you need, you have only to ask for it."

Carolyn took a breath and murmured, "Yes, Stephen."

What was going on with her? She seemed weak-minded or possibly even brainwashed. So unlike Sarah, although their ages were close. What was the difference in their situations?

As Stephen led us down the steps and away from Carolyn's house, he said, "Carolyn had a very difficult childhood and teenage years. She assumes that everyone is ready to hurt her. Even after fourteen years living safely here with us, surrounded by loving family, I think she flashes back sometimes to those bad old days."

"She had a difficult childhood?" I repeated. Maybe her neuroses were the products of childhood trauma, and had nothing to do with Stephen at all.

"Yes," said Stephen. "Terrible years."

"Her parents were abusive?" Kurt asked.

"Abusive, yes. But worse was their neglect. She had to sell herself to stay alive. She was on the streets for many years until she found her way home to us here."

I was shocked at the honest way Stephen simply stated that Carolyn had been a victim of sex trafficking. Did they talk about it openly in the family? I supposed that could be a good thing, considering how often I complained about Mormons never being open about their sex lives, but openness was one thing and re-opening trauma was another.

"You found her on the streets?" Kurt's tone was mild and inoffensive, but I could hear the judgment underneath. He had to be wondering the same thing I was, which was what age Carolyn had been when she married Stephen. Had he taken advantage of a young woman in distress?

One of Stephen's smiles again. "No, no. I skipped an important step in there. When I met Carolyn, she'd already made the decision she wasn't going to sell herself anymore. She was working at a local piano store. They didn't pay her much, but they let her practice after hours, and it was the beginning of a new life for her. I offered to pay her to give lessons to my children up here when it fit into her schedule."

"And then you asked her to marry you?" Kurt's tone was still critical.

"Not for several years, though she fell in love with me after only a few months." He grinned in some kind of shared masculine pride at this.

I wanted to slap him. Had Carolyn fallen in love with him or with his money and the security she thought it might bring her?

"But it was the Spirit that spoke to Rebecca and told her Sarah was to join us. Jennifer agreed, and so I added a third wife with God's grace in 2002," he assured Kurt.

Kurt rolled his eyes toward me at this. I too was beginning to hate the way Stephen used that pseudo-scriptural language in everyday conversation.

We walked down to the rambler next and met Jennifer, who was in her forties and wore stylized cat-eye glasses with jewels on each point. She was enviably trim, perhaps a bit too thin, or so I told myself. I neither saw nor heard children in this house, and there were no signs of toys or other child-related objects. It was also pin-perfect, not a bit of dirt anywhere, no clutter, everything in its place.

Stephen introduced us as Naomi's future in-laws.

"It's good to meet you," Jennifer said, as she offered her hand to shake. "Stephen, I must speak to you privately."

"Right now?" asked Stephen.

"Yes, now."

It was the first time I'd seen any of the wives override Stephen's script for the morning or successfully demand any semblance of privacy, but she pulled him away toward the spotless kitchen. I desperately wanted to tiptoe toward them and see if I could hear anything, but Kurt held my arm.

"Linda, this is not the time for your snooping," he admonished me.

Well, why wasn't it? Didn't he want to know what they were talking about as much as I did?

Jennifer's voice was raised in what sounded like anger, although I couldn't make out any words through the door. Stephen responded with a firm bass.

"Can you believe what we've seen here?" Kurt said softly. "Poor Naomi, having to grow up in this confusing place. No wonder she left the church if it was connected to that for her."

I appreciated his new sympathy for Naomi, but was annoyed that he thought polygamy explained everything about her resignation of her membership. How did he explain Kenneth's?

Kurt started to say something else, but I shushed him as I heard Stephen coming back into the room, trailed by Jennifer, who looked like she had swallowed something very large.

"Can I help?" I asked. "Is something wrong?"

"It's none of your business," Jennifer snapped. Stephen gave her a sharp look and she let her shoulders drop, as if she was putting on some mask right in front of us. "Ah, actually, we were talking about Naomi's upcoming nuptials," she said, then gave us a small, expectant smile. "She was always such a special child. I'm happy that she'll be joining your family and sharing her brilliant mind and sweet heart with you, as well."

The abrupt switch in her behavior was too much for me to take in.

"We're very happy for our son," Kurt said politely.

"Of course. Weddings are a wonderful time for family, aren't they?" I couldn't help but think her tone seemed just a bit condescending.

What was going on here? She was definitely not a cowed, controlled woman, though she was making nice now. Or trying to. Why in the world had Rebecca chosen her as Stephen's second wife?

"Jennifer is an investment genius," Stephen said, as if to divert our attention from the argument they'd had and Jennifer's brash manner. "She helps manage my accounts, as well as those of a few friends. We're very lucky she is so savvy."

Maybe this was the answer to the question about why Jennifer had been his second wife. And also to the question about how Stephen paid for all of the houses and children. But what a cold, calculating way of looking at polygamy—as an institution that needed to be supported financially first and foremost.

"And the children?" Kurt said, who had not, apparently, noticed the lack of toys, though he was staring around the room, as if waiting for children to descend.

Jennifer gave Kurt a sour look. "I don't have children of my own," she said.

Kurt had obviously touched on a sore spot. Maybe he deserved the shortness of her response.

"We have prayed most fervently, but our prayers have not been answered," Stephen said, reaching for Jennifer's hand, though she pulled away as soon as she could. "We must accept God's will for us, whatever it is."

Jennifer's expression as she stared at both Kurt and me was unreadable. "Yes, God's will," she murmured.

"And you're a second mother to the other children, of course, helping them with math homework and such," Stephen added.

"I can help make sure that their futures are secure, which is something their own mothers can't manage," Jennifer said. Her words were disdainful even if her tone was neutral.

"Well, let's move along to the other houses," said Stephen.

"Yes, make sure you visit Joanna in particular. I'm sure she will be delighted to see you after last night," Jennifer said, as she walked to the door and held it open.

"What happened with Joanna last night?" I asked after we had walked outside.

"Nothing," said Stephen, though I could see his fists clench. He wasn't as good at putting on a mask as Jennifer was, I thought. He was angry at Joanna, which only made me more curious to meet her.

CHAPTER 9

Stephen led us on to the final house, the unfinished one, which had patchy aluminum siding on the outside, and bare wood elsewhere. Around it were no flower beds or gardens of any kind, only hard dirt and sagebrush.

"So Joanna is the wife who used to be FLDS?" Kurt asked.

"Yes," Stephen said. "Joanna was married to a Fundamentalist man in Short Creek, Arizona, when she was only fourteen. According to the law of placing, the church authorities chose her husband for her and she had no choice in the matter. He was far older than she was, and her only role once she was married was to give birth to children for him as quickly as possible." He sounded disgusted, but I couldn't help but wonder how differently he saw his own wives' roles. There were lots of children here on the Carter compound.

"So she had her first daughter Grace when she was fifteen," Stephen continued. "By the time she was sixteen, Joanna knew that she had to get out. She fled in the cover of night with her daughter. She came here to Salt Lake City and tried to raise the girl on her own, but she had so few skills. Her education was poor—she could hardly read—and she had no support system because she'd left her family and church behind her. She was terrified of any government assistance because she'd been taught to believe that the government was ruled by Satan, and there was the very real risk she'd be sent home because she was underage."

Rebecca had already mentioned the problem of Joanna's legal emancipation, no doubt something Stephen had helped her with and which had made her even more dependent on and grateful to him. I was angry at the idea of any girl being married so young, and maybe Stephen wanted me to see him as a savior of his wives. He'd helped Carolyn and Joanna have more normal lives than the ones they'd been born into. But I couldn't help but think about the possibility that he had married needy, much-younger women for his own selfish reasons.

"The FLDS believe many of the same things I believe about Wilford Woodruff and the 1890 Manifesto ending polygamy," Stephen said. "But they have some strange ideas about special genetic lineage that mean that there is a lot of intermarriage. As a medical doctor, I can't help but see the mistaken thinking there for what it is. They have many, many children born with defects. There is a baby graveyard in every city they live in, and some-times the elders of the church are even asked to come in and end the suffering of the child and the parents before it happens naturally." He shuddered at this.

Some part of me found it beyond strange that he could look at other people's polygamy and think them so much worse than he was. But at least he had no baby graveyard.

"Even worse is the isolation and control. Boys and girls are not allowed to watch television or use the Internet, so they have no contact with the outside world. They live in isolated com-munities, miles and miles away from the nearest town. All the children work many hours a day to earn money for the large corporations that the elders of the church own, and they are not compensated for their time."

Yes, I knew about the FLDS church and its practices already. But so far much of what he was describing seemed not very different from the Carter family system as Rebecca had described it to me earlier. Did he really see himself as so different?

"The boys are culled regularly when they are of age, to make sure that they don't fall in love with girls marked for the men in authority. When they are sent away, they are given nothing but the clothes on their backs, and they have nothing they can do to earn their way in the world but the crudest labor. I'm sure God does not look on this practice with the least degree of allowance."

Kurt made a grunt of unwilling assent to that.

Stephen picked up a toy that was in the yard and carried it with us as we moved toward the unfinished porch of the farthest house. "As for the girls, they are married so young they cannot object. They have no idea of any life but housework, yard labor, and bearing children. Joanna is unusual in her rebellion. Many girls are tied to so many children by the time they are old enough to think for themselves that they can never escape, not really. It is a travesty. The government should be doing more to stop it, but the group claims religious freedom exemptions all the time for child labor infractions and education failures."

"It is terrible," I agreed, as our walking pace slowed.

"Of course, my own children are very well educated," Stephen said, as if anticipating the comparison. "We homeschool them, but not to handicap them and make them unable to choose any other life, only to make sure that they are able to choose their own topics so their interest in education always remains high."

Hmm. I wasn't sure I believed that was why he homeschooled. Isolation was still a form of social control, no matter how benign it seemed. I was sure that not every branch of Mormonism that continued to practice polygamy was as bad as the FLDS, but I wasn't sure any polygamy could really be less than oppressive to the women involved. And so far, Stephen Carter wasn't disproving my theory in any way.

Approaching the front door, Stephen lowered his voice, as if to keep Joanna from hearing he was talking about her. "We first met Joanna because she had been doing some gardening for our neighbors, the Perezes." He gestured south of the main house, though I couldn't see what neighbors he meant. The property was too big, covered in trees and hills. "Carolyn met her first, when Joanna came up to offer some of her roses. But then Joanna gradually came to visit the house more and more often, bringing little Grace with her. It was Rebecca who insisted that something had to be done about the young woman. Then we helped her find a lawyer and the rest is history." He smiled widely.

"It sounds like you had no choice in the matter," Kurt said skeptically.

"Oh, I wouldn't say that. But it really isn't about my choice. That's why living the Principle is the highest law. We put everything about our lives in God's hands and expect that He will do what is best for us," Stephen said. He stepped up and put the toy down on the front porch.

"How old was Joanna when you married?" I asked, wondering if Stephen was breaking the law here. Statutory rape was still criminal, even if you called it marriage.

"Eighteen years old," Stephen replied, giving me a canny look as if he knew what I was thinking. "That was in 2014."

Eighteen—so he'd just barely avoided marrying a legal minor. It still seemed all too close to breaking the law to me, though.

At that, Stephen knocked on the door, and called, "Joanna, it's me!" He let himself in, and we followed.

Joanna poked her head out from the kitchen. "Come on in here," she called.

The first thing I noticed was the overwhelming smell of roses in the home. Once inside, I saw that on nearly every surface, there were beautiful fresh-cut red, white, pink, and yellow roses of all different sizes. I hadn't seen these kinds of flowers anywhere on the property.

Stephen took us into the kitchen, which had a hole where the dishwasher should have been and no flooring other than cement. Joanna was carrying one of her children on either hip as she maneuvered between what looked like a secondhand stove and sink. Both children were dressed from neck to wrist to ankle in tops and skirts with leggings underneath that I couldn't help but think were completely inappropriate for the summer. The house wasn't air conditioned, so they were sweating onto their mother, who wasn't doing any better. I did notice that both girls had the same blue eyes as Stephen, though their hair was darker than the other children's, like Joanna's.

A slightly older girl was standing by the table, dressed in the same long clothes, up to her neck, past her ankles and wrists, so that she had to push up her sleeves constantly and she seemed to struggle not to trip over her skirt. She also wore a huge white apron that must have been her mother's. She was rolling out sugar cookies. I guessed that she was Grace, the daughter from Joanna's first marriage.

Like her daughters, Joanna wore a loose, long skirt and a long-sleeved, high-necked top. I guess Joanna was used to dressing like the FLDS, so she kept it up even after she had left them. Her dark hair was loose down her back and she wore no makeup.

She was very thin and she looked painfully young to be the mother of three children. But except for the fact that she didn't meet anyone's eyes directly, mine, Kurt's, or Stephen's, she didn't seem to be afraid of Stephen.

"Joanna, this is Kurt and Linda Wallheim, Naomi's in-laws to be," Stephen said.

"Grace and I made these for you," Joanna said without acknowledging our names, though it seemed less from rudeness than simple distractedness. She gestured at a finished plate of sugar cookies on the table. Had she made them or had the little girl? They were all irregular shapes, but when I bit into one it tasted flaky and sweet.

"Thank you. This is delicious," I said, winking at Grace, who had looked over at me. But she did not respond to my friendly gesture, she simply turned back to her work.

"We made them for you because the Spirit whispered to me while I slept that we would have two visitors today," Joanna told us earnestly. The surprise must have been evident on our faces because she added, "I also knew in advance when lightning struck a tree in the gully. And when the mail didn't come last week."

"You know I don't like it when you talk about premonitions," Stephen said, his tone mildly corrective.

"They aren't premonitions or any such nonsense," Joanna said, and her voice sounding older—almost chiding toward Stephen, which wasn't what I'd expected at all. "They're real promptings from the Holy Spirit of Christ."

I wished the Spirit told me practical things like that guests were coming instead of vague feelings of "right" or "wrong." Maybe there was something spiritual for me to learn from this strange, child-like woman.

"That's very scientific," Stephen mocked her without any kindness. "I should bring in someone to do a study on them. But then again, what do you know about science? You've had no education about it at all."

I was taken aback, but Joanna looked smug and superior, not at all hurt. "It's not science. It's the Holy Spirit. Remember back in April when all the milk in all the houses went bad at once? The Spirit had told me it would happen, and I warned all the wives in advance. Don't you remember that, Stephen?"

Stephen seemed to barely be restraining himself from belittling her. But I didn't have any sympathy for his position. I did wonder about what Joanna believed to be her power. I knew that some evangelical traditions spoke about gifts bestowed by Christ, but it wasn't a real part of mainstream Mormonism. I found I wished I could believe it, though—how glorious to have a voice of certainty pointing the way.

"It's a gift," Joanna explained to me and Kurt, "from the Spirit, just like anyone else if you read Christ's promises in the scriptures."

"I see," said Kurt, whom I could see felt sorry for her.

"Joanna, could you send the children outside to play?" Stephen asked. It was a strange thing for him to ask, since he'd been so intent on showing off the children of the other wives.

"All right," she said. I noticed she was very careful to step away from Stephen and put the two toddlers on the floor by Grace, corralling the little girls with her feet. "Grace, can you take the little ones outside?"

"Yes, Mother," Grace said in a grown-up tone, without looking up. "I just need to finish one more cookie."

"Not one more cookie," Joanna said. "Zina and Liza need you."

"Oh, all right." Grace licked her finger, the only sign of her real age, then took off her apron. She gave me a quick, very adult appraising look. Then she picked up the smaller of the two girls in her arms, grabbed hold of the other one by the elbow and took them outside. The last impression I had of her was of eyes so piercingly blue that they would have made her fit right into the family, even if she wasn't genetically related.

"You like it here, don't you, Joanna?" Stephen asked. "It's much better than when you lived with the FLDS?"

Joanna hesitated a moment, and I wondered if she was trying to parse Stephen's tone. I couldn't tell what he wanted her to say. "I like it here, yes," she said.

"And why is that?"

"Because you are good to me," Joanna said, slowly at first, and then warming up to it. "Because you give me freedom and you make sure we always have enough to eat and you are a good father, coming to visit and play with the children almost every day."

It was so obvious this was a learned speech that I cringed at the way Joanna eagerly looked at Stephen for approval.

"Well," he said. "You have certainly had a life without freedom or real education. I've always tried to be fair to you, more than fair. The other wives have complained that I've spoiled you, do you know that?"

Was I imagining a mild threat in what he said? Maybe not, because a tear rolled down Joanna's cheek. "I never want to make you angry with me," Joanna said. "Never."

I remembered Jennifer's insinuation that they had argued last night. I felt like I was listening in on a conversation with only one side in English.

"There now." Stephen bent over and kissed her cheeks. "You just need proper discipline."

"Discipline" did not sound good to me. I looked at Kurt and could see his jaw was clenched. If this were our ward, Kurt could step in and say something. But we were just here for the day and Kurt had no authority to demand a change.

I could only guess that Stephen was doing this in front of us to humiliate Joanna and keep her cowed. I wondered how often that happened here, with the wives being used to embarrass each other.

Stephen was now rubbing a hand down Joanna's back, the picture of sympathy. Ugh!

"I need to be sure of you, Joanna. I'll just have to think of the right thing. Maybe you need more time to yourself so you can think. I could have the older girls come up and fetch your girls to the main house each morning. Would that help?" His voice sounded kind, though his manner was cold.

Joanna had paled dramatically. "I don't need more time to myself," she said. "I need my daughters with me always."

"Do you?" said Stephen. He moved away from her and then turned to Kurt and me. I swear that he was conscious of our attention in this supposedly intimate moment. "I think every mother deserves some time to herself. To go out to a movie or have her hair done. It's difficult when every minute of the day is spent caring for someone else's physical needs. I'm sure you remember that time in your life, don't you, Linda?"

"Yes," I said after a long moment. "I remember it well." But I didn't think it had been the same for me as it was for Joanna.

I hated this place, I thought. If not for Talitha, I would be packing my bags and leaving right now, wedding or no wedding.

"All right. We'll head back to the main house now," Stephen said. "I'll talk to you tomorrow, Joanna."

He turned to the door, but I lingered, trying to think of

something to say to Joanna. Could I let her know that I was safe, if she needed another option for her life and her three daughters? What could I do for her, other than call DCFS, which Naomi had specifically said she wanted not to do? At least not yet.

In that moment, I saw Joanna's body jerk and her eyes roll back in her head. She seemed to gargle in her throat, and then she spat something up. "Wait, Stephen!" she called out.

He stopped, but took a long moment to give her his attention. "What is it you want now, Joanna?"

"It's not for me. I had a vision just then."

Was that what a vision looked like, from the outside? It didn't look pleasant. Unless—could she put on something like that? I didn't believe she was much of an actress based on what I'd seen of her so far.

Joanna extended her hands as if feeling for something in the air, then shuddered and wrapped her arms around her middle. "Stephen, be careful tonight. There may be danger coming for you." Her whispered, dark tone left me with a chill.

Stephen didn't seem affected. In an annoyed, patronizing tone, he said, "All right, Joanna, I'll keep that in mind. Thank you so much for looking out for me." He shook his head and then stepped out the front door, nodding for Kurt and me to follow.

The sun still bright outside, we walked back to the main house. I thought about what it must have been like for Kenneth when he'd come to visit. He'd made it sound so benign, but hadn't he been affected by the power dynamic here? Or maybe it hadn't been the same, given the recent argument that Jennifer and Joanna had apparently had some part in. I hoped very much that Kenneth and Naomi would be able to make their future life with as much distance from this compound as possible.

Stephen stopped at a good vantage point away from the scrub

oak and motioned to the valley. "Whenever I stand here, looking out at the valley that Brigham Young said was reserved for the Saints, I think about how God has reserved this special piece of land for me and my family. I will always give thanks to Him for all that He gives me every day, however long my life lasts under His hand."

"It's a big piece of property. You said you inherited it from your parents?" I asked.

He nodded. "It's all I have left of my family. If my brother had lived, it would have been ours to share."

There was something fierce in his attachment to this land. I couldn't help but wonder if he and his brother would have fought over how to divide it. Surely his brother would have been uncomfortable with Stephen's call to "the Principle."

Kurt cleared his throat. "Do you mind my asking about your finances?" he asked. "As a father myself, I'm concerned about the children."

"I don't have any secrets," Stephen said, which I highly doubted.

"You make enough money as a doctor to manage food and housing, plus some college expenses, for more than twenty children?" That was the accountant coming out. He wanted to know the bottom line here.

Stephen turned to us and I could see his smile even as his face blocked out the sun. "It's a good profession in Utah. Did you know that we as a state have the highest birthrate in the nation?"

"I think I did know that," Kurt said blandly.

"And your investments with Jennifer must help," I added.

"Yes, very much so," said Stephen, glancing at me for a moment before turning back to Kurt. "Shall I show you two my financial statements before we agree to let our children marry?"

"No, no. I didn't mean that," Kurt said, looking more soberly out at the same valley.

Stephen began to walk again. I followed him, thinking I'd very much have liked to see his financial statements. I wanted to know how much he had salted away for retirement and whether the wives had their own bank accounts. Did Joanna have enough money to survive until her three children were in school? What about Carolyn? I'd come because of Talitha, but I couldn't help but think that everyone here needed my help, if only I could figure out what to do for them.

CHAPTER 10

As we were nearly back to the big house, the sound of howling rose from the backyard, growing louder and louder. It was a child's cry of pain.

"Who is that?" I asked, but didn't wait for Stephen to respond. I jogged ahead, Kurt quickly joining me. We found Talitha seated in the reddish dirt behind the main house. As we approached it became clear she was hunched over her cat, Lucy.

When I got closer I could see the cat was dead, eyes and mouth open and lifeless. There was no blood, though, and Talitha didn't seem hurt, which relieved me.

Kurt knelt and put a comforting hand on Talitha's shoulder.

"Let go of me!" she shouted at Kurt, wrenching herself away.

"He's dead, sweetheart," Kurt said, rising and taking a few steps back, knocking into me and then putting an arm around my waist.

"It's not a he. It's Lucy!" Talitha yelled. "And she's not dead. I won't let her be dead!"

"Oh, honey!" I said, wishing I could do something to help her.

Stephen had finally joined us. He didn't seem overly concerned. "All animals die, Talitha. It's why we shouldn't get so close to them."

Talitha looked up at her father, pleading. "Make her come back to life. Put your hands on her and heal her with your priesthood, Daddy." She was still clutching the dead cat to her chest tightly.

I turned to watch Stephen. It sickened me that Talitha thought he could actually do that. Had he told her that he could lay his hands on the dead and resurrect them? Or had she made it up out of her own desperation?

"Talitha, this is a pet, not a human being," Stephen said. "It has no soul to call back from the dead."

I hated him for his callousness. Couldn't he at least tell his young daughter that the cat had died as peacefully as it could have in her loving arms, as it so clearly had?

"I think she does have a soul," Talitha said. "How can she not if I loved her so much? Daddy, I want Lucy to be in my heaven."

The only time Kurt and I had talked about pets in heaven had been when Samuel's rabbit Fluffy had died about ten years ago now. I'd resisted getting any pets for the other boys, but Samuel had been so tender with animals and pleaded so often, I'd eventually given in. She'd only lasted eighteen months. I remember how distraught he was at the thought that his pet was dead forever. So Kurt and I told him that we were sure that a God of love would include pets in heaven, as well, though Mormon doctrine wasn't clear on this topic.

To Talitha, Stephen said firmly, "But you know that Christ did not die for animals to go to heaven, only for us, only for God's children." He gestured to himself, to me and Kurt, and to Talitha.

I wished he hadn't included us in this opinion. I also couldn't help but wonder if this heartless treatment of a sensitive girl like Talitha might lead her to act in the unhappy way Naomi had interpreted as an indicator of abuse.

"Why?" demanded Talitha, holding the cat tighter to her chest. She looked so tightly wound, I thought she might explode. "I love animals, and I want them in heaven with me. Why can't they be there?"

"Let go of that creature immediately, Talitha," Stephen snapped, apparently tired of the conversation. He glanced sharply at us, apparently angry that Kurt and I had seen Talitha defy him.

Talitha turned her back to her father deliberately, hunching closer to the cat so that they were both almost on the ground. She whispered fervently. "I love you and you're going to come back, maybe as my baby sister—"

She was interrupted by Stephen yanking her up by the elbow. The dead cat tumbled out of her grip to the ground.

The girl kicked and screamed, "Lucy!"

Her arms reached for the cat, but Stephen was hauling her back toward the house. Talitha was just at the age when she could still be carried, but she was big enough for it to be a struggle.

I started to run after them, but Kurt pulled me back. "Linda, don't. You have to leave it. You'll only make it worse for her."

I wanted to call DCFS. But as much as I hated how Stephen treated Talitha, I hadn't actually seen any physical abuse. Was that going to happen inside the house where I couldn't see it?

"She's just a little girl," I said tightly, watching Stephen carry Talitha's struggling, squawking form into the house.

"Yes, she is, and he's a grown man. But if you want to do anything to help here, you have to make sure Stephen doesn't see you as the enemy," said Kurt. "Unless you want to leave?"

I swung back to him, furious. "Just because you're not comfortable here, you want to leave? Why don't you think of Talitha?"

"Linda, we haven't seen anything that is illegal. And if Naomi had wanted to call DCFS, she would have done it herself. You know that. If you feel obliged to stay and see more of this—mess—I'll do what I can to help, but I can't pretend I'm comfortable about it." Kurt was pulling at his ever-decreasing thatch of gray hair.

"I have to see more. I can't leave unless I know that girl is safe," I said, even though I wasn't sure at all how I was going to accomplish that.

The sound of Talitha's shrieking was abruptly cut off as the back door to the main house slammed shut.

"Or if you know for sure that she's being abused, Linda? Where does it stop? When you put yourself in danger?" Kurt's hair was standing on end, but his eyes were fierce and bored into mine.

I looked away, focusing on the cat's corpse for a long moment instead of my husband. My own safety could not be my concern. As a mother, I had learned always to put myself second and it wasn't a habit I could forget easily. But for now, I took another calming breath and said, "Let's at least bury her cat."

We'd done that for Fluffy, and for many years Samuel had gone out to look at her grave and remember her. It had helped him, though I think he had stopped thinking about the pet as much in recent years.

"All right." Kurt reached for the cat, then seemed to think better of it and pulled back. "We'll need a shovel and maybe an old blanket." He stood up straight and looked at the house.

It was clear that Kurt wanted to leave. He didn't want any of this to be our responsibility, and I couldn't say I blamed him. But I couldn't just walk away from a little girl who might be in danger.

"I'll go inside and ask," I said, trying to make this easier on him. But Kurt came with me. In the late afternoon light, we crossed the splotchy grass field, which didn't look like it was ever mowed. I went inside the back door while Kurt scraped his shoes on the wooden slats of the porch.

Sarah was in the kitchen, her arms wet with soapy water.

"Talitha's cat Lucy died just now," I told her. She had to have heard Talitha hollering as Stephen brought her inside, but maybe she didn't know what her daughter had been so upset about.

"Oh," Sarah said with a shrug, scrubbing a pan with the rough side of a dish sponge. "Well, everything dies eventually."

Surprised by her response, I said, "Um, I was wondering if Kurt and I could bury the cat. I'm sure it will help Talitha with her grief if she can visit the gravesite." I didn't mean to tell a mother what her own child needed, except that in this case, maybe I had to.

I saw a flash of anger in Sarah's eyes. "If you think that's necessary," she said.

It might not be necessary, but it was a kind gesture for a little girl in pain.

After taking a long, deliberate moment finishing one last dish, Sarah wiped off her hands and showed me and Kurt into the garage, which was right next to the kitchen.

"Thank you," Kurt said to Sarah, rummaging around until he found a shovel. "And if I could have an old blanket, as well? Just to wrap the animal in and move it to the burial spot."

"All right," Sarah said. We followed her back to the entryway and she disappeared upstairs for a few minutes, then came back with what looked like a hand-sewn baby quilt. It was old, but surely too precious for this. "This was Talitha's," she said with what I hoped was not the malevolence it sounded like.

"We couldn't use this on a cat burial," Kurt said, trying to hand it back.

Sarah held up her hands in refusal. "No one's using it anymore. Waste not, want not." She left the baby quilt on the piano bench and walked back into the kitchen.

Practical was one thing. Cruel was another. What had made Sarah act like this toward her own daughter?

As I turned toward the back door, I heard sobbing coming from the second floor. I froze, my heart twisting at the child's pain.

"Amen to the priesthood of that man," Kurt said, quoting from the Doctrine and Covenants, the modern Mormon scripture from Joseph Smith. He was alluding to the scripture about men who use their priesthood to intimidate or manipulate or harm others, and that they would have no sanction from God if they did so.

"He's abusing more than Talitha here," I said. Whether it was physical or not seemed a nitpick to me.

"But he's smart and ruthless. I think you should consider whether we would be better able to help from the outside."

But what about Naomi's worry that all the children would be taken away from their mothers if we went to the authorities? That wasn't what I wanted. It would punish the wives as well as Stephen.

"I'll think about it," I said. But the truth was, I couldn't imagine walking away from this, not unless Talitha was coming with me.

"On with the burial, then," said Kurt.

We trooped outside together. Even though it had been my idea, he carefully used the baby quilt to pick up the cat, then wrapped up the ends so he never had any actual contact with the animal's fur.

"So, where do we bury it?" he asked, staring out at the mountainside. I thought fleetingly how rare it was that he asked me to give him instructions, especially these days. He was very used to being in charge as bishop, and it spilled over into our home life. Maybe that was part of the problem for me, that he could never talk to me as Kurt, my husband, but only as Kurt the bishop. If we could figure out a way around that, maybe we could talk out things about the new policy. But not here. Not now.

I glanced back at the main house where Talitha's room was. "Not too far away, I think."

"Maybe under those scrub oaks?" Kurt said. He gestured to a group of trees right on the foothill of the mountain itself.

"Looks good to me," I said.

Kurt started toward the trees, the small quilted package in the crook of one arm, the shovel in his other hand. I felt a chill run through me as I watched him. I knew it was a cat inside the baby blanket, but it was just the size of a human infant.

We made our way to the scrub oaks Kurt had indicated, and he began digging. I felt useless standing next to him, but there was only one shovel and the dirt was clearly difficult to dig into. I didn't often let myself off of physical labor because I was a woman, but in this case, I let Kurt take over.

I found a seat on one of the large boulders lodged nearby and watched Kurt's steady rhythm. At least things weren't so bad that we couldn't work together to help someone in need, like Talitha. That had to mean something about our marriage, didn't it?

Kurt stopped for a moment to wipe his face. His eyes must be stinging from dripping sweat, but I didn't really think my offering to help would do anything other than delay the burial. Sometimes I felt so helpless and I took it out on Kurt. I knew it wasn't fair, and I tried to think of some way to explain what I was feeling. But I couldn't.

Finally, Kurt had dug deep enough down that he was satisfied, and he carefully placed the bundle in the hole. I stepped in to take the shovel from his hand.

"Linda, I can manage this."

"Let me do something," I said.

At that, Kurt stepped back and let me awkwardly shovel dirt in over the animal's form. When I was finished, we sat for a few minutes together on the boulder, his dirt-crusted hand in mine, which was bleeding slightly from the reopened cut I'd noticed while making Danishes.

I had a distinct memory of the day that we had buried Georgia. We hadn't had a full funeral for her, but our bishop at the time had come, and the three older boys, Joseph, Adam, and Zachary. They'd had no idea how to feel, had seemed more confused than sad at the loss of the baby they'd awaited. I had smelled the same dry, slightly piney scent of soil then, though Kurt and I hadn't dug the grave. I'd held tight to Kurt's hand and I'd always thought of it as the worst day of my life. But we'd been on the same side then. We'd grieved the same loss. We'd faced the same journey forward. Now it wasn't nearly as obvious what we had in common. Our children, yes. But they were grown now, and where did that leave us?

"Will you say a prayer over the grave, please?" I asked.

"Linda, I can't." His voice sounded strangled. "You know, I can't. Not for an animal's grave."

Fine. I hadn't meant an official consecration of the plot, just a prayer. It had been a chance for him to move to my side, and he wouldn't take it. Well, I didn't need his permission to do what I thought was right.

I knelt on the ground and folded my arms, the simple pose of prayer rather than a formal grave dedication. "God, please give this animal peace. She was well loved in this life. And we ask Thee also to give comfort to the little girl Talitha, who misses her cat friend so much."

I waited to feel inspiration, something about what I should do to best help Talitha, but I felt nothing. "Amen," I said at last.

Kurt's voice rang out with mine, and I was both surprised and gratified by his participation, after all.

CHAPTER 11

Following a few moments of shared silence, Kurt and I began to walk back to the house with the shovel. Kurt went through the same ritual at the porch steps with his shoes, and then we took the shovel back to the garage.

"Let's find a bathroom so we can wash up," Kurt said, holding out his filthy hands. Mine weren't nearly as bad, but washing up would be good for me, too.

There was no one in the kitchen this time when we let ourselves into the house, though there was a pot of potatoes boiling, and the room smelled deliciously of roasted pork, which I saw was standing to rest by the stove before being carved. We searched for a bathroom on the main floor, washed thoroughly, then ran into Stephen as he was coming down the stairs.

"Ah, there you two are. I'm sorry about that interruption," he said. He didn't name Talitha or ask about the cat's body that he had left us with. "Before we had dinner, I meant to make sure you felt comfortably settled in the room where you'll be sleeping before we had dinner."

Before Kurt or I had a chance to say object, Stephen called for Sarah and Rebecca. Sarah was already coming up the stairs from the basement, carrying canned green beans, and a few moments later Rebecca appeared on the staircase coming down from the second floor.

"Even if Naomi and Kenneth aren't here, we want to make sure our guests feel welcome to stay the night," Stephen said to Rebecca. "Can you sort out which room would be best? Now if you'll excuse me, I have some business to take care of. I'll be in my basement office." With the matter safely in his wives' hands, Stephen seemed ready to leave us.

I stopped him, reaching out instinctively and putting a hand on his arm.

"Yes?" he said, looking down at his arm as I pulled back my hand.

"Talitha," I said, but the word came out like a bleat because my mouth was dry. I swallowed and tried again. "Is Talitha all right?"

"She'll be fine," Stephen said. "She's up in her room resting." He shook his head, smiling faintly. "Little girls and their little problems. When she wakes up tomorrow she probably won't even remember that cat."

Little problems—so dismissive a phrase. "You mean . . . Is she in bed for the night?" I asked.

"She is very upset right now," Rebecca said sadly. "We hope she'll cry herself to sleep soon."

I fought a wave of frustration—I needed to talk to Talitha.

"No reason to dilly-dally, ladies," Stephen said to his two wives. "Go on, all of you." He made a shooing gesture, then turned and headed down the basement steps Sarah had just come up.

The man seemed to think he could tell Kurt and me what to do as well as his wives. I looked at Kurt, expecting he was going to resist, tell the two women they shouldn't bother with a room because we weren't staying the night. But he didn't say anything, and I thought with relief that Talitha's plight must have changed his mind.

Sarah and Rebecca shared a quick glance, and by some silent agreement Rebecca took the canned beans from Sarah, while Sarah beckoned for us to follow her upstairs. We walked down a hallway of closed doors, stopping at a linen closet so Sarah could take out new sheets and a couple of quilts.

"We buried the cat on the mountain, over by the scrub oaks," Kurt told her as Sarah stacked sheets in the crook of her elbow. "Whenever Talitha is ready, we'll be happy to show her the spot."

"I'm sure knowing that will change everything difficult in her life," Sarah said with clear sarcasm.

In a contest of least happy Stephen Carter wife, Sarah was beating out even Carolyn for first place. And she didn't have pregnancy hormones as an excuse. I wished the woman could overlook her own discontent for her daughter's sake at the moment.

Kurt offered to help carry the quilts, but Sarah refused the assistance. "I don't need a man to help manage the simplest tasks of my life, thank you very much," she said tartly. She led us to the third floor and stopped in front of a door. "Here," she said, opened it, then stepped back to let me enter first.

It was not a typical guest room with a double bed and bland furnishings. This was clearly one of the boys' bedrooms, cluttered with football paraphernalia and cramped by childishly short bunk beds, and I couldn't help but think that Sarah had brought us to the least comfortable room she could as some kind of revenge. For interrupting her routine? Or did she think we were Stephen's allies against her in some way?

I gritted my teeth and decided not to make a fuss over this. Maybe they didn't have a guest room that was any better than this. With so many children, they must not have much extra space. And it wasn't as if I wished that Stephen had given up any of the adult bedrooms he shared with his wives. That would have truly made it impossible for me to stay under his roof.

I looked around the room, amused by the masculine decorating. There were several signed footballs covered in protective plastic domes and signed posters of famous BYU players, including Steve Young and Ty Detmer. I wondered if Stephen was nervous about letting his sons play in a room with so many valuable items.

Sarah had begun to strip the beds of blankets and sheets.

"Can I help?" I asked, secretly guilty she was changing the sheets when I wasn't at all sure Kurt and I would ever use them.

"It'll be faster if I do it myself," Sarah said. She was practiced at the maneuver, as I had never been when my boys had had bunk beds. It was always the upper bunk that was tricky. I felt like I needed eight arms to get everything to lie flat.

"This is Stephen, isn't it?" Kurt said, pointing to a photo of a younger version of Stephen in football gear that looked like it had been taken in the '80s.

"Yes. In his college days," Sarah said.

"How interesting," I murmured in hopes that she would say more.

A big cowbell sounded in the kitchen as Sarah was pulling the second comforter taut across the bed. "Dinner time," she said, and walked out of the bedroom without any further fanfare.

"I need to see Talitha again tonight," I said, when Kurt and I were alone.

Kurt looked around the room, as if measuring it against the mental image he had of our own master bedroom. "I understand that. Maybe you could sneak away during dinner," he suggested.

"Good idea," I agreed.

"I'll see what I can do to cover your absence with Stephen," Kurt said. "But there is no way I'm staying in this house overnight. I've never in my life felt so certain that Satan held sway over the spirit of God in a specific location before. You feel it, too, don't you?"

"Mmm," I said. So he hadn't changed his mind. I wasn't going to argue that the Carter compound had a good spirit about it, but I couldn't leave until I assured myself that Talitha was in no physical danger. The rest I would have to figure out later.

Was there any way I could get Stephen to send her to live with me and Kurt? Our marriage wasn't perfect, but it had to be better than this. But then what about all the other children here, and the wives, too? It was too easy to have my attention fractured. I'd only promised to stay long enough to figure out if Talitha was being hurt. I couldn't fix everything in every family in the world. I wasn't even sure I could fix my own.

I remember Kurt telling me after about six months of being bishop that he'd finally learned that important lesson, that people had to solve their own problems and were only resentful if you tried to tell them what they were doing wrong. Of course, he'd meant adults, not vulnerable children.

"At least no one is starving to death here," I said, as the smell of the roast pork wafted toward us.

Kurt grunted at that and together we walked down to the dining room. The table was really two long wooden tables put together, with a handmade white tablecloth stretched over both. The cloth was all one piece, and had been elaborately cross-stitched with names, a kind of seating chart for the table. There were three real wooden dining room chairs, a few folding chairs, a piano bench, a worn picnic bench, and a long wooden church pew jammed against the wall.

Stephen took one of the wooden chairs and directed me and Kurt to the other two, while Sarah and Rebecca sat on folding chairs. I felt guilty about taking Rebecca's and Sarah's spots, leading them to take Esther's and Lehi's, and on down the line until the five youngest children shared the space of three on the church pew. Kurt tried to stand to insist that Sarah come back to her normal spot, but she refused with a stubborn glee.

Brigham reached in to stick a finger in the bowl of mashed potatoes. Rebecca slapped at his hand, but not before he'd already gotten a hunk of it into his mouth.

Sarah made a sour face, but she didn't seem to feel any obligation to participate in the child management, even of her own children.

I saw Lehi—I think that was his name; the embroidered names were no help because of the mixed up seating arrangement—twist one of the girl's fingers very roughly, for no reason that I could tell. "Maddie is a baby, crying like a baby," he taunted.

Madeleine twisted her mouth to stop herself from crying, and the oldest boy, Nephi, resolved the situation with a threatening finger at his brother. Or half-brother. Whatever the relationship was.

I couldn't help but think that this could easily be my own boys if they'd had so many younger siblings. There were so many odd things about this polygamous group that bothered me, and then a moment like this, that seemed just so—ordinary.

Rebecca clapped her hands loudly. "Manners in front of our company, please," she said. She pointed at Lehi and Brigham, then mimed a smile to Madeleine with fingers at either side of her lips. Madeleine responded by making a false smile that seemed all too much like Sarah's.

I looked at Sarah. Even if she had been in charge of dinner preparation, she didn't seem to be looking after the children at all. I couldn't tell which ones were hers and which ones were Rebecca's based on anything other than my memory of what Stephen had told me. As far as their responses to maternal authority, Rebecca seemed the mother of them all.

Then Stephen Carter stood and stared balefully around the room, the children going absolutely quiet. He bent his head and closed his eyes for prayer. Kurt and I bowed our heads, too, but in that moment, I felt Kurt was right about the spirit of God being pushed away. I felt only a cavernous spiritual darkness here.

Stephen began his prayer with a long list of things he was grateful for, including every child in the room and the two wives who were present. He was grateful for his "abundant wealth," for "our election and calling being made sure," and for God's "saving us from the wrath of hell which so many others must face." The prayer went on and on.

After, there was a period of chaos as serving platters were passed and I noticed that Rebecca was still trying to maintain some control, however badly. I probably could not have done any better in her place.

But I had my own plans, so I ate a small portion of potatoes, roasted pork, and green beans quickly. Then I refilled one of the nearly empty serving plates, stood, and announced I would take it to Talitha.

I could see Stephen was about to object, but Kurt spoke up. "Please pardon Linda. She has no more children of her own at home, and has been so unhappy not to be able to mother anyone. I would be very appreciative if you would let her do this."

I was grateful for Kurt's intervention. For all his dislike of Stephen, Kurt knew how to handle an arrogant man when he was determined to do it. I wondered how many men in church he spoke to like this, men who were not so different from Stephen.

Sarah glanced up at me, as if about to ask if I knew where I was going, and then seemed to decide she wasn't going to help me.

I could manage without her. I hurried upstairs. I wasn't exactly sure which room was Talitha's, but with no one else around, I felt less intrusive opening doors and peering inside. I held the plate full of food in one hand like a waitress and turned doorknobs with the other, calling out "Talitha!" quietly as I went.

After searching the second floor with no luck, I went up to the next floor. The fourth door on the third floor, a couple of doors past the bunkroom where Kurt and I were supposed to spend the night, opened to a room covered in pink and white frills. There was lace everywhere, and the carpet was a dusky shade of rose. Talitha's small figure was obscured by the pink blanket. Long blonde hair splayed over the pillow.

I set down the plate of food on the dresser—white with pink stenciled designs. Then I moved to the bed and put a hand to Talitha's forehead, which was warm, but not hot. She didn't rouse to my touch and was breathing very deeply.

Had Stephen Carter given her drugs to make her sleep this heavily? Had he hurt her physically after he'd left us in the backyard with the cat's body? Her face seemed swollen with crying, but I couldn't guess if she had any other physical harm done to her since I couldn't see her arms and legs under the blanket.

Why didn't they teach us in Relief Society about how to spot signs of abuse, or how to know when to call DCFS without worrying about doing more harm than good?

Reluctantly, I lifted the blanket and saw that Talitha was wearing a short nightie that left her legs mostly bare. Still asleep, she tugged at the blanket, probably because she was cold. But her legs were pale and unbruised as far as I could see. No cuts, no scars except for one line on her calf that was probably from a perfectly natural fall. But how would I know for sure?

"Talitha?" I whispered, next to her ear.

She stirred and moaned something, then tried to turn over.

I shook her shoulder gently. "Talitha, I need to talk to you. Can you wake up a little?"

Her eyes opened again, and I saw that they were rimmed with red. I didn't know if that was a result of drugs or the crying.

"Do you remember me? My name is Linda Wallheim. My son is marrying your sister, Naomi."

No response.

"Did your father punish you?" I asked. I needed her to tell me the truth, but she still might not know me well enough to do it. It was a Catch-22, where she knew Naomi too well to tattle on other family members and me not well enough.

"I'm hungry," said Talitha, tucking the blanket around her legs tightly, ignoring my question.

"Well, lucky for you, I brought this." I offered her the plate of food I hadn't really been sure she would eat. "Do you want me to help?" I asked. "I could feed you."

"Like a baby?" she said, making a funny face.

"Or cut the pork for you?" I tried again.

She shook her head. "I can do it myself."

She sat up and ate very carefully, asking for a napkin, which I had happened to bring, and using it to wipe her lips after nearly every bite. It took her quite some time to get through the food, her hands moving slowly.

She had such a big personality packed into her tiny body, I thought with a smile. Naomi had described Talitha as innocent and carefree, but I wasn't sure that was true. At times she seemed burdened by some invisible weight; and at other times, she seemed wonderfully bright and engaged.

When Talitha was finished eating, I took the plate.

She smiled at me and said, "Do you know where my cat is?" She looked at me with wide eyes and heart-breaking earnestness.

I felt my heart lurch. "Lucy?"

Talitha nodded. "My father doesn't like her to be in the house, but sometimes I sneak her in." She pointed to the open window behind my head. "She knows which window to come in, and I don't let her go into any other rooms."

I hesitated a long moment. Her disorientation made me more certain that Stephen had given her drugs. "You don't remember what happened to Lucy this afternoon?" I asked softly. "Lucy's gone, sweetheart. She died in your arms."

Her mouth rounded in a silent "No." Then tears filled her eyes and started to trace small waterfalls down her cheeks. "I thought it was a bad dream," she got out, half-choking. "I was hoping it was just a bad dream."

"I'm sorry," I said. I reached out my hand for her to hold, but I don't think she noticed, and I let it fall away. I was glad that she had at least been able to enjoy her dinner before she remembered. "My husband found a very nice spot for her grave on the mountain, behind the house. You'll be able to visit her every day if you want. She's wrapped in your own baby quilt. Your mother gave it to us," I said. "It was pink and yellow." Maybe it hadn't been as cruel as I'd thought at the time to choose that particular quilt. I spent a moment reconsidering my view of Sarah, but then pushed it aside. She wasn't important now.

Talitha sniffled, tears dripping down her face.

"Maybe in the morning, we can show you where she's buried," I suggested.

She seemed unable to talk.

I waited until the sobs subsided. "Talitha, I'm worried about you. Is there anything you want to tell me about? Is anyone here at home hurting you?" I felt uncomfortable asking so directly, but I had limited time and had to press the issue.

Talitha looked away and didn't answer.

"I promise not to tell your mother and father," I said. "You can trust me. Naomi sent me. She asked me to make sure you were all right. She's worried about you, too."

Talitha tucked her arms and legs together under the blankets, and pushed her head into the pillow.

"I heard you crying out. Do you remember that? After your father took you inside?" I tried to get her to look me in the eyes. She wouldn't. "Did he hurt you?"

Nothing.

"Talitha, you don't deserve to be hurt. You have to tell some-one if you need help."

I felt sick, my stomach twisting. Was God warning me to stop, or was this His signal that I was right to worry? Sometimes I wished that instead of the Holy Spirit, God would use flash cards. Straightforward instructions on what to do next. Turn left. Turn right.

"I want Naomi," Talitha finally said, her voice small. "She's always gone. But she's the only one who really loves me. She's the one I talk to."

"Naomi will be here in the morning," I said, patting her arm to reassure her. That was what she'd told me, anyway. "All right? You can tell her everything then."

"Really? Tomorrow?"

I nodded.

"Then I just have to sleep and I will see her," she said, and closed her eyes. It seemed she was almost instantly asleep.

I tiptoed out of the room after that and texted Naomi on the way back downstairs to let her know that Talitha's cat had died and that she was waiting for her. Maybe Naomi would know the right thing to say to her sister.

I thought about what I'd seen of Stephen and Talitha. I thought about the way she'd reacted when I asked if someone was hurting her. How could I know for sure if she was safe or not? Naomi had asked me to see to this. I couldn't just walk away and tell her she had to take care of it herself. Somehow, I had to find out more information. And that meant—I had to stay.

I took a deep breath, preparing myself for what I would have to tell Kurt. I didn't think there was any way I could convince him to stay with me, and I knew it was a bad time in our marriage to lay out an ultimatum. But Kurt and I were grownups. Talitha was just a child. When it came to a choice between our welfare and hers, she always had to come first.

CHAPTER 12

I walked the empty plate back to the kitchen, where Kurt met me.

"Nephi, Leah, hi! Good work!" I said to the two children who were finishing up the dishes. I was pleased I'd remembered their names. I was tempted to chat with them, just to put off the fateful conversation with my husband. But there was no point in stalling. Kurt and I were going to argue, and I might as well do it now, before I got more tired and more likely to say something terrible to the man I still truly loved.

So I pulled Kurt, who had been standing on the threshold, into the dining room, which was now empty.

"How is Talitha?" he asked.

"She seems to be well enough," I said. "But she's asking for Naomi, and I'd like to make sure I'm here when Naomi and Kenneth get here tomorrow morning." Was there any chance he'd agree with me?

Kurt's arms were folded across his chest and his face was expressionless. There was my answer. No.

"Linda, I told you that I'm not staying here overnight," he said. "Are you incapable of listening to me anymore?" His voice was uncharacteristically loud, enough that one of the children (I think it was little Rachel) stopped at the bottom of the stairs, gave him a wary look, and then went tiptoeing up.

Maybe I should have been more understanding of his reaching his breaking point, but what about me and mine? I was tired of all the patriarchy and the way women were expected to just fall in line.

I said furiously, "I do listen. I just don't obey you at every turn, Kurt. God gave me my own mind and I'm capable of making my own decisions about right and wrong." Kurt didn't get to tell me what God's will was, not now and not ever. I loved him and I thought he was a good man, but I wasn't under his direction.

"Then why are you always throwing yourself into bad situations?" Kurt demanded. "Do you really believe that's what God wants from you?"

I noticed Nephi and Leah had come out of the kitchen and were looking at us. I was embarrassed to meet their gazes, but they exchanged a glance and disappeared down the basement stairs. I wondered if any of the children would tell the adults about this or if they were used to keeping things to themselves.

"Kurt, let's go out to the truck and talk, all right?" I said. We could at least have some privacy there.

"Because you're embarrassed that Stephen Carter might hear us argue? I don't care what he thinks about me, Linda!".

But I didn't particularly care to be used as a tool for Kurt to show off his machismo, which was what it felt like he was doing.

"Kurt, think about the children," I said softly.

He glanced around, but there weren't any skulking children staring at us now, which he seemed to take as license to continue. "I'm leaving this house tonight and you're coming with me!" he declared.

Oh, really? And how was he going to manage that? Throw me

over his shoulder and carry me away kicking and screaming the way Stephen had done with Talitha? I was pretty sure I out-weighed Kurt by a few pounds.

"Calm down, Kurt. Let's talk about this like reasonable adults," I said, sure that we could ratchet the level of this argu-ment down somehow. We still loved each other more than we were angry at each other. At least I hoped we did. "Look, all I want to do is stay here tonight. I'll come home as soon as I can, tomorrow." I didn't want to directly state that I was looking for signs that something was wrong with Talitha right out here where anyone could eavesdrop, but Kurt knew exactly what I was saying.

He sighed and seemed to shrink, as if he'd gotten sadder and smaller. Nonetheless, he went out the front door, waited for me to come out, then closed it behind me. As we walked toward the truck, he said, all anger gone, "I know that you have a mother's heart and that makes you feel for a little girl like Talitha. But she isn't your daughter, Linda. She isn't your responsibility."

I knew that! I knew that my own daughter was dead. But I was still a mother first and foremost. That's what the church kept telling us, that motherhood was an eternal role, that nurtur-ing children and spreading love was what we would do even when we were in the celestial kingdom, that it was what Heav-enly Mother did. And that wider identity of motherhood meant that my moral responsibilities didn't end with my own children, no matter what was convenient to my husband.

"Kurt, I'm staying here. You can either stay with me or not, it's up to you," I said aloud, feeling firm in this decision. "I'm going to finish what I started."

We reached the truck and he leaned against the passenger side door, his jaw clenched tight. "Linda, are you sure this isn't just about you hurting me because you're angry at me about the policy?"

I wanted to protest immediately, but I made myself consider what he said. He'd asked me weeks ago if I thought Kenneth was marrying a woman from a polygamous family just to tweak us, and I'd told him that was ridiculous, but maybe this suggestion was less ridiculous.

I *was* angry at him. Angry at the way he closed ranks, defending every decision made by the church leaders, whether it made sense or not. I was angry that he hadn't seemed to feel any fury or sorrow about the new policy, hadn't tried to see it from the perspective of all the people it affected, hadn't said one thing about it being wrong or hurtful to Samuel. It felt like he'd left me out to dry, just like he was doing now. Leaving me here because he wanted to be on the side of the right and wasn't willing to accept that sometimes you had to get a little dirty to help people who were in need.

"Kurt, it's complicated," I said, looking up at him, only able to see him from the porch light of the house, his features strangely distorted by the harsh glow.

He put out a hand to touch my face. But I turned my head away from him, backing up a couple of steps until I met the wall. I didn't want him to think that I was giving up and was going to do what he wanted.

And he seemed to have given up trying to convince me. Instead, he said plaintively as a child, "Linda, what can I do to get back to where we used to be?"

It hurt to realize that I had no idea and that maybe we could never go back to where we'd been. But . . . "You could start by seeing the policy change the way I do, the way that Kenneth and Naomi do."

He spread his hands open wide. "We have to accept that God knows best how to make us become like Him, to be worthy of heaven."

And now he was saying exactly what I didn't want to hear. It wasn't that I thought I knew everything. I just called out prejudice when I saw it. The church had changed its stance on what was policy and what was doctrine before now, on polygamy, on blacks and the priesthood, and there was no reason for me to think it wouldn't happen again.

"What about Samuel? You really think that he's supposed to be celibate all his life? Watch his brothers get married and have children and never have any of that, even though the church teaches it's the most important thing in the world for us to do, to have those eternal families?" I asked.

"Samuel can have those things," Kurt said. He sounded desperate. Maybe as desperate as I was. "He might have to work harder to get them. He might spend some years finding just the right woman who understands him, but the church's promise of eternal happiness is available for everyone."

Back to this? With some kind of reparative therapy to "cure" his gayness, Samuel could marry a woman in the temple and be just like our other sons? Like I had tried to marry Ben and make everything work between us. So long as I didn't expect him to have sex with me and enjoy it.

What part of "gay" wasn't Kurt understanding?

I shook my head. "Samuel loves the church so much," I said. "But it seems to me like the church doesn't love Samuel back quite as much. Not as he really is. He has to change himself, pretend to be someone else."

Kurt put thumb and finger to either side of his nose and took a deep breath. "We all have to change," he said. "We're all sinners. We have to give up our sins to get into the celestial kingdom."

I was so tired and frustrated by this. Around and around in circles, that's all that ever happened. "It's not the same and you know it." Giving up sins for Kurt didn't mean never having a satisfying sex life, never truly being in love with his life partner, and never being able to talk about who he was without stigma.

"Does sex matter so much, in the long run?" Kurt's eyes were wide and I recalled in that moment that it had been a long time since we'd had sex. For several months after the policy change, I'd been completely uninterested. There had been a couple of furtive, silent couplings after that, and then—nothing for a long time. Was Kurt saying he was fine with that? I wasn't.

"Kurt, of course it matters," I spluttered.

"Fine." He flushed. "But I just can't accept that anyone would throw away everything that is so good in the church because they wanted more sex."

And yet here we were, in the house of a polygamist who had been excommunicated for his sex life.

"You don't know what it would be like to have sex without sexual attraction," I told him, trying to speak gently so that he wouldn't feel battered by the words that I felt like I was repeating—again. "You don't know what celibacy for your whole adult life would be. And you certainly don't know what it would be like to be told that your natural sexual instincts are wrong and that you have to change them in order to be acceptable to your community. Until you do a little more soul searching about that, I don't think we can talk about this." Why were we rehashing all of this right now? Because it hadn't been resolved. Maybe it never would be and we both would have to accept that, but we hadn't yet.

"But Linda, we're not animals," Kurt said, "We're not just our most base needs. The natural man is an enemy to God." He was quoting scripture at me, the surest way to end any real conversation. Play the "bishop" card and remind your wife that you are in every way considered her spiritual superior.

As I looked at my husband standing there, smelling his unique scent and feeling the warmth leaking from him, it occurred to me to feel some brief pity for Kurt. He hated this compound and all it represented. This wasn't a good moment for him.

But even beyond this moment, Kurt was dealing with other, unresolved problems. His world had been rocked when Samuel came out, and now again with Kenneth's resigning his membership in the church. Maybe somewhere he still held onto the idea that if he was a good father, a good masculine role model, his sons would all turn out heterosexual and perfect, in his own mold. They wouldn't "choose" the wrong path. But now two of his sons had, in completely different ways. And I was threatening to choose my own wrong path, at least the way Kurt saw it.

Beneath the anger was sheer terror, I thought. If I had the time and the energy, I would have tried to reassure him that my staying overnight here didn't mean I was leaving him or the church. It just meant I was changing the terms of my allegiance. A woman promised in the temple to obey her husband as he obeyed God. And in my book, this was where Kurt had stopped obeying the God of love. If only I could get him to see it.

"I'm not going home right now," I said firmly. "This is where I'm supposed to be."

Kurt let out a sigh, like a punctured balloon. "Well, then, I have to do what I know is right," he said. He moved around the truck and climbed in the driver's side, looking across at me through the passenger side window, as if hoping I was still considering getting in.

That was when I remembered that I hadn't ever taken my overnight bag out of the truck. I climbed in and got it.

"I'll need this," I said, feeling terrible that this would be the last thing I said to him. When I had closed the door, Kurt started the engine. I stepped away from the truck.

Then he put his head on the steering wheel and turned the engine off. He climbed out of the truck and walked over to me.

I had a beautiful moment of relief, believing that he had decided to stay with me, after all, that our relationship mattered more than the new policy and his loyalty to the church.

But that wasn't it at all.

"The gate," he said.

I shuddered as I realized what he meant.

"I have to ask Stephen to open it for me."

I tried to think of something I could say that would heal the wound we'd both opened in our marriage. "I love you, Kurt."

He looked up at me and I had never seen his face so ragged. He looked a decade older than he had this morning. I worried about him alone in our house. Kurt hated being alone far more than I did.

"Call me if you want me to come get you. Any time, day or night," he said. He put out a hand as if he was going to offer me a hug, and then pulled it back. I couldn't tell if that was because he was afraid that he wouldn't be able to leave if he touched me or if he thought I didn't deserve his touch in my rebellion.

He walked inside the house and Nephi came out a few moments later, clutching a key and running down the driveway toward the gate as if he'd much rather be outside on a summer night anyway. Kurt and Stephen came down the steps after him, and Stephen followed Kurt to the door of the truck.

"I hope to see you again soon, Kurt. I believe you're a good man," Stephen said graciously, offering his hand.

Kurt very pointedly did not take it, and climbed into the driver's seat. I heard the truck start and listened to it rumble down the driveway as long as I could still hear it.

After that, I was too tired to make polite conversation and went up to the bunk bedroom, though it was only nine, and changed into pajamas for the night. As I lay there on the bottom bunk, trying to sleep, I thought about Talitha, who had lost her cat and might be heartbroken for a long time about it. I thought about Samuel, who'd had a similarly soft heart, not only for animals, but for everyone.

Samuel was always the child you could count on to be kind to the new kid, the odd one out, the kid who was being teased or bullied. He circled around them and made them stronger just by being who he was. I missed him more than I missed any of my other sons, though it felt wrong for a mother to admit that. At this moment I wanted to talk to my youngest, dearest son more than I ever had before.

But he needed to be focused on spiritual work, not his parents' squabbles. A mission was supposed to be a respite from the problems of the real world, from grades in college, from working a job, from the pressure to date and marry. If it was going as well as he said, it might be a rude awakening when he got home and had to face what he was missing as a gay man in a church that had made heterosexuality divine and eternal.

I loved Samuel so much, and I wasn't going to be able to do anything to help him then, not with the new policy in place. He would have to make his own choices, either to leave the church and make his own path as a gay man or to stay and try to make compromises.

But what kind of compromises could I accept? If Samuel tried to marry a woman as I had tried to marry Ben, what would I say? Could I stand by and let that happen without warning her about the consequences?

I wished that Mormonism wasn't synonymous to so many people with prejudice and backwardness and intolerance. I was sick at the idea that my church had turned to hate instead of love. And why?

Because we weren't flexible enough. We waited around for a revelation to tell us how to love, instead of just moving forward with it. Joseph Smith had started the church with the insistence that everyone, even a teenage boy, had the right to ask God for an answer to prayer, but in the last decades, it seemed like the church had become very cautious about any personal revelation and had pushed a level of obedience that had never been part of the original church.

Of course Stephen Carter was the classic example of someone who had gone off the deep end with individual revelation. I wished I could blame him completely for it. But it seemed to me that if Stephen Carter had fallen down some dark tunnel of Mormonism, it was at least partly the fault of a church that was leaving those holes open and trying to ignore they were there rather than trying to fill them up. At this point, there were so many holes in Mormonism I was worried I was about to fall into one myself.

CHAPTER 13

I lay on the lower bunk bed and couldn't sleep, my heart hurting. The sounds of the house had died down and I spent hours tossing and turning. Finally, I decided to get up and go to the bathroom for some water. This was the solution I had often offered to my sons when they were young and said they couldn't sleep. I think the main trick in it was to turn off the part of the brain that was circling around the need to sleep and focus it on something else entirely.

While I was in the bathroom, I heard raised voices downstairs. I checked my watch. It was after midnight. Who was down there? Neither voice was deep enough to be Stephen's.

I turned off the light in the bathroom and listened. I should have gone back to bed, I know. I was here for Talitha, not just to be nosy. That's what I'd told Kurt I was staying for. But I could help Talitha and be nosy, too, couldn't I? Anything I learned about the family might be relevant. At least, that was my excuse as I tiptoed downstairs.

Two women were in the hallway by the back door of the front room. Peeking around the corner, I got a quick glimpse of Sarah's taut back, and Joanna, who must have left her children at home in bed. It was the first time I had seen her without them tugging on her. She looked as overdressed and FLDS as she had earlier, her unbound hair stringy on her back, a worn, long-sleeved flannel nightgown underneath. Sarah was still wearing the dark, modern dress she'd had on when she met us at the door.

Afraid they'd spot me and I'd miss all the interesting gossip, I tried to be very quiet and listened with all my might.

"I need to talk to Stephen," Joanna insisted. Her face was contorted.

"I told you, Stephen will see you on your regular Monday next week. He had to change the chart this week because of the visitors," Sarah said.

There was a chart? Really and truly, a written chart that determined which wife Stephen visited each night?

"I don't see why he still has a night with Rebecca when she's past her years anyway. She can't give him any more children," Joanna said.

My eyebrows rose at this. Was this a rule with polygamists? You didn't have sex with your husband anymore if you couldn't have children? Because it was a waste of sperm he could be using elsewhere?

"Well, he makes the rules here, doesn't he?" Sarah said. "Not you."

"He doesn't even have seven wives. How will he ever become a god?" Joanna complained.

Seven wives? I'd never heard there was a specific number of wives that earned you godhood. So if you had only six, then you were out? And if that was true, then why did so many polygamous men have dozens and dozens of wives if they didn't have to? Maybe because their older wives were out to pasture?

"All that nonsense is FLDS, you know. Stephen doesn't believe any of it. And besides, he was punishing you anyway."

Stephen punished her by not going to her bed? That was interesting.

"I haven't done anything wrong," Joanna said. "But this isn't about that, anyway. He has a dark shadow over him." Her eyes closed and she swayed a little. "You have to tell him."

"That a dark shadow is over him? I don't think I'm going to wake him up for that. I'm not going to be punished for one of your stupid prophecies," Sarah said sourly.

Another reference to punishment. I'd seen Stephen with each of the wives and I'd seen no sign of physical abuse, but there were other ways to abuse and Stephen was smart enough to have found unique ones for each wife.

"Then get Rebecca," Joanna begged. "She understands me."

So Rebecca wasn't just the mother of the children here. She acted like the mother of the wives, too. Or at least Joanna thought of her that way.

But Sarah refused. "I'm not waking her up, and you aren't, either. That would be the same as waking up Stephen, and he doesn't care about your stupid little superstitions." She was mocking Joanna, just as Stephen had done.

"He loves me," Joanna said in reaction. "He loves his children. Even Grace. I know he loves them." She sounded like she was talking from a distance, tinny and unclear.

"You can have his love, then," Sarah said, with a wave of her hands. "But not tonight." She put a hand on Joanna's shoulder and tried to push her toward the door.

Joanna resisted, whirling on Sarah. "My prophecies are true. You know they are. I told you when you were going to be sick last month."

"Phht," Sarah said. "Everyone else had already gotten sick that week. It didn't take a prophecy to see that I would, too."

"But now there's a dark shadow around you, too," Joanna said, a hand to her throat. "It's red and black and splattered, like paint."

"You're crazy, that's what you are," Sarah said. "Stephen might feel sorry for you. He might even see you as a way to have more children. But he isn't stupid. He doesn't believe in your so-called prophecies."

Joanna shook her head slowly, sadly. She turned away from Sarah, her shoulders bowed, defeated. Sarah didn't have to ask her to leave again. She slunk out the back door, and Sarah had to pull it closed behind her.

"Idiot," said Sarah, her lips twisted.

Before she could look up and see me, I scuttled away as quietly as I could manage. Back in bed, I thought about prophecies and women's history of healing blessings in the Mormon church, which had been common in the nineteenth century, but now were outright forbidden.

I thought about charts and menstruation cycles and Joanna's two children with Stephen in a short, two-year marriage. And then I thought of Stephen, who had only five wives, and seven nights in a week, leaving two nights untaken. I fell asleep before I could get beyond that, however.

The next morning, I awoke suddenly to the sound of a feminine voice calling, "Dad, we finally managed to get here! Dad? Where are you?"

I checked my phone then and saw Naomi and Kenneth had both sent me text messages about an hour ago, but I'd slept through them.

There was nothing from Kurt, however.

I got up, quickly threw on the fresh clothes from my overnight bag, and went downstairs.

In the front room, Kenneth looked wonderful, freshly shaved, his hair still wet from the shower. Naomi was holding tightly to Kenneth. She looked like she hadn't slept, dark circles under bloodshot eyes.

"Hi, Mom," said Kenneth. He offered me a hug, which I accepted gratefully. I felt so dislocated here, and now with Kurt gone, Kenneth's touch was an anchor to the present, to reality, to my family.

Naomi fidgeted anxiously beside him. "Where's Dad?" Kenneth asked.

This was not easy. "He went home."

"And left you here alone? Was there some kind of bishop emergency?"

I'd never been one to lie to my children to keep them happy, but in this case, I filed it under "none of my grown son's business," and said, "Something like that."

"How was Talitha last night?" Naomi asked.

I explained about the dead cat and burying it, and also about my visit to Talitha's room with dinner. "She really wanted to see you."

"You're saying you think she was drugged?" asked Naomi, looking furious.

"Maybe," I said, though I wasn't a doctor, or even one in training, as she was.

"I need to talk to my father right now. Have you seen him this morning?" she asked urgently.

"Not yet." I was surprised she wasn't going to see the little girl first.

"He has to be down here somewhere," Naomi said, her tone scalding. "He's always up at the crack of dawn to pray and read scriptures. Mom?" she called.

Rebecca came out of the kitchen. She hadn't come out when Naomi and Kenneth first appeared at the door. Had she just been too caught up in cooking breakfast? Or had she not wanted to talk to her daughter for some reason?

"Naomi, sweetheart!" Rebecca said, stepping forward for a hug.

Naomi ignored the motion and the hug was uncompleted. "Where's Dad?"

"I guess he might be down in his office," Rebecca said. "Although I didn't hear him come down while I was in the kitchen. He doesn't usually sleep in, but I'll go upstairs just to make sure."

Naomi went downstairs while Rebecca went up.

It was only a few moments before I heard a piercing shriek from upstairs that made my heart go cold in my chest. I clutched Kenneth's arm as Naomi came running up from the basement.

"What's wrong?" she asked Kenneth.

"I don't know. That's your mother, isn't it?" he said.

Naomi went rushing upstairs. "Mom?" she called in a panicked tone.

Kenneth loped after her, and I tried to keep up, failing miserably.

By the time I reached the third floor hallway, I could hear Rebecca's loud weeping coming from one of the bedrooms, then Naomi's voice rising over her cries, "Mom, Mom, you've got to—"

I had terrible visions of Talitha, gone cold and white in her bed, and me having to face another dead child's funeral. How could I have left her alone last night? Why hadn't I checked on her before I went to bed? Or when I'd been up and heard the conversation between Sarah and Joanna?

But when I followed Kenneth through the half-open door, where he came to a sudden stop, I saw it wasn't Talitha at all. It wasn't her room, which I'd seen last night. This was obviously the master bedroom. And it was Stephen who was causing the cries.

Rebecca was crouched over her husband, who was lying face up on the floor of the bedroom at the foot of the queen-size bed. Just above the bed was a photo of Stephen surrounded by his loving wives and children, which must have been taken fairly recently.

I smelled something strange, fetid, and the awareness settled in that I was looking at a dead body. Stephen Carter's dead body.

Rebecca, her hands covered in shining red blood, was struggling with something that I realized was a butcher knife lodged in Stephen's chest. She seemed to be trying to pull it out, but her hands kept slipping on it.

"Stephen, Stephen, come back to me," she sobbed as she rocked back and forth.

She really shouldn't have been touching the body, I thought, feeling distant and cold from the horror of the scene. My hands were tingling and I was dizzy and nauseated. I reached out and gripped the side of the door to make sure I didn't fall down.

All of my conflicting feelings for Stephen Carter rose to the surface. He was charming, but also controlling and manipulative. He was a scholar of Mormon history, but had his own reasons for it. He was a father to twenty-one children, and a husband to five wives. He was a doctor, and a good one, from what I'd gathered. He was a child of God, and now he had gone home to God for whatever judgment was just.

CHAPTER 14

I stared at the bulk of the body on the floor. Stephen seemed very large in his death. His muscles were lax, but still, his limbs filled the small space of the room. His eyes were open, and it seemed to me that there was an expression of anger on his face.

I averted my eyes from his dead gaze, eager to look at anything else in the room. I noticed that the rug he was lying on was a handmade rope braid rug, a handicraft that I had never learned, but Rebecca must have. The yellow and green summer colors had been splattered with very dark red blood. That sight made me queasy, but it was less unpleasant than looking directly at Stephen's face.

Naomi was standing in the middle of the room, one hand out, but still as a statue, staring down at her father. Kenneth was at her side.

"Naomi?" He got out.

She turned to him and said with a voice of steel, "Mom. We have to make sure she's all right."

Kenneth stared at his fiancée for one more moment, then moved around her to Rebecca. He crouched down and was about to put a hand to her back, then thought better of it, considering the fact that she had her hand on a knife. "Rebecca, are you all right?" he asked.

I was still trying to figure out what exactly had happened. Her hand was on the bloody knife. Was it possible she had killed Stephen? But surely there hadn't been time between when she'd come up here and when she had shrieked, and I hadn't seen her with a knife going up the stairs. Which meant what? Could she have killed him before she went down calmly to prepare breakfast? She seemed so sincere in her distress.

Still, I could imagine the police coming to take statements and immediately focusing on Rebecca as the prime suspect. It was a damning scene. Why had she put her hands on that knife if she hadn't done it? Wouldn't the natural instinct be away from the evidence of death, not toward it?

The more I thought about it, the more sure I was that Rebecca couldn't kill the man she'd looked at with such admiration yesterday, the father of her children. And everyone here in this house, the children as well as the other wives, needed her here, not in jail somewhere. Even if she was eventually acquitted, if the police took Rebecca away for any period of time, what would happen to those left behind on the compound? The whole family would disintegrate; I was sure of it. None of the other wives would be able to take Rebecca's place.

If Rebecca was gone, I could just imagine what would happen with the rest of the wives, and it wasn't good. Jennifer wouldn't care; she'd stay locked up in her house working on her computer. I couldn't see Joanna, so young and volatile, making the situation any better; she would convince herself she had foreseen divine wrath and would either cause havoc for the other wives or leave entirely. Carolyn would weep and cower some more. And Sarah? Bitter, angry Sarah, trapped caring for all the children, would just tell them the worst stories about their father that she could remember.

This family needed Rebecca to fill the void Stephen's death would create. Rebecca was the one who would think of their needs first and not her own, who would fight to keep them together here. She was the wife I thought was strongest. And maybe that was because she was also the one who was most like me.

Rebecca let go of the knife with a gasp and stared at her now bloodstained hands. "Oh God," she said as if in prayer.

Maybe I was the answer to her prayer. I felt a burning need to help her, even if it meant postponing calling the police. I took a breath and waited for the Holy Spirit to tell me I was wrong, that I had to follow the proper procedure, as Kurt would have done, as he had done when he and I had found a dead body together in the church. He'd coached me through calling the police, not touching the body, dealing with notifying the loved ones.

He wasn't here now and I knew someone should call the police soon, but a little time to figure out what had really happened wouldn't change that much, would it? If I was here to steer the police in the right direction, then Rebecca wouldn't be taken away from the children who needed her so much. And surely if God wanted me to call the police immediately, I'd have felt or heard something. But there was nothing, no spiritual feeling except the need to help Rebecca.

Now Naomi was pulling her mother away from the body, trying to get her to accept a knitted wrap because she was shaking so badly, asking her if she wanted to go downstairs to the kitchen and "wash up." Kenneth had moved to block her view of her husband, good man that he was.

Rebecca wouldn't let herself be moved away, however. "It's all my fault. I did this to him. I failed him," she was saying.

It wasn't really a confession, I was sure. When someone dies, you always feel guilty. When Georgia had died, I blamed myself in every conceivable way, for not going to the hospital sooner, for not eating all the spinach I should have, for the medicine I'd taken for a cold before I knew I was pregnant.

"It should be me dead," Rebecca was moaning. She slapped her own chest and her voice sounded hoarse and raw.

"Mom, maybe you should drink some water," said Naomi. She waved at Kenneth to go get some. He moved around the body and went into the bathroom, but came out with his hands empty. No water cup there, apparently. He hustled downstairs.

My top priority at the moment was to figure out a way to keep Rebecca from being wrongly arrested. On the other hand, I needed to make sure that whoever had committed this crime wasn't still a danger to the rest of the family. So I tried to think about when the murder had to have happened. After Rebecca went down to start breakfast, or she'd have seen the body when she got up, but before Naomi arrived. That had to be a short time window, maybe an hour or less. What else did I know?

Someone had known where to find Stephen, and that he would be alone. There'd been no noise of an argument. Could it be anyone outside the compound? How many people had keys to that gate? I didn't think one of the boys would have been up with a key to the gate so early in the day. So that meant it was most likely someone from the inside, a member of the family.

I heard Kenneth's heavy, hurried footsteps on the stairs and then he reappeared with the promised glass of water.

Rebecca took one sip and then put a hand to her mouth and shook her head adamantly. No more. We didn't want her to throw up on the body.

"Oh, God," she said again. "He deserved better than this. He deserved so much better."

Naomi sighed and patted Rebecca's back, as though the mother had become the child.

I had to figure this out, and quickly. The kitchen knife meant something. It had to have been brought up to the bedroom deliberately, so this wasn't a crime of passion. A knife had been chosen for a reason. It was very personal.

I took a tentative step around Naomi and Rebecca, leaned down and touched Stephen's hand, hoping that I wasn't destroying too much evidence as I did it.

I checked my watch. It was 7:24 now. I remembered reading in one of my mystery books that a body cools about one degree per hour. Stephen felt cool, but not cold. There was no rigor mortis, either. Both of those observations confirmed my guess that this had happened in the early morning.

As much as I wanted to look away, I made myself study Stephen. His hair was dry. He wasn't wearing pajamas, nor was he wearing the clothes he'd had on the day before. The khaki pants looked clean, except for the blood on them, and the light-colored button-down shirt still had fresh ironing creases on the cuffs. Was he just getting ready for his day or had he been expecting someone?

Naomi tried to coax Rebecca out of the room, but Rebecca reached for Stephen again, flinging herself on him and his blood. Naomi and Kenneth worked together to bundle Rebecca into a chair in the corner. I noticed that Sarah hadn't come into the room at the sound of Rebecca's cry, nor had any curious children poked their heads in. It confirmed what I had thought yesterday about the children being used to ignoring adult arguments.

Conscious that the police might frown on this behavior, I nonetheless looked around for Stephen's phone and spotted it on the night table. There was no password locking it, so I easily scrolled through the record of his calls from the last few days.

Mostly they were from the wives, Rebecca from yesterday afternoon asking when he'd be home, Carolyn asking for someone to come lift a box for her, Jennifer reminding him to deposit $300 into his retirement account and something about an appointment Saturday night with an old friend, Joanna telling him she'd be home late last Friday. Sarah hadn't sent him a text in the last week or so, and the only text that had come this morning was from Naomi, telling him she'd be arriving soon, just as she'd told me.

Just before I closed the phone, I saw there was a missed call from "Hector Perez," and it took me a moment to place the name. The neighbors in whose garden Joanna used to work. I would have to follow up on that later.

Rebecca had quieted down at last, no longer sobbing, and her eyes seemed to have glazed over, not really seeing Stephen anymore.

"You should take your mother out of here," I said to Naomi. "You help," I directed Kenneth, because it looked as if Rebecca wasn't going to be able to walk and I didn't think Naomi could carry her alone.

Kenneth hesitated and I said, "Go on."

He seemed surprised that I was taking charge, but it was only until Rebecca was ready to take her rightful place back.

Kenneth hoisted Rebecca out of the chair and in one swift motion got her into his arms, holding her like a baby. Naomi held her mother's hand and whispered calming things to her, making sure her nightgown didn't trip Kenneth up.

And then I was alone in the room, with quiet to think. This was a murder. Someone had planned it out and committed it in cold blood. Which of the other four wives did I think had done it?

Sarah had clearly hated Stephen; for now, she seemed the most likely suspect. I had seen her act angry, cold, unloving, and bitter to different members of her family. But could those difficult emotions blossom into murder?

Jennifer had no motive that I could see. She could have left Stephen any time she wanted without losing children or money. I tried to imagine her involved in a violent crime of passion or premeditation, and could only picture the affectless, almost bored expression behind her cat-eye glasses.

Carolyn was pregnant and dependent both financially and emotionally on Stephen and her place here with the other wives. She had seemed so weak and ineffectual to me. Could I imagine her wielding a kitchen knife, or overpowering the physically intimidating Stephen?

Joanna was barely older than a teenager. Last night, she had come to the house to deliver a second message of danger to Stephen, and I couldn't tell what that meant. That she had some advance knowledge of something? Or was this proof that her gift for seeing the future was real?

I tried to consider if any of the children might be suspects. The grown children I hadn't met, Joseph, Aaron, and Ruth, were the most likely to be physically strong enough to overwhelm their father with a kitchen knife, but they weren't at home. Maybe they could have snuck back onto the compound without being noticed. The only boys living here were surely too young, however. And Talitha, who had been furious at her father about her dead cat, wasn't tall enough to even reach his chest, I didn't think.

Trying to be methodical, I took another careful survey of the room, looking for anything unusual or out of place. Of course, I had never seen the room before, so I had no idea if this was what it usually looked like. The bedcovers were rumpled, unmade, and there were a few items on the carpet by what seemed to be Stephen's side of the bed: a newspaper, books, a copy of the *Ensign*, the official church magazine, though it didn't look like the most recent one. I saw nothing broken and no sign of anything missing, no notable crushed carpet marks.

I turned the lock on the doorknob behind me as I left, thinking that at least I'd leave the scene as undisturbed as possible for when the police eventually arrived. It wouldn't get me out of a stern lecture, I was sure, about tampering with evidence and getting involved in an investigation that should have been left to law enforcement. But if I figured out who was the most likely suspect by then, well, the proof would be in the pudding.

CHAPTER 15

Downstairs, I found Rebecca and Naomi on the couch in the front room. Rebecca's hair was stuck to her face, but at least any spatters of blood on her skin had been cleaned off and she had put on a new dress. She had a wet towel in her hands that she kept wiping them on. She wasn't talking nonsense about being to blame for Stephen's death, though, and that seemed an improvement from my perspective.

At this point, several children were awake and wandering in and out of the kitchen, staring at their mother, but not asking questions. I debated a moment about whether I should stay with Rebecca, but ultimately decided that she would be calmer if the children were calmer, so I went into the kitchen and rescued what I could of the hash browns and pancakes she had been preparing before Naomi and Kenneth arrived and the body was found.

Little Madeleine came in and showed me where the syrup was, never making a sound. She just stood there like a tiny ghost, dressed already for the day in long pants and a white shirt that seemed a little large for her, but was perfectly—even unnaturally—clean.

"Thank you, sweetheart," I said, and my voice seemed to break the spell and make her disappear.

I brought out the food and set it on the table, but instead of ringing the cowbell as Sarah had for dinner last night, I just set some plates out in a stack and some silverware in a pile. I watched as Lehi and Nephi filled plates and headed downstairs with them, looking back guiltily. I guessed they weren't normally allowed to take food from the dining room. They were murmuring to each other; they knew something was off.

I took a plateful of food for myself, feeling strange feeding myself at a time like this, but also aware after having helped with many funerals that the bodies of the living continue to need nourishment, and they collapse if they get nothing. I wrapped some hash browns into a couple of pancakes and ate wolfishly, thinking about how I had scolded my sons when I saw them eat like this, years ago.

I brought out a plate of food for Kenneth and Naomi, but they both refused it. I turned to offer it to Rebecca, but she put a hand to her stomach and looked genuinely close to vomiting, so I put it aside.

"We really need to call the police," Kenneth said.

I tensed, and looked at Rebecca. Her coloring had improved considerably in the twenty minutes I'd been gone. "No police," she said definitively. "They'll take away the children and send us all to jail."

This was an exaggeration of my own fear, but not that far off. I wondered if Stephen had planted this fear in her about the authorities in order to protect himself from ever being called to accountability. But then I reminded myself that polygamists had real reason to be afraid of prosecution.

"We don't have to call the police until you're ready, Mom," said Naomi, though she didn't sound absolutely sure of herself.

"What about the body?" Kenneth said. "We can't just leave it there. It will, well . . ." He trailed off without saying that it was going to start smelling.

"We can think about all that later," I said. I needed to buy just a little more time to talk to the wives and check their alibis and motives.

Rebecca shook her head, her expression hardening. "Not later. No police. Stephen wouldn't have wanted it." Her eyes, I saw, were dry now.

Suddenly I began to consider the possibility that Rebecca had killed Stephen, after all.

"It won't look good if we seem to be hiding something," Kenneth warned.

"No one will know if it looks good or not," Naomi said, now more firm in her decision to back her mother. "Not if they don't know what happened."

"We'll bury him with his brother and his parents," Rebecca said solemnly. "With the babies."

I felt a chill crawl up my back. Babies? What was it I had thought about Stephen at least not having a baby graveyard, unlike the FLDS?

Kenneth threw up his hands. "Hasn't anyone wondered whether this is all illegal?"

"You can bury a body within forty-eight hours in Utah, as long as you bury it in a legal cemetery," Rebecca replied, answering the spoken but not unspoken part of the question—about the legality of covering up a murder. "And part of this property has been designated as that."

How did she know all that? My mind was swirling. I had been so sure Rebecca, the devoted wife, hadn't killed her husband, but now she was insisting on no police involvement at all, and a fast burial, as well. Wouldn't an innocent wife want to see the killer brought to justice? Didn't she worry the rest of the family was in danger until that happened?

"What about life insurance?" Kenneth said, going back to the practical. "You can't collect that without a death certificate."

"We don't need money now," Rebecca said, but she didn't sound as sure as she had before.

"Of course you need the life insurance, Mom," said Naomi. "But maybe there's another way around this." She looked at me for help.

"We can call the police this evening," I suggested, stalling. "After Rebecca has had a chance to tell the other wives and the children."

"No police. At all," Rebecca insisted. "Nephi and Lehi can do the digging. Brigham can help. I'll call them." She tried to stand up, but Naomi held her down.

"Kenneth can take care of the grave digging," she said, looking up at him. "He's bigger and older. "

Kenneth hesitated for a long moment and looked at me.

Would it be a crime if he buried the body? Probably. And if he did, the police could charge us all as accessories. Was I willing to face that? Yes, I was. But my son's facing it was another question.

"Go on," I said, encouraging Kenneth.

He closed his eyes for a moment, his straight back sagging as if I'd taken all the breath out of him. When he opened his eyes again, I couldn't help but think of Kurt when he'd driven off in the truck, looking years older.

"All right," he said. He couldn't have known when he fell in love with Naomi that it would come to this, but he wasn't willing to walk away from her, either, and I had to admire that about my son. Whatever Kurt had said about Kenneth not having commitment, he was wrong.

Naomi stood up. "Then I'll send Nephi to call the wives to a meeting. Mom, you'll be there with me. Linda, can you help Kenneth with . . . the grave?"

"All right," I said reluctantly. I wasn't sure I would add much to the grave digging, considering how badly I'd managed to fill in the cat's grave when Kurt was here. I wished I could be there for the meeting with the wives.

"You're going to have to have a death certificate to probate the will," Kenneth pointed out. I hadn't thought about this problem, but then again, I'd always intended to call the police eventually. It felt like that one decision early on, while Rebecca was still in shock, was making it more and more difficult to go back.

Naomi turned to Rebecca. "Is there anyone who would sign a death certificate for natural causes?" she asked desperately. "One of Dad's colleagues, maybe?"

It would have to be someone who was blind and not very inquisitive, I thought.

"Dr. Benallie," Rebecca said.

"Who is Dr. Benallie?" I asked. And why in the world did Rebecca think she would do something like this?

"She works with Stephen in his practice," Rebecca said, which didn't fully answer my question.

The fact that Rebecca thought she had in hand someone who would write a false death certificate made me go back to the question of whether or not Rebecca had planned this all out. For a moment, I considered calling the police myself. I had my own phone. I could even call Kurt and ask him to come and help deal with things.

But I didn't, because of the reality of how I felt about Stephen Carter.

What if Rebecca really had killed her polygamous husband? What if she had gotten tired of him marrying younger and younger wives? What if she had snapped after the way he had manipulated her and everyone else on the compound? Maybe watching him mistreat Talitha after her cat's death had been too much for her.

Did I really think she deserved to go to jail for that? I had come to like her and feel sympathy for her. Maybe if she had killed Stephen, she was justified in it.

I had never taken the law into my own hands like this before. But I'd never been in a situation like this before. Kurt had left and it seemed that God had kept me here. I didn't feel any sense of divine encouragement, but neither did I feel that sinking sense of darkness that had always told me in the past that I was wrong.

So I exchanged looks with Naomi and Kenneth. Somehow, tacitly, all three of us agreed that we were going to go along with this. God help us all.

"What's Dr. Benallie's number?" asked Naomi.

"Just call the main number for Stephen's office and ask for her. Tell her it's Rebecca Carter calling. She'll speak to you immediately."

Kenneth and I waited as Naomi asked for Dr. Benallie using her mother's name. Then she muted the phone for a moment. "What do I tell her?" she asked. "That he's dead?"

"Just give me the phone," Rebecca said. To my surprise, she very calmly explained that there had been a death "in the family" and asked Dr. Benallie to come see to the "legal details."

"She should be here in a half hour," Rebecca said, handing the phone back to Naomi.

I was astonished and tried to parse what this might mean. Was Dr. Benallie in on the murder somehow?

Sarah came into the living room, scowling at her sister. "It was your day to do breakfast and there are dishes all over the house now. What's the matter this time? Feeling under the weather again?" She sneered. "Looks to me like you're well enough to get out of bed and sit talking with your daughter and her new family."

I was horrified at the rudeness under the circumstances, but before I could say anything, Rebecca said bluntly, "Stephen is dead. In our bedroom."

Sarah's reaction was very slight. She seemed to deflate for a moment, then raised her head so that her chin poked out. "So you left him there?" She didn't ask how he'd died. What did that mean?

"Yes, I did," Rebecca said. "Dr. Benallie is coming to certify his death before we bury him. Will you criticize me for that, too?"

The antagonism between the two sisters had never been more painful to watch. I wished they could have come together in this moment of sorrow, but it wasn't to be.

"I criticize you when you do something wrong. It is not my fault that it happens so often," Sarah said sharply.

"How nice it must be never to do anything wrong," Rebecca said, but her voice was faint. She wasn't really arguing back. It was as if she was accepting that she had done things wrong, even if not this thing.

"Nice is not a word I would have used to describe any part of my life for a very long time," Sarah said. She turned on her heel, but I caught her before she could leave.

"Rebecca is calling the other wives here to tell them the news," I said. "I'm sure you want to be there."

"I'm sure I don't," Sarah said mulishly.

I knew her marriage to Stephen had been miserable, but I still didn't understand her hostility to her sister. I didn't have a sister myself, so maybe I didn't know what it was like. I kept thinking they should be more natural allies.

"Can't you sit with your sister for a little while and offer her some comfort?" I said, pulling Sarah aside and making no effort to temper my critical tone.

"For what? For the death of the man I hated?" Sarah said.

"Hated?" I echoed, and saw Naomi wince

"Yes, I hated him. I think I've hated him since the day I married him and found out who he truly was. And she—helped him keep the secret," Sarah pointed an accusing finger at her older sister. "She colluded with him to lie to me."

I began to see Sarah's side of the story. I don't know why I hadn't before. She must have been quite young when she married, and trusting in her sister's judgment perhaps more than she should have. And this was where it had gotten her. No wonder she was bitter.

"I never lied to you," Rebecca said tiredly.

"You lied to me and you lied to yourself. You lie to everyone every minute of your life!" Sarah shouted.

Naomi had looked away, unable to bear this. Kenneth was stroking her shoulder gently.

"Well, he's gone now," Rebecca said, flinging up her hands in disgust. "Lucky you. You're free."

Sarah's eyed flared with anger. "Free? You call this free? With the children he's chained to me? I'll never be free. But at least I won't have to hear his voice or think about him breathing next to me in bed ever again. I can be happy about that." Sarah jerked her arm out of my grip, crossed the living room, and went out the front door, letting it slam closed. Through the front window I could see her walking angrily down the gravel drive.

Even if I understood her anger a little better now, that didn't mean she hadn't done it. In fact, it might mean she was more likely than ever, both to have killed Stephen with a kitchen knife and to have left him in her sister's bedroom, for her sister to find.

CHAPTER 16

"If we're going to do the funeral tonight," Rebecca said to Kenneth, "you need to get out there and start digging."

I swallowed hard. It was time to face the reality. I was colluding in this now, whether I'd intended for it to go this far or not. Kenneth looked at me, and I nodded to him. This was his family now, and by extension it was mine, too. We were bound forever, even if Kenneth and Naomi didn't plan on marrying in the temple.

Kenneth let go of Naomi and straightened. "All right. Tell me where," he said to Rebecca.

"The graveyard is past the shed, a couple hundred yards down the hill," Rebecca said. "Just follow the stream."

"And a shovel?"

"In the garage," I said, touching his arm. "I'll show you." I led him back through the kitchen and out the garage door.

It was shadowy and cool inside the garage, despite the rising summer sun, and I found myself not wanting to leave and go back out. Or maybe I just didn't want to think about what I was going to tell Kurt. How was he going to feel when he found out I was helping cover up a murder? I'd done things that skirted the law before this, for the sake of someone I thought needed my help, but everything else paled in comparison to this. What had happened to me? Was Kurt right about me being so angry about the policy that I was trying to hurt him back? Or somehow all authority in general?

"Mom, are you really okay with this?" said Kenneth softly.

"You knew Stephen Carter," I said, trying to sound more sure than I was as I stared at the row of rakes, shovels, and picks. "Did you think he was a good person?"

"Not a good person, no. But that doesn't mean I thought he deserved to die with a kitchen knife in his chest." He was pulling at his hair again, that familiar gesture that made my heart ache.

"Do you think Rebecca deserves to end up in prison after living so many years with him and dealing with all of his— machinations?" It seemed the best word to describe what their lives had been like together.

"So you're saying you think she did it?" asked Kenneth, turning around and staring at the door we'd come through.

"No, I'm saying she's the one the police would probably arrest. And then what would happen to everyone else here? You know how attached Naomi is to them. It's not just Talitha she wants to protect, I don't think." I wished right then that I could go back in time and change my choice, that moment when I walked in and found Stephen's dead body. If I'd called the police then, everything would have turned out different. Kenneth and I wouldn't be up to our necks in this and unable to make a better choice. But there was no going back now.

"It's just freaky how she's on board with this," said Kenneth, "almost like they had it planned out in advance. I mean, normal people don't see a murder and think immediately, oh, let's bury the body and just move on with our lives."

I was wondering the same thing. But surely they wouldn't have done it the weekend Kurt and I were supposed to be here.

"Well, the Carters aren't exactly normal people," I said.

"Yeah, I guess I'm getting that loud and clear every second we spend here," Kenneth said.

I looked at him and could see that he was feeling some doubts. It was actually the most normal part of all of this. Whenever you meet the family of someone you love, you question things. You wonder if this is what they will be like, in the end. You worry about all the flaws that are on display and if you've missed something really big.

"Look, Kenneth, now is not the time to walk away. Naomi needs you. She's dealing with hard stuff here, and I know you love her. You're going to be stronger than ever as a couple if you get through this." I was a little surprised at how I was defending the young woman I'd only met twice, but I felt strongly about her already.

Kenneth closed his eyes, nodded, and took a couple of deep breaths. "Right. Okay, I can help Naomi. But it still feels wrong to act as judge and jury and let a murderer go free. What if something else happens and we could have stopped it? We'll never forgive ourselves."

He was right about that. I couldn't just tell myself that Stephen got what he deserved and that it didn't matter who had done this. Even if Rebecca wasn't in danger of being taken from the family, I had to make sure she knew who might be a threat. "Let me take care of it," I said. "I'll figure it out. You dig the grave."

Kenneth's eyebrows rose. "That seems like a slightly unfair division of labor to me."

"You don't know how bad I am at digging," I said.

"Or how good you are at investigating murders, maybe," said Kenneth, looking at me as if he were seeing me for the first time.

But he was the one who had told Naomi I could help her figure out what was wrong with Talitha. Well, I guess my son was going to see me in action now.

He tucked the shovel under one arm and grabbed a pair of gardening gloves, then we headed outside and past the shed, down the hill. I showed Kenneth where Lucy the cat's grave was, in case he needed to show it to Talitha sometime when I wasn't there. I had meant to show her myself, but other things seemed to keep getting in the way.

"You and Dad had a fight, didn't you?" Kenneth asked as we were walking.

Instead of denying it, I said, "It's normal for married people to have conflicts." He was learning that right now.

"If you don't want to talk about whatever happened with Dad, that's fine. I just feel bad because it seems like it's my fault. Mine and Naomi's."

"Of course it's not your fault, Kenneth." My heart burned that he thought it was. Kurt and I were perfectly capable of having a rousing fight without his help.

"Yeah, well, I thought things were pretty messed up to begin with, but I had no idea they'd turn into this. No matter how distanced Naomi tries to be from her family, she keeps getting sucked back into fucked up family stuff."

I wouldn't normally use that word, but in this case it was completely appropriate. "Fucked up family stuff, yes," I said. And Kenneth turned to me with very wide, surprised eyes. I laughed at that. Moms can say the "f" word, too, even Mormon ones.

"Mom, I spent a long time thinking about resigning my church membership," Kenneth said, his tall bulk close enough for me to feel comfort in its size and strength. Just like his father's, I thought.

"I know that," I said.

"No, listen to me. If it were just about me, I'd have done it a long time ago. Even before the policy change. When I got off my mission, I think. But I knew how much it would hurt Dad. And you." Kenneth was looking off into the horizon where the Salt Lake lay instead of at me.

"I love you no matter what, Kenneth. Nothing will change that." I wished Kurt had been there to say the same thing for his part, but the problem was, I wasn't sure that it was true. Did Kurt love Kenneth the same, now that he had left the church? Did he love Samuel the same? I thought he was trying to, but I wasn't sure that was enough.

Kenneth started twirling the shovel, the sun catching it again and again in a kind of visual song. "I remember all through my teenage years, hearing people talk about how it broke parents' hearts when their children chose the wrong path, and how the parents would speak in testimony meeting about praying for their children to come back. I didn't want to be the one you and Dad talked about like that. I didn't want everyone to pity you because of me." Finally, he let the shovel rest on the ground, motionless.

"I won't talk about you like that, Kenneth." But again, I couldn't promise for Kurt.

"The problem with leaving the Mormon church is that it's almost impossible to do without leaving your family at the same time. You have no idea how many stories I've heard from Mormons Anonymous like that. People who just leave both at once, and how disorienting and lonely it is for them for a long time. But it's not any easier for those who try to hold onto their families and then live with the well-meaning emails and 'gifts' for every occasion, all designed to bring the lost sheep home."

"Are you a lost sheep?" I asked Kenneth, forcing him to look me in the eye now.

"Well, yesterday I would have said definitely not. Today, who knows?" he laughed a little hollowly. "But listen, Mom." He looked me straight in the eyes.

Who would have thought there would come a day when it was one of my sons who asked me to listen instead of the other way around? "I'm listening," I said, my heart swollen with feeling for this son of mine.

"I always suspected that if I left, you'd go on loving me without blinking an eye. But I also knew that Dad might not be able to do that, and that the two of you would probably have fights because of me."

I let out a long sigh. "Kenneth, it may look like it's because of you, but what happened between your father and me was about deeper problems. Maybe ones we've been ignoring for most of our marriage." Had I only thought I was really happy with him all those years? Had I just been happy with mothering and with my sons? Or was I exaggerating our problems in the present, because I couldn't see how we'd resolve them in the future?

"Now that I'm out, I feel like I can be my real self. It feels like I can take full breaths for the first time in forever," Kenneth said, and he sounded emotional about it.

"I can breathe," I said defensively.

He laughed. "Yes, Mom. But I'm not like you. I couldn't breathe in there."

I guess I knew what he meant. "I'm glad you've found what you need."

"You want me to do something? Call Dad and apologize?" Kenneth offered.

"Apologize for what? For being true to yourself? No, Kenneth."

After another few minutes, we got down the steepest part of the hill, where the sound of the stream was faint, overcome by the buzzing of insects. I stepped into the cleared section and felt the punishing heat of the July sun in the Utah desert. There were no shade trees overhead, and the overgrown grass only seemed to amplify the heat.

It was more of a cemetery than I had anticipated. There were several large gravestones and a stone angel that looked more frightening than comforting. The angel was wingless, as was traditional in Mormon theology, but it was holding a sword and looked rather martial.

I stood and read the dates on the three large stones:

ELIZABETH CARTER,
BORN DECEMBER 24, 1939, DIED JULY 27, 1981.

RICHARD CARTER,
BORN AUGUST 15, 1938, DIED JULY 27, 1981.

EDWARD CARTER,
BORN AUGUST 15, 1965, DIED JULY 27, 1981.

Ah. Stephen Carter's parents and brother, I assumed. All three dead on the same day, the anniversary of which was coming up soon. They must have all died in the house fire that Stephen Carter had talked about.

There was a fourth gravestone, flat on the ground, and no bigger than a piece of printer paper.

JANE CARTER,

BORN JUNE 4, 2014, DIED JUNE 4, 2014.

From the dates, it sounded like she was stillborn. Rebecca had said "babies," but there was only one stone. Were there others who had been buried without stones for some reason? Maybe if they were preterm?

"I wonder which of the wives was her mother," I said. I could ask that woman in private about what had happened.

"That's the problem with the way we name children," Kenneth said. "Always with the father's last name, like only his legacy counts."

I'd never heard him say anything so feminist before. Was this Naomi's influence? I wanted to cheer. "Are you trying to tell me something?" I asked.

He shrugged and I saw sweat trickling down his face already, before we'd even started digging. "Naomi and I are going to hyphenate our names. It's the only sensible thing to do."

"Carter-Wallheim," I said, trying the sound together.

"Wallheim-Carter," Kenneth corrected me. "After all, there's no reason that the man's name should always go last. That's just a sexist tradition."

I wondered how Kurt would feel about this. But we had four other sons who would keep our name.

"Do you mind, Mom?" Kenneth asked.

It took me a moment to understand what he meant. He had his fingers on the top two buttons of his shirt.

"Go ahead," I said.

After only a few minutes, sweat was running down his back and chest and I thought fleetingly of how much he looked like his father, at least Kurt from twenty years ago.

Couldn't we just go back to then? It had been so much easier to believe, to love. Kurt had been younger and less saggy. I'd loved to look at his body whenever I had the chance. He'd sometimes tease me by flexing a muscle in his chest just to prove how good his control was over every little part.

It wasn't that I thought Kurt was less handsome now. We'd both grown older and frankly, I found him just as physically attractive as ever. But it was different. It wasn't his body alone that turned me on. It was who he was to me, our whole history together, all those little moments when he had been there for me. It was the wisdom that his graying hair and his sagging chest represented. They were scars of time, proof of him letting go of impatience and selfishness and so many traits that the years had smoothed away.

I should call Kurt, I thought sadly. I wanted to talk to him more than anything in the world. I wanted to ask his perspective on the possible motives of each of the wives. But if I called him, he'd lecture me on how we should have called the police. He'd tell me how wrong I had been. He'd play the part of the bishop instead of the husband. He'd use his authority to correct me. I couldn't bear that again.

"I need to go," I said aloud. Not home, though. I needed to get to work on figuring this out so that I could go home after that, and prove I'd been right.

"All right. Good luck, Mom. Or good hunting, whatever they say to detectives in books." He waved at me, and then went back to digging.

Did they say something to detectives in books? Maybe—run away? Save yourselves! If they were smart, they'd say that, anyway.

CHAPTER 17

It occurred to me once I walked away from Kenneth that it would be useful for me to check on the fence perimeter, to see if it was as difficult to penetrate as it seemed. So I turned south of the graveyard and began to do a quick search by sight. There were a couple of spots where I couldn't get to the fence, but I could see it was intact.

And then I saw a small house in the distance, which must have been the neighbors, the Perezes. I didn't immediately see a break in the fence. It wasn't until I got close enough to touch it that I saw that a section had been cut, then replaced. There were flakes of rust on the cut pieces that showed the edges.

Someone had to have made this gate between the Perezes and this property. Did Stephen know about it? Had he made it? And if so, why? I couldn't tell how old it was, but it might have been from when he was "dating" Joanna. The fact that he hadn't had it repaired since then could have meant nothing more than that had forgotten about it.

I trudged back up the hill, continuing to check the fence perimeter, but I found no other places where it had been breached. After that, dripping wet with sweat, I sat down on a boulder for a moment and tried to decide what to do next. Rebecca had called for the wives to meet at the house to tell them about Stephen's death and I'd wished I'd been part of that, though my presence might have made the kinds of reactions I was looking for impossible. Could I nose around in the other houses in the meantime?

In my head, I made a list of possibilities. Frankly, Jennifer's house seemed the most likely to hold secrets. If I could find her financial files, and if I could understand them, there might be a lot there.

And then I remembered Joanna's warning about Stephen in the middle of the night. She was such a strange character. What would I find if I went into her house while she was gone?

I stood up and made my way to the yard by the unfinished house. Before I got there, I saw Joanna herself, herding her children along the stretch of open field toward the main house.

I debated for a moment and decided that talking to her in person, alone, might be more valuable than anything I could find at her house without her. I jogged to catch up to her and touched her arm as they were cresting the hill to the big house's back door.

She turned, her eyes wide, startled. "What is it? I need to go to the house. Rebecca called me for some emergency," she said.

After all her talk about dark shadows, she seemed to have no inkling of why the meeting had been called.

The children in their long dresses were already running ahead toward the back door, which had been left open. For a moment, I wondered what it would be like to be a woman and raise children in a group like this. On the one hand, it would be such a relief to know that there was a babysitter always a moment away, to share the unending responsibilities and maybe find some respite of alone time.

And yet, it would also be difficult to know that your children saw other women as their mothers nearly as much as you, that they could go to someone else and be comforted when they cried.

Being a mother is sometimes a lonely job, but it is always satisfying. Seeing your children eat happily, seeing them sleep peacefully, knowing that they need you and love you desperately. Letting go of the difficulties also seemed to me to be letting go of the treasures.

The back door closed, leaving me and Joanna alone in the yard. "Rebecca is calling all the wives to tell them that Stephen is dead," I said bluntly.

"Oh, my poor Stephen," she said, shaking her head. "How will we go on without him?" She didn't seem distraught, merely concerned.

"You tried to warn him about danger," I said. Standing near her I noticed how small she was—no more than five foot two, and only barely a hundred pounds by my guess.

"Yes." She let out a long breath and began to chew at her fingernail.

"I saw you last night when you came to the house and tried to warn him again." I stared at her, trying to gauge every blink of the eyes. I wanted her to be innocent nearly as much as I wanted Rebecca to be. She was just a child.

"Then you know. I came to tell him about my second vision, nearly the same as the first. If only he had listened to me. He did not believe my gift was a true one. He thought that I was a frightened little girl who wanted to make herself more important." Her hands fluttered in a gesture that seemed very little-girlish.

"Did you go home directly after Sarah sent you home?" I asked.

"Of course." She met my eyes and held my gaze. "I would never leave my children alone in the house for long."

I believed that. Joanna was an odd combination of weakness and strength. She'd left the FLDS and made a new life for herself here. She'd fought to keep Grace, even though it would have been much easier to leave the FLDS if she'd left her daughter behind. She'd married into a difficult situation and she'd had two more children in close succession, and in my book, having children demanded strength of all kinds.

"What about Sarah? Do you think she might have killed Stephen? She seemed very angry with him when I saw her earlier in the day," I said, though she hadn't seemed particularly angry last night. Joanna had said something about seeing a darkness around Sarah, too, something about red and black, but I couldn't remember. What did it mean? That Sarah had blood on her hands?

Joanna considered it for a moment, her face caught in the sunlight and flattened by the lack of shadow in the midday sun. Then she shook her head firmly. "Sarah is always angry. But she has her paintings as an outlet. If Stephen shouts at her or Rebecca nags her, she just disappears into the shed." Joanna nodded to the shed we'd passed on the way up, which I needed to put on my list of snooping spots.

"Then which of the wives do you think is the most likely to have killed Stephen?" I asked, because there was something about Joanna's childishness that brought out blunt honesty in me, as if nothing I said could offend her. I wasn't sure why.

"Jennifer." She offered a ready answer.

"Why Jennifer?" I said, surprised.

"Because she hated him the most. I think she's always hated him."

"But why would she marry him if she hated him?" I asked. I wasn't sure that Joanna really understood all the relationship dynamics here. She was the newest wife, and very young.

Jennifer seemed coldest to me, the least likely to stab someone with a kitchen knife.

"I don't know why, but it's the truth. And she has a murderer's heart." She shivered dramatically.

"Well, I'll think about it." Joanna's testimony wasn't exactly the final clue to present to the police, was it?

"Are you going to find out who killed Stephen?" she asked.

"I'm going to try," I said. "To make sure the rest of you are all safe."

Joanna's eyes shifted for a moment and then I had a weird feeling that made the hair on my arms rise up. I'm not sure I would call it a spiritual feeling because that was usually calm and peaceful to me, filled with love, and this seemed more alien and even eerie.

"Some say the world will end in fire, some say in ice," she said in a low, deadened voice.

"Joanna?" I said.

She didn't respond until I snapped fingers in front of her face. Then she pulled away, blinked several times. "I'm sorry," she said. "What did you say?"

"You quoted that Robert Frost poem. About the world ending in fire or ice. What did you mean?"

She shook her head. "I don't know. I don't remember saying that. Who is Robert Frost?"

With the lack of education among the FLDS, I found I could actually believe she didn't know who Robert Frost was, so I let her go. As strange and unpredictable as she was, she had the least reason to want Stephen dead. She was fragile, young, adoring of Stephen, without worldly skills that would let her survive elsewhere, completely dependent on him financially, though perhaps not as emotionally dependent as Carolyn. But what she'd said about Jennifer was interesting.

Before I went back down to the cemetery, I checked the door to Sarah's painting shed, but it was locked and I couldn't see in very well with the light at this angle. I sighed. I'd just have to make an excuse to see inside later. I also needed a chance to talk to Sarah about last night and about who she thought was the most likely to have wanted Stephen dead.

I stumbled my way down the trail again to check on Kenneth, who was sitting on the side of a knee-deep hole long enough to fit a full-grown man lying outstretched.

"You okay?" I asked.

"I'm fine." He held up his hands, which were blistered despite the gardening gloves he'd been wearing. "Just taking a break. Are you finished with your detecting?"

"Not by a long shot," I said, but I needed time to think for a bit. Did I really think Jennifer was a more likely suspect than Sarah? And what was it about Joanna that made me believe her gift was real?

Since he looked to be so close to done, I stayed with Kenneth as he went back to work and finished digging about forty minutes later. I reached down and helped him out of the hole, only narrowly avoiding being pulled back in myself. Maybe it wasn't exactly six feet deep, but it was pretty close.

"Now what?" he asked.

"Now we go back and wait until they're ready for the body to be buried," I said.

Kenneth wiped at his forehead and then stared at me. "You, wait? I don't think I've ever seen you do that."

I made a face at him. I could wait. If I had to. And in this case, it wasn't going to be just waiting. There'd be plenty of poking around mixed in there, too.

CHAPTER 18

Kenneth used his shirt to dry off the sweat, then pulled it back on as we walked back to the house.

Rebecca and the other wives, including Joanna, were in the front room now, talking to the gathered and silent children, none of whom seemed to have been crying or in shock over their father's sudden death.

After what Joanna had said, I took a chance to observe Jennifer, who looked cool and collected. "Stephen's will made provisions for the families," she was saying to Rebecca, who had just asked her a question I hadn't caught. "You'll all be staying in the homes here. There's no worry about that."

So she had seen Stephen's will, apparently, and knew what was in it. Did it benefit Jennifer herself? Could that be a motive for murder? I needed to see the will somehow. I wondered how I could manage that.

I stayed as the children, including Talitha, were dismissed and led outside by the two oldest girls, Leah and Esther. Once the house was quiet again, the wives, along with Naomi, drew closer to discuss adult concerns.

Jennifer glanced at me, as if about to ask me to leave, when Rebecca said pre-emptively, "I'd like her to stay."

"Why? She has nothing to do with any of this," said Jennifer.

"I think it's wise for us to have someone here who can see things from another perspective. She may see things that none of the rest of us would think of."

I wasn't sure if this was Rebecca trying to help me learn the truth or if she was starting to be nervous about the fact that I knew about Stephen's murder and could call the police. I might get myself in trouble, too, but she would be much worse off than I would. They all would.

Kenneth returned from cleaning himself up and stood at Naomi's side. Jennifer hesitated, looking from me to him. After a moment, she started going through a step-by-step plan for the financial future, including tax payments for the property and houses, children's college funds, medical insurance payments and emergency funds, car and house repairs, and on and on. The assumption seemed to be that everyone would stay here, which was surely what Stephen would have wanted.

Sarah looked as angry as ever, holding herself apart from the others by the stairs to the upper floors. Would she stay on? If so, Rebecca was in for years more of accusations and recriminations from her younger sister. I couldn't envy her that.

Joanna, on the other hand, seemed at peace. She listened politely and without asking questions.

Carolyn looked a wreck. Her face was tear streaked, splotched with red, and her lower lip had been chewed to bleeding. She was seated on the couch with a hand on her pregnant belly, wincing every time the baby kicked, which was clearly visible under the thin knit shirt she wore. Her hair hadn't been done this morning, neither washed nor combed, and it stuck out on one side of her head.

Jennifer asked if there were any immediate financial needs

she was unaware of. When no one raised a hand, she suggested that they speak to Rebecca if they wanted more than their usual allowances deposited in their accounts each month.

I listened for a while, but eventually remembered Stephen mentioning that basement office. There seemed less to be learned from watching the wives here than I'd originally thought, and this was an ideal chance for me to look into his private files, while the wives were busy.

So I stood up and headed downstairs quietly, closing the door to the basement behind me. I paused for a moment, just in case someone noticed me, but no one seemed to. I suppose they were all too focused on one another.

I descended into a great room filled with huge beanbags and scattered with pillows and blankets. Probably the result of my taking the bunk room last night, I thought without too much guilt, since it looked from the general disarray like the boys had had a good time down here. I continued on past a bathroom, a couple of unfinished bedrooms, a furnace room, and at the other end of the hall, a locked door.

After a short search, I found a key on top of the door jamb and let myself in. The office had a utilitarian folding table in the center, as well as a rolling, well-worn fake leather chair next to it. Along the wall, there were four metal filing cabinets in various colors, most of them dented badly with overuse. The table itself was covered in papers stacked to either side, with pens and pencils in the middle.

On the bookshelf under the small high window, I found copies of Fawn Brodie's *No Man Knows My History* and Jon Krakauer's *Under the Banner of Heaven*. They both looked well-read, and when I flipped through I found what had to be Stephen's writing in the margins. Mostly his comments were refutations, but it was interesting he had read the controversial anti-Mormon books.

I opened the drawers of the first filing cabinet and found mostly family photos from the years when Stephen and Rebecca were still monogamous, photos of the new family when Naomi was a baby and a toddler, then portraits adding another baby, and then another—Joseph and Aaron, I guessed.

At the bottom of the cabinet, under some old newspapers, I found a half-empty bottle of whiskey and an open pack of cigarettes. Both were against the Word of Wisdom, the Mormon health code. Once you're excommunicated, I suppose there's less reason to follow the Word of Wisdom so strictly since you can't go to the temple anyway. But I'd have thought Stephen was the kind of person who followed every law to a T in any case, just because he wanted to prove he was better than anyone else.

Then again, the Word of Wisdom had been considered just that—advice, not a law, until the 1900s. Maybe Stephen was just going back to the old days of Mormonism, when you could smoke and drink all week, go to the temple for your endowments on Saturday, and then be at church on Sunday, repenting of your wrongs.

I left the cigarettes and whiskey where they were, then moved onto the next cabinet. I went to the bottom drawer first this time, and found several large manila envelopes with cardboard protectors. I opened them and saw a letter addressed to Stephen Carter by a previous president of the Church of Jesus Christ of Latter-Day Saints. I read through it, then stared at the name and the signature for a long time.

The letter hadn't been printed. It was on official letterhead, but handwritten. If the police wanted to, they could probably get a handwriting analyst to say if it was authentic or not. Not that it seemed to have anything to do with the murder. This president was dead now, so maybe it shouldn't matter to me, but it did. I did not want to believe the letter was real.

It began with a personal note of thanks to Stephen for continuing to live "the celestial law of marriage," "the true Principle of heaven," despite the "arrows of the adversary" that were slung against him, and "the fear of the law." I was shocked and nauseated at this. Could this prophet, whom I'd admired as a child, really have approved of Stephen's way of life?

What a scandal, if this was released to the press! Of course, the church would disavow the letter. And they might be right to do so. I let go of my anger as I acknowledged I had no reason to trust Stephen Carter; this was just the sort of thing he might have invented to convince his wives—or people like me and Kurt—that he was doing what was righteous.

I looked in the other envelope and found a priesthood line of authority, which for Mormon men is kind of like a divine right of kings. Since we believe that John the Baptist and the apostle Peter came down from heaven—literally as resurrected beings—to put their hands on the heads of Joseph Smith and Oliver Cowdery and restore the proper priesthood power that had been lost to all other Christian churches, a priesthood line of authority was an important document for many Mormon men. Kurt had a priesthood line of authority in his office at the church building, going back to his father, and his grandfather, and from there, to Heber J. Grant, who eventually went back to Joseph Smith, the apostle Peter, and then Jesus Christ.

But for Stephen Carter's line of authority, only two names were listed: Stephen Carter's and Jesus Christ's. Somehow, it was actually a relief to me to see this ridiculously self-aggrandizing document in the same file as that letter. This must be the reason he believed he had authority above the leaders of the church. But who would believe it was real? How hard could it be to fake a priesthood line of authority? You could probably fill in a template online and print them off in the thousands if you wanted.

I looked in the upper drawers of the same cabinet and found a marriage certificate—an official, legal one to Rebecca. Since there were no others, it seemed Stephen hadn't bothered with extralegal ones for the other "spiritual" wives, despite the ceremony he'd said he'd had Rebecca officiate. I wondered why, briefly, until I found a copy of a will that had been signed and dated on January 2, 2016. Just a few months ago, but maybe it was something that Stephen did regularly.

As I read the will, I wished desperately that Kurt were there to decipher it for me, or someone else who knew legalese better than I did. But as far as I could tell, it left the compound, the main house, and all the other houses, to Rebecca alone. It also left all his investment accounts, his retirement benefits, and any money in his current savings or checking accounts to Rebecca, with some language about sharing fairly with all other remaining dependents, presumably meaning wives as well as children.

In one sense, this will seemed only fair to Rebecca. She was the one who had borne so much with him. She was his legal wife, and if Stephen had tried to leave something to any of his other wives, the will could have been challenged in court for all I knew. Stephen must have thought he could rely on Rebecca to be fair when it came to keeping the wives in their houses and helping with funds to raise the children.

Actually, now that I thought about it, this was the obvious choice. If Stephen had bequeathed money or houses to each wife separately, they would have had the freedom to sell and move away. This way, Stephen maintained control of the whole family through Rebecca, beyond the grave.

In the back of my mind, I admitted that this also gave Rebecca a strong financial motive to kill Stephen. If the police were here, this document surely would have clinched their case against her. I put it back where I'd found it.

I looked through the remaining drawers in the final cabinet, and found a file with Naomi's name on it. I pulled it out, aware that I might well be invading the privacy of my future daughter-in-law, but I felt the circumstances demanded the breach. I had expected to find childish pictures she'd drawn or letters she'd written to her father. I wasn't prepared to see a careful accounting of the money she'd been receiving from him since her second year of college. Nearly a hundred thousand dollars in total, and the last payment had been made only last month. I saw a list of hours spent at home during the weekends which seemed to offset her debt in a small amount. Was that really why Naomi kept coming home? She'd have to keep doing it until her nineties at this rate to pay Stephen back.

From the way she spoke of her father, I'd assumed that Naomi had severed ties, especially financial ones. I hadn't thought much about where she got the money for med school. Loans or scholarships, I'd assumed. But no. Despite the fact that she had resigned from the Mormon church and that she had told me that she had also rejected her father's lifestyle, she was still taking money from him. Did Kenneth know about this? Was it my place to tell him? I didn't know.

The one worry of mine it eased was that Naomi might have had something to do with her father's death. This file seemed to make it clear that she had no motive. Financially, she would be much worse off without Stephen around.

After that, I looked through some more files and found one labeled INVESTMENTS. I took it out and tried to make sense of it. It looked to me like there was something like two million dollars scattered through various stocks, including tobacco companies, companies known for selling alcohol and spirits, several large media corporations that were known for pornography, and a number of oil companies.

On one level, it bothered me that any Mormon would invest in such things, but it seemed just another layer of Stephen's hypocrisy. And they had certainly brought Stephen significant returns over the years. His return was more than ten times his investment. Was that Jennifer's work? Did it mean she had the least reason of any of them to want Stephen dead? All those investments would be under Rebecca's purview now. She might be able to talk Rebecca into letting her have the same control as before, or she might not.

I poked around on the desk and in one of the envelopes on the top, I found a letter to a lawyer that was dated Sunday, the day before we'd come over. It was a request for a change of will, "as they had discussed," and it was signed. But I had no idea what the requested change had been and I felt a burning frustration over that. All my snooping, and it had only led to more questions than ever.

Had Rebecca been about to be disinherited in favor of one of the other wives? If so, why? Or perhaps Stephen had simply decided to leave the other wives their own houses. But that didn't seem to jibe with what I had known of him. He would have wanted to manipulate them somehow. But then who would get control? Perhaps Jennifer, since she was the one who knew the most about money.

I remembered then the hushed conversation Stephen and

Jennifer had had when he took me and Kurt over to meet her at her house. The argument with Joanna she'd mentioned. It had happened the same day as this letter was dated, but it wasn't necessarily related. I definitely needed to talk to Jennifer alone.

As I went back upstairs, I realized the afternoon was wearing away. I thought about texting Kurt, at least, to tell him I wouldn't be home tonight. Was he expecting me? Would he be worried about me if I didn't show up? Would he come back here to help me? I wished he would, but I couldn't find it in myself to beg him for anything. My pride wouldn't permit me to accept blame for everything just to make peace.

CHAPTER 19

The other wives were gone by the time I went back upstairs to the living room, but Rebecca was still on the couch, alone. I sat down beside her. She seemed older and sadder than she had been before, though not as helpless and lost as when she'd first found Stephen's body.

After a long period of silence, I said, "I saw the will. You inherit everything." I watched for her reaction.

She didn't flinch. "I didn't kill him," she said, staring at her hands.

"Why was Stephen planning to change his will? I saw his letter to his lawyer, never sent, down in his office. From Sunday night."

Rebecca stiffened. "What letter?"

Did she really not know about it? "All it says is to go ahead with the changes, as they'd discussed. But it doesn't say what they are. You didn't talk to Stephen about it?"

She seemed stunned. "No. He never told me. Years ago, he promised me that I would get everything in the will, that he would never change that. I was supposed to help the other wives stay here, so the children could grow up together. Not that we ever thought something like this would happen."

I wanted to believe her. "It can't be a coincidence that he was murdered just before changing his will."

"Probably not," said Rebecca. "But he didn't talk to me about it." She stared at me for a long moment. "Naomi told me that you've investigated murders before, that you've solved crimes the police couldn't."

I put up my hands. "I don't know if I'd go that far," I said.

"I want you to help us here. We need to know the truth about what happened. The police would ruin everything, but if I know who it is, I can act swiftly to provide closure."

I wasn't sure what she meant by that. She'd throw the killer and her children out of the compound? Or let her stay and black-mail her into good behavior?

This was a dangerous suggestion, and I knew it. But I went along with it anyway because this was a mother talking, who didn't think about anything but her children's well-being. As a mother, I understood Rebecca. I thought she was right, and we would understand the nuances better than anyone outside the compound could.

But I had to make one caveat. "Rebecca, you should know that if I find out it was you, I have to call the police." Even if that meant I had to face legal consequences myself.

She looked at me squarely, as if she'd prepared for this moment. Her face was blank, no love nor hate in it, just earnest-ness. "I didn't kill my husband. I loved him dearly."

I believed her. "Then I will do my best to find out who did it."

She gave me a tremulous half-smile, and reached to hold my hand between both of hers. "Thank you. I will never forget this. I know that you had misgivings when you came here. I know that Kenneth must have warned you about us."

"Kenneth loves Naomi," I said diplomatically.

"Yes," she said. "I know he does. And I know you love him. A mother's love for her child never ends, no matter what difficulty it leads to."

On that rather mysterious note, we were interrupted by a knock at the door.

Rebecca stood and walked across the room to open it. I followed her and she introduced me to Dr. Allyson Benallie, who had a wide, flat face, long gray hair pulled back into a bun, and light brown skin. It took me a moment to realize that she was Native American. The name Benallie was vaguely familiar—Navajo? The Mormon church had done some extensive school-year fostering with Navajo children to white families in Utah during the 1970s, though it had stopped now. Dr. Benallie was the right age to have been part of the Indian Placement Program.

"So, the man has died," was the first thing Dr. Benallie said.

"Good to see you, Allyson," Rebecca said coolly. Her tone made me wonder what in the world their relationship was like.

"And you, Rebecca," said Dr. Benallie, as Rebecca directed us up the stairs to Stephen's body.

On the third floor, Rebecca led us down the hallway to the locked bedroom and opened the door. She glanced around, probably to make sure there were no children nearby, then quickly ushered the two of us inside and closed the door behind her.

The rank smell of death was stronger now, and the body looked grayer, though it still seemed quite large. Dr. Benallie leaned over the body and without any squeamishness, simply pulled out the knife that had been stuck in his chest. The sucking sound as she did so was something I would prefer never to hear again. A little more blood leaked out of the chest wound, but not much.

I felt again the sense of loss and the confusion of emotions. Was I genuinely grieved he was dead, or was there a little relief in there? Was that why I was helping Rebecca move forward with this strange plan of trying to cover up the murder, because I was glad Stephen Carter was gone?

Dr. Benallie handed the knife to Rebecca. "Best clean that and return it to where it belongs. I assume it's yours."

Rebecca stared at the bloodied knife and nodded after a moment.

"Will you ever be able to use it again?" asked Dr. Benallie, which seemed a strange question to me while standing over a corpse.

"It would be a waste not to," Rebecca said, which was perhaps just as strange. She moved into the bathroom and I could hear the water in the sink turn on.

I thought of all the evidence she was destroying. But at this point it seemed likely the police would never know.

"Who are you?" asked Dr. Benallie abruptly, staring at me. She had closed Stephen's eyes and stood up. "You said your name was Linda? You're too old to be one of his new wives."

"No, my husband is . . ." I trailed off because it was too complicated. I stuck with, "Stephen's daughter Naomi is engaged to my son Kenneth."

"Ah, family, then," said Dr. Benallie, and that seemed the end of her interest in the conversation.

Rebecca came back with the clean knife. "It's nicked," she commented, "but I'll sharpen it with a stone and it will be nearly good as new."

Dr. Benallie wasted no time in issuing a matter-of-fact list of next steps Rebecca needed to undertake to cover up this crime. It made me wonder if she had done all this before, she was so specific and insistent.

"Roll the body up in the rug to carry it out. Then burn the rug once the body is buried, and clean in here with bleach and replace it with another area rug, so you don't have any curious carpet delivery people asking questions about why you're only replacing one room's carpet. What about the grave?"

"It's been prepared," I said, not mentioning Kenneth specifically. "I think it's deep enough."

Dr. Benallie tilted her head to the side, considering my admission to participating in the cover-up. "I always wondered how Stephen would end up. I can't say I'm surprised about this." She turned to Rebecca. "Though I'm sorry for you, Rebecca, if you're grieving."

"I am," she said. "Of course I am."

"If you say so," said Dr. Benallie. She stared at the body again.

The woman was practical to the point of coldness. While she and I agreed generally on our opinion of Stephen, I disliked her manner toward Rebecca. I also wondered why it was that she knew so well exactly what Rebecca should do to cover up the murder. Could she have been involved? It seemed from her appearance at the door that she had a key to the compound gate, unless I was missing something.

"You'll write up the death certificate, then?" I asked, probing her to see how far she would really go.

"Yes. I'll simply say he died of heart failure," Dr. Benallie said. "So long as no one has reason to question it, I'll keep my license and you can keep your secrets." She looked at Rebecca and something passed between them that I did not understand.

"Thank you." Rebecca was tearful again. "You'll never know how grateful I am for this."

At that point, I couldn't stop myself from blurting out, "Why are you doing this? What was Stephen to you besides a col-league?"

Dr. Benallie smiled wistfully. "Stephen and I were engaged to be married eleven or twelve years ago." She shifted and I caught a glimpse of a large turquoise necklace tucked in her blouse.

"But you never married?" I asked. Surely someone would have mentioned a sixth wife, even if she didn't live at the com-pound.

"No. We broke up rather acrimoniously, at least on my side," she said. "I realized that he would have told me anything to get me to marry him. He had a way of seeing what a woman most needed to hear to keep her coming back for more. He could see weaknesses and he manipulated them."

I glanced at Rebecca to see if she would contradict this, but she was impassively listening.

"He kept telling me that our marriage would be the fulfillment of the promises in The Book of Mormon to the descendants of the Lamanites. He said that he had had a dream and he saw Samuel the Lamanite speaking to him, telling him I was his granddaughter, and that he had permission to marry me from the prophet himself, if only he promised to treat me like a prin-cess. An Indian princess." She spat out the last words, her hatred clear.

"So you're doing this to get back at him?" I asked. She was willing to risk her medical license to get back at a man already dead?

"I owe Rebecca," said Dr. Benallie.

I glanced at Rebecca.

"It wasn't much," she said.

"It was enough," said Dr. Benallie. She looked at me and

admitted, "Stephen nearly separated me from the practice back then. It would have been the end of my career, and at a time in my life that I would have had to declare bankruptcy with all of my medical school debts."

I was a little surprised at this, but more that Dr. Benallie was grateful enough to Rebecca's intervention to help her now. After all, remaining with the practice meant that Dr. Benallie had had to continue to deal with Stephen every day of her life since the broken engagement. Had her financial solvency really been worth that?

"You have a key to the gate," I pointed out, easing into my next question. "You came in without having to wait for someone to open it."

It took a moment for her to parse what I was saying. Then she gave me a strange rictus grin, all her teeth showing. "You think I killed him?"

It would have been an easy answer, sparing the wives any more fuss. The scorned woman, no threat to anyone anymore, and we could all move on.

But Dr. Benallie shook her head. "I didn't do it. But I can't say I wouldn't shake the hand of whoever did. In this case, murder is only justice for an evil man."

She looked at Rebecca and I found it difficult to understand the relationship between one woman who had loved Stephen and the other, who had hated him. Rebecca didn't defend Stephen, at least not now.

"And now we're all free," Dr. Benallie said, walking out of the room.

"Some of us more than others," Rebecca said, with a hint of bitterness I had never heard from her before. She sounded so much like Sarah in that moment.

I followed the two women into the hallway. Rebecca carefully closed and locked the door behind us. In silence, the three of us went down the stairs. Dr. Benallie left without another word. In a few minutes, I heard her driving away on the gravel road.

CHAPTER 20

I had just begun to wonder where Kenneth and Naomi were when the back door slammed and Sarah came in, looking wild and flushed. She smelled of paint. "Did you do it?" she shouted at Rebecca.

At first I thought she was accusing Rebecca of murdering Stephen.

"Do what?" Rebecca asked.

"My paintings," Sarah rasped, then burst into tears.

"Something happened to your paintings? Sarah, I'm so sorry." Rebecca's whole body had changed, had become attuned to her sister's distress. There could be no doubt that Rebecca loved her younger sister, even if the feeling was not entirely returned.

Sarah bit her lower lip. "It must have happened in the night. They were fine yesterday, but just now I went in and saw they'd been torn to shreds. Stephen must have done it himself before he died. Bastard," she swore.

If Stephen had done it, was it punishment for some misdeed of Sarah's? Could the paintings have something to do with Stephen's death? Or was it a coincidence that the two events had happened on the same day?

"I don't think Stephen would have done that," said Rebecca. "He—"

"It's exactly what he would have done and you know it!" Sarah declared, shaking her fist. "He knew exactly how much my paintings meant to me and how to hurt me through them."

"How many were destroyed? Were they torn or—" I stopped myself from asking if they'd been cut with a knife.

I was trying to think of a timeline. Joanna had been here at the main house that night around midnight. She had seemed to go back to her own house, but she could have gone to the shed. And Joanna hadn't prophesied about a dark shadow over Stephen only. Joanna's prophecy about Sarah and black and red—was that supposed to be paint? Could Joanna have been the vandal? Sarah hadn't leaped to the conclusion, though, so I kept quiet.

"It doesn't matter anymore," Sarah spat. "The only thing that matters now is getting out of here. I'm taking the paintings that he didn't destroy with me. And Talitha, since I brought her here with me. She doesn't belong to him, either—she belongs to me."

Talitha, bright and sensitive girl that she was, with Sarah, the bitter, callous mother? I shuddered at the thought.

"Sarah, please," said Rebecca, looking at me.

Did she think I could help?

It only turned Sarah's attention to me. "Do you know that Stephen took each of the other children away from me, nearly from the moment of their birth? He gave them to Rebecca because he said I was unfit to be their mother. He said I was too emotional."

I'd been so curious about this lifestyle and now I began to wish that I didn't know any of this, that I'd never become involved at all. It was too horrible.

"It wasn't like that. He wanted me to help you, to watch over you," said Rebecca. She had one hand outstretched to her sister, but she had not moved close enough to touch her. She feared being rebuffed, clearly.

"He told me over and over again that I was a terrible mother. And maybe I was. Maybe I still am. So you can have them. All the others. I'm only taking Talitha," Sarah said furiously.

I wanted to say something, to do something, to end this terrible quarrel, but I couldn't help but think about the possibility of Sarah's guilt. She hadn't known about the paintings, but she could have killed Stephen for other reasons, couldn't she?

"I'm going to have my own life at last. And you can't stop me!" Sarah declared, then stormed off upstairs in the direction of Talitha's room.

Rebecca gave me a pleading look before she also disappeared upstairs, and I was left standing alone in the living room, my mind turning, unsure of any next step I should take.

Eventually I heard raised voices, including Naomi's. Kenneth came downstairs. "Mom, do you know what's going on? Talitha's distraught. Her mother says she is taking her away. Naomi is refusing to let her go. She told Sarah she would take Talitha over her dead body."

"There was an argument between Sarah and Rebecca," I summed up for Kenneth.

"But Sarah can't just make Talitha leave with her, can she? We have to stop her," Kenneth insisted.

If the police were here, what would they say? But the police weren't here. And Sarah was Talitha's mother, biologically at least.

I sighed. "Does Talitha want to go with her?" Maybe she would be better off away from here. Though with volatile Sarah—I doubted it. What other choices did she have?

Kenneth grimaced. "She's upstairs right now begging Naomi to let her stay here. She wants to be where her cat Lucy is buried."

I hoped that didn't mean that Sarah was going to disinter the cat's body to take with them. "Sarah is Talitha's mother. I'm not sure we can stop her," I said. All Sarah had to do was threaten to call the police and Rebecca might well be willing to sacrifice one child to save the rest of the family. I hated to think about it that way, but she was the one who had put herself in this situation, even if I had helped her move forward with it.

"Don't you think everyone should take some time to calm down and think this over?" Kenneth said.

That was a sensible suggestion. For a moment, I thought about offering to take Talitha home with me for a cooling-off period. Then she could have some space to make a decision about where she wanted to live without pressure from either side. And if only for a little while, I could be a mother again, which had always been my best skill. But Kurt and I had fought so terribly. It wasn't a good time to bring a child into that.

"I'm going to ask Naomi if she thinks we should take Talitha in, at least for a while," Kenneth said, his voice deep and gravelly. "What do you think?"

I was stunned, and then very proud of him. He'd had a few doubts about Naomi and her family just a few hours ago, but he had moved past them. Talitha would be much better off with her favorite sister.

"I think that is very noble of you, Kenneth," I said, struggling against tears.

He rolled his eyes. "Not noble, Mom. I love Naomi, and I love Talitha, too. Naomi has practically been Talitha's mother ever since she was born. Sarah doesn't have a maternal bone in her body."

No, I thought. Sarah wasn't a mother in spirit. She was still a child herself, whatever her age.

"Are you going to stay for the funeral?" asked Kenneth.

"I'm staying until I find out who murdered Stephen." For the mothers, and for me. As for Kurt, he would have to wait for me to come home and figure out things with him.

CHAPTER 21

Rebecca dispatched Lehi and Brigham to help Kenneth take the body to the grave. The two boys looked pale but determined. I didn't think Rebecca had told them anything about the murder, and the knife wound wasn't visible, since Rebecca had already wrapped Stephen in the rope braid rug and tied it with bungee cords herself. But still, this was their father who was dead, and they had to handle the body.

Kenneth looked at me and I nodded. This was it, the moment that we both decided we were in this for the long haul, that we were going to face whatever consequences there were for helping to cover up this murder.

Kenneth took a deep breath. "Boys, this is men's work and you should be proud to do it, no matter how hard it is," he said.

The two boys said nothing, just following Kenneth down the stairs, grunting with effort.

I didn't know if Rebecca had asked the older girls to keep the younger children occupied in the basement for this, but none of them was watching during the twenty minutes it took to maneuver the body outside. I watched until I couldn't see them out the back door anymore, then sat down on the couch in the living room and prayed that I hadn't just done the worst thing a mother could do to her son, leading him to sin—or possibly to jail.

When the three came back, Kenneth ushered Lehi and Brigham to the bathroom to wash up.

Then Rebecca rang the cowbell and the children streamed up from downstairs with the older girls. We all sat down in the dining room for a rather grim, cold dinner of ham sandwiches and deviled eggs.

"Tonight is your father's funeral," Rebecca said after the too-quiet dinner. "We're going to wait in the backyard until everyone is ready to go down together."

The children trooped silently out to the backyard with Rebecca and then waited there for the other wives and children to gather. When Jennifer, Joanna, and Carolyn had arrived, along with their children, we all began the descent together. I noticed that Sarah wasn't here, and that Naomi and Talitha weren't, either. Good, I thought. Naomi could make sure that Talitha didn't get taken away while Rebecca and the rest of the family were busy with the funeral.

In the dimming light, I watched as several of the younger girls, Judith and Martha and Madeleine and Hannah, held and released one another's hands, making snaking patterns with their arms. It looked like a game they had been playing for a long time together, and I was relieved to see them act like children, at least for a little while.

I noticed that Joanna's children remained at her side, the least integrated of them all even when we reached the gravestones around the open grave. Not far from her, I noticed a man who looked like he could have been Stephen's brother, and I gave a start.

A much younger brother, I chided myself when I looked more

carefully. He was standing next to another young man who looked very much like Stephen, although not as strikingly as the first. They must be the two oldest sons, Joseph and Aaron, who were at the U. Presumably Rebecca had informed them of the death of their father and they had arrived just in time for the funeral. Did they know anything about the proposed will change? Did either of them have any idea which of the wives might have wanted Stephen dead? That would have to wait until after the funeral.

Away from the city here in the mountains, the air smelled clean and fresh. We were high enough that the exhaust of cars and trains and the industrial plants to the north were below us.

As we stood looking out over the valley, I wondered for a moment what it had been like in 1847, when Brigham Young had famously said, "This is the place." The desert landscape then must have seemed extreme—sagebrush and tumbleweed, no buildings in sight. The canal system that kept the pioneers alive hadn't been cut into the land yet. Desert colors of red and gray and brown would have been all that met the eye.

I could imagine women weeping when they were assigned a piece of land to cultivate to keep their family alive. How long until they managed to harvest food from the ground? How many hours a day did they work in hopes that the next year would bring them more than this one had? And when they were asked to share their husbands in polygamous marriages, not to mention their food, their land, their hopes and dreams—how had they borne it?

As soon as everyone had collected around the grave, Carolyn led everyone in singing the famous Mormon hymn "Come, Come, Ye Saints."

Come, come ye saints, no toil nor labor fear;
But with joy wend your way.
Though hard to you this journey may appear,
Grace shall be as your day.
'Tis better far for us to strive
Our useless cares from us to drive;
Do this, and joy your hearts will swell—
All is well! All is well!

The hymn had been written on the plains, as the Mormon pioneers walked day after day, often twenty miles a day, through unsettled territory. They slept at night with the sounds of wolves in their ears, and the fear of Indians in their hearts. For protection, the wagons were circled—quite literally—and the people slept underneath the wide wooden slats to escape bad weather.

When the weather was good, fires were lit in the center of the circle, and the meager food cooked over them. Mostly, the pioneers ate fried cakes made of flour and water. When they were desperate, they tried to eat what plants they found on the trail, and those experiments often ended with vomiting or worse.

The penultimate verse of "Come, Come Ye Saints" was about dying on the plains and how it wouldn't be so bad, since God would reward His chosen people and they wouldn't have to suffer anymore. Grim stuff, but it was part of our history.

When I taught in the Primary, I was astonished at some of the horrible stories that were told in the children's manuals. Women who died in childbirth on the trail, whose husbands and other children left the body behind, then came back later to reclaim it only to find no trace of the bones. Small children who froze to death in the middle of the night and whose parents woke next to corpses. Older children set to walk last behind the rest of the train to gather oxen droppings to dry for fuel, who disappeared by day's end and were never found again. Taken by Indians? By wolves? Lost and calling out for help somewhere?

Mormons are extraordinarily proud of their heritage, and they tend to see persecution of any kind as proof of their righteousness. Maybe being excommunicated had made Stephen Carter feel himself even more justified in his lifestyle, as a descendant of these people who had been chased away from every place they had tried to settle.

As I scanned the group, I noticed two other people I had never met, an older, Hispanic-looking man and a beautiful, dark-haired and dark-eyed young woman whom I guessed to be in her late teens. These must be the Perezes. Had they come up through the break in the fence I'd noticed earlier, or the long way around on the road? I wondered if they knew that Stephen had been murdered and if either of them was likely to go to the police. I sincerely hoped not, now that Kenneth and I were too far involved in this to get out easily. But I would need to talk to them about Stephen, too.

After the song there was a long silence until Rebecca Carter came to stand in front of the mounded grave that Kenneth had filled in over the body. She took charge, silhouetted by the falling sun. Light glowed around her head and shoulders as though she'd been marked as an angel.

She thanked everyone for coming, but she did not eulogize her husband. She did not tell us the story of Stephen's early years or their marriage. She said simply that she honored Stephen, her husband, the father of her children, in death as she had honored him in life, with the best of herself. She held up her hands and asked God to take Stephen's soul to Himself. And then she moved aside, as if to encourage anyone else to speak.

None of the other wives stepped forward.

I noticed Carolyn was holding her belly and looking at the ground. I couldn't imagine being pregnant and attending my husband's funeral, knowing that I would have to face the labor and delivery on my own. I hoped the other wives would be there for her when she delivered in a few months.

Jennifer was dressed in a somber black gown that looked out of place at this ad-hoc and informal outdoor funeral. But she looked less like a grieving widow than like a friend of the family who had attended to be supportive. I could read no emotion on her face, except perhaps an occasional flicker of stifled boredom.

Joanna seemed more worn than tearful, her children clinging to her except for Grace, who stood like a soldier at attention in her overly adult clothing.

After a few minutes, one of Rebecca's older sons—Aaron, as he announced himself—stood up and said, through tears, that his father was the "best man I've ever known." He didn't seem able to get anything else out. His brother Joseph was standing by his side with his lips tightly clenched together, as if he didn't trust himself to say anything.

I couldn't help but think about what Kurt's funeral might be like, what I hoped was a long way off. Would our sons speak at it? What would Samuel and Kenneth say? What would I?

We stood around for a while in the silence, and then people decided to disperse, mothers herding the children home for bed. I had a choice to make, between the two sons and the Perezes. Which ones should I talk to first? Surely, in Mormonism, it was always family first.

CHAPTER 22

I hurried to overtake Joseph and Aaron, who were walking away together. "Excuse me, but I don't think we've met," I said, planting myself directly in the path to the house. I stuck out my hand. "Linda Wallheim. I'm to be Naomi's mother-in-law and your father had invited me over to visit the family when this tragedy occurred."

"You already know I'm Aaron," said the son who had spoken at the funeral. He was shorter and thinner than his father or his brother. "And this is Joseph," he said, nodding to his brother.

Now that I looked at Joseph up close, he no longer looked as much like his father. For one thing, I could see that his nose was different; it had been broken and not set properly. His face wasn't as sharp as Stephen's had been, either. And Aaron's was even more softly shaped.

They both shook my hand, though Joseph seemed slightly uncomfortable about it.

"I'm so sorry for your loss," I said, hoping they didn't notice how perfunctory my tone sounded. "My sincere sympathies. I know so much is going to fall to you now as oldest sons."

Joseph stared at me with suspicion.

"Of course we are sad that our father has gone from this life," said Aaron. "But none of us can ever know when God will choose to bring us home, and we who remain must be comforted by the knowledge that we will all be together in the glorious celestial kingdom."

"Glorious," murmured Joseph, and I had the first glimpse into his eyes as they met mine. He looked as bored as Jennifer had at the funeral, and as disconnected.

"I hope your mother and the other . . . children can depend on you for your support," I said blandly. It felt too awkward somehow to mention the other wives, as well.

I had addressed both of them, but Aaron replied as if I had spoken to him alone. "Well, I'll see what I can do," he said. "I'm very busy right now with summer courses. I'm sure you can guess how demanding the pre-med program is. And I assume that my father's insurance policy will take care of the family."

"You assume?" I said, because this was what I'd been meaning to ask from the beginning. "Your father never talked to you about the provisions in his will?" While I was thinking about this, I realized both of them must have their own keys to the gate, and although I'd originally thought of the wives as the only suspects, either of them could have snuck in and killed their father and snuck out again. It might even explain why Rebecca wanted to prevent a police investigation, if she suspected her beloved older sons of the murder.

"My father didn't consider either of us to be adults worth talking to about anything of importance," Joseph said loudly. So it wasn't grief that had kept his jaw clenched throughout the funeral. He must have spent the whole time trying to keep his anger in, and now it was exploding out of him.

"He loved us and made sure we had everything we needed," Aaron said, facing his brother. His hands were in fists; he was geared up for a confrontation. "You know that he was a fine father and a fine man."

"Well, that is certainly what he would have said of himself," Joseph said, with dark humor. "It's nice to know that you still agree with him about everything."

"He was a good father," Aaron repeated, turning to me. He was even more defensive sounding now. "He paid for our college tuition and room and board. He made our lives very easy, with no strings attached."

Joseph rolled his eyes. "No strings. You're right there. They were nets, not strings, big enough to pull whole planets in. We were never children, not to him. We were the manifestation of his future power in the world. He molded us and punished us and manipulated us so that we would be what he wanted us to be, and even now, I can't see a way to escape his plan for me."

He couldn't just drop out of school and do something else? I found I didn't like either of the sons, who seemed to see everything in the world only as it related to themselves. Though Joseph hated his father, he was like him in many ways, including his tendency to speechify normal conversation.

"So you didn't know about the will?" I asked, trying to get them back to my original point.

"I assume—didn't he leave everything to Mom?" said Aaron, turning back to me.

"There's some question about whether he changed his will recently." I was watching them both closely, but saw no flicker of guilt on either of their faces.

"Why would he do that?" said Aaron, who seemed genuinely confused now.

I didn't know. That was why I was asking. "Did he speak to either of you about it?" I looked at Joseph.

"He said something about changing our monthly allowances the last time I talked to him."

"When was that?" I asked.

"A couple of days ago," Joseph admitted, squinting in concentration, trying to remember. "But I thought it was just his usual threats that we had to get perfect grades and so on."

"What did he say?" I asked, since this sounded like it was on the same timeline as the will and the argument between Stephen and Joanna.

Joseph shrugged. "That there were changes coming. I figured he meant another wife and kids. Maybe he was changing his will to include her, whoever she was." He made an ugly face.

Another wife? I hadn't heard anything about that from anyone else, and I was inclined to dismiss it from Joseph, who so clearly had a chip on his shoulder about his father.

I took a deep breath and asked, "Did your mother tell you anything about your father's death?"

"A heart attack," Aaron said.

Ah, so she had lied to them, as well. I had assumed she had lied to the small children, but not to the grown ones.

"Did you know if there was a specific new woman your father was, uh, dating?" I asked, picking up on the thread of what Joseph had said.

"He said something about her being a neighbor. I thought maybe it was the girl who was here." He glanced around, but the Perezes appeared to have gone back to their house.

"Isn't she a little young for a man your father's age?" I asked.

"You don't know my father if you think that," Joseph said, shaking his head.

Aaron gave his brother a disgusted look. "He's talking about our neighbor Maria. She's only sixteen—the same as Esther."

Joseph shrugged, apparently unaffected by the idea of his father marrying someone the same age as one of his little sisters. "The younger the better for our father. They were easier for him to con."

"He wasn't conning them!" Aaron interjected. "They just had fewer set ideas about what marriage should be. He said they were more flexible."

"More flexible, yeah, I'll say." Joseph guffawed at this and even I blushed at the unintended innuendo.

"That's not what I meant." Aaron had reddened a little.

"Do you mind if I ask you where you were last night and this morning?" I asked.

Joseph looked at me long and hard. "I was at a party," he said finally. "Why?"

Did he know that his father hadn't died of a heart attack? I wouldn't be able to tell if he was lying to me. "What about this morning?"

"The party went all night," he said. Aaron shot him a reproving look. "Not that it's any of your business. Why do you want to know?"

"I was wondering if you'd had a chance to talk to your father before he died," I said carefully. "What about you, Aaron?"

"I didn't talk to him," Aaron said, and he seemed genuinely bereft. "I thought about coming home for dinner, too, but instead I just studied all night."

I didn't think he had killed his father, but I asked anyway, "What about this morning?"

"I didn't wake up until Naomi called with the news," he said. "And then it was too late."

I said goodnight and let them walk away. I wasn't certain they were telling the truth, but I wasn't going to get any closer without having to explain why I was asking. And besides, I had no way of confirming their alibis, anyway. Too bad I couldn't ask for witness phone numbers like the police could

I considered just going straight to bed. It was nearly nine, and I was exhausted from not sleeping well the night before and all the events of today. But the longer I put off talking to the Perezes, the longer it would be until I could go home. I hoped they had more to offer than the two older sons had, though. It felt like I was circling around the truth and then always finding myself back at the beginning with nothing to show for all my time and effort. Not to mention my frustration.

CHAPTER 23

I made my way slowly in the dark back to the fence perimeter, and had to take two tries at what I thought was the break before I found the right opening in the fence. I had to duck to get through it.

I could see a figure in the backyard, apparently digging in the flower beds that ran along the house. Evening gardening made sense; I knew the heat of the summer sun could be brutal. At first I assumed it was Mr. Perez, but as I got closer, I could see he was too tall and too young to be the man I'd seen at the funeral just an hour ago. Who was he?

"Hello?" I called out. When he turned to face me, I waved. "I'm from Stephen Carter's house." I hoped he didn't know all the wives by sight or he'd know I wasn't one of them, and then I'd have a long explanation to give.

"Hello," the man said.

I drew closer and in the light from the house I realized he was a white man with broad shoulders, though he wasn't particularly tall. I guessed he was in his early fifties, with a full head of graying hair tied back in a ponytail. He looked nothing like the old man and the teenage girl who had come to the funeral, and I was suddenly unsure of his identity.

"I'm here to talk to the Perezes, if I you don't think it's too late," I said.

"Go around to the front and knock on the door. They're both still awake," said the man. Then before I could ask his name, he took off his gloves and offered his hand. "John Edwards," he said. "I was assigned as Hector's home teacher.

"Linda Wallheim," I said in return. A home teacher—that meant the Perezes were Mormons.

"Nice to meet you, Linda," he said with a nod. "I help Hector out with the garden now and then, when I can fit it in with my other work schedule. Hector loves his garden so much and when he started to get older he really needed help to keep it up."

I was absurdly pleased that Mr. Perez was being looked out for by the local Mormon ward. A man of his age needed someone to check in on him. "That's very nice of you," I said. I surveyed the well-kept beds around me. There were roses of all colors here. I remembered then that Joanna had roses in her room. The Perezes must be close family friends indeed. Could what Joseph had said be true—that Stephen had been courting their teenage daughter?

"Do you mind if I ask you a question?"

"I suppose," he said, looking at the darkening sky.

"It's about Maria Perez." .

"Maria's a very good girl. A loyal granddaughter. A good student," he said.

I hadn't meant for him to feel obliged to defend her. How could I put this? "Have you noticed the break in the fence back there?" I asked, motioning north to the perimeter.

"Of course. Stephen made it so that Joanna could come back and forth and visit Maria. You didn't think Maria did it herself, did you?"

"No, no." That wasn't what I was getting at. "I was wondering whether Stephen ever visited."

"Oh, well, I know he's not officially a member of the ward anymore, but he's always been a good neighbor to the Perezes. He comes down sometimes and chats with me to make sure Hector is being looked after." He smiled gently and I had the feeling he really had gotten along with Stephen, despite the excommunication. He was talking about him in present tense, which I guessed meant he didn't know about the funeral. I didn't correct him. I was more concerned about Maria.

So I tried again. "Does Maria date?"

He tilted his head and looked at me oddly. "Not that I've noticed. Hector doesn't approve of his granddaughter going out at her age."

That sounded exactly like what a man of that generation would say. Poor Maria, if she wasn't allowed to date at all. "Did you ever think that Hector—Mr. Perez—had cause to be angry at Stephen? Did he ever say anything to you about him doing anything improper?"

John Edwards's eyebrows rose. "No, but he might not have. That would be a private thing, not to be shared with a family friend like me."

A private thing Hector Perez might feel obliged to deal with on his own? With a kitchen knife in the morning before anyone else appeared? With the break in the fence, he wouldn't have needed a key.

"How long have you known Hector Perez?"

"Oh, a few years," was the answer.

"And what do you think of him?"

"He's the most kind-hearted man I've ever met." John Edwards gave me an affectionate smile.

"Well, thank you," I said.

"Why don't I walk you around to the front?" he asked. "It's getting dark and there are some tricky spots in the lawn."

"Thank you so much," I said. He offered me his arm, and I could feel the strong muscles there. I thought for a moment about Kurt and how much I missed him.

When we got to the front of the house, he stopped. "Good night, Linda," he said.

"Good night," I echoed.

I wished I'd learned more from him, but at least I did know that Stephen had come to visit. I stepped up to the porch and took a few moments to orient myself.

I noticed that the Perez house was smaller than any of Stephen Carter's homes and looked like it had been built long before them, with old red brick and white trim that hadn't been updated in decades. The windows and the door were tiny and I suspected the house had been built in the 1800s by people who were much smaller than we were now.

I rang the bell and after a long minute, the porch light flicked on and the elderly Hispanic man I'd seen at the funeral answered the door. He was only about five foot five and had a thick, gray-flecked handlebar mustache. He sported cowboy boots and a cowboy shirt over Wrangler jeans, and I wondered if he thought they were actually comfortable to wear in this heat or if he was trying to fit in with some perceived cowboy dress code in Utah.

"Mr. Perez?" I asked. Even setting aside what John Edwards had said about Hector Perez being the kindest man he knew, the idea of this man killing Stephen now seemed ridiculous, considering his size and age. But he had been one of Stephen's last phone calls. Maybe he had something to tell me that would help.

"Yes. How can I help you?" he said with a noticeable accent.

His tanned skin was spotted with age, and his head was nearly entirely bald with a few white wisps around the ears.

I put out my hand and introduced myself again. "Linda Wallheim. I'm a friend of the Carters." I nodded up the hill. "I think we saw each other at the funeral just now."

He looked more carefully at me. "Ah, yes. I remember now." I wasn't sure that he really did remember. How old was he? Seventy? Eighty? He could be a hundred, for all the wrinkles on his face. "Very terrible, what happened, Stephen dying and leaving so many grieving behind," he said.

"Yes. Terrible," I said, then quickly added, "I'm sorry to disturb you, but Rebecca thought that you might have talked to Stephen the day he died. She was hoping that there might be some last message he had given to you." I was working wildly to come up with a reason for what were sure to be intrusive questions.

"Stephen spoke to Maria on Monday morning," Mr. Perez said. He turned around and called for Maria quite loudly. He took a step back into the house and gestured for me to enter. "Come in, come in."

I wasn't going to wait for a second invitation.

Inside, the house smelled heavily of perfume, and of a stale mustiness. The couches he led me to were covered twice, once in plastic, and a second time in crocheted blankets of red and orange and yellow flower patches. They looked very worn, but I could see the beauty in the pattern, the petals standing up as if to greet the morning sun.

In a few moments, the young woman I'd seen at the funeral came down the stairs. Up close, she looked even younger than she had before. Her skin was perfection, without a mole or freckle, without a line anywhere, and she had that willowy figure of youth. Her long dark hair was very straight, though it might have been flat-ironed that way. She wore heavy black eyeliner. She was possibly the last person I would have imagined might have been interested in a man of Stephen Carter's age or situation in life.

"Abuelo?" she said in a low voice.

"Mrs. Wallheim has come to ask you about Stephen. Rebecca sent her," said Mr. Perez.

Her mouth tightened into an "Oh," but there was no sound.

"I understand that Stephen was here on Monday," I said.

"He was in a hurry, yes, Maria? He said that he had visitors coming and he had to prepare for them," said Mr. Perez.

"I think so, yes," she agreed.

On Monday Kurt and I must have interrupted Stephen's visit here, which was why he had been late when we arrived.

"You must be very upset," I said to Maria.

"Yes, of course. I will miss him, as will Abuelo." Her English was perfectly Midwestern, with a few hints of Utah twang in it.

The way she turned to her grandfather again made it clear that she thought that he and Stephen were closer than she and Stephen were. Which made me wonder what Stephen had really been doing here.

"Did Joanna come with you?" Maria asked, looking behind me to the door.

"No," I said. "I'm sorry." Of course, she and Joanna would be closer in age and must be friendly.

"Oh, well, I miss her. Will you tell her I hope she will come soon? I have a video I want to show her on YouTube."

Considering her FLDS background and old-fashioned clothing, I was surprised that Joanna would be interested in anything on the Internet, but I nodded. "I'll tell her when I go back. Right now I'm wondering if Stephen said anything special to you on that last day, something I could pass along to Rebecca to remember him by." It was lame, but it was the best thing I could think of to get her to talk to me about Stephen.

"To me?" Maria said. "Why would he do that?"

"Stephen loved you, Maria," said Mr. Perez. "You know that he did."

"And I loved him, like an uncle, Abuelo." She sounded cautious now, as if she didn't want to offend her grandfather, but she also wasn't far from disgust.

"It would have grown into more than that, Maria. Stephen was waiting for you to be ready."

So Stephen had been grooming a teenager? Was that what he'd done with Joanna, too, planting the idea of marriage and then waiting until she was eighteen? At least now I had a reason Stephen might have wanted to change his will, if he was planning to take on Maria as a sixth wife. Then again, why would he change the will now to include her if he was going to wait two more years before they got married? This wasn't quite adding up.

Maria stared at her grandfather. "Stephen was nearly as old as you are. He was your friend, not mine. I'm only sixteen. I'm going to college. I'm going to have a job, a life. And when I get married, if I get married, it will be to someone my own age who I choose myself." She looked and saw me, and then flushed with embarrassment that I'd overheard her scolding her grandfather.

Mr. Perez tsked at her. "He was not nearly as old as I am, Maria. He was a young man, still vigorous. In his prime. And he had much to offer you." He turned to me. "These teenagers, they do not understand the real world, do they? They do not see the danger in it, and how they need protection."

I had no idea how to answer that. It was uncomfortable for him to be involving me in the conversation, but also useful that it was unfolding in front of me.

He turned back to Maria, whose jaw was tight. "Maria, he would have built you your own house. He would have provided handsomely for your children in time. My great-grandchildren."

"Children? With Stephen Carter?" said Maria, shuddering.

"You do not know what's good for you, Maria. I do. I have lived much longer than you have. I have watched my son and daughter-in-law both die, and they made me promise I would make sure that you had a better life than they did. Stephen was my way to honor my promise to them. I am not going to be here much longer, you know."

Maria seemed caught between shouting at her grandfather and comforting him. She chose comforting in the end, going to his side and wrapping an arm around him. "Don't say that. You'll be here for a long time yet. Long enough that you don't need to worry about marrying me off like that." She seemed to remember I was still in the room. "This must all seem crazy to you. I don't know what Stephen thought, but whatever it was, I didn't know anything about it."

"Of course not," I said sympathetically. Her grandfather hadn't killed Stephen, I decided. He'd approved of the relationship Stephen intended. And Maria wouldn't have killed Stephen, either, since she didn't seem to even know what was going on. It seemed like coming here had just steered me back at the wives for my list of suspects.

"Excuse me. I'm going to bed now. I'm very tired and it has been a difficult day," Maria said. She hurried upstairs after a long look at her grandfather, leaving me alone with him.

I tried to think of anything else I could ask. Was it possible

Mr. Perez knew anything useful about the murder? I couldn't ask him if he knew who'd killed Stephen without revealing that he'd been buried without a police investigation. "Mr. Perez? What did you think of Stephen Carter?" So vague it might yield nothing.

"I thought he was a great man. A true Mormon, with courage to live as God meant us to, from the beginning," said Mr. Perez warmly.

"Do you mind if I ask if you were born here? And if you're a member of the Mormon church?"

"Of course I am a member of the church. But I was born in Mexico, to parents sealed in the covenant. I came to the United States to be near the temples. But I did not know that so many had fallen away from the true Principle," said Mr. Perez.

What? He was a polygamist, too? I knew that many polygamous Mormons had fled to Mexico in 1890 to continue to live the Principle there long after it was illegal in Utah. How old was Hector Perez? Old enough to have been taught to believe in polygamy, apparently.

"Did you have more than one wife yourself?" I asked.

"I had two," he said, "though they both died before I came here. I had so few years with them. They taught me so much about being selfless. I came here to the United States when Maria was a baby, when she and I were all that was left." His hands moved to his chest as if to cradle a child in his arms. "Stephen and I had written many letters to each other and he had invited me many times to come here. This house was old and inexpensive. I improved it greatly, back in those days, when I had energy to do my own work."

I had not expected this long-term relationship with Stephen. He might know more about Stephen's life than anyone else.

"How long ago did you first come in contact with Stephen?" I asked.

"Oh, more than thirty years," Mr. Perez answered. "We wrote each other letters, we studied God and the Principle together. He wanted to know about how I had been raised in the Principle, and we told each other about our families and our plans."

I tried to cover my surprise. "Thirty years? So was that before he married Rebecca?"

"Yes, before that. He was so happy to find a willing woman. He knew she would see the truth of the Principle. I felt so much joy for him when I heard he was getting married. She's a good woman, Rebecca."

I was turning over what I had just learned—Stephen hadn't just come across polygamy ten years after he and Rebecca were married. He had known all along he planned to practice polygamy. He had just been waiting for the right time to tell his wife about it and convince her he was right—a time after they already had children and a life together. I wanted to run up and shout the truth at Rebecca, so that she knew what kind of a man Stephen was. But it wouldn't help her now.

"Were his parents polygamous?" I asked, though Mr. Perez might not know this.

"No. But Stephen told me about his childhood, how his parents died in a house fire, leaving him alone in the world, poor boy." Hector Perez put a hand to his heart.

"His parents and his brother," I said, because I'd heard the story before.

"Brother? No, Stephen was an only child. His mother could not have children for many years. And then, like Abraham and Sarah, his mother was blessed to conceive in her old age, and she had Stephen, a blessed child. It was one of the reasons that he believed so strongly in the Principle, because he knew that in order for his father to have posterity like the sands of the sea, he himself would have to have more than one wife."

What twisted version of Mormonism was this? And it was somehow combined with Stephen's past, from which he had for some reason erased his brother. Stephen had been excommunicated from his ward for polygamy, but it seemed that Hector Perez had not. Maybe John Edwards had never talked to Hector Perez enough to know about his past polygamy? Or had he thought he was too old to be disciplined for something he was no longer practicing?

I supposed I could understand John Edwards's covering up the truth for an old man to allow him to remain in the church he loved for the last few years of his life, but it made me wonder again about the bishop of this ward and the "wink-nod" attitude about polygamy that Naomi had mentioned. Maybe it was something Kurt would eventually need to bring up with higher authorities in the church—if I ever had a chance to tell my husband about all of this.

Disgusted, and with my mind's wheel spinning, I said a quick farewell to Mr. Perez and made my way back through the opening in the fence, up the hill, past the now empty graveyard, and toward the main house, tripping twice over rocks I couldn't see in the twilight.

CHAPTER 24

I had intended to head directly to the bunk room and sleep, but I saw the lights on in the shed and figured now was my chance to go in and see Sarah in her element. It occurred to me then that maybe it would be wise for me to see what exactly had happened there.

I knocked on the door of the shed lightly.

Sarah opened it a moment later, obviously surprised to see me. "Yes?" She only allowed me to see her face through the crack in the door.

"I was hoping to see some of your paintings," I said. "If you'd be willing to show me some of the remaining ones."

"It's a mess right now," she said, glancing behind her. But she stepped back, allowing me inside.

I took in the space itself. The one overhead light was rather harsh. The shed was divided into different sections. I saw there was a small refrigerator and a portable cook top, along with a cabinet that had a couple of dirty pans and dishes on top of it and a sink under the window. I could see a tiny door that was probably a bathroom. Sarah could really retreat here for days on end if she wanted to.

On the other side of the room, there were several large, blank canvases, as well as cans of paint neatly ordered on shelves. But there were also piles of ruined canvases heaped together, scraps floating in the flow of air from the space heater. Sarah was carefully keeping away from the pile of ruined things, as if touching them would hurt her all over again. I felt sympathy for her then, dealing with this invasion and cruelty, whoever it had come from.

"Did any of your work survive?" I asked Sarah, investing my voice with all my compassion. "I'd love to see something."

"All my favorites, the new things, are gone, but I'll see what I can find," Sarah said in a muted tone. She was so different here, vulnerable and hurt. Who had done this to her? Stephen, as she thought? Did that lead me back to her as the best suspect for the murder? Not if she hadn't found the destruction until today, as she said she had.

Sarah picked through some paintings and I felt sorrow on her behalf as more scraps of ruined canvases fell to the cement floor. They had been cut by a knife, I thought. Repeatedly, and with some viciousness.

"Were you an artist before you married Stephen?" I asked, genuinely curious.

Sarah's tone was distant as she picked through the stack of canvases. "I dabbled a bit. I never finished college."

"Oh? Why was that?" I asked.

She stiffened at my question and let go of the canvases. "I got pregnant when I was a sophomore and dropped out of school."

I had guessed as much—Talitha didn't look much like Stephen, whose genes were too obvious on all the other children's faces, and I'd wondered if an out-of-wedlock pregnancy had been part of how Sarah had ended up here on the Carter compound. "What about the father?" I asked nosily.

Sarah made a sound of disgust, apparently at her past,

youthful self. "Same old story. I fell in love with another student. I thought he loved me, too. But I was an idiot, didn't know anything about birth control because my Mormon parents hadn't bothered to tell me about it. And I got pregnant."

"You didn't consider an . . ." I trailed off, finding it hard to say the word "abortion" out loud after years of avoiding the word in Mormon settings. It wasn't against Mormon doctrine to use birth control, at least not anymore, but Mormons were certainly still encouraged to have large families and to start at a young age. As for abortion, the Mormon church allowed it only in cases of rape, incest, and risk to the mother's life. Even then, you had to get clearance from your bishop if you wanted to keep a temple recommend and avoid discipline.

"No. I don't know why. I fell in love with my baby before she was even born. I thought her father would feel the same way about her, which was idiotic of me, I know." She made a derisive sound. "The day after I told him, he disappeared. Talitha and I have never heard from him again."

She paused a moment and I wanted to say that I was sorry, but surely that would sound condescending to her so instead I said, "What about your parents?" Why hadn't they been a backup for her?

"My parents only wanted to offer me a place to stay if I repented of my sins and gave the baby up for adoption." She was staring at her hands. I knew the Mormon church encouraged adoption for unmarried mothers, but it shouldn't have been forced. I was suddenly so angry at those parents from so many years ago. What might Sarah's life have been like if they hadn't been so judgmental? "I was sure I'd never have my own life again after that," Sarah said. "So I . . ."

She paused, and I filled the silence. "So you married Stephen."

Sarah nodded and the worn defeat in her eyes startled me. It might have been the look of a woman twice her age. "Yes, I married Stephen. I was so naïve."

If her parents had been here, I would have given them a piece of my mind. No young woman should have to go through so much in such a short period of time—getting pregnant, getting dumped, losing her family and their financial support, having to abandon her education, feeling backed into a drastically different lifestyle and nearly new religion, all at once.

After a moment, she added, "I will give him this much, Stephen never shamed me about the pregnancy. He said that all children are welcomed by God. I think that was part of the attraction. My parents could barely look at me or my stomach. But Stephen thought it was beautiful."

Because it was proof she could bear him more children, proof she would stay bound to him, I thought furiously. He had taken advantage of a vulnerable young woman and shackled her to a life of isolation and servitude. If she had killed him, did she really deserve punishment?

"And you haven't seen your parents since then?" I asked, wondering if she was planning to take Talitha and live with them now.

She shook her head. "They cut Rebecca off when Stephen began practicing polygamy. It's been the same for me. The only grandchildren who've ever met them are the older ones, and that was years ago." She had a tight hold on one of the paintings and I was worried that she might rip it with her own grip.

Judge your children and if they don't come up to your standard, cut them off? That was what Jesus said, wasn't it?

"Were you never happy with Stephen?" I asked.

"Not for a moment," Sarah said, finding a ripped piece of

canvas on the floor and tearing it in a vicious gesture, then flinging it at the pile nearby. "It was better at first. Then Stephen acted like all his rules were just suggestions. But after Talitha was born, he became very rigid. Punitive."

"Did he hurt you?" I asked.

Sarah rubbed at a visibly twitching muscle in her neck. "Oh, he never harmed me physically. He didn't have to. He had a thousand other ways to make my life miserable. When he said the word, the other wives would refuse to speak to me, actually turn their backs on me. Car privileges would be suspended for months on end, and he would take away my key so that I couldn't get out of the compound at all. I'd be put on constant laundry and kitchen duty, never even allowed to go outside and breathe fresh air, my hands getting so dried that my skin would crack and bleed. He wouldn't even let me put any cream on them."

And this was the man whose home I had decided to stay in, while Kurt left in protest. I quailed at the idea that anyone might think that I approved of him.

"Sometimes, if I had done something truly heinous, like speak back to Stephen, they would send Talitha away to one of the other houses and I wouldn't see her for weeks at a time. My milk dried up when she was only a few weeks old because I kept speaking back to him. I just couldn't keep my damned mouth shut." She looked down at her chest, pressing gently against her left breast as if she remembered how it had felt bursting with milk that no child would drink.

My God, if even half of what she said was true, this was a true horror story. And I'd let Stephen Carter blather on to me about "the Principle." I'd thought of Sarah as cold and unpleasant, as bitter. I'd thought of Rebecca as the "good" sister. But how could she have allowed this?

"Did you ever try to leave?" I asked. I knew that abused women sometimes had been so messed up mentally they couldn't see a way out. And this young woman had been betrayed by everyone around her.

"Well, by the time my milk had dried up, I was pregnant again."

"So soon?" I asked. It wasn't impossible, but it was unusual.

She shrugged. "Then I was in an even worse situation than before. Stephen was on Talitha's birth certificate as the father and he told me he would seek custody of both children if I left, and that the state would give it to him because I had no means of support for them. And that I was crazy. He said that enough that I started to believe him." She spoke flatly, as if she had become separated from her own feelings.

"You're not crazy," I said then. Just angry, I thought. With good cause.

"My art was the one indulgence he allowed me. Maybe because he knew that without that, I'd have killed myself." Her mouth twisted with a weird half-smile. "He would tell me how lucky I was that he was willing to pay for the expensive canvases and the oil paints. He'd tell me how unlikely it was that I'd ever get a job that could pay for such a hobby, considering I didn't even have a college degree."

"Had he ruined your paintings before?" I asked.

Sarah hesitated. "No," she said, as if surprised at her own words. "He actually let me keep a lock on the door, though he must have had a key. I'd locked it last night before I went to bed, and it was locked when I came in again this morning, so whoever did this had a key. If it wasn't Stephen, it was someone who had a spare I didn't know existed until now."

"Did he like your paintings?" I asked.

"He said I was gifted, but that I needed more discipline." She laughed harshly. "I do need more discipline. I need more time, too. But I've done what I could and I am proud of myself. The only thing I'm truly proud of, I think. You don't give birth to paintings whether you want to or not. You have to try to grow them."

I felt such sympathy for her. I wanted to reach out and console her, but I didn't think she would welcome a comforting gesture.

"Anyway, I stayed here for eight years, and it was always just when I thought about leaving that I got pregnant again. It wasn't until three years ago I started refusing Stephen in bed. I used a knife the first time to make sure he got the message."

I wondered what kind of knife it had been. A kitchen knife, by any chance?

She made a sharp motion with one hand. "But it didn't matter. I was just as stuck as before. God, I hated him. I wished him dead a thousand times, but figured God didn't listen to a woman like me. I guess I was wrong again, wasn't I?" That odd half-smile, again, as she stared at me and waited for a response.

She had just told me she wanted Stephen dead. Did that count as a confession?

"I don't think Stephen's death was an answer to prayer," I said.

Sarah let out a brittle laugh. "No, I suppose not. God doesn't use kitchen knives, does He? Too lowly for His tastes. He'd create a hurricane to destroy the whole compound while He was at it, wouldn't He?"

Sarah hadn't really confessed to anything other than wishing Stephen was dead, which wasn't criminal. I thought about Maria and about Stephen's tendency to prey on young, vulnerable women.

"Did you hear anything about a change in Stephen's will?" I asked.

"What? Did he not leave everything to Rebecca?" Sarah asked. She smiled. "Well, I can't say I'm sorry for her."

So she didn't know anything about it. If she had, she'd have known the will hadn't been changed, and that Rebecca got everything, after all.

"I heard you and Joanna talking the night before Stephen was murdered," I said after a moment, trying to cover all the bases.

"So?" Sarah seemed to think back for a moment. "Joanna's stupid premonition came true that time, I guess."

"It didn't come true at other times?" I asked.

Sarah waved a hand dismissively. "Oh, she always claimed that it did. She'd twist whatever she said into being whatever happened in the end."

So she didn't believe the gift was real, but that wasn't a surprise.

"Did you go to bed right after Joanna left?" I asked.

Sarah shook her head. She wasn't stupid. She knew what I was getting at. "I didn't wait around the bedroom for five hours until I could sneak in and stab him, if that's what you're asking."

"Who do you think did it, then?"

"I don't know and I don't care," she said. And then, moving on to something that actually interested her, she took out two paintings and showed them to me. One was about the size of a chest of drawers; the other big enough to cover nearly the entire wall of a shed. Both were splattered with rich shades of color, thick enough with paint I could see waves of it.

I was so stunned that I couldn't say anything for a long moment. The paintings were far better than I had thought they would be. I'd expected something more pedestrian, but Sarah's use of color was astonishing. It stirred a wildfire of emotion in me that I hadn't known paint and canvas alone could evoke.

"These are both amazing. You are very talented."

I tried to remember the few art classes I'd had in college. These paintings were definitely abstracts, but I wasn't sure "modern" would be the right word to describe them. Maybe "primitive"? The larger painting had only shades of red, but the gradations were such that I felt like the paint was every shade of rage captured in one canvas.

The smaller painting, meanwhile, was full of blues and made me think of the sea. I felt touched with calm when I looked at it, and I thought for a moment I could hear the rhythm of waves hitting the shore.

I pointed to the blue one. "The ocean?" I asked quietly, not wanting to let go of the feeling it evoked in me. Kurt and I had gone to a beach in California for our honeymoon, and this reminded me vividly of the physical pleasure of those few days and the heady sense of being special and loved above anyone else in the world.

Sarah seemed to soften, which was the first time I'd seen anything like that in her. I thought for that moment how young she still was. She said, "Yes. I'm from California. My parents used to take me to the beach nearly every day. I miss it in ways I never thought I would."

The enveloping love I felt in that painting made me think better of her parents, at least a little. "Have you ever had a gallery show your paintings?" I asked. It seemed a crime that the rest of the world would never see these, or experience the feelings I had just felt on seeing them—both good and bad. Kurt would love these, and I was sad again for a moment that he wasn't here with me to enjoy them.

"No, of course not. Stephen said my work was private and besides, he didn't want to spend money arranging it." That bitterness in Sarah's voice again.

Stephen had made so much money in his investments that that shouldn't have been an issue. Did she know that, too?

Stephen had been a terrible husband to Sarah. But she was also now in dire financial straits, with no more skills to make a living than she'd had in high school and with a lot more responsibilities. That didn't mean she hadn't killed Stephen, but it meant I didn't believe she had planned it. But she was the wife with the strongest motive, and she certainly had the personality to kill someone in the heat of the moment. I felt I had to ask her again.

"Sarah, did you take that knife out of the kitchen? Did you use it to kill Stephen?"

Sarah put down her paintings then. Ignoring my question, she turned away and began to clean the bristles of some brushes that were soaking in a bucket. The smell of turpentine was strong.

"Sarah, did you kill Stephen with that kitchen knife?" I asked again, insistent.

She whirled at me. "Did I kill him? I wish to God I had," she said. She was on the verge of tears. "If I had, I might have some self-respect left. But no, I didn't do it." Her voice cracked.

And still I pressed, God forgive me. I gripped her hands and forced her to look me in the eye. "Are you sure? Would you remember it if you had? Would you admit it?" Could she have had some kind of mental break after she'd found her paintings ruined?

"Are you joking? If I'd killed Stephen, I'd trumpet it from the rooftops," she said. "I wouldn't care if I went to prison, either. Better that than here."

I let out a breath and found I believed her. Which meant I could let her go. Though it left me with more work to do, I was relieved that she wasn't the culprit, since she had been so much a victim. At least she might find peace once she was gone from here.

I asked her one more question before I left her alone. "Do you know who did kill him?"

She shook her head. "If it wasn't God Himself, giving us all justice at last, you mean?"

In my experience, God's justice was not so swift or clear as that.

CHAPTER 25

I left her in the shed, continuing to clean brushes, and walked back to the house. At last, I headed up to bed myself and wondered what I had accomplished today.

I'd found Stephen's will and a letter saying he'd planned to change it. I'd learned that Joanna thought Jennifer had the best motive for murder. I'd met Dr. Benallie, Stephen's business partner and former fiancée, who hated him, but claimed innocence of the murder. I'd talked to Joseph and Aaron, who told me about Stephen's interest in Maria Perez. From Hector Perez, I'd found out that Stephen had been planning to be polygamous long before he told Rebecca about it. And from Sarah, I'd found out that Stephen had been a controlling and manipulative husband whom I wished I had never met.

As I stared up at the bunk bed above me, I thought about my own husband, whose sins had shrunk in comparison to Stephen's. Was he still angry at me? He hadn't sent a text or tried to call me since he left. It was hard to believe it had only been about thirty hours since then. It felt like weeks had gone by in my life without him. This was my second night away from home and I had no idea what he must be thinking of me. I missed the physicality of his presence in the bed next to me, his smell, and the pattern of his breathing.

Just as I was drifting off, Rebecca cracked the bedroom door open and poked her head in, her expression cautious. "I'm so sorry to bother you when you're trying to sleep, but I'm wondering if I can talk to you for a moment? It's important."

"All right," I said, wishing she hadn't asked. I'd been so sympathetic to her at first, but that feeling had changed, especially after my conversation with Sarah. There were too many problems here for her to ignore them and still talk about the holiness of the Principle.

I sat up too quickly, knocking my head on the upper bunk pretty hard. I rubbed at it and tried not to let the tears of pain well up.

"Are you all right? Should I get you some ice?" Rebecca asked.

"Just give me a minute," I said, holding a finger up as I put my head to my knees. I counted to ten, like I told my boys to do when they were in pain. My head was still throbbing, but I didn't feel quite the same need to curse.

"We always tried to get the boys out of these bunk beds by the time they were tall enough to start doing that," said Rebecca with a gentle smile of memory. She sat down on the only chair in the room as I rose, ducking to avoid bumping my head again. It was uncomfortable leaning against the bunk, but there was nowhere else to sit. Well, it would keep me awake, anyway.

"I have a confession to make." Rebecca looked around the room nervously, as if expecting someone to rush in on us.

"Go ahead." I had been so sure at first that Rebecca wasn't guilty. But maybe I'd been wrong again. It was strange that I felt so unthreatened, despite the fact that the door was closed and Rebecca had me here alone, in a quiet house after dark.

"I don't want you to think worse of me than you already do. I've made mistakes in my life, but I've tried so hard to do what is right. But there are times when my weaker side just takes over." She was digging her fingernails into her palms as if in punishment for her crimes.

"I believe you've tried to do right," I said, offering her the kindest interpretation of her actions that I could think of.

Rebecca gave a sad laugh. "Tried being the operative word there, I suppose."

I didn't know if she was about to confess to murder—I certainly hoped not—but whatever it was she wanted to say, I was sure it would help my investigation and bring me some much-needed clarity. "Sometimes life is complicated," I offered, trying to sound as sympathetic as possible.

She pushed her hair back and toyed with one of the knick-knacks on the dresser. Finally, she said, "I love Sarah so much. Sometimes it frightens me how much. Maybe she wouldn't be able to make me so angry with her foolish choices if I didn't love her as I did. And wish more for her." She leaned back against the chair, pensive.

The sisters' relationship was still a mystery to me. Rebecca said she loved Sarah, but I knew now she had also betrayed her in terrible ways—at least, from Sarah's perspective. Was Stephen's mistreatment of Sarah enough of a reason for Rebecca to kill him? My mind was struggling to make sense of everything I had discovered so far—all the hints and half-truths. What if the sisters had plotted together? Sarah had convinced me of her innocence back in the shed, and I'd been so sure of Rebecca's innocence this whole time. But maybe they had both tricked me. Cautiously, I said, "I think the more we love someone, the more difficult it can be to do what is best for them."

Rebecca twitched briefly. Then she said, "Yes."

There was a long silence. I felt like screaming my frustration. Last night had ended with Kurt and me fighting and him driving off and leaving me here. Then I'd woken up to a dead body, and I'd been going nonstop since then. I was exhausted physically, emotionally, and spiritually. Why wouldn't she just tell me what had really happened? Then I could go home and clean my hands of this whole thing.

When Rebecca finally spoke, her voice was so low it was almost inaudible and I spent a moment putting the sounds all together.

"I was the one who ruined Sarah's paintings," Rebecca said.

"What? Why?" This was not the confession I had expected. I stood up and paced. I was so sick of all the secrets that were hidden here, coming out one by one, each one darker than the last. Did everyone have secrets like this that came out eventually, even if there wasn't a murder in their midst?

Rebecca looked at the floor. "She woke me up that night, the night before Stephen was—killed. She was in a rage because she said that she was being wasted here, that it was all my fault. The same things she always says, but it was the last straw for me, I guess. She demanded that I get her money so she could take real lessons and buy more canvases. She said she wasn't going to end up like me, a dried-up old woman who had nothing in her life but memories of her children, who had left her."

I stopped, silent, sure this was the moment that the rest of the confession I'd been expecting would finally come out. If Rebecca could have taken a kitchen knife and been that vicious to those paintings, how much more would it have taken for her to use the knife on Stephen? Maybe she had been in the kind of rage that knows no bounds.

Rebecca continued, "I waited until she went to bed and then I rummaged in Stephen's drawers until I found the shed key. I let myself in, and used one of the knives that was already in there. It felt so good, tearing and ripping at those things she had made that I never would."

I was stunned. This didn't sound like the Rebecca I thought I knew, the loving mother who cared for everyone on the compound. "But why? Why would you do that?"

"I don't know. I don't know. She just loves her paintings so much. More than anyone—any*thing*, I mean—and . . . " Rebecca hesitated and looked at me, her eyes pleading. I wondered what my expression must be. It couldn't have been particularly sympathetic. I'd seen Sarah's talent and how much those paintings meant to her. Destroying them was truly cruel and it shocked me that Rebecca was capable of that. "Maybe I always thought it was unfair that she was so gifted and I wasn't," Rebecca finished quickly.

I didn't know what to say. Why was she telling me about this at all? Did Rebecca want me to offer her some kind of absolution? It wasn't really a Mormon theological concept. Besides, I wasn't the one she needed to confess to, but I could see why she wasn't eager to tell Sarah.

Then Rebecca said, "I should let you go to sleep now," and waved me back to bed.

"Wait!" I said, and called her back.

She turned, eyes clouded with grief and guilt.

"You really didn't come here to tell me you killed Stephen?" I asked.

"What? No." Her expression fluttered from shock to hurt. "No,

I told you from the beginning, I didn't kill him. Why would I ask you to stay to find out the truth if I'd done it myself?"

"Maybe because you were trying to point me in the wrong direction. Keep me busy as long as you could and make sure Kenneth and I were implicated in the cover up so we wouldn't call the police when we found out the truth." Which was why she'd felt free to tell me tonight. Except that she hadn't told me that at all.

"No. I didn't kill him. It wasn't even the same knife that I used, though I checked to make sure. I don't know why I did that," she said dully.

Did I believe her still or not? In any case, I didn't stop her from leaving, and narrowly avoided beaning myself on the upper bunk again as I climbed back in. I wasn't ready to leave, though I wasn't sure any more if that was about finding out who was the murderer or about not wanting to go home to Kurt as embarrassed as I felt right now. I hadn't realized how compromised my point of view had become since my arrival here. I had been so sympathetic to Rebecca from the beginning. Naomi wanted me to come because she thought she was too close to the inside to see objectively, but wasn't I now in the same place?

I finally went to sleep and dreamed of paintings burning. I didn't think it was anything like Joanna's apparently very real prophetic gift, but when I woke in the middle of the night, I wished desperately Kurt were there to curl around me and assure me that it had only been a dream. I'd go home tomorrow, I promised myself. And then I'd say whatever needed to be said to Kurt to make things right again.

BUT I WAS destined not to get much sleep that night—again. In the wee hours, I jerked awake to the sound of the bedroom door opening again, and my name being called.

It was Naomi, who was carrying a large black bag. She was white-lipped with tension.

"I need your help," she said. "Carolyn's gone into labor and she won't go to the hospital."

"Isn't she early?" I tried to think what day it was. Wednesday?

"Yes, eight weeks early." Naomi's voice was strained—and maybe even a little afraid.

"You're going to deliver her at home?" In Utah it was still legal to deliver at home. Whether it was sane to do so was another question.

"If you'll help me," she said. She waited for me to get up, which I did, throwing on a robe over my nightgown. Then she motioned for me to follow her to the stairs and out the back door.

She explained further as we crossed the yard. "Dad usually delivered the wives at home because he had all the equipment here. And last time Carolyn went to the hospital, it turned out badly for her. She seems to think that it was because she wasn't faithful enough."

"I don't have any training," I said nervously.

"You're sensible and steady," said Naomi, her face unclear in the dim light of the morning. "That's what I need. I helped my father deliver enough times that I think unless there's something drastically wrong, it should be fine."

It sunk in now that she could have asked her mother or any of the other wives to help, but she hadn't. She'd asked me. I felt touched at the gesture, and a little nervous about making sure she didn't end up regretting her choice.

"Why wouldn't your father just deliver all his wives at the hospital? Wouldn't that make more sense, when he already had privileges there? It would have just been routine."

Naomi shook her head, looking at the ground instead of at

me, minding her step over the uneven soil. "He always said that the pioneers delivered their babies at home and that was good enough for them. If there was a problem, he'd go in, but that only happened a couple of times."

Control again, I thought. He wanted even more control than he'd have in a hospital. It was more than a little frightening.

"What about Dr. Benallie? Would she be willing to come and help?" I asked as we moved across the yard, Naomi moving with the confidence that came from growing up here and me struggling to follow on the uneven ground. I checked my watch and saw it was just past 4 A.M., and there was a bit of light behind the mountains, signaling an early summer dawn.

"Dr. Benallie?" Naomi said, and shook her head with a short laugh. "No."

"But she came when—" I didn't finish.

"She's on probation at the hospital. Part of a settlement for a malpractice suit."

So maybe her medical license was already in jeopardy and it hadn't felt like as much of a risk to falsify the death certificate for Stephen?

"We'll have to check if she's bleeding," Naomi said as we reached the steps of Carolyn's small house. "If she has a placental separation, I can't help her here. She needs a hospital, and I'll insist she goes there."

I'd had nightmares about hospitals after Georgia's birth, but I couldn't imagine taking the risk of delivering at home after that. I'd wanted even more medical intervention, not less.

"Linda, are you with me?" asked Naomi at the door of the house.

"I'm with you," I said, trying to infuse my voice with certainty

I did not feel. I did not understand the women here, though I kept trying to.

Naomi opened the door and because it was the one thing I'd always relied on in uncertainty, I whispered a prayer:

Heavenly Father, please let Carolyn and the baby live. She has suffered too much already. Everyone here has.

My lips felt numb and I had none of my normal sense of confirmation that God had heard the prayer.

Heavenly Mother, I said in my mind, redirecting my prayer to the half of the godhead I thought might listen to me more right now, even if it was highly unorthodox. *You know what it's like to give birth. You know how a mother feels about an unborn child. Please, give us all the strength to make it through this day, whatever it brings. Let us bring solace and joy to each other as women. Amen.*

It wasn't the prayer I'd intended to say, but it was the one that had come to me. I felt comfort, but also a sense of foreboding. I thought of Joanna, who thought she could see the future. I wondered what warnings she'd be giving me right now if she were here.

CHAPTER 26

Without knocking, Naomi opened the bedroom door and we saw Carolyn leaning over the bed. Naomi looked at me and I could see the fear in her eyes immediately. As for Carolyn, her face was gray, and there was a pool of fluid on the carpet beneath her. I saw the pink-tinged smear staining her temple garments, which she still wore despite the circumstances. How she had gotten them as a polygamist, however sympathetic her bishop was, I could only guess at. You were supposed to have a temple recommend to purchase them from the Distribution Center and these didn't seem homemade to me.

It was stupid for me to focus on such things, but it was the only way I could manage to not start crying immediately as I felt a wave of emotion flood my senses. Childbirth should be a holy time, but to me, it was always a time of sorrow combined with terror at my own lack of power over the universe.

Naomi crouched next to Carolyn, trying to help her pant through the next contraction.

After all my attempts to steel myself, my knees buckled and I ended up leaning on the bed next to Carolyn. But Carolyn deserved my help, and by God, I was going to give it to her as much as I could manage. If I had no strength to stand, at least I could find the strength to speak.

So I looked into Carolyn's brown eyes, took her hand in mine, and said, "You are strong, Carolyn. You can do this."

Carolyn took a deep breath as the contraction subsided. "It's too early," she whispered to Naomi, who was palpating the outside of Carolyn's unmoving abdomen. "I'm not due for eight more weeks. Will the baby be all right?"

I could see Naomi hesitate, then make the decision. She met Carolyn's eyes squarely, pasted a reassuring smile on her face and said, "Yes, everything's fine. The baby's fine for now. You just need to concentrate on getting through the contractions."

"You're sure?" Carolyn said.

"Of course I'm sure." Naomi reached over and rubbed Carolyn's back.

Carolyn looked at me for confirmation and I didn't know what to say. My mouth went dry and I thought about the doctor in that horrible hospital room telling me rather bluntly that my baby had already died. I had been in pain from labor and couldn't help thinking that maybe he could have let me hope for just a few hours longer, to get through the delivery. But I didn't really know for sure that there was no hope here, as there had been none for me. Just because Naomi was worried didn't mean the baby was dead, did it?

"Everything will be all right," I told her, my voice wobbling as I spoke.

After that, Naomi helped Carolyn back onto the bed.

"I've always labored leaning over the bed like that before," Carolyn murmured.

"Well, we don't want to speed things up at the moment," Naomi said, and I had no idea if this was the truth or not. "The baby is early and your body isn't quite prepared."

Another contraction came and went as Carolyn tried to pant through it. "It's coming soon no matter what position I'm in, I think," she said.

Naomi pulled off Carolyn's temple garment bottoms, though Carolyn reached for them and folded them under one arm. I wasn't sure why she thought she should keep them close to her. Did she think that would somehow protect her? Some Mormons cling to the idea that garments offered physical protection against harm, not just spiritual protection. In this case, I had no interest in taking any comfort away from Carolyn. She deserved everything she could hold onto.

Naomi opened the black bag that must have been Stephen's and set out a tray by the bed, including a scalpel, a pair of medical scissors to cut the umbilical cord, and a clamp for the stump. She'd been away at school for years now—how long had it been since she had done a live delivery with her father?

I stayed beside Carolyn, trying to focus her on her breathing.

"The children?" she whispered hoarsely, when another contraction was over.

"They're still asleep for now," Naomi said, "but I woke up Esther to come over and help as soon as she could dress. She should be here before anyone wakes."

And as she spoke, I heard the doors open downstairs and the sound of footsteps going into the kitchen beneath us.

Then there was another contraction to draw my attention back. It was a long one and Carolyn held my hand the whole time, pressing it to the point that it was almost all pins and needles. Good. If that helped her, it didn't matter what it did to me.

"I feel like I'm almost ready to push," Carolyn said, when she was done.

I helped move her hair out of her face, which was wet

with sweat, and wiped her forehead with a towel by the side of the bed.

"I need to see how far you're dilated," Naomi said, and moved around to the bottom of the bed. "I'm putting my hand inside of you. I hope it's not too cold. Just relax," she said, trying to talk the other woman through each step.

She would be a good OB/GYN, I thought. I always appreciated the ones who talked me through what they were doing, instead of the ones who just took it for granted that I knew what was going on—or that I didn't want to know.

"The baby's things—are—in—nursery—one door down— left," Carolyn gasped out, reaching for me. "Will you go get them?"

I glanced at Naomi, whose bleak eyes held mine for a moment, and then she nodded. I knew then that she had already diagnosed a stillbirth was coming. I had felt it in my heart before, and now I had confirmation in my mind. That was how the scriptures said you knew the truth, if it was in heart and mind.

I somehow managed to get to my feet. It wasn't a graceful walk, but I made it down the hall, my heart pinched in my chest every step of the way.

The nursery was recently vacated, it seemed to me as I looked around, the crib bottom still down to its lowest notch, to keep a toddler contained, rather than up to make it easier to reach an immobile newborn.

I let out a little sob, away from Carolyn's hearing, and then stuffed my feelings back inside. I grabbed the tiny sleeper, red with white trim, and the pack of diapers that were on the top of the baby dresser.

Then I heard a long, pained groan in the next room, and rushed out, holding the baby items to my chest.

"Go ahead and push, Carolyn," Naomi was saying when I got back. "You're fully dilated."

Urgently, Naomi motioned me back to the bed and I put the things down on the floor next to us.

"Behind her," said Naomi. "Help her with pressure to her lower back. She needs someone to help support her with each push. It takes a lot of strength to deliver a baby."

Kurt had taken that position behind me during the births of our sons. With Georgia, too. His strong hands and the whisper of his voice in my ear came back to me. I missed him so much.

"Now, Linda," said Naomi.

So I maneuvered myself into position and put my hands on Carolyn's back. She groaned and pushed.

"Good. Rest for a moment," Naomi said when the contraction was over. She brushed back her own hair impatiently.

The tears began to flow then and I didn't even try to stop them anymore. There was no hope of that. I wept and I did what Naomi asked. I felt as if I were flickering back and forth between my own past and into Carolyn's present.

Kurt behind me, weeping, the smell of his clean sweat as his body was pushed to its limits along with mine. And then the moment when Georgia came into the world, the moment that changed both of us forever. Sometimes I wondered if any problems I had, with Kurt, with the church, were really all related to that one moment when I had become broken, when our whole family had become broken.

Carolyn was delivered of a stillborn son three minutes later. He was tiny, and the umbilical cord was wrapped around his neck. It was not a pretty sight.

I was surprised, somehow, because Georgia had been so beautiful. There had been no real reason for her death in utero, except that the doctor said she had gone too late and the placenta had stopped working. From what he said, it seemed clear to me at the time that my infant daughter had slowly suffocated over a period of hours inside of me, unable to cry out or demand help.

My tiny daughter had been so perfect at birth; I could almost believe when I held her that she might yet take a breath. Kurt and I had wept over her, until it seemed that everything I drank that day had tasted of salty tears. We had taken a few solemn pictures of her, of us together, though those photos were now in a box in our basement that contained everything of Georgia's.

I remembered Kurt holding our dead daughter and ritually blessing her with hands on her head, after he got special permission from our bishop to do so. He had loved her. I knew that from the way that he held her so gently, as if she were still alive and needed that special newborn tenderness. He had touched her tiny fingers and toes, as he had with our sons, counting them to make sure she had all ten. It had been half a day before she had turned so cold that I was certain she was dead, and Kurt was able to convince me that we could leave her in the hospital, for her body to be taken to the mortuary who had promised to pick her up.

There was very little lifelike about Carolyn's baby, however. I remembered now counselors coming to warn me, before Georgia was delivered, how gray and gruesome a stillborn baby might look. I had not remembered what they'd said in all these years, because in the end, Georgia had not looked like they'd described.

I had never thought to thank God that my daughter had died with so little trauma visible. Through my tears, I did so now.

I wished I could have been stronger for Carolyn, but in that last moment I was unable to help her sit up to deliver the afterbirth. I was sobbing for two lost babies (hers and mine) who might never know each other in any world, mortal or immortal.

By the time I was capable of moving again, Naomi had already wrapped the baby tightly in a serviceable, white blanket and handed him to Carolyn. At least the blanket covered up much of the damage to his deteriorating head.

I put a hand on Carolyn's arm. "It's not your fault," I said. "Whatever you think right now, remember that. It's not your fault." It was what I wish someone had told me at that time, but I wasn't sure hearing it from someone else would have helped me—or would help Carolyn. A mother can never see a child dead in her arms and not believe it her fault, surely.

Carolyn looked up at me. "Thank you," she whispered, and we shared a moment of utter unity then, the kind that no one ever wants to share, but no one can ever forget.

Then I wiped at my face and turned to Naomi. "What can I do?" I asked, trying to signify that I was ready to be of use again.

Naomi's eyes whipped over me, and I flinched from the disgust in them. She had wanted me to be stronger—had expected it of me, and I had failed her.

"You can take this and dispose of it," she said, handing me the mess of the afterbirth. I tried to clear my head, focusing on my task, wondering if there was something special I was supposed to do with it. If Carolyn had been delivered in a hospital, the afterbirth would have been medical waste. But what would it harm going out with the trash? I hoped it wasn't illegal, but I had no idea what else to do.

Downstairs in the kitchen, I greeted Esther with a mumble. Then I opened the back door and used the big trash can there. Somehow it surprised me that the big plastic can looked nearly identical to the one I used at my own house. But of course the Carters still needed the city to take the trash. It was so ordinary, and so practical. I found myself sobbing again as I reached for the door to go back inside.

I was angry by then, angry at a Heavenly Father who would do this to a woman already grieving the loss of her husband— however complicated their relationship—and who had only wanted to love and care for this child she had spent months sacrificing her own health and comfort for.

I was angry that Naomi had pretended things would be fine and that I had followed her lead.

I was angry at Kurt for not being here when I needed him.

I was angry at Kenneth for getting me mixed up in this whole thing.

I was angry at Joseph Smith and Brigham Young and every Mormon who had ever thought that polygamy was a sacred practice.

And I was angry at myself, for not getting out of this while I could.

After I'd kicked the side of the house hard enough to turn the anger into pain, which then faded, I went back inside and heard the sounds of a child's inquisitive voice, answered by the older Esther in the kitchen. I checked the time and saw it was now past 6:00 A.M.

Back upstairs, Carolyn was now weeping openly, her labor pain giving way to grief. I held her from behind and resisted the impulse to repeat the stupid things people had said to me, that she would see her son again in the next life, that she would raise him there, that she was sealed to him in the eternities. Those things might be true, but none of them changed the reality that right now, her baby son was gone.

Naomi worked at cleaning up the bloodied bedding and remaking the bed without asking Carolyn to move more than a few inches this way and that. Then she disappeared, presumably to put the sheets in the washing machine.

"You know what this is like," Carolyn said softly to me, twisting her head so that she could look into my eyes. "Don't you?"

I nodded. "My daughter was stillborn more than twenty years ago," I admitted.

"Did your husband know it would happen?".

That I hadn't expected. "What? No. Of course not." Why would she ask such a thing?

"Do you believe it was a punishment? That your daughter was born dead?" Carolyn pressed. Her face was bruised and there were huge dark circles under her eyes, but her eyes were fever-bright.

"No," I said. And then added, "Not anymore."

We could hear the sounds of children laughing downstairs, and of footsteps. They were playing some sort of chasing game. I wished they weren't, because it felt wrong that anyone anywhere could be laughing at a time like this.

But of course Esther was just trying to take care of the younger children as she had been asked. And there were people all over the world who were laughing, perhaps celebrating the best achievements of their lives. Right now. While we wept.

That was what life was, this grandest of contradictions, joy and sorrow combined in one. There was no separating it, not really. The more we loved life, the more we suffered. The less we loved, the less we laughed.

"Stephen told me this would happen. Months ago," Carolyn whispered, her voice hoarse with laboring. "He told me that I was to be punished. He said that this child would be a boy and that he would never take a breath."

I felt my stomach clench. What a thing to say to a vulnerable, pregnant woman! For a moment, I wished Stephen was alive again so I could stab him myself with that kitchen knife.

"What was he punishing you for?" I asked, and then wondered if it was only curiosity that was making me ask.

Carolyn bit her lower lip, hesitating. Did she think I would judge her as harshly as Stephen had? "I told him that I didn't want any more children after this one. I wanted an operation. Or at least some kind of medicine to prevent it. There are so many children here, and I'm not—I'm not as patient with them as I should be."

Stephen probably thought he was the only person who should be in charge of the number of children that came out of Carolyn's body.

"He couldn't have possibly known what would happen," I said, pressing a comforting hand into Carolyn's. "It's just a coincidence. A terrible coincidence."

Had Stephen planned to kill the child if it hadn't been stillborn to prove that he had been right about the future? Or would he have pardoned Carolyn sometime later and removed the curse from the unborn child? The more I learned about the man, the more of a monster he seemed to be. Not complex at all, but just an expert at hiding and manipulating the truth.

Or—it occurred to me to wonder if Joanna had predicted Carolyn's stillbirth, which Stephen had simply taken credit for. Was this proof her spiritual gift was real? I would have to ask her myself.

"You don't think he is up in heaven, now, watching to see that his prophecy came true?" Carolyn said.

"No. No." I had to force my hands to unclench, because I was about to tear the clean bedsheets. "Carolyn, Stephen never had that kind of power and he certainly doesn't now."

I stayed with Carolyn, my mind whirling with thoughts of Stephen's murder, of Joanna's gift, money and power, and my own sins, until Carolyn blessedly fell asleep.

When Naomi returned, she beckoned to me to head out with her. Moving slowly, I extricated myself from the awkward position I'd been in, trying to circle Carolyn with some sense of love and comfort. I felt completely drained of energy and my head buzzed with hunger as if I'd been fasting for a full day.

"We have to decide what to do with the baby's body," Naomi said.

We wouldn't have to report this child's death, either, I supposed. But in this case, no one needed a death certificate for a stillborn child. Georgia didn't have one, either, and she had been born properly in a hospital.

"Bury him in the graveyard with the others?" I said tentatively, wondering about how our relationship would work now that she had seen me at my worst, and I secretly knew too much about her reliance on her father's wealth.

"I don't think we should do a funeral. It wasn't ever really alive," Naomi said.

"Don't you say that!" I snapped at her, surprised at the surge of anger I felt. "To Carolyn, he was alive. She felt that little boy move within her for seven months or more. He was her son as much as any child could be!" Of course Naomi couldn't understand, never having had or lost a child herself, but couldn't she try a little harder?

Naomi put up her hands wearily. "All right. If you say so."

I felt bad for the ferocity of my reaction then, but I didn't have the strength to explain it to her. I would have to tell her about Georgia later.

"Let Carolyn hold the baby for as long as she wants today," I said, sure of myself. In this, I had far more experience than Naomi did.

"The body is pretty far gone," Naomi said.

Why did she have to talk about it as a "body" and not as a child? Was that what they taught you in medical school? My doctor had acted like that, too. As if it was just a procedure to him, just so much human flesh to be disposed of. I hadn't remembered that until now, either.

Maybe it was a coping mechanism for a professional who would see many deaths in the course of their career, but it wasn't one I admired.

"Give her time to let go," I said as calmly as I could manage. "When she's ready, then you can bury him and ask her for a name to put on a stone. But first make sure you ask her if she wants any pictures taken to remember him by."

"Pictures?" asked Naomi, disbelieving. "Of that?"

"Yes, of him," I said coldly. "And make sure they dig a new grave. That boy shouldn't have to share his grave with Stephen." Though it would be easier to simply dig up the soil over his grave because it was already soft. The little boy whose death had been predicted by a vengeful father deserved better than that and I was going to make sure he had everything I could give him, however small it was.

CHAPTER 27

I was still shaking with emotion as I walked away from Carolyn's house. I wanted to go home to my normal life, to a husband who didn't need to be in control of my every action and thought, and who genuinely cared for and grieved with me. Whatever my disagreements with Kurt about the policy, he was a good husband and father. He loved Samuel and Kenneth and he was going to figure out a way to stretch his faith around them both. Maybe he was taking a different path than I was, but I had to respect that.

I had promised to solve Stephen's murder before I left, and now I desperately wanted to go home. So I pushed myself to focus. I'd been asking everyone about the changes to the will except the one person I should have: Jennifer. She was the investment broker. She was far more likely to have known about Stephen's financial situation than anyone else. So I headed toward her house. It occurred to me that maybe I had been avoiding talking to her just because I disliked her so much.

Jennifer was standing on the porch, staring at the rising rose of sun in the eastern mountains.

"How is Carolyn?" was the first thing she said to me.

They say news flies in a small town. In a compound like this, it must get around so fast it was practically time travel. "The baby was stillborn," I said.

Jennifer nodded. "Yes, I'd heard."

"It must be particularly painful to you when one of the other wives loses a child," I said, watching her carefully. "Especially when you couldn't have children of your own." I was needling her—I could tell she clearly disliked children and probably never wanted any.

She frowned and then recovered. "It just wasn't to be, I suppose. Stephen always said that we had to look to God for answers to such difficult questions."

I was curious about why she had married Stephen when he, from what I had heard, must have expected her to give him more children. What had Jennifer really wanted from this marriage, this lifestyle? And had Stephen at some point discovered he had been duped when she gave him no children to be his in heaven?

"It bothered Stephen, though, didn't it?" I pressed. The wooden floor of the porch, I noticed, looked like it had been replaced recently. Stephen didn't stint Jennifer for anything, though Joanna's house was still unfinished.

"Of course it bothered him. Being a god means having posterity for eternity. Filling the universe with your offspring." Her voice sounded distant and she had a hand on the door to the house.

I couldn't make her stay and talk to me, but I was hoping she wouldn't escape into the house too soon. I spoke bluntly. "You disappointed him as a wife, then. Not giving him children." This would have been cruel if Jennifer were the woman that Stephen had thought she was, but she showed no reaction at all.

"I'm sure I disappointed Stephen in more than just that one way," Jennifer said, smiling as if it were a joke.

There was something very strange about their relationship, about the fact that she had been the first woman to agree to enter into a polygamous marriage with Stephen and Rebecca. She just wasn't the same type as the others who had joined. She wasn't needy at all, nor did she seem to be cowed by Stephen.

"You made sure you didn't have children?" I guessed.

"That was the simplest part. A little pill each morning," said Jennifer with a faint smile. "Stephen never found out, at least not until a few weeks ago. And by then, what did it matter? I'm too old to have children now."

A few weeks ago? Was this what had precipitated the murder? "Then why did you marry him in the first place?"

Jennifer was quiet for a long moment. "Why do you think?" she asked.

"Money," I guessed out loud.

"Well, if that was so, it wasn't as if he had anything to complain about in the deal," she said, grimacing. Was she another wife who had denied Stephen her bed eventually?

"But surely you could have made money on your own," I said.

She looked at the door jamb, pressed her finger into a bit of wood hanging out of it, and then held it out to me to see the splinter there. "Of course. But I'm not like other people. I learned that early on in life. I didn't want friends or relationships. I never cared about feelings or security, whatever it is that makes other people do what they do."

She studied the splinter, but didn't take it out. It must hurt, and it was strange to see her so curious about her own physical pain, without ever reacting to it. "Stephen's proposition of marriage gave me a chance to live here." She gestured widely to take in the expanse of the compound. "I've been able to have quiet almost all the time. And in addition to that, no one bothers me to go on dates or to spend time doing things I'm not interested in."

I stared at her and wondered if she was what a psychologist would call a sociopath. I'd read about them in books and I'd always felt sick at their lack of sympathy for others. But I'd met Jennifer several times now and never guessed this about her. She really seemed to feel nothing, at least not in any normal sense.

"It went much better with Stephen than I ever imagined. Once I understood him, he was easy to manage. He had his ego, but if I stroked it with a few words, or let him stroke me a few times a month"—she glanced sideways at me at this, but showed no embarrassment—"that was all it took. And he didn't ask twice about all the money I was investing for him, never looked carefully at my yearly reports. He trusted me, if you can believe it. Me." She shrugged and smiled again, that cold, wide smile. It reminded me of what Joanna had said about Jennifer having a murderer's heart.

My stomach clenched and I wondered if I was in danger. I could see no real reason for Jennifer to want to kill Stephen, since she had so clearly thought she was getting the better end of the bargain between them. But if there was any person on this compound I was truly afraid of now, it was Jennifer. Was it possible she had just decided to kill Stephen to see how it would feel?

"You knew Stephen was thinking of changing his will," I said, sure she had. She knew everything. Rebecca might be the mother of the compound, but Jennifer was the queen.

She shrugged, unashamed. "He was old friends with a lawyer from college. He asked me to make an appointment with him to change the will. As if I was his secretary."

The appointment with an old friend that she'd messaged him about, I thought. It was with a lawyer about the will. "Why did he want to change it?"

"He said he'd decided that he was going to put Aaron in charge of distributing funds if he died, and that each of the children who was verified to be his would get an equal portion."

I thought for a moment. "But what about Talitha? What about Grace?"

"What about me?" She met my eyes and I thought again of how cold she was. She didn't seem to care about the children's welfare at all, only her own.

"Was this to punish Sarah?" I asked. Cutting Talitha out of the will would have been a blow to Sarah, surely.

"Well, Stephen had discovered the truth about Sarah and Rebecca." She spoke so casually, though she watched me to see my reaction.

"What truth?" I asked, trying to hide the lurch in my stomach. Rebecca and Sarah. There had always been something wrong in their relationship, something too fraught, too emotional, and I'd known it. Rebecca had admitted as much to me last night when she'd told me about destroying Sarah's paintings.

"You never thought about how they look so much alike?" she asked.

"They're sisters. A lot of sisters look alike," I said, still pushing away what Jennifer was hinting at. It was too much. I'd liked Rebecca and I had done so much to help her cover up Stephen's murder because I connected to her as a mother, but what kind of mother could allow what Jennifer was suggesting?

"Did you never think about the age difference between Sarah and Rebecca? Fifteen years," Jennifer went on.

"Yes," I said.

A gust of wind mussed Jennifer's hair and she smoothed it back carefully. She was so calm, even amused. "I've seen the genealogy. One of the perks of that Mormon obsession with records. They were easy to find. Rebecca's mother was born in 1930. Rebecca was born in 1970, a surprise child at the end of what looked like a childless marriage. Sarah was born in 1985." Jennifer looked at me meaningfully.

I did the math in my head as Jennifer watched me, clearly giving me extra time in case I was very slow. So Rebecca's mother would have been fifty-five when Sarah was born. That made it pretty much impossible for her to conceive without intervention that would probably not have existed at the time.

Rebecca was not Sarah's sister, but her mother. I was rocked to my core. Everything I had thought about the two of them, about Stephen, about Talitha: it was all wrong. Her own daughter had married her husband? Why wasn't Rebecca disgusted by that? It was practically incest.

"You told Stephen," I said, sure she had done it for some reason of her own.

"I was trying to get him to change the will to my benefit. He came up with the idea about the children and the will on Saturday night, after he had that argument with Joanna. I tried to convince the other wives to talk him out of it, but they wouldn't listen to me. I tried to talk him out of it on Monday, too, when he came to visit me here with you and your oh-so-righteous husband in tow."

I felt a twinge of pain at this reference to Kurt, but it did explain something else I'd been meaning to ask Jennifer. Had I at last caught the tail of the right dog here? This had to have all led to Stephen's death.

"You told all the other wives that Stephen was going to change his will?" This was finally the last thing I was looking for, the timeline that made sense for the murder.

"No. Only Carolyn and Joanna. I didn't want Rebecca or Sarah to know about it. Sarah doesn't know the truth yet about Rebecca, and I thought it would upset her and make her unmanageable. She can be very annoying when she is like that."

For some reason Stephen had decided to change his will in favor of his own biological children, which certainly would not have benefited Jennifer since she hadn't given him any. So she had told Stephen about Rebecca and Sarah's being mother and daughter, hoping to get him to change the will in her favor instead. Why would she kill him before she'd been able to convince him to make the changes she wanted?

She'd have waited until she succeeded, and she certainly would have believed she could eventually wear him down. Carolyn and Joanna knew about the change to the will, and Joanna had argued with Stephen over it, presumably because her daughter Grace would be cut out. But what about Sarah? Could she have found out that Talitha was going to be cut out? Was her threat to take Talitha away just that, a threat, when really she was planning to stay because that was the only way she could get some of Stephen's money?

I still didn't have the full picture here, but I was close. I just had to poke at a few more things, and I was sure this would break wide open. What would happen after that, I didn't know, but I would be done with it and could go home to Kurt. I could shake the dust off my feet, as they say in the scriptures, from this evil place.

Jennifer tugged at the splinter in her finger, licking at the blood that came out. Then she went inside, leaving me outside with what felt like as many questions as she'd given me answers.

CHAPTER 28

I wanted to go back to the main house and get some more sleep to make up for what I'd missed during the night. What I did instead was go directly from Jennifer's house to Joanna's. It was only 10 A.M., but it felt much later. I walked inside without knocking, and found Joanna in the kitchen, finishing up dishes by hand.

"Still no dishwasher?" I spoke softly, trying to avoid startling her.

She looked over her shoulder at me and did not seem surprised at my presence. Maybe she'd had a premonition I was coming? "Stephen kept saying he would buy me one, but he never got around to it. Now I'll probably never get one."

She put down the dishrag and braced a hand again her lower back to support it. I felt instant sympathy. When my children were small and I picked them up and carried them around all day long, I had done the same thing. I'd always been in pain, and there had always been more to do after the children were in bed. It's very physical labor, mothering.

I sat down and waited until Joanna was finished. I felt guilty for not offering to help, but wasn't sure she would want my interference. I was also trying to figure out exactly how to put into words my accusation about the will being changed and the argument with Stephen that had followed.

When Joanna finally came and sat next to me, she was silent, and closed her eyes for long enough that I wondered if she had fallen asleep sitting up. Then she let out a long breath and opened her eyes to look at me.

"My gift warned me you would come today and why," she said. "You don't have to beat around the bush with me." Her eyes seemed very intense. "You want to know if I killed Stephen."

Well, that was blunt. "Did you?" I said, trying to stare into her eyes and discern her motives—as I'd come to believe that was my spiritual gift.

"No, I did not," Joanna said. The words were clear and steady. "But even if I didn't hold the knife, I can see how the others might feel I am to blame."

"What do you mean?" I asked. She was such a strange woman, never going quite where I expected her to go in conversation.

She clasped her hands in a prayer pose. "I should have made him listen to me about the danger. Why else did God give me those visions except to share the information with others? To prevent Satan's evil from blossoming into fruit in this world."

She had such colorful turns of phrase, but they were ominous, as well. I reached across the table and patted her shoulder. "I'm sure God won't hold you accountable for that mistake." I hoped that was the right thing to say to her. "Maybe you saw the vision to prepare yourself and your children for what would happen afterward."

But her expression was closed and unforgiving as she shook her head. "The burden of not getting Stephen to listen to me will always be mine to carry. So if you need to tell the other wives whose fault it was, you can tell them it was me."

"I won't do that, Joanna." I wanted to take her home with me and mother her, the same impulse I'd felt with Talitha. She was not much older than my own Samuel. She could be my own daughter, if I'd had another one after Georgia's death.

"Thank you for saying that. You don't know how much it means to me." She sounded choked up and ready to cry.

"I remember that you had a vision about Sarah, too?" I said. "The night before Stephen died, you said you saw her in a shadow of black and red." I wasn't sure I had it right.

She nodded. "Yes. That shadow is still over her. I see it every time we meet." She shuddered.

"Oh. I thought that maybe—it was about her paintings being torn to pieces." I watched Joanna closely to see if she showed any foreknowledge of the situation. Did she know that Sarah was Rebecca's daughter? Was there any way she could have guessed that Rebecca would do what she had done? Or precipitated it by returning to talk to Rebecca about Sarah's paintings?

"Her paintings? No, the shadow is far more than that. She is filled with darkness because she has no purpose in life. The black and red I saw in her were the cracks in her soul. She is bleeding out her very heart in her anger at the world itself. She cannot see any of the good in her life, and she will throw it all away because of that."

This was rather more perceptive about Sarah than I'd have expected from Joanna. There was a sound at the kitchen door and we both turned to see Grace.

"You're supposed to be playing with the little girls," said Joanna, but there was no anger in her tone.

"I had a vision, Mama, just like you," Grace said, her expression alight, her eyes wide and her hands splayed dramatically. "You were in danger and I had to help you."

"Well, it's not true right now." Joanna pulled her chair away from the table and patted her lap. "Where are the others?"

"They're in the playpens, taking their naps," said Grace.

"All right. Come here and I'll hold you for a little while," said Joanna

"Did your mother have visions, as well?" I asked Joanna, wondering if the gift ran in the family.

"What? Oh, no. Never." Joanna was stroking Grace's hair as the little girl sprawled across her mother's lap.

In this awkward position, I could see what Grace was wearing underneath her dress and leggings, and it seemed to be long, white underwear of some kind. But that made no sense. I guessed that Joanna might have worn long underwear as an FLDS woman, and now I wondered if she was still wearing them herself. But why would she make smaller garments for her daughter and force her to wear them every day, even in the summer?

Joanna drew my attention back to her by saying, "My mother spent most of her time in bed every day. She'd been put out to pasture by then, because I was the youngest. She said she was ill, but I knew she was just lazy."

"Put out to pasture" was a cruel way of saying what Joanna had mentioned before, about Rebecca being too old to have children. There was surely more to her mother's story, but I still had to ask her about the changes to the will she'd heard about from Jennifer.

"Have you thought about whether or not you're going to stay here now?" I asked, again trying to ease toward the harder questions.

"I've thought about nothing else," Joanna said. Another sigh. "You know, what I miss most about the ward in Short Creek is the sense of purpose. Everything you did was part of God's work.

There was nothing that was mindless. Washing dishes, feeding children, changing diapers—it was all God's work, all glorious."

For just a moment, looking at her, I had a glimpse of what she felt she had lost. The same brightness she exuded when she talked about her visions had come back to her.

"I'm sorry," I said, though I wasn't entirely sure what I was sorry for.

"Well, I just have to believe that I'm still part of God's plan, even if it's changed a little," she said sadly.

"Mama, you said that it's impossible for us to not be part of God's plan," Grace piped up, her head rising out of the relaxed pose she'd been in.

"Of course, that's true. God knows all that we will ever do, so how can we ever thwart Him?" said Joanna.

"And you said that Papa will find us again," Grace added.

"In heaven," said Joanna soothingly. "We will see Stephen again in heaven."

Grace settled again, and I couldn't help but question why Stephen would cut this little girl out of his will. It seemed needlessly cruel and it made me wonder about her biological father. Grace had been just a baby when Joanna left the FLDS. She wouldn't remember him, whoever he was.

"I think you did the right thing to leave Short Creek. I'm sure it's difficult to adjust to life on the outside, but you're doing well, Joanna," I said.

Joanna flinched at that and I wondered how I could have put it better.

"You did nothing wrong," I tried again. "They were the ones who treated you badly. You had to leave to protect yourself and Grace."

Grace squirmed in her lap and scooted away to entertain herself in her own room.

"I know that," Joanna said, when we were alone again. "I know that God had called me to another work."

"Did you have a vision that you were supposed to leave?" Maybe you would need something like that to give you the strength to do what Joanna had done.

"Of course I did. I would never do anything without the knowledge of God's approval."

Which made me ask, "How long have you had the gift of visions?"

"As long as I can remember. Since I was Grace's age, at least." She sighed. "But I learned not to talk about it. It made people in Short Creek uncomfortable. They said that I was taking too much to myself."

"That must have been so hard," I said.

"It was. Until I married. And then—" Joanna's face reddened as if she had been slapped.

"What? What happened then? Did your first husband mistreat you?" It seemed like it must have been even worse than most FLDS marriages, none of which sounded ideal to me.

Joanna hesitated. "No, he—he believed me. I loved him so much for that. So much."

"What made you leave?"

She didn't answer, but her lips were pressed firmly together, as if against a wave of pain. "I need to tell you that I have a feeling that you should go home," Joanna said. The words were spoken shyly, as if she was embarrassed to say them, but her body was tense.

"I will go soon," I said. As soon as I'd figured this out. I was so close now. Wasn't I? "I just need to ask you about Stephen's will. I spoke to Jennifer a few minutes ago and she mentioned telling you Stephen was planning to change it. Instead of Rebecca inheriting everything, he had intended to leave things in trust to each of the children individually." I meant to keep going, but Joanna had clenched her fists together and was shaking visibly.

"Linda, listen to me, please. I had a vision. About you. You're in danger here. You should go home now, as soon as you can."

I felt a tingling rush through me. "Danger? What kind of danger? From whom?"

"I don't know who wants to hurt you. I only know—" She began choking, then retching, doubled over.

I patted her back to calm her down. "It's okay. It's going to be okay," I said.

She sagged against me, exhausted, but pulled herself upright a moment later. "I'm sorry. I didn't mean to do that."

"No, I'm glad that you told me. What did you see?"

"Only a muddled shape." Joanna's hands shook as she tried to demonstrate, then dropped to the table as she gave up. "It was too dark to see clearly. The darkness is always evil. God can't see through the minds of those who have fallen to Satan."

This was a bit of theology I hadn't heard before. "Then how will I be hurt?"

"I don't know." She sounded desperately unhappy and I decided not to push her any harder. She was already at her limit.

"All right. I'll go home as soon as I can," I said. But I couldn't leave it at that. "Is anyone else in danger? Do I need to warn someone?" I was thinking about Rebecca and Talitha. Maybe Naomi, too.

"You and your son, Kenneth," said Joanna.

There was almost nothing she could have said that would have made me want to move faster.

CHAPTER 29

I got back to the main house, but the doorbell rang before I'd had a chance to find Kenneth and talk about the best way to make an exit. I could hear the children in the basement rough-housing, but no adult appeared to answer the door. I was reminded briefly of the fact that it was Sarah who'd invited Kurt and me inside when we'd arrived on Monday, not Rebecca. Answering the door didn't seem to be a top priority here. Then again, maybe it wasn't a habit since few people would ever get as far as the door?

I opened it myself and to my surprise saw Dr. Benallie.

"Ah, you're still here," she said when she saw me.

Not for much longer, I hoped.

"Can I get someone for you? Rebecca, maybe?" I asked, though I wasn't sure where Rebecca was.

"I'm here to check on Carolyn. Rebecca texted me that she'd given birth this morning with Naomi's assistance. I thought she should have a follow-up with a real OB/GYN."

I was a little suspicious of this since Naomi had been so certain that Dr. Benallie wouldn't come to help. "I thought there was something wrong with your license," I said mildly.

She drew herself up to her full height, which was a couple

inches taller than me. "I'm a skilled doctor. Do you want Carolyn to have a follow-up or not?"

I considered for a moment the likelihood that Carolyn would go to anyone else, and then sighed. Not that I really had any right to stop Dr. Benallie from going to see her in the first place, but I felt protective of her. I knew what she was going through right now.

"Oh, good, Linda let you in," said Rebecca, as she came in from the backyard. She looked sweaty and there were leaves in her hair and dirt under her fingernails. I guessed she'd been working in the vegetable garden, and when I turned, I saw she was carrying a cloth sack on her back that bulged with tomatoes. "Do you mind waiting here while I get a drink?" she asked us both.

"Of course not," said Dr. Benallie.

We waited uncomfortably for Rebecca to go into the kitchen and get her drink, then clean her hands. I tried to think of something polite and innocuous to say to Dr. Benallie, but failed.

Finally, Rebecca came back out. "Thank you so much for waiting," she said, though her hair was still filled with leaves. Her face, at least, was not as red or sweaty. She must have rinsed it with her hands and dried it off. "If you two will follow me. I'm sure Carolyn will appreciate your support, too, Linda."

Which made it impossible for me to explain that I was ready to leave. How long would this take?

Rebecca led us back into the yard where the heat was rising. It was going to be the kind of hot day where they tell the elderly to stay indoors for their own safety.

"How are things at the office?" Rebecca asked.

"Fine. We're figuring out how to shuffle patients around to new doctors now that Stephen is gone," Dr. Benallie said bluntly.

Rebecca took in a sharp breath and marched ahead, not looking back.

When we were about halfway there, Dr. Benallie reached for my arm and pulled me to the side by a tree. "I have to tell you something," she said.

"What is it?" I said, curious. I thought Rebecca would notice we weren't following her, but she didn't. She went straight into Carolyn's house while I was watching.

"I know you're helping Rebecca tie things up here. So there's something you should know." The grip on my arm tightened and Dr. Benallie had an expression on her face like a child keeping a secret. She said, "I've been looking through Stephen's birth records for the last couple of years, the ones that are still in his office. Cleaning up."

"And?" I asked, a little breathless. I'd known I had to be missing something. Ready to leave or not, I had to find out about this.

Dr. Benallie glanced at Carolyn's house, but Rebecca still hadn't come out. "About two years ago, one of his patients had a baby with Trisomy 18, a nearly inevitably fatal condition." She spoke coldly, clinically. "There were several ultrasounds before the birth which all clearly indicated it."

"That's tragic," I murmured, feeling sick at the thought of what it would be like as a mother to know that the child you were carrying would not live past birth. How to measure the grief of mothers, I did not know. Was my grief at Georgia's unexpected death worse than this mother's? Or Carolyn's, whose son's death had been prophesied?

"But the baby was born and survived. She is miraculously still alive, in fact." Dr. Benallie made a dramatic sweep of her arms and looked up at heaven, but only for a moment. Then she pinned me with her eyes. "A two-year-old with blonde hair and blue eyes. There's a recent photo of her in the file."

Blonde hair and blue eyes were common in Utah. What was she saying?

"Her parents are both dark-haired and dark-eyed," Dr. Benallie went on.

"Genetics are funny that way," I said.

"I remembered that Carolyn was due at nearly the same time that same year, in June of 2014. But she had a stillborn daughter, if I recall correctly. Though those records are mysteriously missing from Stephen's office."

"Maybe Stephen didn't keep the records from his own children's births there." I had a flash of memory of his basement office. Were they there?

"All of his other children have birth records there, despite the fact that he delivered almost all of them at home," said Dr. Benallie in a clipped tone.

Suddenly, my mind leaped to the tiny gravestone I'd seen along with the ones for Stephen's parents and brother. "Jane Carter," I said aloud. "Born and died 2014."

"You've seen the grave, then?" She showed animation for the first time since she arrived, her eyes wide, her body leaning closer to me.

"Yes, it's down with the others in the family graveyard."

"Well, I'm guessing the date on it was June fourth."

I wasn't certain, but that sounded correct. "But—" What was she saying? That Stephen had taken Carolyn's healthy baby away from her and given it to one of his patients? Why would he do that? Just to torture Carolyn? Or was it to make himself look better as a doctor who could deliver a healthy child even when the ultrasound technician had delivered a fatal diagnosis?

Dr. Benallie smiled widely, and it chilled me. "Back when I thought I was going to marry him, Stephen told me that he loved each of his wives dearly, but that he had to make sure that they always knew he was in charge. It bothered me even then, but I thought he was explaining about how he managed a difficult situation. He said that his wives had to know they couldn't conspire against him, because he would bring the wrath of God down on their heads, and on the heads of their children."

In the brief silence of the summer morning in this quiet place, I could hear Carolyn's broken voice in my mind, telling me that Stephen had predicted her son would be stillborn, and that it was a punishment for some misdeed of hers. Had this been the second time he'd done the same thing? I put a hand to my stomach to quell the sour bile rising.

"But how could he know they'd be born on the same day?" I asked.

"Because he was in charge of the induction schedule, and when Carolyn went into labor, Stephen changed the other schedule to match. He told the woman in question that if she delivered a little early there would be a better chance the baby would live," said Dr. Benallie coldly.

"And then Stephen switched the babies in the hospital?" Hadn't anyone noticed?

"Doctors can do things in a hospital that no one asks questions about."

"The parents didn't wonder about the child's coloring? And the disappearance of all the problems the ultrasound saw?"

Dr. Benallie shrugged. Clearly, she thought they were idiots, but if someone had given me a baby girl after Georgia had died, wouldn't I have just thought it was a miracle and taken her home as my own?

"You can't tell Carolyn," I said, glancing up at the house. Was that why Dr. Benallie had come? She seemed to be telling me as a dry run. Or maybe she wanted to be talked out of this. Maybe she had some better side of her nature that I hadn't seen until now.

"Why not?" That cold voice again. "Carolyn should hire a lawyer and get her daughter back. The girl is only two years old. She should be with her mother."

"Carolyn needs time to recover before she can deal with something like this," I said, watching the woman carefully to see if she would listen to me. She could have no idea how fragile Carolyn was now.

She frowned at me. "How much time?"

"A month or two at least," I said, thinking how ridiculous it was to pretend Carolyn would be emotionally healed in only a few months.

"If there's to be a legal claim on little Jane, I'd need to exhume the body of the stillborn child buried here," Dr. Benallie was saying. "We can prove that there is no DNA link to Stephen or Carolyn, and from there, we can demand a DNA sample from the other girl. It would go to the courts after that. If Carolyn's rights were terminated without her knowledge or consent, she should get her daughter back."

I didn't know if Dr. Benallie was right about the legalities here or not. I also wasn't sure it was in Carolyn's best interest to embark on a long and possibly difficult legal case at this point in her life. I was pretty sure Dr. Benallie wasn't doing any of this because she felt bad for Carolyn, but because she wanted more vengeance on Stephen Carter.

"You don't have proof about any of this," I said.

"No, not yet. Not until I get permission from Rebecca for the exhumation."

And Dr. Benallie had leverage over Rebecca—she had falsified the death certificate, and that had bound us all to her. But hadn't it also bound her to us?

I steeled myself to play as ruthlessly as Dr. Benallie was playing. "Do you think this means Carolyn is probably the one who killed Stephen?" I asked.

She stared at me. "What?"

"If Carolyn had somehow found out about what Stephen had done to her daughter, it means she has the strongest motive to kill him of any of the wives. I thought at first she was too physically weak, with the pregnancy, but they say that a mother's anger can give a woman amazing physical capacity. That knife that was in Stephen's chest could have been put there by Carolyn." Bluff, pure bluff.

"I sincerely doubt it," said Dr. Benallie, glancing toward Carolyn's house again.

I made sure my voice didn't waiver. "But if Rebecca decides Carolyn murdered Stephen, she may be angry enough to call the police, after all. And then what will happen to you and that falsified death certificate you wrote up?"

Dr. Benallie's face went very still, though a slight touch of wind picked up her hair and danced it around her face.

I went on, "You might lose your license to practice forever. Just to put a woman in jail who killed a man who stole her baby and gave it to someone else. Is that really what you want to do?"

She put her arms over her chest. "You'll say almost anything to get me to stop, won't you?"

She was right on that point. "If I have to choose between you and the vulnerable women and children here, I will choose them. You got out. They didn't." She was stronger than they were, even if she had stayed in Stephen's circle for reasons I didn't understand.

Dr. Benallie stared at me for a long moment and I didn't like the twisted expression. Finally, she said, "I'm beginning to wonder if you had a hand in Stephen's death yourself. You should think about that before you call the police. Why shouldn't they see you as a suspect, along with all the rest of us? You hated him, too."

What? I had hated him, but I hadn't killed him. No one could think that I had, surely. Except that Kurt hadn't been in that bunk room with me to give me an alibi. I had been right by Stephen's bedroom. I could have snuck two doors down and . . .

No, I wasn't going to let her shake me. I wasn't doing any of this for myself. And I was doing the right thing.

"These women have suffered enough," I said, trying to put steel into my voice. "You should leave them be."

"Fine." Dr. Benallie shouldered her purse, her annoyance clear. "I'll be leaving now, then."

"No," I said. "Carolyn still needs to see a doctor to make sure everything is all right physically, just as you said was the reason you were coming in the first place."

So we both walked up to the house, passing Carolyn's children in the yard. The oldest of Carolyn's children, Elizabeth, was climbing one of the trees. Jonathan and Noah were wrestling in the shade beneath Elizabeth. Judith was trying to read a book. I looked into the heavens and asked God for some advice about what to do about Carolyn's missing and supposedly dead daughter.

Was I really supposed to destroy another family to bring another child to this polygamous compound where everything was so disastrous? I just couldn't stomach it. And I felt no dark cloud over my mind, and assumed that meant God was agreeing with my choice. These children were Carolyn's without dispute. They would have to be enough for her.

Without any conversation, Dr. Benallie moved past me as we entered the house, and went up to the bedroom, where she got out her equipment. She sent me and Rebecca away so Carolyn could have privacy, but I listened at the door to make sure that was all she was doing.

"Everything all right?" Rebecca asked curiously.

"I'm sure it is," I said. The conversation sounded perfectly normal.

I looked at Rebecca's eager expression and wondered if she listened in regularly to the other wives. That was the atmosphere of suspicion here. I hated it. I thought again of Joanna's warning that I should leave. Maybe it wasn't physical danger she had been warning me of, but this contamination of suspicion.

When Dr. Benallie invited Rebecca and me back in, she was finishing up her final instructions. "You need to take care of yourself just as you would after any birth, Carolyn. No heavy lifting, no significant physical exercise for six weeks, and plenty of fluids and food. Do you want me to show you how to bind your breasts? The milk should dry up in a week or so."

I thought I could hear a little compassion in Dr. Benallie's tone at this and thanked her for that in my heart.

Carolyn said a few words, but I had the sense she wasn't taking in much. In the end, Rebecca stayed to help with some laundry and dishes while I walked with Dr. Benallie back to the gravel road and her car, to make sure she was truly gone.

CHAPTER 30

As I approached the main house I heard a commotion coming from the front room.

When I got there to see what was going on, I found Sarah had her purse in one hand, clearly on her way out the door, and her other hand around Talitha's arm. Talitha was dressed in boyish shorts and a T-shirt, her mouth twisted in a stubborn line.

"You'll do as I tell you to. I'm your mother!" Sarah said.

"I don't want to," Talitha said in return.

"Well, sometimes you have to do things you don't want to." Sarah punctuated this by tugging Talitha's arm hard, jerking her toward the door.

Talitha caught the edge of the door frame. "I don't want to. I want to stay here."

Sarah let go of Talitha's arm and yanked on her hands clamped to the door frame. Talitha, in turn, used her feet to jam herself further.

It was a ridiculous protest. I remembered my sons doing similar things when I'd tried to discipline them without Kurt—they never treated Kurt that way for some reason. He spoke in that low, masculine voice and they jumped to pay attention.

But in this case, my sympathies were entirely with Talitha.

"Let me go!" Talitha cried loudly.

"Sarah," I said, coming up behind them, "you should really—"

I don't think Sarah had registered that I was nearby. Tired of pulling on Talitha, she reared back and slapped the girl hard across the face.

"You will do as I say!" she said in a tone so vicious that I was shocked to stillness. All this time, I'd seen Sarah's anger and her moodiness, but it hadn't clicked in my head that she was the one who had been abusing Talitha all along.

"You've always been disobedient and willful, a wicked spirit!" Sarah shouted, and slapped her daughter again.

Blood spurted down Talitha's bone-white face and I stared at it like it was one of Sarah's paintings.

I should have done something to stop that second blow. If Kurt were here, he'd have simply stood between them, and his bulk would have intimidated Sarah into stepping back. But it took me until Sarah raised her arm to strike a third blow before I managed to put myself between Sarah and Talitha, feeling a drop of warm blood fall on my arm from the gash I could see opening on Talitha right cheekbone.

"Sarah, she's a child. You're hurting her!" I said in horror.

Sarah looked up at me and her eyes seemed wild. "Of course I'm hurting her," she said. "And I'll hurt her some more if she doesn't obey me."

"Let her go right now!" I demanded, and pulled at the hand that Sarah had latched onto Talitha's shoulder.

"She's mine." Sarah's face was beet-red and she was shaking with emotion. "She's my daughter. She's the only one who is mine, and I'm taking her with me."

Talitha had bared her teeth like a dog—or a cat, I suppose.

"Look, why don't you stay a few more days?" I asked, grasping at anything that would get Sarah to stop. "Until we have a chance to sit down and talk things out with you and Talitha and Rebecca?"

As soon as I said the name "Rebecca," Sarah's whole body spasmed. "I'm not giving her Talitha. I'm not!" Sarah said hysterically. At least she had stopped hitting Talitha. She had let go of the little girl, who had collapsed on the floor.

I heard footsteps coming from the stairs, and in a moment, Naomi was cradling Talitha in her lap. Kenneth was behind her, a wall of masculine strength protecting both of them.

"There is no other choice," Sarah said, but she sounded defeated. She sagged against the wall, the angry energy drained out of her.

Naomi was examining Talitha's face gingerly. The skin on her lower left cheek was broken from the sharp stone on Sarah's wedding ring and there was blood dribbling down to the girl's chin and staining the pink T-shirt below.

"Is she all right?" Sarah asked faintly. It seemed ironic, when she had done this to her daughter herself. But I saw no regret or apology in her, only exhaustion.

I tried to recall Talitha's behavior around her mother before this. Had it been fearful? I hadn't noticed. After all my excuses to Kurt about staying here for Talitha's sake, I'd been too caught up in the drama surrounding Stephen to protect the little girl I'd vowed to Naomi to help. I couldn't help but think that Georgia must be watching me from heaven and thinking she was lucky to have been spared living with me as a mother. If I couldn't protect Talitha when I had been warned she was being abused, how could I have protected my own daughter, if she had lived?

Naomi sent Kenneth to the kitchen to get a bag of ice for the wound, cocooning Talitha with her own body.

"Does she need to go to the hospital?" I whispered, not trusting myself anymore to make a decision.

Naomi shook her head. "There's a lot of blood, but the cut isn't big enough for stitches. I think she'll heal on her own well enough," she said. Neither of us said anything about contacting DCFS. I looked at Naomi and I could see the guilt in her eyes. We both should have known better. The abuser isn't always the obvious choice.

After Kenneth brought the ice, he helped Naomi carry Talitha to one of the couches and she reclined there, very stoically saying she was fine and she just wanted to go get dressed and eat lunch with everyone else. Sarah stayed where she was, sitting like a child on the floor by the door with her legs splayed out in front of her.

Rebecca came back from Carolyn's house then. I watched her reaction when she saw Talitha's face. She whitened and looked at Sarah, the weight of guilt on her features familiar to me now.

She'd known, I thought. All this time, she'd known and covered for her sister—no, her daughter whom she did not dare acknowledge as such.

"I fell," Talitha said in a very practiced tone. Clearly, she knew better than to point a finger at her mother and my heart burst at the thought that she had lived her whole life like this, knowing that even adults who had seen what happened would likely not take her side.

"I see," Rebecca said. "Is there anything special you need? Some Tylenol? A juice drink so you don't have to sit up to eat?"

"I just want regular food," Talitha said. "I'm hungry."

"Grilled cheese sandwiches?" asked Rebecca, brightening. "With potato chips?"

"And dip," Talitha said, nodding with a little smile on her face.

I had the sickening sense that this was a routine between them, a favorite treat in exchange for her silence and "good" behavior despite what had been done to her.

No wonder the poor girl had been so attached to her pet cat. No wonder she had wanted so much to believe that Lucy would be in heaven with her. The way that Mormons talked about forever families must be terrifying to a girl like Talitha who was abused and encouraged to be silent by all the adults around her who were supposed to be her eternal family. The cat had been her buffer against all of that.

But did anyone here really want to spend eternity with anyone else? I wasn't convinced that they did.

"I'll set the table," Sarah offered, standing up at last, and straightening her dress. She was strangely and suddenly calm. She went into the kitchen with Rebecca, leaving me alone with Kenneth, Naomi, and Talitha.

I couldn't help but revise in my head the story of her miserable life here that Sarah had recited for me in her painting shed. Stephen might have had good reason to take away Talitha when she was a baby and give her to the other wives to be looked after—maybe Sarah had been dangerous to her baby. And the minor infractions for which Stephen had meted out his punishments were perhaps not so minor. I had never liked Stephen Carter, but I had to remember that at least Sarah's view of him was not to be totally relied on.

"Kenneth," I heard Naomi say, "we have to do something now. Something legally binding, not just taking her in for a few weeks." She was trying to speak quietly enough that Talitha didn't pay attention, but I could see Talitha had gone tense with alertness.

"She comes home with us today. Permanently," Kenneth said firmly. "We can figure out the legalities of the adoption as we go."

My emotions swelled in that moment. He and Naomi were very young and it would be difficult for them financially to manage a ten-year-old girl while they were still starting out. But Talitha was clearly so emotionally connected to Naomi. It was the right solution for her, and I found I cared much less about what either Sarah or Rebecca thought of it.

"Do you want to come live with us, Talitha?" Naomi asked the little girl, walking over to the couch and gently pulling the ice pack away from her face.

"But you don't live together, right? You're not married yet, are you?" Talitha said.

It was quite a practical question.

"We could move up our wedding date, couldn't we, Kenneth?" Naomi said.

"We'll get married tomorrow if we need to," Kenneth said gravely.

I didn't know if it could happen that quickly in Utah. But they could make a quick trip to Vegas, I supposed. My heart sank at the idea of them getting married without me and Kurt and the rest of our sons to witness the ceremony. But a child's welfare was at stake here. Besides, we could do a second wedding or a reception later that everyone could publicly cry and laugh at.

"We don't have any space for her right now," Naomi pointed out. "I have my one bedroom, and you have a one bedroom. Where would Talitha sleep?"

"I could sleep on the couch at your place," Kenneth volunteered. "For the next couple of weeks. You two can share the bed. And I can start looking for a two bedroom for all of us. It shouldn't take too long to find something."

I thought of offering them the empty bedrooms in our house, but knew immediately that Kenneth would reject the offer. There was no privacy for them there, and of course, the relationship between Kurt and Kenneth would not benefit from that kind of close living. Still, I ached not being able to help mother Talitha in the way I wanted. And Naomi and Kenneth, too, for that matter.

"But what about your honeymoon?" Talitha said. Her lower lip was wobbling. "You don't want me around for all that."

The fact that Talitha was thinking about the needs of the adults, and about their sex life no less, was disturbing to me, almost as disturbing as the physical abuse had been.

"Of course we do," Naomi said, and she and Kenneth joined together to give Talitha a big hug.

Sarah came past us from the kitchen toward the dining area with plates for the table. I could see her tense at the sight of the new threesome, snuggled together. "What's going on?" she asked.

Naomi pulled away from Talitha, making sure with a glance that Kenneth was still with her, then helped Sarah with the plates. "Let's just talk about the next few weeks, Sarah. I'm sure you need some time to get settled in your new life."

Sarah grunted at this. Would she really let her daughter go? I couldn't see any evidence that Sarah was concerned about Talitha's well-being, only her sense of ownership.

"Talitha can stay with Kenneth and me for a while, not here with Rebecca and the others, and we'll discuss a permanent solution later. All right?" said Naomi gently.

I got up and took the remaining plates from Sarah, who seemed to have stopped in her tracks before she reached the table. She was looking out the window by the front door, her throat moving as if she was swallowing many different answers to Naomi's words.

Finally, she got out, "You may think I'm selfish, but it's the first time in more than eleven years I've done anything for myself."

The words seemed to hang in the air, until they fell, unanswered.

In that moment, I couldn't help but feel sorry for Sarah, too, despite her treatment of Talitha. Her parents had pushed her away when she was pregnant, and her biological mother had allowed her into this terrible situation that had only made things worse for her. I couldn't excuse her, but I could pity her.

"I love you, Talitha," Sarah said, looking like she had shrunk several inches. She stepped closer to her daughter and held out her hands for a hug, but Talitha only turned her face into Kenneth's shoulder.

At that, Sarah's face became its own study in cold emotion. Lunch seemed to be forgotten. She didn't glance back once at the table or the kitchen. She simply went to the door, her jaw set, and swept out without another word.

I moved to the window to see what I believed was the family's only car rattle by.

"Godspeed," Rebecca said, before I realized she was standing there beside me, watching her daughter drive away, her shoulders shaking with sobs.

It was only then that I thought of Joanna's warning again. I should leave for many reasons. Whoever had killed Stephen, I hadn't been able to figure it out. Rebecca would have to figure it out on her own, if she really wanted to know the truth.

At least Talitha, who was the original reason I'd come, was safe now, and Naomi and Kenneth had made a big step in their future.

CHAPTER 31

It was time to call Kurt and tell him I was ready for him to come get me. I dialed the number, waiting with a thumping heart for Kurt to answer.

"Hello? Linda? Are you all right?" Kurt said. "Do you want me to come pick you up now?"

I started crying at the sound of his familiar voice. All I could manage verbally was a vaguely affirmative, mucusy "Mmm-hmmm."

"What happened?" Kurt asked in that solid voice I loved so much, and had missed almost unbearably. This was the man who had been with me through Georgia's stillbirth, through every moment of our five sons' lives. Even if I wasn't home, I felt home in his love.

"Stephen's dead," I got out.

"What? How? When?"

I couldn't find it in myself to repeat the lie that Rebecca had offered, that Stephen had had a heart attack. "He was murdered," I said.

I heard something loud in the background. Maybe Kurt smashing his desk with his fist? "How does this always happen to you?" he asked.

"I don't know," I said. I really didn't. It was either really bad luck or God wanted me in particular locations at particular times and seemed to be arranging for it to happen.

"Are the police there right now?" Kurt asked. "Will they let you leave if I come up?"

How could I tell my husband that I hadn't called the police and had, in fact, cooperated in covering up the murder? "It happened Tuesday morning and the investigation is still ongoing. But they've had the funeral already," I said. This list of questions wasn't what I had wanted when I called Kurt, but I'd known it would happen. It was part of why I'd delayed this moment.

Kurt let out a long breath. "Is that why you've stayed so long? To help his wives deal with the funeral and such?"

"Yes." That was mostly true.

"Well, I can come up immediately, then. There's nothing going on in the ward that can't wait."

I felt a wave of relief and love for him. He wasn't demanding an apology. He wanted everything to go back to the way it had been between us before, just as much as I did. It wasn't going to be that easy, but at least it was a start.

"Thank you," I said. "And . . . well, just thank you." He was always there for me. He really was.

"Do they know who murdered him? Was it one of the wives?"

"I guess I don't really know."

"And you're not trying to find out?" He sounded surprised, and a little amused.

The man was my sanity, I thought. "I'm trying," I said. "But failing, sadly."

"Does it by any chance have anything to do with the FLDS?" asked Kurt.

It was such an odd question. "Why would you ask that?"

"Linda, I did some online research on Stephen Carter and his history after I left. I was worried about you, and about him." Now he sounded embarrassed. My Kurt had done some investigating on his own? It did seem out of character for him.

"What did you find?" I asked, my curiosity leaping to the forefront of my emotions again.

"Well, first of all, I found out about the house fire Stephen mentioned," Kurt said. "They only ever found the two adult bodies in there."

"What? Not his brother?" I thought back to what Hector Perez had said. "Was he an only child after all?"

"No, why would you think that?"

I didn't have time to go into my talk with Hector Perez, so I said, "What happened to his brother, then?" What was his name? Edward, wasn't it? I tried to bring up the image of the tombstone, but failed.

"Well, in the newspaper article I found online, Stephen is quoted as saying that his parents had told him to get his younger brother out first, which he did. And by the time he tried to go back for the adults, it was too late. The flames were too high."

Then why was there a gravestone for his brother? "Did the brother die soon after, from injuries related to the fire or something?" I asked.

"No, Linda. He's alive."

I felt my chest constrict. This mattered. This could be the piece of information that solved the case. And I hadn't had it the day before because I wasn't talking to Kurt. My pride, it seemed, had gotten in the way.

"Linda, he's not only alive, he's close by. Edward Carter owns a residence in Short Creek, Arizona, though he also seems to own a house in Spanish Fork."

"He lives in Short Creek?" That made no sense. Short Creek was a very closed community, only for the FLDS. My mind leaped to Joanna, who had grown up in Short Creek.

"That's what I'm trying to tell you," Kurt said urgently, "Edward and Stephen were both in foster care for a number of years with a Grace and Thomas Jeffs, who are some of the Jeffs of FLDS fame. They're apparently cousins of Stephen's mother, and they took Edward back after the fire. To Short Creek."

"Grace," I murmured. Joanna's oldest daughter was named Grace. The one born while she was still part of the FLDS. It could be a coincidence. But my gut told me it wasn't. "But if the Jeffs took in Edward after the fire, why didn't they take Stephen, too?"

"An article I read about the fire said that Stephen was eighteen by that time, which means he had aged out of the system. I suppose he could have petitioned for guardianship of his brother as a young man."

"But instead he went to medical school," I said, "and buried any memories of his brother in the backyard."

Based on what Stephen had told us and Hector Perez, he was more than happy to erase his brother from his life in one way or another. But how might Edward feel about that? If Edward had left Short Creek at some point and discovered Stephen's financial success, not to mention his ownership of the property that had once belonged to their parents and should perhaps have been split between them, he could easily have been angry about it. Could it have led to a murderous rage?

I'd been so focused on one of the wives doing the deed that I hadn't thought about the possibility that she was just an accessory to it. Those damned keys to the gate. I'd gotten so focused on them and on the insular nature of life on the compound. Of course any of the wives could have opened up the gate for someone else. But I hadn't given much thought to that because the wives were so isolated here. Who could they have known outside the compound who would be willing to commit murder? It had seemed much more likely that one of them would have done it themselves.

Now I had a new possibility: that one of them had been married to a man who hated Stephen and had probably spent years waiting for the right moment to take his revenge.

Joanna had to have been part of this. She could have easily let Edward Carter onto the property Tuesday morning. Her reasons I could only guess at. Did she hate Stephen more than I had ever suspected?

Then I remembered suddenly that Joanna had said her first husband believed in her gift of prophecy. What if she had never truly left him—or the FLDS?

She had acted as if she had escaped, but the way she wore her hair, the way she dressed, and the way she dressed her children had all pointed to the fact that she had never really changed her beliefs from her FLDS days. How long had this particular revenge been in the making? Joanna must have known Stephen was going to be attacked. When she'd warned Stephen of danger while Kurt and I were there, and that night, when she came to the house and argued with Sarah—she had to have been trying to save him. It hadn't been a premonition at all.

She had also tried to warn me to leave because I was in danger, I remembered then. I felt a tingling sensation as she'd also told me to take Kenneth out of the compound with me. What was going on here? What else was she planning?

"I have to go," I said to Kurt.

"Linda, promise me you'll be safe until I can get there." His voice seemed very far away.

"I'll try," I said, and hung up the phone.

After what Joanna had already told me, and with the track record I knew her premonitions had, I should have gone out of the house right away. I should have found Kenneth and Naomi and told them to go home now and take Talitha with them. I should have warned everyone else in the house while I was at it.

But before I left, I had to talk to Rebecca. After all, Rebecca might have only wanted to cover it up when she thought that it was one of the wives who had killed him. When she found out it was likely Stephen's long lost FLDS brother, I was pretty sure she would change her mind.

CHAPTER 32

I went downstairs, thinking that I was most likely to find Rebecca in the kitchen. It smelled as if someone had burned something, but no one was there. One of the children must have tried a baking experiment, then cleared out before the evidence was discovered. I checked to make sure the oven was off, then hurried back upstairs to look for Rebecca.

I eventually found her upstairs in the master bedroom, looking through the night table on Stephen's side of the bed. There were several envelopes, including one large manila one.

"I have something important I need to tell you," I said. "About Stephen. And his brother."

"His dead brother, Edward? Oh, you don't need to bother." She shook her head and put her hands on my shoulders. "Linda, I'm so sorry I've gotten you involved in all of this. I should have encouraged you to go home two days ago, but I have to admit, I was really enjoying having an adult woman around who wasn't one of the wives I have to take care of all the time. Sometimes I really miss my old life, before all this happened. The regular Mormon world of Relief Society activities and lessons and meals. You know what I mean?"

I knew what she meant. "You really do want to know about—" I started again, but she hadn't seemed to hear me.

She let go of me turned to the side. "First, can you look at this? I don't understand it at all and it was on Stephen's night table, marked Saturday afternoon mail delivery, which might mean it's important or might not. I just need to know if I should throw it away or keep it," Rebecca said. She handed the manila envelope and its contents to me.

I glanced at the document purely so that I could tell Rebecca it wasn't nearly as important as what I'd found out about Stephen's past. My eyes were getting older and I couldn't see things as well, though I was vain enough not to carry reading glasses with me everywhere. I did have them at home.

I squinted at the page, but the more I read, the less sure I was about this not being important. The first page was simply a form letter, explaining that these were the results of a DNA test on paternity for three children, Grace, Eliza, and Zina Carter—Joanna's children. The letter recommended that Stephen, to whom the letter was addressed, read through everything before he came to any conclusions.

Each page after that was labeled with a different one of Joanna's children's names and contained two columns. One had a bunch of letters and numbers in it and the other column indicated whether or not the child and Stephen were a match. There were scientific explanations underneath each chart, but I have to admit, I couldn't really follow them.

For Grace, one marker out of fifteen matched Stephen's; for Eliza, there were two matches, and for Zina only one again. I had no idea if that was normal or not for any random group of people.

I'd already known that Grace wasn't Stephen's biological daughter. She was born when Joanna still lived with the FLDS and her father was Joanna's ex-husband. The real question was why Grace had almost the same number of genetic marker matches with Stephen as the other two children. I wasn't a scientist and knew nothing about genetics, but something was taking shape in my brain connected to the truth about Stephen's brother Edward.

"Does this mean they're not Stephen's children, any of them?" asked Rebecca, tapping at the final page that said the results were all "negative."

"I think so," I said.

"Then who's the father?"

I remembered then what Jennifer had said about the will being changed to benefit only Stephen's own genetic children. I'd thought that was a dig at Sarah, through Talitha. But now it seemed clear it was about Joanna's children, none of whom were genetically Stephen's.

How had he ever begun to suspect it? Had he heard Joanna talking on the phone to the other man? Had he followed Joanna out of the compound when she went to visit Edward? She must have visited him plenty if she'd had two children with him. How close was he? Had she gone all the way down to Spanish Fork or had he found a closer way to keep in touch with her? It would have been easier for her if he had, even if it were only temporary, and a lie. A neighbor. Or a delivery man. Or . . .

And then the last piece of the puzzle fell into place. Mr. John Edwards, the kind gardener I'd met at the Perezes, the man who had taken over Joanna's own position there, and who continued to send up flowers to her to enjoy here. I remembered his prominent nose, his wide shoulders without much height. I hadn't thought then that he looked like Stephen, but bringing up the image in my mind and comparing it to the photograph of Stephen hanging just above the bed, I realized that John Edwards had to be Edward Carter, Stephen's brother. He had to have planned all of this, not just Stephen's murder, but Joanna's first meeting with him, their marriage.

And Joanna, whom I had always thought innocent, had colluded with him. Were her premonitions just an act? Was there an evil mind at work behind her dreamy exterior or was she just a manipulated pawn, moved about between two men? I really had no idea, and I wasn't sure that it mattered anymore.

My eyes were watering, and that was when I noticed that the smoke had been getting worse all this time. It couldn't possibly have come from a minor food mishap in the kitchen. This was a real fire.

Suddenly, I remembered Joanna's quoting Robert Frost's poem, "Some say the world will end in fire."

"Mom, what are you doing in here?" I looked up to see Kenneth standing in the doorway with Naomi. His nostrils flared. "We need to get everyone out of the house. Now."

"Hurry, Mom!" Naomi said to Rebecca.

Rebecca looked up then and put the papers aside. "What's happening?" She seemed frozen again, reverted to the child she had been when Stephen's body had been found.

"It's the house," said Naomi, "It's on fire and we need to get out of here."

She herded her mother out the door and I followed close behind.

In the hallway, the smoke was worse. I had to assume that Edward Carter had set the fire, a last revenge against his brother, who had taken this property from him after the first fire killed their parents and changed both their lives forever. Whether Joanna had helped him, I didn't know. But somehow she had known there was going to be a fire.

Naomi turned to Kenneth. "You get Talitha and check for any children who might still be upstairs. I'll make sure our moms get out and we'll look for any other kids on our way through the house."

He nodded and they embraced but quickly separated again. Then Kenneth turned to me and put a hand on my back. "Mom, be careful."

"Don't worry about me. Worry about the children." Their lives couldn't be the price of the legacy of hate between Stephen and Edward, played out on this property where they'd once lived together, and where their parents had died.

I made my way downstairs with Naomi and Rebecca, pausing a moment to call 911 on my cell phone, explaining where the compound was and which house was on fire. Then I helped Naomi with Rebecca as she bumped confusedly from one of us to the other. I could hear Kenneth opening and closing bedroom doors behind us, calling out in case any children weren't already outside.

We were at the front door when I remembered that Rebecca had left the manila envelope with the DNA evidence in it upstairs. That was evidence the police would need if they wanted to prosecute Edward Carter. I'd been convinced not to call the police in the first place because I wanted to make sure that Rebecca wasn't convicted of the crime. Now I knew who had done it and I couldn't just let a murderer go free. I had to get those papers.

Naomi opened the door. The hot midday air felt refreshing compared to the smokey heat inside the house. It beckoned to me and I was so tempted to go into it. But I resisted the temptation and told Naomi, "I'll be right back. I just have to go get something."

"But—" Naomi started to say.

I didn't give her a chance to say anything else. I hurried back to the staircase, so much smoke swirling now that I had to put my hands to the walls to make sure I knew where they were. I took the steps slowly, glad that there weren't children rushing down past me. I counted steps to the second floor, then counted again to the third floor. I listened for any sound of Kenneth's voice, but I didn't hear it. I hoped he had headed outside after finding no one in the house.

I made my way down to what I thought should be the door that led to Stephen's bedroom, opened it, and stepped back as the smoke swirled out. This was not the bedroom I recognized. I must not have gone far enough.

Not bothering to close the door behind me, I moved down the hallway to the next room. It was the third room that was the right one, which I might have remembered if I hadn't been so addled by smoke inhalation. I stepped inside and could see the bed and the photo of Stephen with his entire family above the bed, fire licking up on the eastern side of the wall.

Where had Rebecca put the manila envelope and the pages inside it? I looked at the floor, but couldn't see anything but the carpet smoldering. Was it back on the nightstand? Had everything already been incinerated?

This was what Kurt complained about when I investigated things. I was so convinced I could figure things out that I went to extremes, like coming back into this burning house. Like not calling the police in the first place. I should go back downstairs, let the police figure this out on their own. Surely the laboratory where Stephen had sent the DNA samples would have kept records and be able to produce a duplicate.

Then I saw the envelope tucked underneath the bed skirt. I bent over, picked it up, and collapsed. I coughed horribly, and couldn't seem to clear my throat. Was I about to die here because I had been stupid enough to imagine that a piece of evidence against a murderer was worth risking my life?

I don't know how long I lay there, but I heard a familiar, rough voice some eternity later and felt myself being picked up into the arms of my husband, who had arrived at last. Kurt was trying to carry me away, but I'd lost the envelope and the papers. I struggled weakly against him and reached for them. He didn't argue with me, just grabbed what I'd pointed at, thrust it into my hands, and then picked me up again.

I sincerely hoped he didn't end up with a herniated disc because of this. The whole ward would blame me, and with good reason. Of course we both had to get out alive first.

He carried me down two flights of stairs, then let me down once we were on the main floor, where the smoke wasn't as bad. He put his face close to mine and kissed me firmly on the lips.

It was ridiculous and unlike Kurt and perfect.

"Shouldn't we get out of here?" I asked after a moment, my voice hoarse.

He smiled at that, then held my hand (or possibly was just making sure that I couldn't wander off again) as we ran out the front door.

Outside, I heard the sound of a siren approaching. Rebecca was on the gravel road, clutching her knees to her chest, sobbing something about the house. Kenneth was there, more smoke-smeared than he'd been before, but counting children with Naomi, who was holding tight to Talitha's hand.

There was the crashing sound of the gate breaking down under the firetruck, and it occurred to me to wonder how Kurt had gotten in without a key, but I didn't have the energy to ask the question. There was something symbolic about seeing the firetruck arrive in front of the burning main house, and looking up to see the gravel road open to the mountain. Everyone here was free now, free and safe and alive.

"What was so important about those papers?" asked Kurt.

I looked down at them, hoping that I hadn't ended up risking my life for what turned out to be a phone bill. No, they were the pages about the DNA analysis of the three children who weren't Stephen's. I folded them back together with shaking hands and tucked them inside the singed manila envelope.

"We'll see," I said. My throat felt too sore to try to explain it all now.

"You look terrible," said Kurt.

I laughed a little. "Thanks," I said in a low tone.

He was holding so tightly to me that my arm had gone numb, but I didn't ask him to let go. "I was sure when I saw the smoke coming out of the house that you were dead inside of it. I drove around the whole area and when I saw that other house nearby, I just took a chance and hoped I'd find a way from that backyard to this one, and I did."

I couldn't help but think that perhaps Kurt had been guided by inspiration to find that hole in the fence. It had been used for great evil, and now for good, as well. "You're right where you're supposed to be now," I said. "And so am I."

I wasn't sure how we were going to figure out our problems, but the one thing I knew now was that I didn't want to live without Kurt. He had come for me when I asked him to, and I wasn't going to let go of him again.

"Linda, I love you," he said, as if he thought this was his last chance to say it. "And whatever's wrong between us, I promise I'll fix it. Somehow, I will."

It was just like Kurt to think it was his job to fix things, I thought. But what I said was, "I love you, too."

After that, the EMTs came over to check everyone for smoke inhalation and it turned out I failed the test, which meant I got an oxygen mask and an invitation to ride in the ambulance to the hospital for treatment.

Kurt got in beside me.

"Do you want me to give you a healing blessing?" he asked, as the doors closed.

I nodded and felt a deep calm and sense of rightness as Kurt anointed me with consecrated oil from the tiny flask he kept always on his keychain, then spoke aloud a blessing of healing and comfort. I don't remember any of the words, only the relief that I could let go and let someone else take care of everything.

CHAPTER 33

I woke in a hospital room some time Thursday morning, I guessed. Kurt was there, slumped in a chair, asleep. I felt guilty waking him, and only meant to shift my position a little so that the arm that had gone to pins and needles came back to life. But as soon as I moved, Kurt started and stood up, coming toward me.

"Are they all right? All of them?" I asked.

He nodded. "The children are all accounted for and safe. A few of them were treated for smoke inhalation on site, but you're the only one who ended up in the hospital."

It occurred to me then that the reason I'd ended up here was the manila envelope with the evidence against Joanna and Edward Carter I'd thought was so important. I patted around the hospital bed for it, then realized how foolish I must look.

Kurt met my eyes with a look of chagrin. "They already came to take the papers you saved from the fire."

"Who? The police?"

He nodded. "I don't know if it really mattered that you saved them, but they insisted that it was part of the Stephen Carter murder case. I figured you had meant for the police to have the papers, despite the fact that you kept the truth from them for so

long." His tone was mildly annoyed, which meant he was showing some restraint, and I appreciated that.

I could have defended my choices, but I didn't bother. I'd
wanted to save Talitha, and even if I hadn't noticed what her own
mother was doing to her until it was happening right in front of
me, she was going to be better off with Kenneth and Naomi. I'd
figured out that Joanna and Edward were involved in the murder,
even if I had been rather late. And I'd had the presence of mind
to call 911 in the midst of the fire. I wasn't entirely embarrassed
about my part in all of this.

"You said all the children were accounted for? What about
Joanna's?"

He sighed. "You really need to know all the details right now,
don't you?"

I nodded. "I really do."

"All right. She and Edward Carter were apprehended on I-15,
heading south toward Short Creek with their three young children. The two of them will be arraigned for the murder of
Stephen Carter and the arson on the house."

I let out a long breath. It was finished now. I'd done what I
could do and maybe I hadn't done it the best way, but no one else
had died and the real murderers were in custody. That seemed
something to be proud of.

"I'm not sure what Joanna's role was," I said. She had known
about the crimes before they happened, but maybe she had just
been Edward's pawn. How guilty could she be, given the way that
she had been taught to follow orders all her life and never have a
thought of her own? I was still trying to figure out if any part of
her spiritual gift had been real, or if it had all just been part of the
charade. I wanted to believe that one trapped young woman could
see the future, I guess. Maybe I wanted to believe it too much.

"It's hard to believe she was completely ignorant of what Edward Carter had planned," Kurt said.

I hadn't yet told him about the Robert Frost poem quote or her warning to me and Kenneth. "Knowing about it is not the same as being responsible," I said. And I wondered if Mormon women were the same as the women in FLDS, kept from leadership and thus from responsibility.

"I did more research on the FLDS while you were sleeping," Kurt said. "It sounds like the young men are taught from birth to evade the law as much as they can, because the government itself is supposedly in the hands of Satan. They call it 'bleeding the beast' and they break child labor laws, school laws, food stamp rules, anything they can. Then they give the profit to the one man in charge. I think Edward Carter just decided that it was time for him to use the same attitude for his own cause."

It sounded like he and his brother had a lot in common. Stephen had been the king of his castle and fiefdom. Edward had made himself prophet and president of his own church, even if that only contained five people: himself and Joanna and the three children.

"Do you think Joanna was planted for two whole years to bring this to pass?" I asked. "Or do you think she really did get away and he found her again?" My encounter with the Perezes made me think the former, but I could be wrong.

"I don't know. But it might ease your mind to know that a couple of good pro bono lawyers who've had experience defending women in polygamous cults are volunteering to defend Joanna," said Kurt. I couldn't tell how he felt about this.

I was relieved, though. At least a good defense would be some way to right the balance of the scales, though I didn't really know what a fair result for Joanna would be in all this.

"Are the police going to arrest anyone for obstruction? Or conspiracy to conceal a crime?" I asked, wondering if I was going to be headed to jail immediately after this, where I would find Kenneth and Rebecca had adjoining cells. I also wondered how difficult it would be to prosecute Edward and Joanna, given how contaminated much of the evidence would now be.

"They're disinterring the body right now, but Rebecca took the blame for everything. She said that the two young boys, Lehi and Nephi, dug the grave on her orders and that she dragged the body into it herself," Kurt explained. But I was pretty sure he had a good idea what had really happened there.

I was surprised for a moment that Rebecca would implicate her own children in any of this, then remembered that they were minors and were unlikely to face any charges. If it were otherwise, Kenneth or I would have had to step forward to try to shield them from prosecution.

"It's a mess, isn't it?" I said. Rebecca might well end up serving time. And Dr. Benallie couldn't be shielded, either, after all my threats to keep her from telling Carolyn the truth about her supposedly stillborn child. That was likely to break wide open, too, and there was no more I could do to help Carolyn now.

"A mess is a nice word for it. Why in God's name you allowed that to happen, I don't know. Did you really think you'd do a better job of the investigation than the police?"

Well, maybe it looked ridiculous now. At the time, it had seemed to make sense.

"I was so sure it was one of the wives. I thought I just had to figure out which one before I left," I tried to explain. "I thought they might have had a good reason. Those poor women." I had been trying to help them. Or had I been trying to help myself? To make myself feel useful and righteous?

"Yes, poor Joanna, who nearly killed everyone in that burning house, including you," Kurt said, rubbing at his head.

Yes, poor Joanna. "She is hardly more than a child," I said, my voice hoarse with tears. So many children in that compound, so many victims.

Kurt sighed. "You're right, I suppose. But the most I can do is pray for her to get the help she needs. And pray you get well enough to never do something crazy like this all over again."

It was useless to promise that I would never do anything like this again, so I was silent. I listened to the sounds of the hospital. Beeping, swishing, dripping medication. Squeaky shoes and squeaky wheels outside my room. Life. My life. And Kurt was still with me, despite it all.

"You've talked to Kenneth and Naomi about their plan to adopt Talitha?" I asked, aware that I was changing the subject.

"Yes," Kurt said.

So that was done, and Kurt looked happy about it. Good. There would probably be a strain for a long time between father and son, because of Kenneth leaving the Mormon church, but I had hope that it would heal, in time.

"You know, while you were gone, I spent a lot of time thinking about the policy," said Kurt.

I widened my eyes at this. I hadn't thought the hospital would be the ideal place for a discussion of this depth, but on the other hand, if Kurt was willing to bring up the topic again, maybe I could at least listen.

"I never intended to imply that I would pressure Samuel to marry a woman. I know how hard that was on you, with your— uh, Ben," he said. Kurt still didn't like to talk about Ben Tookey as my first husband.

"Samuel always wants to please you. You have to be careful

about what you hint at with him. He can be very sensitive," I said gently.

Kurt rubbed at his hair. One of these days, he was going to go completely bald and then what would he do when he was thinking? Rub his eyebrows instead?

"I only want him to be happy. I want for him what I want for all my sons. I want for him what I have for myself." He looked me in the eyes and I felt a warmth spread through me at what he was saying. He was happy with me. Or he had been, before the new policy had gotten in the way.

"I know, but it's different for Samuel."

"I can't see the church suddenly changing its doctrine," he said, his lips twisting glumly. "It's too deep. Heavenly Father and Heavenly Mother, the temple ceremonies, they're all based on the idea of opposite sex marriage and complementarity between husband and wife. I don't see how it can work with husband and husband."

I thought about how the church had struggled to change doctrine when the revelation about blacks and the priesthood had come in 1978. Nearly forty years later, and God was still always depicted as white and The Book of Mormon still hinted that white skin was better than dark skin, even after some changes to the text. "I don't know either," I said.

Kurt looked at me, holding my gaze with his warm eyes. "I don't want Samuel to think he's lesser in any way. I don't want him to think that he has to die in order to be made into something that can be allowed in the kingdom. I can't bear the thought of anyone believing that."

I let out a long, slow breath. Why couldn't we have had this conversation months ago? I guess maybe it took this long for Kurt to see all the implications of the policy. He hadn't been thinking about us having a gay son for nearly as long as I had. He hadn't been thinking about LGBTQ issues since before we were married like I had, either.

"You can start by doing something in the ward. Something better than that talk last month," I suggested.

"Like what?" asked Kurt. "I'm trying to be sensitive. Tell me what you think I can do that will be supportive of our son and not end up with me being released as bishop and possibly excommunicated."

I hadn't ever asked him to do something that would end like that. I just wanted understanding. "You could wear a rainbow ribbon," I said.

He flinched. It took me a moment to figure out why. Some people might think wearing the ribbon was a protest. So I said, "Not to show you're trying to get the apostles to change the policy, but just to show people that you're a safe place, that they can talk to you if they have questions or just need someone to listen without judging them."

Kurt considered this for a long moment. "I'm not interested in protesting anything. I love the church. I love the brethren. I truly believe that they are doing the best they can for everyone. Until God gives them new revelation, they have to do the best they can, and the policy was supposed—"

I held up my hand. I couldn't hear his defense of it again. "Please," I said, "Can we just go back to the loving part? You love the church. You love Samuel. You love me. You're trying to love people as Christ would, right?"

He nodded. "But that doesn't mean—"

"Maybe neither of us knows what it really means to love as Christ would. But let's both try a little harder to find out." I certainly hadn't shown myself to be an expert at listening to the spirit of God when it came to Stephen Carter's family. I'd gotten so many things wrong because of my own prejudices and expectations. I was willing to accept that other people got things wrong, too.

Kurt leaned in and held my hand in his. His touch reminded me of how he'd found me in the fire. It reminded me of his touch on my back as I labored to give birth to Georgia, a child I'd already been told was dead. It reminded me of his touch when we had knelt across the altar in the temple to be sealed together.

Mormonism was all about binding people in love, not in coercion, and not against their own desires. At some point, we'd figure out how to work the doctrine around that one abiding principle. I hoped we would, anyway, and I fell back asleep in the sweet assurance that I could let go, for just a little while, and trust that God would be able to handle this on His own, without me.

CHAPTER 34

I got out of the hospital on Friday evening and Kurt took me home and treated me as if he were trying to keep me wrapped in my hospital bubble packaging. I slept snugged up close to him for weeks before he would let it go any farther than that. Our sex life was still not what it had once been, but it was something.

There were no legal consequences from concealing Stephen's death for Kenneth and me, though Rebecca was fined and asked to do a certain number of hours of community service. Because of her lawyer, the police eventually let Joanna return home to Short Creek, though there was an ongoing custody battle over her three children, who were still in the care of the state.

Edward Carter, on the other hand, was awaiting trial for murder and arson. Dr. Benallie hadn't been arrested, though she had lost her license, since this was not the first case of her doing something outside the bounds of the law. I wondered at Stephen's choice of her as a potential partner. He seemed to have two models for wives, the ones he could manipulate and the ones who could benefit him in specific ways. Dr. Benallie might have been his idea of someone who could help him in shady medical plans that had only ever come to fruition with Carolyn's lost baby. As far as the baby was concerned, I'd heard nothing of a lawsuit for custody, and I tried not to think too much about all of that, since it wasn't my business anymore. It really never had been.

The Monday after the fire, Kenneth enrolled Talitha in school near a condo he and Naomi were now planning to buy in Sandy. It would be a thirty-minute drive for him to work and her to medical school, but the schools were better south of the city, and they were willing to make the sacrifice for Talitha's sake. An official adoption was months off, but they had legal custody of her now that Sarah had signed papers relinquishing her own rights as a mother.

It seemed like everything was neatly tied up, except that the more I thought about the Carters, the less I could sleep. I was far away from the madness of the compound, but I'd lie in bed beside Kurt and start to smell the smoke from the burning house again. Even though I tried to relax, I could feel smoke around me, suffocating me. I could see the glint of kitchen knives. I could smell blood. I was barefoot and walking through blood-drenched carpet, going more and more slowly as it pulled me down.

When I actually managed to fall asleep, it was worse. In my dreams, I was frantically searching my burning house, or another house, or a park, or a car. There were children missing, dying, and I had to rescue them. But I couldn't find them.

Sometimes the children were my own, younger versions of Adam and Joseph and Zachary and Kenneth and Samuel. Sometimes the children were left in my care by another mother, and I had somehow forgotten about them, and suddenly their mother reappeared with an expression of fury and horror. I had forgotten her children! I had left them in danger! How dared I be safe myself?

I wanted to call Anna up and talk all this through with her on one of our walks. But every time I tried to do that, I found myself paralyzed and speechless, unable to figure out a way to explain to her why what she'd said to me at church had hurt me so deeply. Going back to church also seemed a monumental task. I had skipped church the first week under Kurt's insistence that I needed rest, and the weeks went on after that, each one making it easier than the last to stay at home.

When Kurt was at work, I spent time playing the piano and found some solace in that. It had been years since I had practiced seriously. And maybe this didn't count as serious practice, either. It was pure therapy. I was pounding the keys, playing old familiar songs again and again. I wasn't worried about technique or scales. I didn't even care how the music sounded. I just needed it to be louder and more intense than my own thoughts. I was trying to stop thinking, to simply be.

Naomi came over for lunch in August to discuss final arrangements for the wedding. I was thrilled to see her, but I had to stifle the impulse to dump on her all my fears. She wanted a sane mother-in-law and I had to at least try to pretend to be one. Besides, though she hadn't talked about it with me, I was sure she must be struggling to deal with everything that had happened to her and Kenneth, and to her family.

We talked about the wedding for a few minutes. Details, lists, names. I could manage that. Then I asked her about Kenneth, having worried over the secret I'd kept from him all these weeks. "Does he know about the money you were taking?"

"The money I took from my father to get through school?" asked Naomi, her face bright with surprise.

I nodded. I'd even kept this truth from Kurt, for fear that he would somehow try to use it to sabotage the wedding.

"He knows. I told him after we started the adoption papers.

I wish I'd told him before. I was supposed to pay the family back later by helping him with some of the home births he thought would come up. I just kept thinking that it wouldn't happen, that the wives would get too old. I didn't want to think about how much longer he could keep having more children if he married younger and younger women." She played with her engagement ring, twisting it in that way only a woman who is still getting used to it will do.

"Did Kenneth get mad that you'd hidden that from him?" I asked.

She let out a breath, nodding. "It was pretty bad. But he did say that he remembered you telling him that all normal couples have disagreements. It's the ones who learn how to deal with the conflict who survive and thrive, not the ones who avoid it." She looked at me, clearly hoping I would say something comforting.

"It's certainly true of my marriage. We've fought plenty and we still love each other." As I said it, I realized that this was partly true because the more we felt free to fight, the more we trusted each other. Or I hoped that we did.

"Well, thank you for the advice," she said, her eyes shining. "I think you may have saved my marriage in advance."

After that, we veered into a discussion about Talitha, who was "frighteningly quiet and good," according to Naomi. She always did her homework. She helped around the house. She never watched television, played on the Internet, or asked to go out, and she seemed to have no interest in making friends at school.

"I wonder if she is just too used to being hurt by the people who are supposed to love her to make any new connections," Naomi said. "I want to make everything better, but it's going to take a long time."

Yes, it would, and the worst part was that she might have to accept that there were some things she could never fix. But I didn't say that.

"I think she's a very lucky girl, with you and Kenneth as her parents." I patted Naomi's hand.

"Thank you," she said. "You always know the right thing to say."

I wasn't sure that was true.

Then with a sigh, Naomi admitted, "Sarah has disappeared. Not a word from her to anyone. I don't even know if she's still in Utah."

Poor Sarah. She had been through too much. But maybe it was best for her to be on her own for a while. And that could be a good thing for Talitha, too. I didn't know if Naomi had guessed at the truth about Sarah and Rebecca's biological relationship, and I didn't want to talk about it in any case, so I left it alone.

"Rebecca has come to visit Talitha once, but she's so busy with the other children that she doesn't have time for more than that. I wonder sometimes if she can possibly have enough time to give to that many children," Naomi said.

It was a good question, though in some sense I thought that children would take up as much time as you could give them. There was never a point where they thought you'd given them too much attention.

We were quiet for a long moment.

"Sometimes I wonder if I should just give up school. At least for a few years, until Talitha is settled," she said at last, her head low and her eyes not meeting mine.

I hadn't expected this. Naomi had seemed like such a modern woman to me, throwing off the ideals of my generation. It was something I had noticed more and more in the church, and outside of it. Younger women seemed to have no understanding of why a woman would choose only to stay at home, giving up all ambitions outside of motherhood.

Sometimes I was jealous of them, because they seemed to be able to become mothers without giving up what I had. At other times, I felt sorry for them because they had so much to do, so many responsibilities. I had loved being a stay-at-home mother. I had found deep meaning and spiritual purpose in it at the time. But looking back, I also wondered if I had ignored too many other things going on around me. Politics, inside and outside the church, bigger issues that had been brewing for a long time and now had gaped open a maw large enough to threaten everything. If I'd faced those issues earlier, maybe I wouldn't be in the position I was in now. But on the other hand, I had five wonderful grown sons, and I couldn't regret that.

"I can help," I offered impulsively, and it was the first time I'd felt the energy to help someone else since the fire. "If you need someone to care for Talitha. She's a great kid and I'd be happy to watch her for you on a regular basis, if you need me."

Naomi's face brightened and she seemed younger, or at least less weighed down. "Really?"

I nodded heartily.

She grabbed my hand enthusiastically. "Thank you so much! I've been worrying over how I can juggle all these things."

"You know, being a mother doesn't mean you can't rely on other people for help. It's not necessarily a sacrifice for other people to be involved in your family," I said. It could be a gift to someone like me, who was still looking for ways to be a mother.

"Can I call you Mom?" Naomi choked a bit.

It felt so good to fold her into my arms and feel like I was widening the circle of my family yet again. I should have told her to call me Mom long before now.

"I'd be honored," I said.

She pulled back so she could look at me directly. "I'd heard people say that when you marry, you marry the whole family. That used to frighten me. I worried as much about anyone needing to fall in love with my family as I did about falling in love with someone else's family. And I worried that my love had already been stretched to the limit with so many siblings, so many mothers. Maybe there was no more space in my heart for anyone else."

"But it isn't like that, is it?" I said.

Naomi wiped at her eyes. "No," she said, "it isn't."

CHAPTER 35

As a Mormon bishop, Kurt was authorized to officiate at weddings anywhere, not just in our home chapel. He had never done it for a couple that wasn't Mormon before, but there was no reason why he couldn't (so long as it wasn't a same-sex marriage, according to the new policy's rules). Kenneth and Naomi asked him to officiate in the Draper City Park on the 26th of August, 2016. We didn't want to have to try to squeeze both of our large families into a restaurant, so I had reserved several pavilions for the catering service to deliver the wedding banquet to us there.

It was painful to let someone else do all the cooking, but Kurt had insisted, and he was right that I simply couldn't have managed everything on my own this time. I'd tried before, with Adam and Marie's wedding, and with Joseph and Willow's, but in both of those cases, I'd had months and months in advance to plan and cook and put things in freezers to prepare. And I had been younger then. And not just out of the hospital and dealing with a lot of emotional baggage.

Dawn was bright and early on the day of the wedding, and there wasn't a cloud in the sky. There was no inversion clouding the skies and making it difficult to breathe either, which felt like a blessing from God. I spent a moment staring down into the valley from my bedroom window and thought how different Utah in the summer was from Utah in the winter. The glint of light off the lake brightened everything, and the sky stretched from the Wasatch Mountains in the east to the smaller Oquirrh Range in the west, creating a safe space that the pioneers had needed when they arrived, battered from mobs in Nauvoo. I needed this space, too.

Kurt and I dressed in our wedding clothes, me in a rose-colored, flowing mother-of-the-groom gown and him in a matching tie with his black suit and the rainbow ribbon he had started to wear with his suit every week to church. Except for a couple of teenagers throwing a Frisbee around, we of the wedding party were the only people at the park that morning.

Naomi had chosen a vibrant pink bridal gown that fell to just below her knees. Her blonde hair was down, and it blew in the light breeze. She wore sandals of a natural leather color with no heels. Kenneth wore a beige linen suit. I stared at him when I first saw him, surprised at how good he looked. With a slightly rumpled white shirt underneath, my son looked at ease despite the formal wear. His deep tan was set off by the lighter colors, and there was a faint scar on his cheek that I knew had come from the fire.

Talitha wore a paler shade of pink than Naomi did, and braided into her hair was a crown of real daisies. I didn't know whether Naomi had managed that herself or knew someone who was a fabulous hair stylist. Like the child she was, Talitha giggled as she ran around in the park, diving into the grass. I was pretty sure there would be green stains on her dress, but Naomi didn't scold her. Whatever Talitha's scars were from her father's death, her mother's abuse, and her childhood in polygamy, none of them seemed apparent today.

My sons Adam, Joseph, and Zachary had gotten here early enough to help set up chairs. I think they had tried to make the two sides look even by spreading out the chairs on our side, but it wasn't possible, considering how many people were on Naomi's side. I hadn't invited my extended family and Kurt's parents and brother were dead. That meant twenty chairs versus fifty, all in rows.

I thought of Samuel, and missed him deeply. Kurt and I hadn't bothered to ask the Boston area mission president if Samuel could come home for the wedding since it was so unlikely that it would be approved. For a funeral, perhaps, but a wedding, no. I'd written him a redacted version of the events at the Stephen Carter compound so he wouldn't feel left out. He probably understood me well enough to know how much I'd left unsaid, but we could talk about the details after his mission, if he wanted them.

Kenneth introduced me to some of his friends, one of his college roommates, and several of the people who worked at his coin laundry business with him. Naomi introduced me to a couple of classmates she'd invited, as well.

To my surprise, Anna Torstensen was seated in the back, as well. She smiled at me and I could see the strain in her face. Kurt must have told her about the wedding and made sure she was invited. He'd taken a risk, but I was glad to see her there. I went over to help her find a seat. She leaned close to me and hugged me for a long time without saying a word.

Emotions rode over me one after another: fury, desolation, loneliness, loss, fear, and then a more lasting wave of love.

"Thank you for coming," I said.

"I wouldn't miss it for the world," she said.

I opened my mouth twice to say something, and nothing came out.

"I miss our walks," she said at last.

"I do, too." That was a beginning, at least.

"Maybe you could come over for tea next week? I have some new recipes I could share with you," she offered.

"That sounds nice." It did. Tea was just what I needed. I didn't know what we would talk about, but we would figure it out as we went.

"I want you to know that I've never judged you through this. I hope you haven't judged me."

I had judged her. Maybe unfairly. I let out a long breath, and let go of—something. "I love you, Anna," I said. Wasn't that enough? Wasn't it more than enough?

I got up after that, wiping at my wet face, glad I hadn't bothered with makeup since I suspected today would be a day for crying anyway. I moved away from Anna and our side of the chairs, then maneuvered my way to the front and caught Rebecca's eye.

She nodded to me and I thought that she looked much the same as she had before, an older woman with too much responsibility on her back and too many regrets haunting her dreams. On the other hand, several rows back, Carolyn looked much better than the last time I had seen her, without the shadows under her eyes and the physical strain of pregnancy and loss. I didn't know how much truth about the "stillborn" daughter had come out when Dr. Benallie had been questioned by the police about Stephen's murder, but I hoped Carolyn had been strong enough to deal with what had.

The children on Naomi's side of the family were dressed in sober church clothes with pink roses pinned on their shirts that I suspected had come from the Perezes' garden. I was surprised at how quiet and well-behaved they were, and then a little disturbed by it. They'd been trained to obey too well. I hoped they didn't think of this ceremony as anything like the too-recent funeral they'd been to for their father.

I sat down on our side in the front, with an up-front view of Kurt as officiator, and Kenneth at his side. I felt a moment of peace, and more than that, sheer joy and satisfaction. There are few enough moments in life like this, where you feel that everything you've done has been worth it, that you've received more than you ever deserved. It might not last, but I was going to hold that sense close to my heart. I was a mother, and this was a mother's reward.

The music began, a single violin playing a Csárdás. I didn't recognize the violinist, and he was so talented that I wondered if it was someone Kenneth or Naomi knew personally or if they'd hired him. With the music playing and everyone standing and turned to watch her, Naomi walked down the aisle. Talitha walked just in front of her, throwing rose petals with abandon.

This was very little like a temple wedding, where everyone would have been dressed in white and the couple kneeling across an altar with mirrors indicating eternity behind them each. But there was something sacred about this moment, even so.

When Naomi reached Kenneth, she touched his hand, and then let go so that Talitha could squeeze between them. Kurt looked a bit disconcerted, but after a moment he began his lecture on marriage before the official ceremony. He had tailored this one specifically to Kenneth and Naomi, throwing out all of his old set pieces about eternal life and the temple. He had asked me to look over his paragraphs in their early stages to be sure he was on the right track, but I hadn't seen it all together. Tears came to me again as he began.

"Marriage is our refuge within the storm of life. Marriage to the right person brings us peace when peace seems impossible. Marriage makes us grow when we want to stay the same. Marriage teaches us what love is—and what love isn't.

"Marriage is the reason we want to stay in bed some days, and the reason we get up other days. Marriage is the best of us and the worst of us, and we make an offering of those together to our beloved. And we accept their offering in return, and vow to be more ourselves than we have ever been before."

I hoped that this was still true of our marriage, too.

Kurt turned and spoke directly to Kenneth. "Son, you and I have had our differences. But here we are together. My marriage to your mother is part of what has bound us and will always bind us. But now you are binding yourself to another. And so I must say goodbye to my son, and welcome the man he is becoming. You are no longer mine to care for and advise, but you will always be part of my heart.

"You are the head of your own marriage now. You must ask the questions, and figure out the answers. You must find a way to love as deeply as you are capable—to be as kind and gentle and as understanding as you can. Remember how blessed this day is, and that each day is as blessed as this day, if you make it so—for her and for you."

It was a patriarchal way to perceive marriage, but I hoped that Kenneth would receive it in the spirit in which Kurt intended it.

Kurt turned to Naomi. "First of all, I wasn't sure I'd ever see Kenneth married off safely, so thank you."

That got a laugh out of the crowd.

"I know Kenneth very well. Better than you do, in some ways, but certainly not in every way. And as each year passes, you will know him better and I will know him less well. And that's as it should be. But remember this: his flaws are mine. I did my best to teach him, but I could only teach what I knew. The lessons you teach him, he will have to teach me in turn. And believe me, my wife will be glad about that."

More chuckles at that. This wasn't the kind of wedding Kurt would normally have done in a chapel. I liked the more casual, self-deprecating, funnier version of Kurt officiating here.

"All I can say now is, good luck! Kenneth loves you, which shows he got some good sense from me, at least. You love him, which shows—I don't know what." This got another laugh from the crowd. "There will be days when he may seem angry at you, but you should know it isn't you he's shouting at. It's himself. Don't let him get away with it. Tell him that you love him and remind him that marriage makes you one so he never has to be afraid of being alone again," Kurt continued, his expression earnest once more.

Never alone again. Yes, though I had been pushing Kurt away for months, I had never really been alone. And that was a good thing. I was weeping with joy for my son and new daughter-in-law, but also for me and for Kurt and for the enduring power of our marriage.

Then Kenneth and Naomi had their own vows to share.

"I will love you and cherish you until I die," Naomi said solemnly and simply, and she put the ring on Kenneth's finger.

"You are my one and only," Kenneth said, putting the ring on Naomi's finger.

After these simple words, Kurt pronounced them husband and wife, and that was it. We all clapped and stood for them as they walked back down the aisle and over to the gazebo that was waiting for them to greet their guests.

I went and took Kurt's arm. "Good work," I said, as I watched the catering truck pull into the parking lot nearby.

"It didn't feel like it was right until the moment I stood up there and started. I was sure I was going to offend everyone and end up with no one left in their chairs at all. Not even you," Kurt said.

"Well, you said exactly the right things. You made Kenneth and Naomi feel both loved and welcomed." And no pressure to return to Mormonism, which I knew was quite difficult for him.

"Thank you," Kurt said with emotion in his voice. After a moment, he added, "Although, you know, I can't say I really take credit for all of it. Mostly, I just let myself say what I thought you would say if you were marrying them."

"Ah," I said, smiling. "Well, no wonder it turned out so well, then."

There was a moment of his hand on mine when I felt that we were one, as Kurt had said marriage could make you. Maybe it wasn't meant to last for more than a moment or two, so that it was always something you held close, and tried to get back to.

"Talitha is going to be quite a handful in a few years," Kurt said, after he wiped the tears from his own face.

She was now plucking flowers out of the pots and throwing excess petals at her cousins and younger siblings.

"She's a handful now," I said.

And she was going to be our handful for the next week, as Kenneth and Naomi went on their honeymoon. I was looking forward to every minute of that time with her, time to be a mother again.

Maybe it was what I needed to heal, to find myself again. If loving service was the heart of Mormonism, maybe I just needed to get back to that and forget all the rest.

The food arrived at the tables set up on the grass, and I sat next to Anna as we ate and she commented on what she thought she or I would have done better ourselves. I danced with Kenneth, and Kurt took the traditional father-daughter dance with Naomi. We ate good food, toasted with soda, juice, and no alcohol as per the negotiation between Kenneth and Kurt.

For a few sacred hours, I felt as much a part of an eternal family in that park with my sons around me, my baby granddaughter and my adoptive granddaughter-to-be, my daughters-in-law, and my best friend as I ever had. Heaven might be better than this, but I couldn't imagine it if it was.

AUTHOR'S NOTE

When I began writing this book about dealing with the effects of Mormon polygamy in the modern era, I knew very little of the historical facts that I discovered in the course of my research. Though the church insists that polygamy ended in 1890, I found that it persisted into the twentieth century, a fact that the official documents of the church obscured for most of my adult life.

Over the course of writing this book, I also sought out polygamists who consider themselves part of the larger Mormon community and began to listen to their stories. Some are FLDS, and their stories were often heartbreaking. Some have left; others continue within the community for various reasons. Then there were other groups, the Apostolic United Brethren (AUB), the True and Living Church (TLC), and Centennial Park groups. The neglect of children, the abuse of women, the lack of education—these are all real problems, not to mention the emotional scars that come from a controlling community.

I've read exposés about the sex lives of the men involved in these unions, but have also heard from those who truly consider polygamy to be a holy practice and who claim they are not involved in abusive relationships (yes, I am also skeptical of this, but I have tried to let people speak for themselves and not impose my own judgments on them). I also spent time watching *Escaping Polygamy* on A&E, which is about the Kingston clan, and which is just as horrible as Stephen Carter's independent polygamous group, though perhaps wealthier and more complicated.

And then there are the independent polygamists whose experiences I used to build Stephen's purported conversion to polygamy, which he shares with Rebecca. If you listened to these people speak, you might feel, as I did, torn by your assumptions about abuse and control and the clear-eyed, open-hearted people in front of you. I try hard not to judge others in the practice of their religion. Polygamists who eschew child marriage are, at least, avoiding the worst aspects, as are those who make sure that wives and children are well educated.

Of course, I am writing mystery novels and when there is a crime like murder, there have to be multiple motives and multiple possible suspects, so in each draft my Stephen became more and more a villain. I do not mean in writing this novel to indict all polygamists everywhere. Perhaps there are some who could come to a more egalitarian polygamy, though I'm not sure what it would look like in the end. While Stephen Carter's polygamous ideas are loosely based on the claims made by the original leaders of the FLDS church and some of its offshoots, he is his own prophet, as his brother is. This seems to be fairly typical of fundamentalist religions in my study of the history of Mormon Fundamentalists, each group claiming the "true authority" of previous leaders, and pointing the finger at others who have gone astray, even as the mainstream LDS church thinks of all of them as apostates and reprobates.

I should also note that I wrote the first draft of this novel (then called *Family Bonds*) in 2014 and subsequent drafts in early 2015. By November 2015, when the "Exclusion Policy," as opponents have begun to call it, was leaked to the press by ex-Mormon blogger John Dehlin, I thought the book was nearly finished. When it came back for plot edits, I found I couldn't see any way to write this story set in this time frame, with Samuel openly gay and headed on a mission, without having Linda deal with the new policy in some way.

As I went through thirteen more drafts of the book in the next six months, I desperately tried to iron out my own emotional feelings as I wrote through Linda's. As in other books, Linda is not me, but perhaps she is more like me in this book than she has been in any other. My experience with Mama Dragons mirrors Linda's, and some of my new friends in progressive Mormonism appear in this book, including Mitch Mayne. These are friends to whom I have clung as I have felt like the walls of my religion have been crashing in on me.

I have also included here a glimpse into my own experience with home birth. I delivered two of my five children at home with a lay midwife, one with a certified nurse midwife in a free standing clinic, one at a hospital with a certified nurse midwife, and one in an emergency transport at a hospital after things nearly went bad at home. My stillborn daughter's heartbeat was gone before I tried to deliver again with a midwife at home, but I have always wondered if I had chosen to deliver with a doctor, if she might have been induced earlier and saved. This leaves me in a strange position of ambivalence about home birth.

I thought that *The Bishop's Wife* was as much a book that exposed myself as I would ever write. It turns out I was wrong. This book is far more personal and has been far more painful and difficult to write than any other. Thank you for reading it and for being willing to sit through this sifting of my thoughts on marriage, religious freedom, gender equality, and ultimately, devout faith. I'm once again trying to be better and more faithful, and mostly failing.

I need to thank my editor, Juliet Grames, for her many drafts of patient editing of this book. Also, Amara Hoshiro, who helped edit early drafts; Jennifer Ambrose Lyford, who did an emergency final edit to fix the ending; and my agent, Jenn Udden, who did several ultra-fast edits to come my rescue, as well. Thanks to the whole team at Soho, including Meredith Barnes, Rudy Martinez, Bronwen Hruska, Paul Oliver, Abby Koski, and Rachel Kowal.

BIBLIOGRAPHY

These are some of the resources I used as background for this book. If you're interested in learning more, I highly recommend the book section as being more detailed and accurate. The Internet resources are quick and easy ways to get an overview.

Books on Mormonism and Polygamy:

Hales, Brian. *Modern Polygamy and Mormon Fundamentalism: The Generations After the Manifesto*. Greg Kofford Books, March 29, 2007.

Hales, Brian C. and Laura H. *Joseph Smith's Polygamy: Toward a Better Understanding*. Greg Kofford Books, Vols 1-3, April 14, 2015.

Hardy, B. Carmon. *Solemn Covenant: The Mormon Polygamous Passage*. UI Press, April 1992.

Krakauer, Jon. *Under the Banner of Heaven: A Violent History*. Anchor, June 8, 2004.

Pearson, Carol Lynn. *The Ghost of Eternal Polygamy*. Pivot Point Books, July 2016.

Quinn, D. Michael. *The Mormon Hierarchy: Extensions of Power*. Signature Books, 1997.

Quinn, D. Michael, ed., *The New Mormon History: Revisionist Essays on the Past*. Salt Lake City, Signature Books, 1992.

Internet Resources on Mormon Polygamy:

Park, Lindsay Hansen. *Year of Polygamy*, podcast audio, http://www.yearofpolygamy.com/

"Plural Marriage and Families in Early Utah." The Church of Jesus Christ of Latter-Day Saints, https://www.lds.org/topics/plural-marriage-and-families-in-early-utah?lang=eng.

"Plural Marriage in Kirtland and Nauvoo." The Church of Jesus Christ of Latter-Day Saints, https://www.lds.org/topics/plural-marriage-in-kirtland-and-nauvoo?lang=eng.

Quinn, D. Michael. "LDS Church Authority and New Plural Marriages, 1890-1904." *Dialogue: A Journal of Mormon Thought*, Spring 1985, http://www.lds-mormon.com/quinn_polygamy.shtml.

Quinn, D. Michael. "The Mormons Interview." *PBS* transcript of interview, conducted on January 6, 2006, http://www.pbs.org/mormons/interviews/quinn.html.

Other Mormon History Topics in Books:

Brodie, Fawn. *No Man Knows My Name: The Life of Joseph Smith*. Vintage, August 1, 1995.

Brooks, Juanita. *Mountain Meadows Massacre*. University of Oklahoma Press, May 15, 1991.

Bushman, Richard Lyman. *Joseph Smith: Rough Stone Rolling*. Vintage, March 13, 2007.

Farland, David. *In the Company of Angels*. David Farland Entertainment, July 23, 2009.

King, Linda Newell and Valeen Tippetts Avery. *Mormon Enigma: Emma Hale Smith*. University of Illinois Press, June 1, 1994.

Prince, Greg. *Leonard Arrington and the Writing of Mormon History*. University of Utah Press, June 30, 2016.

Riess, Jana. *Mormonism for Dummies*. For Dummies, February 25, 2005.

Smith, Joseph and B.H. Roberts. *The History of the Church. 7 Vols.* Chickadee Publishers, July 12, 2014.

Snow, Erastus and Orson Hyde. *The Complete Journal of Discourses*. Chickadee Publishers, July 12, 2014.

Stegner, Wallace. *The Gathering of Zion: The Story of the Mormon Trail*. Bison Books. April 1, 1992.

Internet Resources on Mormon History Topics:

"Do Mormons Believe That Adam is God." Brigham Young University. http://www.physics.byu.edu/faculty/colton/personal/lds/adamisgod.htm.

"Fundamentalist Mormon Beliefs Explained For Us – 'Sister Wives.'" Sister Wives Blog, July 10, 2011. http://sisterwivesblog.blogspot.com/2011/07/fundamentalist-mormon-beliefs-explained.html.

"The Grand Destiny of the Faithful: Teachings of Presidents of the Church: Lorenzo Snow." The Church of Jesus Christ of Latter-Day Saints, 2011. https://www.lds.org/manual/teachings-of-presidents-of-the-church-lorenzo-snow/chapter-5-the-grand-destiny-of-the-faithful?lang=eng.

"Mormon Fundamentalism." Wikipedia, June 12, 2016. https://en.wikipedia.org/wiki/Mormon_fundamentalism.

The Mountain Meadows Massacre. http://mountainmeadowsmassacre.com/.

Oswaks, Molly. "Tiny Tombstones: Inside the FLDS Graveyard for Babies Born from Incest." *Vice*, March 9, 2016. https://broadly.vice.com/en_us/article/tiny-tombstones-inside-the-flds-graveyard-for-babies-born-from-incest.

"Race and the Priesthood." The Church of Jesus Christ of Latter-Day Saints. https://www.lds.org/topics/race-and-the-priesthood?lang=eng

Snow, Lowell M. "Blood Atone   yclopedia of
Mormonism, Brigham Young Un   sity, 1992. http://eom.byu.
edu/index.php/Blood_Atonement.

Stack, Peggy Fletcher. "Shocking Historical Finding: Mormon
Icon Eliza R. Snow Was Gang-raped by Missouri Ruffians," The
Salt Lake Tribune, March, 3 2016, http://www.sltrib.com/
home/3613791-155/shocking-historical-finding-mormon-
icon-eliza.

"Was Joseph sealed to other wives before being sealed to
Emma?" Fair Mormon, December 25, 2014. http://
en.fairmormon.org/Joseph_Smith/Polygamy/Hiding_the_
truth/Did_Emma_know.

"9 Things You Didn't Know About the FLDS." ABC News, May 7,
2015. http://abcnews.go.com/US/things-didnt-flds-church/
story?id=30827256.